Fortitude by Hugh Walpole

Sir Hugh Seymour Walpole, CBE was born in Auckland, New Zealand, on March 13th, 1884.

His parents had moved to New Zealand in 1877, but his mother, Mildred, unable to settle there, eventually persuaded her husband, Somerset, an Anglican clergyman, to accept another post, this time in New York in 1889. Walpole's early years involved being educated by a Governess until, in 1893, his parents decided he needed an English education and the young Walpole was sent to England.

He first attended a preparatory school in Truro. He naturally missed his family but was reasonably happy. A move to Sir William Borlase's Grammar School in Marlow in 1895, found him bullied, frightened and miserable.

The following year, 1897, the Walpole's returned to England and Walpole was moved to be a day boy at Durham School. His sense of isolation increased. His refuge was the local library and reading.

From 1903 to 1906 Walpole studied history at Emmanuel College, Cambridge and there, in 1905, had his first work published, the critical essay "Two Meredithian Heroes".

Walpole was also attempting to cope with and come to terms with his homosexual feelings and to find "that perfect friend".

After a short spell tutoring in Germany and then teaching French at Epsom in 1908 he found the desire to fully immerse himself in the literary world. He moved to London to become a book reviewer for The Standard and to write fiction in his spare time. In 1909, he published his first novel, The Wooden Horse. The book received good reviews but sold little.

Better was to come in 1911 when he published Mr Perrin and Mr Traill. In early 1914 Henry James wrote an article for The Times Literary Supplement surveying the younger generation of British novelists. Walpole was greatly encouraged that one of the greatest living authors had publicly ranked him among the finest young British novelists.

As war approached, Walpole realised that his poor eyesight would disqualify him from service and accepted an appointment, based in Moscow, reporting for The Saturday Review and The Daily Mail. Although allowed to visit the front in Poland, these dispatches were not enough to stop hostile comments at home that he was not 'doing his bit' for the war effort.

Walpole was ready with a counter; an appointment as a Russian officer, in the Sanitar. He explained they were "part of the Red Cross that does the rough work at the front, carrying men out of the trenches, helping at the base hospitals in every sort of way, doing every kind of rough job".

During a skirmish in June 1915 Walpole rescued a wounded soldier; his Russian comrades refused to help and this meant Walpole had to carry one end of a stretcher, dragging the man to safety. He was awarded the Cross of Saint George. By late 1917 it was clear to Walpole, and the authorities, that his work was at an end. In London Walpole joined the Foreign Office and remained there until resigning in February 1919. For his wartime work he was awarded the CBE in 1918.

Walpole continued to write and publish and now also began a career on the highly lucrative lecture tour in the United States.

In 1924 Walpole moved to a house, Brackenburn, near Keswick in the Lake District. Although he maintained a flat in Piccadilly, Brackenburn was to be his main home for the rest of his life.

At the end of 1924 Walpole met Harold Cheevers, who soon became his friend and constant companion and remained so for the rest of his life; "that perfect friend".

Hollywood, in the shape of MGM, invited him in 1934 to write the script for a film of David Copperfield. He also had a small acting role in the film.

In 1937 Walpole was offered a knighthood. He accepted although Kipling, Hardy, Galsworthy had all refused. "I'm not of their class... Besides I shall like being a knight," he said.

Unfortunately his health was undermined by diabetes made worse by the frenetic pace of his life. Sir Hugh Seymour Walpole, CBE died of a heart attack at Brackenburn, aged 57 on June 1st, 1941. He was buried in St John's churchyard in Keswick.

Index of Contents

BOOK I: SCAW HOUSE
CHAPTER I - INTRODUCTION TO COURAGE
CHAPTER II - HOW THE WESTCOTT FAMILY SAT UP FOR PETER
CHAPTER III - OF THE DARK SHOP OF ZACHARY TAN, AND OF THE DECISIONS THAT THE PEOPLE IN SCAW HOUSE CAME TO CONCERNING PETER
CHAPTER IV - IN WHICH "DAWSON'S," AS THE GATE OF LIFE, IS PROVED A DISAPPOINTMENT
CHAPTER V - DAWSON'S, THE GATE INTO HELL
CHAPTER VI- A LOOKING-GLASS, A SILVER MATCH-BOX, A GLASS OF WHISKY, AND VOX POPULI
CHAPTER VII - PRIDE OF LIFE
CHAPTER VIII - PETER AND HIS MOTHER
CHAPTER IX - THE THREE WESTCOTTS
CHAPTER X - SUNLIGHT, LIMELIGHT, DAYLIGHT
CHAPTER XI - ALL KINDS OF FOG IN THE CHARING CROSS ROAD
CHAPTER XII - BROCKETT'S: ITS CHARACTERS AND ESPECIALLY MRS. BROCKETT
BOOK II: THE BOOKSHOP
CHAPTER I - "REUBEN HALLARD"
CHAPTER II - THE MAN ON THE LION
CHAPTER III - ROYAL PERSONAGES ARE COMING
CHAPTER IV - A LITTLE DUST
CHAPTER V - A NARROW STREET
CHAPTER VI - THE WORLD AND BUCKET LANE
CHAPTER VII - DEVIL'S MARCH
CHAPTER VIII - STEPHEN'S CHAPTER
BOOK III: THE ROUNDABOUT
CHAPTER I - NO. 72, CHEYNE WALK

CHAPTER II - A CHAPTER ABOUT SUCCESS: HOW TO WIN IT, HOW TO KEEP IT—WITH A NOTE AT THE END FROM HENRY GALLEON
CHAPTER III - THE ENCOUNTER
CHAPTER IV - THE ROUNDABOUT
CHAPTER V - THE IN-BETWEENS
CHAPTER VI - BIRTH OF THE HEIR
CHAPTER VII - DECLARATION OF HAPPINESS
CHAPTER VIII - BLINDS DOWN
CHAPTER IX - WILD MEN
CHAPTER X - ROCKING THE ROUNDABOUT
CHAPTER XI - WHY?
CHAPTER XII - A WOMAN CALLED ROSE BENNETT
CHAPTER XIII - "MORTIMER STANT"
CHAPTER XIV- PETER BUYS A PRESENT
CHAPTER XV - MR. WESTCOTT SENIOR CALLS CHECKMATE
BOOK IV: SCAW HOUSE
CHAPTER I - THE SEA
CHAPTER II - SCAW HOUSE
CHAPTER III - NORAH MONOGUE
CHAPTER IV - THE GREY HILL
HUGH WALPOLE – A SHORT BIOGRAPHY
HUGH WALPOLE – A CONCISE BIBLIOGRAPHY

BOOK I — SCAW HOUSE

CHAPTER I

INTRODUCTION TO COURAGE

I

"'Tisn't life that matters! 'Tis the courage you bring to it" ... this from old Frosted Moses in the warm corner by the door. There might have been an answer, but Dicky Tasset, the Town Idiot, filled in the pause with the tale that he was telling Mother Figgis. "And I ran—a mile or more with the stars dotted all over the ground for yer pickin', as yer might say...."

A little boy, Peter Westcott, heard what old Frosted Moses had said, and turned it over in his mind. He was twelve years old, was short and thick-necked, and just now looked very small because he was perched on so high a chair. It was one of the four ancient chairs that Sam Figgis always kept in the great kitchen behind the taproom. He kept them there partly because they were so very old and partly because they fell in so pleasantly with the ancient colour and strength of the black smoky rafters. The four ancient chairs were carved up the legs with faces and arms and strange crawling animals and their backs were twisted into the oddest shapes and were uncomfortable to lean against, but Peter Westcott sat up very straight with his little legs dangling in front of him and his grey eyes all over the room at once. He could not see all of the room because there were depths that the darkness seized and filled, and the great fiery place, with its black-stained settle, was full of mysterious shadows. A huge fire was burning and leaping in the fastnesses of that stone cavity, and it was by the light of this alone that the room was illumined—and this had the effect as Peter noticed, of making certain people, like Mother Figgis and Jane Clewer, quite monstrous, and fantastic with their skirts and hair and their shadows on the wall. Before Frosted Moses had said that sentence about Courage, Peter had been taking the room in. Because he had been there very often before he knew every flagstone in the floor and every rafter in the roof and all the sporting pictures on the walls, and the long shining row of mugs and coloured plates by the fire-place and the cured hams hanging from the ceiling ... but to-night was Christmas Eve and a very especial occasion, and he was sure to be beaten when he got home, and so must make the very most of his time. He watched the door also for Stephen Brant, who was late, but might arrive at any moment. Had it not been for Stephen Brant Peter knew that he would not have been allowed there at all. The Order of the Kitchen was jealously guarded and Sam Figgis, the Inn-keeper, would have considered so small a child a nuisance, but Stephen was the most popular man in the county, and he had promised that Peter would be quiet—and he was quiet, even at that age; no one could be so quiet as Peter when he chose. And then they liked the boy after a time. He was never in the way, and he was wonderfully wise for his years: he was a strong kid, too, and had muscles....

So Peter crept there when he could, although it very often meant a beating afterwards, but the Kitchen was worth a good many beatings, and he would have gone through Hell—and did indeed go through his own special Hell on many occasions—to be in Stephen's company. They were all nice to him even when Stephen wasn't there, but there were other reasons, besides the people, that drew Peter to the place.

It was partly perhaps because The Bending Mule was built right out into the sea, being surrounded on three sides by water. This was all twenty years ago, and I believe that now the Inn has been turned into an Arts Club, and there are tea-parties and weekly fashion papers where there had once been those bloody fights and Mother Figgis sitting like some witch over the fire; but it is no matter. Treliss is changed, of course, and so is the world, and there are politeness and sentiment where once there were oaths and ferocity, and there is much soap instead of grimy hands and unwashen faces ... and the fishing is sadly on the decline, but there are good drapers' shops in the town.

For Peter the charm of the place was that "he was out at sea." One could hear quite distinctly the lap of the waves against the walls and on stormy nights the water screamed and fought and raged outside and rolled in thundering echoes along the shore. To-night everything was still, and the snow was falling heavily, solemnly over the town.

The snow, and the black sea, and the lights that rose tier on tier like crowds at a circus, could be seen through the uncurtained windows.

The snow and quiet of the world "out-along" made the lights and warmth of the room the more comforting and exciting, and Sam Figgis had hung holly about the walls and dangled a huge bunch of mistletoe from the middle beam and poor Jane Clewer was always walking under it accidentally and waiting a little, but nobody kissed her. These things Peter noticed; he also noticed that Dicky the Idiot was allowed to be present as a very great favour because it was Christmas Eve and snowing so hard, that the room was more crowded than he had ever seen it, and that Mother Figgis, with her round face and her gnarled and knotted hands, was at her very merriest and in the best of tempers. All these things Peter had noticed before Frosted Moses (so called because of his long white beard and wonderful age) made his remark about Courage, but as soon as that remark was made Peter's thoughts were on to it as the hounds are on to a fox.

"'Tisn't life that matters, but the Courage yer bring to it...."

That, of course, at once explained everything. It explained his own father and his home, it explained poor Mrs. Prothero and her two sons who were drowned, it explained Stephen's cousin who was never free from the most painful rheumatics, and it explained Stephen himself who was never afraid of any one or anything. Peter stared at Frosted Moses, whose white beard was shining in the fire-place and his boots were like large black boats; but the old man was drawing at his pipe, and had made his remark apparently in connection with nothing at all. Peter was also disappointed to see that the room at large had paid no attention to the declaration.

Courage. That was what they were all there for, and soon, later in the evening, he would take his beating like a man, and would not cry out as he had done the last time. And then, at the thought of the beating, he shivered a little on his tall chair and his two short legs in their black stockings beat against the wooden bars, and wished that he might have stayed in some dark corner of The Bending Mule during the rest of the night and not go home until the morning—or, indeed, a very much better and happier thing, never go home again at all. He would get a worse beating for staying out so late, but it was something of a comfort to reflect that he would have been beaten in any case; old Simon Parlow, who taught him mathematics and Latin, with a little geography and history during six days of the week, had given him that morning a letter to his father directed in the old man's most beautiful handwriting to the effect that Master Westcott had made no progress at all in his sums during the last fortnight, had indeed made no attempt at progress, and had given William Daffoll, the rector's son, a bleeding nose last Wednesday when he ought to have been adding, dividing, and subtracting. Old Parlow had shown him the letter so that Peter knew that there was no escape, unless indeed Peter destroyed the paper, and that only meant that punishment was deferred.

Yes, it meant a beating, and Peter had hung about the town and the shore all the afternoon and evening because he was afraid. This fact of his fear puzzled him and he had often considered the matter. He was not, in any other way, a coward, and he had done, on many occasions, things that other friends of his own age had hung back from, but the thought of his father made him quite sick with fear somewhere in the middle of his stomach. He considered the matter very carefully and he decided at last (and he was very young for so terrible a discovery) that it was because his father liked beating him that he was afraid. He knew that his father liked it because he had watched his mouth and had heard the noise that came through his lips. And this, again, was rather strange because his father did not look as though he would like it; he had a cold face like a stone and was always in black clothes, but he did not, as a rule, show that he was pleased or angry or sorry—he never showed things.

Now these words of Frosted Moses explained everything. It was because his father knew that it was Courage that mattered that he liked to beat Peter ... it was good for Peter to learn Courage.

"'Tisn't life that matters" ... it isn't a beating that matters....

Frosted Moses was a great deal wiser than old Simon Parlow, who, in spite of his knowing so much about sums, knew nothing whatever about life. He knew nothing whatever about Courage either and shook like a leaf when his sister, Miss Jessel Parlow, was angry with him, as she very often had reason to be. Peter despised the old man with his long yellow tooth that hung over his lower lip, and his dirty grey hair that strayed from under his greasy black velvet cap (like wisps of hay). Peter never cared anything for the words or the deeds of old Parlow.... But Frosted Moses! ... he had lived for ever, and people said that he could never die. Peter had heard that he had been in the Ark with Noah, and he had often wished to ask him questions about that interesting period, about Ham, Shem and Japheth, and about the animals. Of course, therefore, he knew everything about Life, and this remark of his about Courage was worth considering. Peter watched him very solemnly and noticed how his white beard shone in the fire-light, how there was a red handkerchief falling out of one enormous pocket, and how there was a big silver ring on one brown and bony finger ... and then the crowd of sailors at the door parted, and Stephen Brant came in.

II

Stephen Brant, the most wonderful person in the world! Always, through life, Peter must have his most wonderful person, and sometimes those Heroes knew of it and lived up to his worshipping and sometimes they knew of it and could not live up to it, but most frequently they never knew because Peter did not let them see. This Hero worship is at the back of a great deal that happened to Peter, of a great deal of his sorrow, and of all of his joy, and he would not have been Peter without it; very often these Heroes, poor things, came tumbling from their pedestals, often they came, in very shame, down of their own accord, and perhaps of them all Stephen only was worthy of his elevation, and he never knew that he was elevated.

He knew now, of course, that Peter loved him; but Peter was a little boy, and was taken by persons who were strong and liked a laugh and were kind in little ways. Stephen knew that when Peter grew older he must love other and wiser people. He was a very large man, six foot three and broad, with a brown beard, and grey eyes like Peter's. He had been a fisherman, but now he was a farmer, because it paid better—he had an old mother, one enemy, and very many friends; he had loved a girl, and she had been engaged to him for two years, but another man had taken her away and married her—and that is why he had an enemy. He greeted his friends and kissed poor Jane Clewer under the mistletoe, and then kissed old Mother Figgis, who pushed him away with a laugh and "Coom up there—where are yer at?"—and Peter watched him until his turn also should come. His legs were beating the wooden bars again with excitement, but he would not say anything. He saw Stephen as something very much larger and more stupendous than any one else in the room. There were men there bigger of body perhaps, and men who were richer—Stephen had only four cows on his farm and he never did much with his hay—but there was no one who could change a room simply by entering it as Stephen could.

At last the moment came—Stephen turned round—"Why, boy!"

Peter was glad that the rest of the room was busied once more with its talking, laughing, and drinking, and some old man (sitting on a table and his nose coming through the tobacco-smoke like a rat through a hole in the wall) had struck up a tune on a fiddle. Peter was glad, because no one watched them together. He liked to meet Stephen in private. He buried his small hand in the brown depths of Stephen's large one, and then as Stephen looked uncertainly round the room, he whispered: "Steve— my chair, and me sitting on you—please."

It was a piece of impertinence to call him "Steve," of course, and when other people were there it was "Mr. Brant," but in their own privacy it was their own affair. Peter slipped down from his chair, and Stephen sat down on it, and then Peter was lifted up and leant his head back somewhere against the middle button of Stephen's waistcoat, just where his heart was noisiest, and he could feel the hard outline of Stephen's enormous silver watch that his family had had, so Stephen said, for a hundred years. Now was the blissful time, the perfect moment. The rest of the world was busied with life—the window showed the dull and then suddenly shining flakes of snow, the lights and the limitless sea—the room showed the sanded floor, the crowd of fishermen drinking, their feet moving already to the tune of the fiddle, the fisher girls with their coloured shawls, the great, swinging smoky lamp, the huge fire, Dicky the fool, Mother Figgis, fat Sam the host, old Frosted Moses ... the gay romantic world—and these two in their corner, and Peter so happy that no beatings in the world could terrify.

"But, boy," says Stephen, bending down so that the end of his beard tickles Peter's neck, "what are yer doing here so late? Your father...?"

"I'm going back to be beaten, of course."

"If yer go now perhaps yer won't be beaten so bad?"

"Oh, Steve! ... I'm staying ... like this ... always."

But Peter knew, in spite of the way that the big brown hand pressed his white one in sympathy, that Stephen was worried and that he was thinking of something. He knew, although he could not see, that Stephen's eyes were staring right across the room and that they were looking, in the way that they had, past walls and windows and streets—somewhere for something....

Peter knew a little about Stephen's trouble. He did not understand it altogether, but he had seen the change in Stephen, and he knew that he was often very sad, and that moods came upon him when he could do nothing but think and watch and wait—and then his face grew very grey and his eyes very hard, and his hands were clenched. Peter knew that Stephen had an enemy, and that one day he would meet him.

Some of the men and girls were dancing now in the middle of the room. The floor and the walls shook a little with the noise that the heavy boots of the fishermen made and the smoky lamp swung from side to side. The heat was great and some one opened the window and the snow came swirling, in little waves and eddies, in and out, blown by the breeze—dark and heavy outside against the clouded sky, white and delicate and swiftly vanishing in the room. Dicky the Fool came across the floor and talked to Stephen in his smiling, rambling way. People pitied Dicky and shook their heads when his name was mentioned, but Peter never could understand this because the Fool seemed always to be happy and cheerful, and he saw so many things that other people never saw at all. It was only when he was drunk that he was unhappy, and he was pleased with such very little things, and he told such wonderful stories.

Stephen was always kind to the Fool, and the Fool worshipped him, but to-night Peter saw that he was paying no heed to the Fool's talk. The Fool had a story about three stars that he had seen rolling down the Grey Hill, and behold, when they got to the bottom—"little bright nickety things, like new saxpennies—it was suddenly so dark that Dicky had to light his lantern and grope his way home with that, and all the frogs began croaking down in the marsh 'something terrible'—now what was the meaning of that?"

But Stephen was paying no attention. His eyes were set on the open window and the drifting snow. Men came in stamping their great boots on the floor and rubbing their hands together—the fiddle was playing more madly than ever—and at every moment some couple would stop under the mistletoe and the girl would scream and laugh, and the man's kiss could be heard all over the room; through the open window came the sound of church bells.

Stephen bent down and whispered in the boy's ear: "Yer'd best be going now, Peter, lad. 'Tis half-past nine and, chance, if yer go back now yer lickin' 'ull not be so bad."

But Peter whispered back: "Not yet, Stephen—a little while longer."

Peter was tremendously excited. He could never remember being quite so excited before. It was all very thrilling, of course, with the dancing and the music and the lights, but there was more than that in it. Stephen was so unlike himself, but then possibly Christmas made him sad, because he would be thinking of last Christmas and the happy time that he had had because his girl had been with him—but there was more than that in it. Then, suddenly, a curious thing happened to Peter. He was not asleep, he was not even drowsy—he was sitting with his eyes wide open, staring at the window. He saw the window with its dark frame, and he saw the snow .. and then, in an instant, the room, the people, the music, the tramping of feet, the roar of voices, these things were all swept away, and instead there was absolute stillness, only the noise that a little wind makes when it rustles through the blades of grass, and above him rose the Grey Hill with its funny sugar-loaf top and against it heavy black clouds were driving— outlined sharply against the sky was the straight stone pillar that stood in the summit of the Grey Hill and was called by the people the Giant's Finger. He could hear some sheep crying in the distance and the tinkling of their bells. Then suddenly the picture was swept away, and the room and the people and the dancing were before him and around him once more. He was not surprised by this—it had happened to him before at the most curious times, he had seen, in the same way, the Grey Hill and the Giant's Finger and he had felt the cold wind about his neck, and always something had happened.

"Stephen," he whispered, "Stephen—"

But Stephen's hand was crushing his hand like an iron glove, and Stephen's eyes were staring, like the eyes of a wild animal, at the door. A man, a short, square man with a muffler round his throat, and a little mouth and little ears, had come in and was standing by the door, looking round the room.

Stephen whispered gently in Peter's ear: "Run home, Peter boy," and he kissed him very softly on the cheek—then he put him down on the floor.

Stephen rose from his chair and stood for an instant staring at the door. Then he walked across the room, brushing the people aside, and tapped the little man with the muffler on the shoulder:

"Samuel Burstead," he said, "good evenin' to yer."

III

All the room seemed to cease moving and talking at the moment when Stephen Brant said that. They stood where they were like the people in the Sleeping Beauty, and Peter climbed up on to his chair again to see what was going to happen. He pulled up his stockings, and then sat forward in his chair with his eyes gazing at Stephen and his hands very tightly clenched. When, afterwards, he grew up and thought at all about his childhood, this scene always remained, over and beyond all the others. He wondered sometimes why it was that he remembered it all so clearly, that he had it so dramatically and forcibly before him, when many more recent happenings were clouded and dull, but when he was older he knew that it was because it stood for so much of his life, it was because that Christmas Eve in those dim days was really the beginning of everything, and in the later interpretation of it so much might be understood.

But, to a boy of that age, the things that stood out were not, of necessity, the right things and any unreality that it might have had was due perhaps to his fastening on the incidental, fantastic things that a small child notices, always more vividly than a grown person. In the very first instant of Stephen's speaking to the man with the muffler it was Dicky the Fool's open mouth and staring eyes that showed Peter how important it was. The Fool had risen from his chair and was standing leaning forward, his back black against the blazing fire, his silly mouth agape and great terror in his eyes. Being odd in his mind, he felt perhaps something in the air that the others did not feel, and Peter seemed to catch fright from his staring eyes.

The man at the door had turned round when Stephen Brant spoke to him, and had pushed his way out of the crowd of men and stood alone fingering his neck.

"I'm here, Stephen Brant, if yer want me."

Sam Figgis came forward then and said something to Stephen, and then shrugged his shoulders and went back to his wife. He seemed to feel that no one could interfere between the two men—it was too late for interference. Then things happened very quickly. Peter saw that they had all—men and women—crowded back against the benches and the wall and were watching, very silently and with great excitement. He found it very difficult to see, but he bent his head and peered through the legs of a big fisherman in front of him. He was shaking all over his body. Stephen had never before appeared so terrible to him; he had seen him when he was very angry and when he was cross and ill-tempered, but now he was very ominous in his quiet way, and his eyes seemed to have changed colour. The small boy could only see the middle of the floor and pieces of legs and skirts and trousers, but he knew by the feeling in the room that Stephen and the little man were going to fight. Then he moved his head round and saw between two shoulders, and he saw that the two men were stripping to the waist. The centre of the room was cleared, and Sam Figgis came forward to speak to Stephen again, and this time there was more noise, and the people began to shout out loud and the men grew more and more excited. There had often been fights in that room before, and Peter had witnessed one or two, but there had never been this solemnity and ceremony—every one was very grave. It did not occur to Peter that it was odd that it should be allowed; no one thought of policemen twenty years ago in Treliss and Sam Figgis was more of a monarch in The Bending Mule than Queen Victoria. And now two of the famous old chairs were placed at opposite corners, and quite silently two men, with serious faces, as though this were the most important hour of their life, stood behind them. Stephen and the other man, stripped to their short woollen drawers, came into the middle of the room. Stephen had hair all over his chest, and his arms and his neck were tremendous; and Peter as he looked at him thought that he must be the strongest man in the world. His enemy was smooth and shiny, but he seemed very strong, and you could see the muscles of his arms and legs move under his skin. Some one had marked a circle with chalk, and all the men and women, quite silent now, made a dark line along the wall. The lamp in the middle of the room was still swinging a little, and they had forgotten to close the window, so that the snow, which was falling more lightly now, came in little clouds with breaths of wind, into the room—and the bells were yet pealing and could be heard very plainly against the silence.

Then Sam Figgis, who was standing with his legs wide apart, said something that Peter could not catch, and a little sigh of excitement went up all round the room. Peter, who was clutching his chair with both hands, and choking, very painfully, in his throat, knew, although he had no reason for his knowledge, that the little man with the shining chest meant to kill Stephen if he could.

The two men moved round the circle very slowly with their fists clenched and their eyes watching every movement—then, suddenly, they closed. At once Peter saw that the little man was very clever, cleverer than Stephen. He moved with amazing quickness. Stephen's blows came like sledge-hammers, and sometimes they fell with a dull heavy sound on the other man's face and on his chest, but more often they missed altogether. The man seemed to be everywhere at once, and although the blows that he gave Stephen seemed to have little effect yet he got past the other's defence again and again.

Then, again, the figures in front of Peter closed in and he saw nothing. He stood on his chair—no one noticed him now—but he could not see. His face was very white, and his stockings had fallen down over his boots, but with every movement he was growing more afraid. He caught an instant's vision of Stephen's face, and he saw that it was white and that he was breathing hard. The room seemed to be ominously silent, and then men would break out into strange threatening sounds, and Peter could see one woman—a young girl—with a red shawl about her shoulders, her back against the wall, staring with a white face.

He could not see—he could not see....

He murmured once very politely—he thought he said it aloud but it was really under his breath: "Please, please—would you mind—if you stood aside—just a little...." but the man in front of him was absorbed and heard nothing. Then he knew that there was a pause, he caught a glimpse of the brick floor and he saw that Stephen was sitting back in his chair—his face was white, and blood was trickling out from the corner of his mouth on to his beard. Then Peter remembered old Frosted Moses' words: "The courage you bring to it...." and he sat back in his chair again and, with hands clenched, waited. He would be brave, braver than he had ever been before, and perhaps in some strange way his bravery would help Stephen. He determined with all the power that he had to be brave. They had begun again, he heard the sound of the blows, the movement of the men's feet on the rough brick of the floor; people cried out, the man in front of him pressed forward and he had a sudden view. Stephen was on one knee and his head was down and the other man was standing over him. It was all over—Stephen was beaten—Stephen would be killed, and in another minute Peter would have pushed past the people and run into the middle of the room, but Sam Figgis had again come forward, and the two men were in their chairs again. There followed another terrible time when Peter could see nothing. He waited—he could hear them moving again, the noise of their breathing and of their feet, the men in the crowd were pressing nearer, but there was no word spoken.

He must see—at all costs he must see. And he climbed down from his chair, and crept unnoticed towards the front. Nobody saw him or realised him.... Stephen was bending back, he seemed to be slowly sinking down. The other man, from whose face blood was now streaming, was pressing on to him. Peter knew that it was all over and that there was no hope; there was a dreadful cold, hard pain in his throat, and he could scarcely see. Courage! he must have it for Stephen. With every bit of his soul and his mind and his body he was brave. He stood taut—his little legs stiff beneath him and flung defiance at the world. He and Stephen were fighting that shiny man together—both of them—now. Courage! Stephen's head lifted a little, and then slowly Peter saw him pulling his body together—he grew rigid, he raised his head, and, as a tree falls, his fist crashed into his enemy's face. The man dropped without a word and lay motionless. It was over. Stephen gravely watched for a moment the senseless body and then sat back in his chair, his head bowed on his chest.

The fight had not, perhaps, been like that—there must have been many other things that happened, but that was always how Peter remembered it. And now there was confusion—a great deal of noise and people talking very loudly, but Stephen said nothing at all. He did not look at the body again, but when he had recovered a little, still without a word to any one and with his eyes grave and without expression, he moved to the corner where his clothes lay.

"'E's not dead."

"No—give 'im room there, he's moving," and from the back of the crowd the Fool's silly face, peering over...

Peter crept unnoticed to the door. The clocks were striking ten, and some one in the street was singing. He pulled up his stockings and fastened his garters, then he slipped out into the snow and saw that the sky was full of stars and that the storm had passed.

CHAPTER II

HOW THE WESTCOTT FAMILY SAT UP FOR PETER

I

The boy always reckoned that, walking one's quickest, it took half an hour from the door of The Bending Mule to Scaw House, where his father lived. If a person ran all the way twenty minutes would perhaps cover it, but, most of the time, the road went up hill and that made running difficult; he had certainly no intention of running to-night, there were too many things to think about. That meant, then, that he would arrive home about half-past ten, and there would be his aunt and his grandfather and his father sitting up waiting for him.

The world was very silent, and the snow lay on the round cobbles of the steep street with a bright shining whiteness against the black houses and the dark night sky. Treliss' principal street was deserted; all down the hill red lights showed in the windows and voices could be heard, singing and laughing, because on Christmas Eve there would be parties and merrymakings. Peter looked a tiny and rather desolate figure against the snow as he climbed the hill. There was a long way to go. There would be Green Street at the top, past the post office, then down again into the Square where the Tower was, then through winding turnings up the hill past the gates and dark trees of The Man at Arms, then past the old wall of the town and along the wide high road that runs above the sea until at last one struck the common, and, hidden in a black clump of trees (so black on a night like this), the grim grey stones of Scaw House.

Peter was not afraid of being alone, although when snow had fallen everything seemed strange and monstrous, the trees were like animals, and the paths of all the world were swept away. But he was not afraid of ghosts; he was too accustomed to their perpetual company; old Frosted Moses and Dicky, and even men like Stephen, had seen ghosts so often, and Peter himself could tell odd stories about the Grey Hill—no, ghosts held no terror. But, very slowly, the shadow of all that he must very soon go through was creeping about him. When he first came out of The Bending Mule he still was as though he were in a dream. Everything that had happened there that evening had been so strange, so amazing, that it belonged to the world of dreams—it was of the very stuff of them, and that vision of Stephen, naked, bleeding, so huge and so terrible, was not to be easily forgotten.

But, as he climbed the steep street, Peter knew that however great a dream that might be, there was to be no dreaming at all about his meeting with his father, and old Frosted Moses' philosophy would be very sadly needed. As he climbed the hill the reaction from the excitement of his late adventure suddenly made him very miserable indeed, so that he had an immediate impulse to cry, but he stood still in the middle of the street and made fists with his hands and called himself "a damned gawky idiot," words that he had admired in the mouth of Sam Figgis some days before. "Gawky" was certainly the last thing that he was, but it was a nice queer word, and it helped him a great deal.

The worst of everything was that he had had a number of beatings lately and the world could not possibly go on, as far as he was concerned, if he had many more. Every beating made matters worse and his own desperate attempts to be good and to merit rewards rather than chastisement met with no success. The hopeless fact of it all was that it had very little to do with his own actions; his father behaved in the same way to every one, and Mrs. Trussit, the housekeeper, old Curtis the gardener, Aunt Jessie, and all the servants, shook under his tongue and the cold glitter of his eyes, and certainly the maids would long ago have given notice and departed were it not that they were all afraid to face him. Peter knew that that was true, because Mrs. Trussit had told him so. It was this hopeless feeling of indiscriminate punishment that made everything so bad. Until he was eight years old Peter had not been beaten at all, but when he was very young indeed he had learnt to crawl away when he heard his father's step, and he had never cried as a baby because his nurse's white scared face had frightened him so. And then, of course, there was his mother, his poor mother—that was another reason for silence. He never saw his mother for more than a minute at a time because she was ill, had been ill for as long as he could remember. When he was younger he had been taken into his mother's room once or twice a week by Mrs. Trussit, and he had bent down and kissed that white tired face, and he had smelt the curious smell in the room of flowers and medicine, and he had heard his mother's voice, very far away and very soft, and he had crept out again. When he was older his aunt told him sometimes to go and see his mother, and he would creep in alone, but he never could say anything because of the whiteness of the room and the sense of something sacred like church froze his speech. He had never seen his father and mother together.

His mornings were always spent with old Parlow, and in the afternoon he was allowed to ramble about by himself, so that it was only at mealtimes and during the horrible half-hour after supper before he went up to bed that he saw his father.

He really saw more of old Curtis the gardener, but half an hour with his father could seem a very long time. Throughout the rest of his life that half-hour after supper remained at the back of his mind—and he never forgot its slightest detail. The hideous dining-room with the large photographs of old grandfather and grandmother Westcott in ill-fitting clothes and heavy gilt frames, the white marble clock on the mantelpiece, a clock that would tick solemnly for twenty minutes and then give a little run and a jump for no reason at all, the straight horsehair sofa so black and uncomfortable with its hard wooden back, the big dining-room table with its green cloth (faded a little in the middle where a pot with a fern in it always stood) and his aunt with her frizzy yellow hair, her black mittens and her long bony fingers playing her interminable Patience, and then two arm-chairs by the fire, in one of them old grandfather Westcott, almost invisible beneath a load of rugs and cushions and only the white hairs on the top of his head sticking out like some strange plant, and in the other chair his father, motionless, reading the Cornish Times—last of all, sitting up straight with his work in front of him, afraid to move, afraid to cough, sometimes with pins and needles, sometimes with a maddening impulse to sneeze, always with fascinated glances out of the corner of his eye at his father—Peter himself. How happy he was when the marble clock struck nine, and he was released! How snug and friendly his little attic bedroom was with its funny diamond-paned window under the shelving roof with all the view of the common and the distant hills that covered Truro! There, at any rate, he was free!

He was passing now through the Square, and he stopped for an instant and looked up at the old weather-beaten Tower that guarded one side of it, and looked so fine and stately now with the white snow at its foot and the gleaming sheet of stars at its back. That old Tower had stood a good number of beatings in its day—it knew well enough what courage was—and so Peter, as he turned up the hill, squared his shoulders and set his teeth. But in some way that he was too young to understand he felt that it was not the beating itself that frightened him most, but rather all the circumstances that attended it—it was even the dark house, the band of trees about it, that first dreadful moment when he would hear his knock echo through the passages, and then the patter of Mrs. Trussit's slippers as she came to open the door for him—then Mrs. Trussit's fat arm and the candle raised above her head, and "Oh, it's you, Mr. Peter," and then the opening of the dining-room door and "It's Master Peter, sir," and then that vision of the marble clock and his father's face behind the paper. These things were unfair and more than any one deserved. He had had beatings on several occasions when he had merited no punishment at all, but it did not make things any better that on this occasion he did deserve it; it only made that feeling inside his chest that everything was so hopeless that nothing whatever mattered, and that it was always more fun to be beaten for a sheep than a lamb, stronger than ever.

But the world—or at any rate the Scaw House portion of it—could not move in this same round eternally. Something would happen, and the vague, half-confessed intention that had been in his mind for some time now was a little more defined. One day, like his three companions, Tom Jones, Peregrine Pickle and David Copperfield, he would run into the world and seek his fortune, and then, afterwards, he would write his book of adventures as they had done. His heart beat at the thought, and he passed the high gates and dark trees of The Man at Arms with quick step and head high. He was growing old—twelve was an age—and there would soon be a time when beatings must no longer be endured. He shivered when he thought of what would happen then—the mere idea of defying his father sent shudders down his back, but he was twelve, he would soon be thirteen....

But this Scaw House, with its strange silence and distresses, was only half his life. There was the other existence that he had down in the town, out at Stephen's farm, wandering alone on the Grey Hill, roaming about along the beach and in amongst the caves, tramping out to The Hearty Cow, a little inn amongst the gorse, ten miles away, or looking for the lost church among the sand-dunes at Porthperran. All these things had nothing whatever to do with his father and old Parlow and his lessons—and it was undoubtedly this other sort of life that he would lead, with the gipsies and the tramps, when the time came for him to run away. He knew no other children of his own age, but he did not want them; he liked best to talk to old Curtis the gardener, to Dicky the Idiot, to Sam Figgis when that splendid person would permit it—and, of course, to Stephen.

He passed the old town wall and stepped out into the high road. Far below him was the sea, above him a sky scattered with shining stars and around him a white dim world. Turning a corner the road lay straight before him and to the right along the common was the black clump of trees that hid his home. He discovered that he was very tired, it had been a most exhausting day with old Parlow so cross in the morning and the scene in the inn at night—and now—!

His steps fell slower and slower as he passed along the road. One hot hand was clutching Parlow's note and in his throat there was a sharp pain that made it difficult to swallow, and his eyes were burning.

Suppose he never went home at all! Supposing he went off to Stephen's farm!—it was a long way and he might lose his way in the snow, but his heart beat like a hammer when he thought of Stephen coming to the door and of the little spare room where Stephen put his guests to sleep. But no—Stephen would not want him to-night; he would be very tired and would rather be alone; and then there would be the morning, when it would be every bit as bad, and perhaps worse. But if he ran away altogether? ... He stopped in the middle of the road and thought about it—the noise of the sea came up to him like the march of men and with it the sick melancholy moan of the Bell Rock, but the rest of the world was holding its breath, so still it seemed. But whither should he run? He could not run so far away that his father could not find him—his father's arm stretched to everywhere in the world. And then it was cowardly to run away. Where was that courage of which he had been thinking so much? So he shook his little shoulders and pulled up those stockings again and turned up the little side road, usually so full of ruts and stones and now so level and white with the hard snow. Now that his mind was made up, he marched forward with unfaltering step and clanged the iron gates behind him so that they made a horrible noise, and stepped through the desolate garden up the gravel path.

The house looked black and grim, but there were lights behind the dining-room windows—it was there that they were sitting, of course.

As he stood on his toes to reach the knocker a shooting star flashed past above his head, and he could hear the bare branches of the trees knocking against one another in the wind that always seemed to be whistling round the house. The noise echoed terribly through the building, and then there was a silence that was even more terrible. He could fancy how his aunt would start and put down her Patience cards for a moment and look, in her scared way, at the window—he knew that his father would not move from behind his paper, and that there would be no other sound unless his grandfather awoke. He heard Mrs. Trussit's steps down the passage, then locks were turned, the great door swung slowly open, and he saw her, as he had pictured it, with a candle in her hand raised above her head, peering into the dark.

"Oh! it's you, Master Peter," and she stood aside, without another word, to let him in. He slipped past her, silently, into the hall and, after a second's pause, she followed him in, banging the hall door behind her. Then she opened the dining-room door announcing, grimly, "It's Master Peter come in, sir." The marble clock struck half-past ten as she spoke.

He stood just inside the door blinking a little at the sudden light and twisting his cloth cap round and round in his hands. He couldn't see anything at first, and he could not collect his thoughts. At last he said, in a very little voice:

"I've come back, father."

The lights settled before his eyes, and he saw them all exactly as he had thought they would be. His father had not looked up from his paper, and Peter could see the round bald patch on the top of his head. Aunt Jessie was talking to herself about her cards in a very agitated whisper—"Now it's the King I want—how provoking! Ah, there's the seven of spades, and the six and the five—oh dear! it's a club," and not looking up at all.

No one answered his remark, and the silence was broken by his grandfather waking up; a shrill piping voice came from out of the rugs. "Oh! dear, what a doze I've had! It must be eight o'clock! What a doze for an old man to have! on such a cold night too," and then fell asleep again immediately.

At last Peter spoke again in a voice that seemed to come from quite another person.

"Father—I've come back!"

His father very slowly put down his newspaper and looked at him as though he were conscious of him for the first time. When he spoke it was as though his voice came out of the ceiling or the floor because his face did not seem to move at all.

"Where have you been?"

"In the town, father."

"Come here."

He crossed the room and stood in front of the fire between his father and grandfather. He was tremendously conscious of the grim and dusty cactus plant that stood on a little table by the window.

"What have you been doing in the town?"

"I have been in The Bending Mule, father."

"Why did you not come home before?"

There was no answer.

"You knew that you ought to come home?"

"Yes, father. I have a letter for you from Mr. Parlow. He said that I was to tell you that I have done my sums very badly this week and that I gave Willie Daffoll a bleeding nose on Wednesday—"

"Yes—have you any excuse for these things?"

"No, father."

"Very well. You may go up to your room. I will come up to you there."

"Yes, father."

He crossed the room very slowly, closed the door softly behind him, and then climbed the dark stairs to his attic.

II

He went trembling up to his room, and the match-box shook in his hand as he lit his candle. It was only the very worst beatings that happened in his bedroom, his father's gloomy and solemn study serving as a background on more unimportant occasions. He could only remember two other beatings in the attics, and they had both been very bad ones. He closed his door and then stood in the middle of the room; the little diamond-paned window was open and the glittering of the myriad stars flung a light over his room and shone on the little bracket of books above his bed (a Bible, an "Arabian Nights," and tattered copies of "David Copperfield," "Vanity Fair," "Peregrine Pickle," "Tom Jones," and "Harry Lorrequer"), on the little washing stand, a chest of drawers, a cane-bottomed chair, and the little bed. There were no pictures on the walls because of the sloping roof, but there were two china vases on the mantelpiece, and they were painted a very bright blue with yellow flowers on them.

They had been given to Peter by Mrs. Flanders, the Rector's wife, who had rather a kind feeling for Peter, and would have been friendly to him had he allowed her. He took off his jacket and put it on again, he stood uncertainly in the middle of the floor, and wondered whether he ought to undress or no. There was no question about it now, he was horribly, dreadfully afraid. That wisdom of old Frosted Moses seemed a very long ago, and it was of very little use. If it had all happened at once after he had come in then he might have endured it, but this waiting and listening with the candle guttering was too much for him. His father was so very strong—he had Peter's figure and was not very tall and was very broad in the back; Peter had seen him once when he was stripped, and the thought of it always frightened him.

His face was white and his teeth would chatter although he bit his lips and his fingers shook as he undressed, and his stud slipped and he could not undo his braces—and always his ears were open for the sound of the step on the stairs.

At last he was in his night-shirt, and a very melancholy figure he looked as he stood shivering in the middle of the floor. It was not only that he was going to be beaten, it was also that he was so lonely. Stephen seemed so dreadfully far away and he had other things to think about; he wondered whether his mother in that strange white room ever thought of him, his teeth were chattering, so that his whole head shook, but he was afraid to get into bed because then he might go to sleep and it would be so frightening to be woken by his father.

The clock downstairs struck eleven, and he heard his father's footstep. The door opened, and his father came in holding in his hand the cane that Peter knew so well.

"Are you there?" the voice was very cold.

"Yes, father."

"Do you know that you ought to be home before six?"

"Yes, father."

"And that I dislike your going to The Bending Mule?"

"Yes, father."

"And that I insist on your doing your work for Mr. Parlow?"

"Yes, father."

"And that you are not to fight the other boys in the town?"

"Yes, father."

"Why do you disobey me like this?"

"I don't know. I try to be good."

"You are growing into an idle, wicked boy. You are a great trouble to your mother and myself."

"Yes, father. I want to be better."

Even now he could admire his father's strength, the bull-neck, the dark close-cropped hair, but he was cold, and the blood had come where he bit his lip—because he must not cry.

"You must learn obedience. Take off your nightshirt."

He took it off, and was a very small naked figure in the starlight, but his head was up now and he faced his father.

"Bend over the bed."

He bent over the bed, and the air from the window cut his naked back. He buried his head in the counterpane and fastened his teeth in it so that he should not cry out....

During the first three cuts he did not stir, then an intolerable pain seemed to move through his body—it was as though a knife were cutting his body in half. But it was more than that—there was terror with him now in the room; he heard that little singing noise that came through his father's lips—he knew that his father was smiling.

At the succeeding strokes his flesh quivered and shrank together and then opened again—the pain was intolerable; his teeth met through the coverlet and grated on one another; but before his eyes was the picture of Stephen slowly straightening himself before his enemy and then that swinging blow—he would not cry. He seemed to be sharing his punishment with Stephen, and they were marching, hand in hand, down a road lined with red-hot pokers.

His back was on fire, and his head was bursting and the soles of his feet were very, very cold.

Then he heard, from a long way away, his father's voice:

"Now you will not disobey me again."

The door closed. Very slowly he raised himself, but moving was torture; he put on his night-shirt and then quickly caught back a scream as it touched his back. He moved to the window and closed it, then he climbed very slowly on to his bed, and the tears that he had held back came, slowly at first, and then more rapidly, at last in torrents. It was not the pain, although that was bad, but it was the misery and the desolation and the great heaviness of a world that held out no hope, no comfort, but only a great cloud of unrelieved unhappiness.

At last, sick with crying, he fell asleep.

The first shadow of light was stealing across the white undulating common and creeping through the bare trees of the desolate garden when four dark figures, one tall, two fat, and one small, stole softly up the garden path. They halted beneath the windows of the house; the snow had ceased falling, and their breath rose in clouds above their heads. They danced a little in the snow and drove their hands together, and then the tall figure said:

"Now, Tom Prother, out with thy musick." One of the fat figures felt in his coat and produced four papers, and these were handed round.

"Bill, my son, it's for thee to lead off at thy brightest, mind ye. Let 'em have it praper."

The small figure came forward and began; at first his voice was thin and quavering, but in the second line it gathered courage and rang out full and bold:

As oi sat under a sicymore tree A sicymore tree, a sicymore tree, Oi looked me out upon the sea On Christ's Sunday at morn.

"Well for thee, lad," said the tall figure approvingly, "but the cold is creepin' from the tips o' my fingers till my singin' voice is most frozen. Now, altogether."

And the birds in the silent garden woke amongst the ivy on the distant wall and listened:

Oi saw three ships a-sailin' there— A sailin' there, a-sailin' there, Jesu, Mary, and Joseph they bare On Christ's Sunday at morn.

A small boy curled up, like the birds, under the roof stirred uneasily in his sleep and then slowly woke. He moved, and gave a little cry because his back hurt him, then he remembered everything. The voices came up to him from the garden:

Joseph did whistle and Mary did sing,
Mary did sing, Mary did sing,
And all the bells on earth did ring
For joy our Lord was born.

O they sail'd in to Bethlehem,
To Bethlehem, to Bethlehem;
Saint Michael was the steersman,
Saint John sate in the horn.

And all the bells on earth did ring,
On earth did ring, on earth did ring;
"Welcome be thou Heaven's King,
On Christ's Sunday at morn."

He got slowly out of bed and went to the window. The light was coming in broad bands from the East and he could hear the birds in the ivy. The four black figures stood out against the white shadowy garden and their heads were bent together. He opened his window, and the fresh morning air swept about his face.

He could hear the whispers of the singers as they chose another carol and suddenly above the dark iron gates of the garden appeared the broad red face of the sun.

CHAPTER III

OF THE DARK SHOP OF ZACHARY TAN, AND OF THE DECISIONS THAT THE PEOPLE IN SCAW HOUSE CAME TO CONCERNING PETER

I

But it was of the nature of the whole of life that these things should pass. "Look back on this bitterness a year hence and see how trivial it seems" was one of the little wisdoms that helped Peter's courage in after years. And to a boy of twelve years a beating is forgotten with amazing quickness, especially if it is a week of holiday and there have been other beatings not so very long before.

It left things behind it, of course. It was the worst beating that Peter had ever had, and that was something, but its occurrence marked more than a mere crescendo of pain, and that evening stood for some new resolution that he did not rightly understand yet—something that was in its beginning the mere planting of a seed. But he had certainly met the affair in a new way and, although in the week that followed he saw his father very seldom and spoke to him not at all beyond "Good morning" and "Good night," he fancied that he was in greater favour with him than he had ever been before.

There were always days of silence after a beating, and that was more markedly the case now when it was a week of holidays and no Parlow to go to. Peter did not mind the silence—it was perhaps safer— and so long as he was home by six o'clock he could spend the day where he pleased. He asked Mrs. Trussit about the carol-singers. There was a little room, the housekeeper's room, to which he crept when he thought that it was safe to do so. She was a different Mrs. Trussit within the boundary of her kingdom—a very cosy kingdom with pink wall-paper, a dark red sofa, a canary in a cage, and a fire very lively in the grate. From the depths of a big arm-chair, her black silk dress rustling a little every now and then, her knitting needles clinking in the firelight, Mrs. Trussit held many conversations in a subdued voice with Peter, who sat on the table and swung his legs. She was valuable from two points of view—as an Historian and an Encyclopædia. She had been, in the first place, in the most wonderful houses—The Earl of Twinkerton's, Bambary House, Wiltshire, was the greatest of these, and she had been there for ten years; there were also Lady Mettlesham, the Duchess of Cranburn, and, to Peter, the most interesting of all, Mr. Henry Galleon, the famous novelist who was so famous that American ladies used to creep into his garden and pick leaves off his laurels.

Peter had from her a dazzling picture of wonderful houses—of staircases and garden walks, of thousands and thousands of shining rooms, of family portraits, and footmen with beautiful legs. Above it all was "my lady" who was always beautiful and stately and, of course, devoted to Mrs. Trussit. Why that good woman left these noble mansions for so dreary a place as Scaw House Peter never could understand, and for many years that remained a mystery to him—but in awed whispers he asked her questions about the lords and ladies of the land and especially about the famous novelist and, from the answers given to him, constructed a complete and most romantic picture of the Peerage.

But, as an Encyclopædia, Mrs. Trussit was even more interesting. She had apparently discovered at an early age that the golden rule of life was never to confess yourself defeated by any question whatever, and there was therefore nothing that he could ask her for which she had not an immediate answer ready. Her brow was always unruffled, her black shining hair brushed neatly back and parted down the middle, her large flat face always composed and placid, and her voice never raised above a whisper. The only sign that she ever gave of disturbance was a little clucking noise that she made in her mouth like an aroused hen. Peter's time in the little pink sitting-room was sometimes exceedingly short and he used to make the most of it by shooting questions at the good lady at an astonishing rate, and he was sometimes irritated by her slow and placid replies:

"What kind of stockings did Mr. Galleon wear?"

"He didn't wear stockings unless, as you might say, in country attire, and then, if I remember correctly, they were grey."

"Had he any children?"

"There was one little dear when I had the honour of being in the house—and since then I have heard that there are two more."

"Mrs. Trussit, where do children come from?"

"They are brought by God's good angels when we are all asleep in the night time."

"Oh!" (this rather doubtfully). A pause—then "Did the Earl of Twinkerton have hot or cold baths?"

"Cold in the morning, I believe, with the chill off and hot at night before dressing for dinner. He was a very cleanly gentleman."

"Mrs. Trussit, where is Patagonia? It came in the history this morning."

"North of the Caribbean Sea, I believe, my dear."

And so on, and Peter never forgot any of her answers. About the carol-singers she was a little irritable. They had woken her it seemed from a very delightful sleep, and she considered the whole affair "savoured of Paganism." And then Peter found suddenly that he didn't wish to talk about the carol-singers at all because the things that he felt about them were, in some curious way, not the things that he could say to Mrs. Trussit.

She was very kind to him during that Christmas week and gave him mixed biscuits out of a brightly shining tin that she kept in a cupboard in her room. But outside the gates of her citadel she was a very different person, spoke to Peter but rarely, and then always with majesty and from a long way away. Her attitude to the little maid-of-all-work was something very wonderful indeed, and even to Aunt Jessie her tone might be considered patronising.

But indeed to Aunt Jessie it was very difficult to be anything else. Aunt Jessie was a poor creature, as Peter discovered very early in life. He found that she never had any answers ready to the questions that he asked her and that she hesitated when he wished to know whether he might do a thing or no. She was always trembling and shaking, and no strong-minded person ever wore mittens. He had a great contempt for his aunt....

On New Year's Eve, the last day but one of release from old Parlow, Mr. Westcott spent the day doing business in Truro, and at once the atmosphere over Scaw House seemed to lighten. The snow had melted away, and there was a ridiculous feeling of spring in the air; ridiculous because it was still December, but Cornwall is often surprisingly warm in the heart of winter, and the sun was shining as ardently as though it were the middle of June. The sunlight flooded the dining-room and roused old grandfather Westcott to unwonted life, so that he stirred in his chair and was quite unusually talkative.

He stopped Peter after breakfast, as he was going out of the room and called him to his side:

"Is that the sun, boy?"

"Yes, grandfather."

"Deary me, to think of that and me a poor, broken, old man not able to move an arm or foot."

He raised himself amongst his cushions, and Peter saw an old yellow wrinkled face with the skin drawn tight over the cheekbones and little black shining eyes like drops of ink. A wrinkled claw shot out and clutched Peter's hand.

"Do you love your grandfather, boy?"

"Of course, grandfather."

"That's right, that's right—on a nice sunny morning, too. Do you love your father, boy?"

"Of course, grandfather."

"He, he—oh, yes—all the Westcotts love their fathers. He loved his father when he was young, didn't he? Oh, yes, I should rather think so."

And his voice rose into a shrill scream so that Peter jumped. Then he began to look Peter up and down.

"You'll be strong, boy, when you're a man—oh, yes, I should rather think so—I was strong once.... Do you hear that?... I was strong once, he, he!"

And here grandfather Westcott, overcome by his chuckling, began to cough so badly that Peter was afraid that he was going to be ill, and considered running for Aunt Jessie.

"Hit my back, boy—huh, huh! Ugh, ugh! That's right, hit it hard—that's better—ugh, ugh! Oh! deary me! that's better—what a nasty cough, oh, deary me, what a nasty cough! I was strong once, boy, hegh, hegh! Indeed I was, just like your father—and he'll be just like me, one day! Oh! yes, he will—blast his bones! He, he! We all come to it—all of us strong men, and we're cruel and hard, and won't give a poor old man enough for his breakfast—and then suddenly we're old ourselves, and what fun that is! Oh! Yes, your father will be old one day!" and suddenly, delighted with the thought, the old man slipped down beneath his cushions and was fast asleep.

And Peter went out into the sunlight.

II

Peter looked very different at different times. When he was happy his cheeks were flooded with colour, his eyes shone, and his mouth smiled. He was happy now, and he forgot as he came out into the garden that he had promised his aunt that he would go in and see his mother for a few minutes. Old Curtis, wearing the enormous sun-hat that he always had flapping about his head and his trousers tied below his knees with string in the most ridiculous way, was sweeping the garden path. He never did very much work, and the garden was in a shocking state of neglect, but he told delightful stories. To-day, however, he was in a bad temper and would pay no attention to Peter at all, and so Peter left him and went out into the high road.

It was two miles across the common to Stephen's farm and it took the boy nearly an hour, because the ground was uneven and there were walls to climb, and also because he was thinking of what his grandfather had said. Would his father one day be old and silly like his grandfather? Did every one get old and silly like that? and, if so, what was the use of being born at all? But what happened to all his father's strength? Where did it all go to? In some curious undefined way he resented his grandfather's remarks. He could have loved and admired his father immensely had he been allowed to, but even if that were not permitted he could stand up for him when he was attacked. What right had his silly old grandfather to talk like that?... His father would one day be old? And Stephen, would he be old, too? Did all strength go?

Peter was crossing a ploughed field, and the rich brown earth heaved in a great circle against the sky and in the depth of its furrows there were mysterious velvet shadows—the brown hedges stood back against the sky line. The world was so fresh and clean and strong this morning that the figure and voice of his grandfather hung unpleasantly about him and depressed him. There were so many things that he wanted to know and so few people to tell him, and he turned through the white gates of Stephen's farm with a consciousness that since Christmas Eve the world had begun to be a new place.

Stephen was sitting in the upstairs room scratching his head over his accounts, whilst his old mother sat dozing, with her knitting fallen on to her lap by the fire. The window was open, and all the sound and smells of the farm came into the room. The room was an old one with brown oaken rafters and whitewashed walls, a long oaken table down the middle of it, and a view over the farmyard and the sweeping fields beyond it, lost at last, in the distant purple hills. Peter was given a chair opposite the old lady, who was nearly eighty, and wore a beautiful white cap, and she woke up and talked incessantly, because she was very garrulous by nature and didn't care in the least to whom she talked. Peter politely listened to what she had to say, although he understood little of it, and his eyes were watching for the moment when the accounts should be finished and Stephen free.

"Ay," said the old lady, "and it were good Mr. Tenement were the rector in those days, I remember, and he gave us a roaring discourse many's the Sunday. Church is not what it was, with all this singing and what not and the clothes the young women wear—I remember..."

But Stephen had closed his books with a bang and given his figures up in despair. "I don't know how it is, boy," he said, "but they're at something different every time yer look at 'em—they're one too many for me, that's certain."

One of Stephen's eyes was still nearly closed, and both eyes were black and blue, and his right cheek had a bad bruise on it, but Peter thought it was wiser not to allude to the encounter. The farm was exceedingly interesting, and then there was dinner, and it was not until the meal had been cleared away that Peter remembered that he wanted to ask some questions, and then Stephen interrupted him with:

"Like to go to Zachary Tan's with me this afternoon, boy? I've got to be lookin' in."

Peter jumped to his feet with excitement.

"Oh! Steve! This afternoon—this very afternoon?"

It was the most exciting thing possible. Zachary Tan's was the curiosity shop of Treliss and famous even twenty years ago throughout the south country. It is still there, I believe, although Zachary himself is dead and with him has departed most of the atmosphere of the place, and it is now smart and prosperous, although in those days it was dark and dingy enough. No one knew whence Zachary had come, and he was one of the mysteries of a place that deals, even now, in mysteries. He had arrived as a young man with a basket over his back thirty years before Peter saw the light, when Treliss was a little fishing village and Mr. Bannister, Junior, had not cast his enterprising eye over The Man at Arms. Zachary had beads and silks, and little silver images in his basket, and he had stayed there in a little room over the shop, and things had prospered with him. The inhabitants of the place had never trusted him, but they were always interested. "Thiccy Zachary be a poor trade," they had said at first, "poor trade" signifying anything or anybody not entirely approved of—but they had hung about his shop, had bought his silks and little ornaments, and had talked to him sometimes with eyes open and mouth agape at the things that he could tell them. And then people had come from Truro and Pendragon and even Bodmin and, finally, Exeter, because they had heard of the things that he had for sale. No one knew where he found his treasures, for he was always in his shop, smiling and amiable, but sometimes gentlemen would come from London, and he had strange friends like Mr. Andreas Morelli, concerning whose life a book has already been written. Zachary Tan's shop became at last the word in Treliss for all that was strange and unusual—the strongest link with London and other curious places. He had a little back room behind his shop, where he would welcome his friends, give them something to drink and talk about the world. He was always so friendly that people thought that he must wish for things in return, but he never asked for anything, nor did he speak about himself at all. As for his portrait, he had a pale face, a big beak nose, very black hair that hung over his forehead and was always untidy, a blue velvet jacket, black trousers, green slippers, and small feet.

He also wore two rings and blew his long nose in silk handkerchiefs of the most wonderful colours. All these things may seem of the slenderest importance, but they are not insignificant if one considers their effect upon Peter. Zachary was the most romantic figure that he had yet encountered; to walk through the shop with its gold and its silver, its dust and its jewels, into the dark little room beyond; to hear this wonderful person talk, to meet men who lived in London, to listen by the light of flickering candles and with one's eyes fixed upon portraits of ladies dancing in the slenderest attire, this was indeed Life, and Life such as The Bending Mule, Scaw House, and even Stephen's farm itself could not offer.

Peter often wondered why Stephen and Zachary were friends, because they seemed to have little enough in common, but Stephen was a silent man, who liked all kinds of company, and Peter noticed that Zachary was always very polite and obliging to Stephen.

Stephen was very silent going across the Common and down the high road into the town, but Peter knew him too well by this time to interrupt his thoughts. He was thinking perhaps about his accounts that would not come right or about the fight and Burstead his enemy.

Everybody had their troubles that they thought about and every one had their secrets, the things that they kept to themselves—even Aunt Jessie and old Curtis the gardener—one must either be as clever as Zachary Tan or as foolish as Dicky the Idiot to know very much about people. Zachary, Peter had noticed, was one of the persons who always listened to everything that Dicky had to say, and treated him with the greatest seriousness, even when he seemed to be talking about the wildest things—and it was a great many years after this that Peter discovered that it was only the wisest people who knew how very important fools were. Zachary's shop was at the very bottom of Poppero Street, the steep and cobbled street that goes straight down to the little wooden jetty where the fishing boats lie, and you could see the sea like a square handkerchief between the houses on either side. Many of the houses in Poppero Street are built a little below the level of the pathway, and you must go down steps to reach the door. Zachary's shop was like this, and it had a green door with a bright brass knocker. There were always many things jumbled together in the window—candlesticks, china shepherds and shepherdesses, rings and necklaces, cups and saucers, little brass figures, coins, snuff-boxes, match-boxes, charms, and old blue china plates, and at the back a complete suit of armour that had been there ever since Zachary had first opened his shop.

Of course, inside there were a thousand and one things of the most exciting kind, but Stephen, an enormous figure in the low-roofed shop, brushed past the pale-faced youth whom Zachary now hired to assist with the customers and passed into the dark room beyond, Peter close at his heels.

There were two silver candlesticks lighted on the mantelpiece, and there were two more in the centre of the green baize table and round the fire were seated four men. One of them Zachary himself, another was pleasant little Mr. Bannister, host of The Man at Arms, another was old Frosted Moses, sucking as usual at his great pipe, and the fourth was a stranger.

Zachary rose and came forward smiling. "Ah, Mr. Brant, delighted to see you, I'm sure. Brought the boy with you? Excellent, excellent. Mr. Bannister and Mr. Tathero (old Moses' society name) you know, of course; this is Mr. Emilio Zanti, a friend of mine from London."

The stranger, who was an enormous fat man with a bald head and an eager smile rose and shook hands with Stephen, he also shook hands with Peter as though it had been the ambition of his life to meet that small and rather defiant person.

He also embarrassed Peter very much by addressing him as though he were grown up, and listening courteously to everything that he had to say. Peter decided that he did not like him—but "a gentleman from London" was always an exciting introduction. The boy was able very quickly to obliterate himself by sitting down somewhere in a corner and remaining absolutely silent and perhaps that was the reason that he was admitted to so many elderly gatherings—he was never in the way. He slipped quickly into a chair, hidden in the shadow of the wall, but close to the elbow of "the gentleman from London," whose face he watched with the greatest curiosity. Stephen was silent, and Frosted Moses very rarely said anything at all, so that the conversation speedily became a dialogue between Zachary and the foreign gentleman, with occasional appeals to Mr. Brant for his unbiassed opinion. Peter's whole memory of the incident was vague and uncertain, although in after years he often tried very hard to recall it all to mind. He was excited by the mere atmosphere of the place, by the silver candlesticks, the dancing ladies on the walls, Zachary's blue coat, and the sense of all the wonderful things in the shop beyond. He had no instinct that it was all important beyond the knowledge that it roused a great many things in him that the rest of his life left untouched and anything to do with "London," a city, as he knew from Tom Jones and David Copperfield, of extraordinary excitement and adventure, was an event. He watched Mr. Emilio Zanti closely, and he decided that his smile was not real, and that it must be very unpleasant to have a bald head. He also noticed that he said things in a funny way: like "ze beautiful country zat you 'ave 'ere with its sea and its woods" and "I 'ave the greatest re-spect for ze Englishman"—also his hands were very fat and he wore rings like Zachary.

Sometimes Peter fancied that his words meant a great deal more than they seemed to mean. He laughed when there was really nothing to laugh at and he tried to make Stephen talk, but Stephen was very silent. On the whole the conversation was dull, Peter thought, and once he nodded and was very nearly asleep, and fancied that the gentleman from London was spreading like a balloon and filling all the room. There was no mention of London at all.

Peter wondered for what purpose Stephen had come there, because he sat looking at the fire with his brown hands spread out over his great knees, thinking apparently all his own thoughts.

Then suddenly there came a moment. The London gentleman, Mr. Emilio Zanti, turned round quite quickly and said, like a shot out of a gun: "And what does our little friend think of it?"

Peter did not know to what he was referring, and looked embarrassed. He was also conscious that Zachary was watching him keenly.

"Ah, 'e does not understand, our little friend. But with life, what is it that you will do when you are grown up, my boy?" and he put his fat hand on Peter's knee. Peter disliked him more than ever, but he answered:

"I don't know—I haven't settled yet."

"Ah, it is early days," said Mr. Zanti, nodding his head, "there is much time, of course. But what is the thing that our little friend would care, most of all, to do?"

"To go to school," said Peter, without any hesitation, and both Zachary and Mr. Zanti laughed a great deal more than was in the least necessary.

"And then—afterwards?" said Mr. Zanti.

"To go to London," said Peter, stiffly, feeling in some undefined way that they were laughing at him and that something was going on that he did not understand.

"Ho! that is good," said Mr. Emilio, slapping his knees and rocking in his chair with merriment. "Ho! that is very good. He knows a thing or two, our young friend here. Ho, yes! don't you mistake!" For a little while he could not speak for laughing, and the tears rolled down his fat cheeks. "And what is it that you will do when you are there, my friend?" he said at last.

"I will have adventures," said Peter, growing a little bolder at the thought of London and its golden streets. And then, suddenly, when he heard this, curious Mr. Zanti grew very grave indeed, and his eyes were very large, and he put a finger mysteriously to his nose. Then he leant right over Peter and almost whispered in his ear.

"And you shall—of course you shall. You shall come to London and 'ave adventures—'eaps and 'eaps and 'eaps. Oh, yes, bless my soul, shan't he, Mr. Tan? Dear me, yes—London, my young friend, is the most wonderful place. In one week, if you are clever, you 'ave made thousands of pounds—thousands and thousands. Is it not so, Mr. Tan? When you are just a little bit older, a few years—then you shall come. And you ask for your friend, Mr. Emilio Zanti—because I like you. We will be friends, is not that so?"

And he held out his large fat hand and grasped Peter's small and rather damp one. Then he bent even closer, still holding Peter's hand: "Do you know one thing?" he whispered.

"No," replied Peter, husky with awe.

"It is this, that when you think of Mr. Zanti and of London and of adventures, you will look in a looking-glass—any looking-glass, and you will see—what you will see," and he nodded all over his fat face.

Peter was entirely overcome by this last astonishing statement, and was very relieved to hear numbers of clocks in the curiosity shop strike five o'clock. He got off his chair, said good-bye very politely indeed, and hurried up the dark street.

For the moment even his beloved Stephen was forgotten, and looking-glasses, the face of Mr. Emilio Zanti, London streets, and Zachary's silver candlesticks were mingled confusedly in his brain.

III

And indeed throughout the dreary supper Peter's brain was in a whirl. It often happened that supper passed without a word of conversation from first to last. His father very rarely said anything, Peter never said anything at all, and if Aunt Jessie did venture on a little conversation she received so slender an encouragement that she always forsook the attempt after a very short time. It was a miserable meal.

It was cold beef and beetroot and blanc-mange with a very, very little strawberry jam round the edges of the glass dish, and there was a hard red cheese and little stiff woolly biscuits.

But old grandfather Westcott was always hungry, and his querulous complaints were as regular an accompaniment to the evening meal as the ticking of the marble clock. But his beef had to be cut up for him into very tiny pieces and that gave Aunt Jessie a great deal of work, so that his appeals for a second helping were considered abominable selfishness.

"Oh, my dear, just a leetle piece of beef" (this from the very heart of the cushions). "Just the leetlest piece of beef for a poor old man—such a leetle piece he had, and he's had such a hunger." No answer to this and at last a strange noise from the cushions like the sound of dogs quarrelling. At last again, "Oh, just the leetlest piece of beef for a poor old man—" and then whimpering and "poor old man" repeated at intervals that lengthened gradually into sleep.

At last the meal was over, the things had been cleared away, and Peter was bending over a sum in preparation for lessons on Monday. Such a sum—add this and this and this and this and then divide it by that and multiply the result by this!... and the figures (bad ill-written figures) crept over the page and there were smudgy finger marks, and always between every other line "London, looking-glasses, and fat Mr. Zanti laughing until the tears ran down his face." Such a strange world where all these things could be so curiously confused, all of them, one supposed, having their purpose and meaning—even grandfather—and even 2469 X 2312 X 6201, and ever so many more until they ran races round the page and up and down and in and out.

And then suddenly into the middle of the silence his father's voice:

"What are you doing there?"

"Sums, father—for Monday."

"You won't go back on Monday" (and this without the Cornish Times moving an inch).

"Not go back?"

"No. You are going away to school—to Devonshire—on Tuesday week."

And Peter's pencil fell clattering on to the paper, and the answer to that sum is still an open question.

CHAPTER IV

IN WHICH "DAWSON'S," AS THE GATE OF LIFE, IS PROVED A DISAPPOINTMENT

I

It was, of course, very strange that this should come so swiftly after the meeting with the London gentleman—it was almost as though he had known about it, because it was a first step towards that London that he had so confidently promised. To Peter school meant the immediate supply of the two things that he wanted more than anything in the world—Friendship and Knowledge; not knowledge of the tiresome kind, Knowledge that had to do with the Kings of Israel and the capital of Italy, but rather the experience that other gentlemen of his own age had already gathered during their journey through the world. Stephen, Zachary, Moses, Dicky, Mrs. Trussit, old Curtis, even Aunt Jessie—all these people had knowledge, of course, but they would not give it you—they would not talk to you as though they were at your stage of the journey, they could not exchange opinions with you, they could not share in your wild surmises, they could not sympathise with your hatred of addition, multiplication, and subtraction. The fellow victims at old Parlow's might have been expected to do these things, but they were too young, too uninterested, too unenterprising. One wanted real boys—boys with excitement and sympathy... real boys.

He had wanted it, far, far more terribly than any one had known. He had sat, sometimes, in the dark, in his bedroom, and thought about it until he had very nearly cried, because he wanted it so badly, and now it had suddenly come out of the clouds... bang!

II

That last week went with a rattling speed and provided a number of most interesting situations. In the first place there was the joy—a simple but delightful one—on Monday morning, of thinking of those "others" who were entering, with laggard foot, into old Parlow's study—that study with the shining map of Europe on the wall, a bust of Julius Cæsar (conquered Britain? B.C.), and the worn red carpet. They would all be there. They would wonder where he was, and on discovering that he would never come again, Willie Daffoll, of recent tragic memory, would be pleased because now he would be chief and leader. Well, let him!... Yes, that was all very pleasant to think of.

There was further the thought that school might not, after all, be exactly what Peter imagined it. The pictures in his mind were evolved from his reading of "David Copperfield." There would be people like Steerforth and dear Traddles, there would be a master who played the flute, there would be rebellions and riots—would there?

Mrs. Trussit was of little value on this occasion:

"Mrs. Trussit, were you ever at school?"

"No, Master Peter, I was never at school. My good mother, who died at the ripe old age of ninety-two with all her faculties, gave me a liberal and handsome education with her own hands."

"Do you think it will be like 'David Copperfield'?"

Mrs. Trussit was ignorant of the work in question. "Of course, Master Peter. How can you ask such a thing? They are all like that, I believe. But, there, run away now. It's time for me to be looking after your mother's supper," &c. &c.

Mrs. Trussit obviously knew nothing whatever about it, although Peter heard her once murmuring "Poor lamb" as she gave him mixed biscuits out of her tin.

Stephen also was of little use, and he didn't seem especially glad when he heard about it.

"And it's a good school, do you think?" he said.

"Of course," said Peter valiantly, "one of the very best. It's in Devonshire, and I leave by the eight o'clock train" (this very importantly).

The fact of the matter was that Peter was so greatly excited by it all that abandoning even Stephen was a minor sorrow. It was a dreadful pity of course, but Peter intended to write most wonderful letters, and there would be the joyful meeting when the holidays came round, and he would be a more sensible person for Stephen to have for a friend after he'd seen the world.

"Dear Stephen—I shall write every week—every Friday I expect. That will be a good day to choose."

"Yes—that'll be a good day. Well, 'ere's the end of yer as yer are. It'll be another Peter coming back, maybe. Up along they'll change yer."

"But never me and you, Steve. I shall love you always."

The man seized him almost fiercely by the shoulders and looked him in the face. "Promise me that, boy," he said, "promise me that. Yer most all I've got now. But I'm a fool to ask yer—of course yer'll change. I'm an ignorant fool."

They were standing in the middle of one of Stephen's brown ploughed fields, and the cold, sharp day was drawing to a close as the mist stole up from the ground and the dim sun sank behind the hedgerows.

Peter in the school years that followed always had this picture of Stephen standing in the middle of his field—Stephen's rough, red brown clothes, his beard that curled a little, his brown corduroys that smelt of sheep and hay, the shining brass buttons of his coat, his broad back and large brown hands, his mild blue eyes and nose suddenly square at the end where it ought to have been round—this Stephen Brant raised from the very heart of the land, something as strong and primitive as the oaks and corn and running stream that made his background.

Stephen suddenly caught up Peter and kissed him so that the boy cried out. Then he turned abruptly and left him, and Peter did not see him again.

He said his farewells to the town, tenderly and gravely—the cobbled streets, the dear market-place, and the Tower, The Bending Mule (here there were farewells to be said to Mr. and Mrs. Figgis and old Moses); the wooden jetty, and the fishing-boats—then the beach and the caves and the sea....

Last of all, the Grey Hill. Peter climbed it on the last afternoon of all. He was quite alone, and the world was very still; he could not hear the sea at all. At last he was at the top and leant his back against the Giant's Finger. Looking round there are the hills that guard Truro, there are the woods where the rabbits are, there is the sea, and a wonderful view of Treliss rising into a peak which is The Man at Arms—and the smoke of the town mingled with the grey uncertain clouds, and the clouds mingled with the sea, and the only certain and assured thing was the strength of the Giant's Finger. That at least he could feel cold and hard against his hands. He felt curiously solemn and grave, and even a little tearful—and he stole down, through the dusk, softly as though his finger were on his lips.

And then after this a multitude of hurrying sensations with their climax in a very, very early morning, when one dressed with a candle, when one's box was corded and one's attic looked strangely bare, when there was a surprising amount to eat at breakfast, when one stole downstairs softly. He had said good-bye to his mother on the previous evening, and she had kissed him, and he had felt uncomfortable and shy.

Then there were Mrs. Trussit and his aunt to see him off, there was a cab and, most wonderful of all, there was his father coming in the cab. That was a dreadful thing and the journey to the station seemed endless because of it. His father was perfectly silent, and any thrill that Peter might have snatched from the engines, the porters, the whistles, and his own especial carriage were negatived by this paralysing occurrence. He would have liked to have said something himself, but he could only think of things that were quite impossible like "How funny Mrs. Trussit's nose is early in the morning," "I wonder what old Parlow's doing."

It was terrible.

He was in his carriage—they were hurrying, every one was hurrying.

His father suddenly spoke.

"The guard will see to you. You change at Exeter. Your aunt has given you sandwiches." A little pause, and then: "You've got pluck. You stood that beating well." Then the stern face passed, and the grave awful figure faded slowly down the platform.

Peter felt suddenly, utterly, completely miserable, and alone. Two tears rolled slowly down his cheeks. He blew his nose, and the train started.

III

And so this first run into liberty begins with tears and a choke in the throat and a sudden panting desire to be back in the dark passages of Scaw House. Nor did the fleeting swiftness of the new country please him. Suddenly one was leaving behind all those known paths and views, so dimly commonplace in the having of them, so rosily romantic in the tragic wanting of them!

How curious that Mrs. Trussit, his aunt, and his father should appear now pathetically affectionate in their farewells of him! They were not—to that he could swear—and yet back he would run did Honour and Destiny allow him. Above all, how he would have run now to Stephen.

He felt like a sharp wound the horrible selfishness and indifference of his parting when Stephen's beard had been pressed so roughly against his face that it had hurt him—and he had had nothing to say. He would write that very night if They—the unknown Gods to whose kingdom he journeyed—would allow him. This comforted him a little and the spirit of adventure stirred in him anew. He wiped his eyes for the last time with the crumpled ball of his handkerchief, sniffed three times defiantly, and settled to a summary of the passing country, cows, and hills and hedges, presently the pleasing bustle of Truro station, and then again the cows and hills and hedges. On parting from Cornwall he discovered a new sensation, and was surprised that he should feel it. He did not know, as a definite fact, the exact moment when that merging of Cornwall into Devon came, and yet, strangely in his spirit, he was conscious of it. Now he was in a foreign country, and it was almost as though his own land had cast him out so that the sharp appealing farewell to the Grey Hill, Treliss, and the sea was even more poignant than his farewell to his friends had been. Once more, at the thought of all the ways that he loved Cornwall, the choking sob was in his throat and the hot tears were in his eyes, and his hands were clenched. And then he remembered that London was not in Cornwall, and if he were ever going to get there at all he must not mind this parting.

"What the devil are you crying about?" came suddenly from the other side of the carriage. He looked up, and saw that there was an old gentleman sitting in the opposite corner. He had a red fat face and beautiful white hair.

"I'm not crying," said Peter, rather defiantly.

"Oh! yes, you are—or you were. Supposing you share my lunch and see whether that will make things any better."

"Thank you very much, but I have some sandwiches," said Peter, feeling for the paper packet and finding it.

"Well, supposing you come over here and eat yours with me. And if you could manage to help me with any of mine I should be greatly indebted. I can't bear having my meals alone, you know."

How can one possibly resist it when the Olympians come down so amiably from their heights and offer us their hospitality? Moreover the Old Gentleman had, from his bag, produced the most wonderfully shaped parcels. There was certainly a meal, and Aunt Jessie's sandwiches would assuredly be thick and probably no mustard!

So Peter slipped across and sat next to the Old Gentleman, and even shared a rug. He ultimately shared a great many other things, like chicken and tongue, apples and pears and plum cake.

"Of course," said the Old Gentleman, "you are going to school and probably for the first time—and therefore your legs are as weak as pins, you have a cold pain in the middle of your chest, and you have an intense desire to see your mother again."

Peter admitted that this was true, although it wasn't his mother whom he wished to see so much as a friend of his called Stephen, and, one or two places like the Grey Hill and The Bending Mule. All this interested the Old Gentleman very much.

"You, too, were at school?" Peter inquired politely.

"I was," said the Old Gentleman.

"And was it like David Copperfield?" said Peter.

"Parts of it—the nice parts. School was the best, the very best time of my life, my boy, and so you'll find it."

This was immensely reassuring, and Peter felt very much cheered. "You will make all the friends of your life there. You will learn to be a man. Dear me!" The Old Gentleman coughed. "I don't know what I would have done without school. You must have courage, you know," he added.

"I heard some one say once," said Peter, "that courage is the most important thing to have. It isn't life that matters, but courage, this man said."

"Bless my soul," the Old Gentleman said, "how old are you, boy?"

"Twelve—nearly thirteen," answered Peter.

"Well, the more you see of boys the better. You might be forty by the way you talk. You want games and fellows of your own age, that's what you want. Why I never heard of such a thing, talking about life at your age."

Peter felt that he had done something very wrong, although he hadn't the least idea of his crime, so he turned the conversation.

"I should like very much," he said, "to hear about your school if you wouldn't mind."

Then the Old Gentleman began in the most wonderful way, and to hear him talk you would imagine that school was the paradise to which all good boys were sent—a deliriously delightful place, with a shop full of sweets, games without end, friends galore, and a little work now and then to prevent one's being bored.

Peter listened most attentively with his head against the Old Gentleman's very warm coat, and then the warmth and the movement of the train caused the voice to swim further and further away into distance.

"Bless my soul!" Peter heard as though it had been whispered at the end of the train.

"Here's Exeter, young man. Your father said you were to change here."

A rubbing of eyes, and behold a stout guard in front of the door and no sign of the Old Gentleman whatever, but when he felt for his ticket in his side pocket he found also a glittering sovereign that had certainly not been there when he went asleep.

All this was very encouraging, and Peter followed the guard across the Exeter platform hopefully and expectantly. Right down the platform, on a side line, was a little train that reminded Peter of the Treliss to Truro one, so helpless and incapable did it look. The guard put him and his luggage into a carriage and then left him with a last word as to Salton being his destination. He waited here a very long time and nothing happened. He must have slept again, because when he next looked out of the window the platform was full of people.

He realised with terror that they were, many of them, boys—boys with friends and boys without. He watched them with a great feeling of desolation and homesickness as they flung themselves into carriages and shouted at one another.

A small boy with a very red face and a round fat body, attended by a tall, thin lady in black, got into the carriage, and behaving as if Peter weren't there at all, leaned out of the window.

"All right, mater. That's all right. I'll tell 'em about the socks—old Mother Gill will look after that."

"You won't forget to send me a post card to-night, Will, dear, will you?"

"No, mater, that's all right. I say, don't you bother to wait if you want to be off."

"No, dear, I'd like to wait. Don't forget to give father's letter to Mr. Raggett."

"All right. I say it's rotten for you waiting about, really. Give my love to Floss!"

"Well, perhaps I had better go. This train seems to be late. Good-bye, dearest boy."

An interval, during which the stout boy leaned out of the window and was embraced. Soon his bowler hat was flung wildly on to the rack and he was leaning out of the window, screaming:

"Cocker! I say, Cocker! Cocker! Oh! dash it, he's going in there. Cocker! Cocker! Hullo, Bisket! going strong? Cocker! Oh! there he is! Hullo, old man! Thought I should miss you. Come on in here! Thought I'd never get rid of the mater. They do hang about!"

A small boy with his hat on one side got into the carriage, stepped on Peter's feet without apologising, and then the two gentlemen sat down at the other end of the carriage and exchanged experiences.

"What sort of hols.?"

"Oh, pretty rotten! Got nothing for Christmas at all except a measly knife or two—governor played it awfully low down."

"I rather scored because my sister had a ripping writing case sent to her, and I gave her a rotten old book in exchange, and she jolly well had to."

And so it continued. To Peter it was completely unintelligible. The boys at old Parlow's had never talked like this. He was suddenly flung into a foreign country. The dismay in his heart grew as he remembered that he was going into this life entirely alone and without a friend in the world. He felt that he would, had it been possible, gladly have exchanged this dreadful plunge for a beating from his father.

At any rate, after that there were friends to whom one might go—after this?...

As the train dragged slowly and painfully along the dreariness and the loneliness increased. The dusk fell, and they stopped, as it seemed, every other minute, and always Peter thought that it must be Salton and prepared to get out. The two boys in his carriage paid no attention to him whatever, and their voices continued incessantly, and always the little train jolted along sleepily wandering through the dark country and carrying him to unknown terrors. But he set his teeth hard and remembered what the Old Gentleman had told him. He would fight it out and see it through.

"'Tisn't Life that matters, but the Courage—"

And then suddenly the train stopped, the two boys flung themselves at the window, and the porter outside, like a magician who kept a rabbit in a bag, suddenly shouted "Salton!" After that there were mixed impressions. He stood alone on the dark, windy platform whilst dark figures passed and repassed him. Then a tall, thin Somebody said "Are you Westcott?" and Peter said "Yes," and he was conveyed to a large wagonette already crowded with boys. Then there was a great deal of squeezing, a great deal of noise, and some one in authority said from somewhere, "Less noise, please."

The wagonette started in a jolting uncertain way, and then they seemed to go on for ever and ever between dark sweet-smelling hedges with black trees that swept their heads, and the faint blue of the evening sky on the horizon. Every one was very quiet now, and Peter fell asleep once more and dreamed of the Old Gentleman, plum cake, and Stephen.

A sudden pause—the sound of an iron gate being swung back, and Peter was awake again to see that they were driving up to a dark heavy building that looked like a hospital or a prison.

"The new boys please follow me," and he found himself, still struggling with sleep, blinded by the sudden light, following, with some ten others, a long and thin gentleman who wore a pince-nez. His strongest feeling was that he was very cold and that he hated everybody and everything. He heard many voices somewhere in the distance, doors were being continually opened and shut, and little winds blew down the dismal passages. They were suddenly in a study lined with books and a stout rubicund gentleman with a gold watch chain and a habit (as Peter at once discovered) of whistling through his teeth was writing at a table.

He turned round when he heard them enter and watched them for a moment as they stood by the door.

"Well, boys" (his voice came from somewhere near his watch chain), "come and shake hands. How are you all?"

Some eager boy in the front row, with a pleasant smile and a shrill piping voice said, "Very well, thank you, sir," and Peter immediately hated him.

Then they shook hands and their names were written in a book. The stout gentleman said, "Well, boys, here you all are. Your first term, you know—very important. Work and play—work and play. Work first and play afterwards, and then we'll be friends. Oh, yes! Supper at nine. Prayers at nine-thirty."

They were all bundled out, and the tall man with pince-nez said: "Now, boys, you have an hour before supper," and left them without another word in a long dark passage. The passage was hung with greatcoats and down each side of it were play-boxes. At the other end, mistily and vaguely, figures passed.

Peter sat down on one of the play-boxes and saw, to his disgust, that the eager boy with the piping voice sat down also.

"I say," said the piping boy, "don't you like school awfully?"

"No, I hate it," said Peter.

"Oh, I say! What's your name?"

"Peter."

"Peter! Oh! but your other name. The fellows will rag you most awfully if you tell them your Christian name."

"Westcott, then."

"Mine's Cheeseman. I'm going to like everybody here and get on. I say, shall we be chums?"

"No."

"Oh, I say! Why not?"

"Because I don't like you."

"Oh, I say!"

"In another minute I'll break your neck."

"Oh! I say!" The piping boy sprang up from the play-box and stood away. "All right, you needn't be ratty about it! I'll tell the fellows you said your name was Peter! They'll give it you."

And the piping boy moved down the passage whistling casually.

After this, silence, and only all the greatcoats swaying a little in the draught and bulging out and then thinning again as though there were two persons inside them. Peter sat quite motionless for a long time with his face in his hands. He was very tired and very cold and very hungry.

A crowd advanced towards him—five or six boys, and one large fat boy was holding the piping one by the ear.

"Oh, I say! Let me go! Let me go! I'll do your boots up, really I will. I'll do whatever you like! Oh! I say! There's a new boy. He says his name is Peter!"

So did the wretched piping one endeavour to divert attention from his own person. The fat boy, accompanied by a complacent satellite, approached Peter.

"Hullo, you. What's your name?"

"Westcott."

"'Tisn't. It's Peter."

"Peter Westcott."

"Well, Mr. Peter Westcott, stand up when you're spoken to by your betters. I say, hack him up, you fellows."

Peter was "hacked" up.

"Now, what do you mean by not speaking when you're spoken to?"

Peter stood square and faced him.

"Oh! you won't speak, won't you? See if this will do it."

Peter's arm and ear were twisted; he was also hit in the mouth.

He was still silent.

Some one in the back of the crowd said, "Oh, come on, you chaps—let's leave this kid, the other fellow's more fun."

And they passed on bearing the piping one with them.

Peter sat down again; he was feeling sick and his head ached. He buried his head in the greatcoat that hung above him, and cried quite silently for a very long time.

A bell rang, and boys ran past him, and he ran with them. He found that it was supper and that he was sitting with the other new boys at the bottom of the table, but he could not eat and his head was swimming. Then there were prayers and, as he knelt on the hard floor with his head against the form, some one stuck a pin into the soft part of his leg and gave him great pain.

Then at last, and all this time he had spoken to no one, upstairs to bed. A tall, thin woman in shining black was at the head of the stairs—she read out to the new boys the numbers of their dormitories in a harsh, metallic voice. Peter went to his, and found it a long room with twenty beds, twenty washing basins, and twenty chairs.

One last incident.

He slept and was dreaming. He was climbing the Grey Hill and Stephen was following him, calling on him. He remembered in his dream that he had not written Stephen the letter that he had promised, and he turned back down the hill. Then suddenly the ground began to toss under his feet, he cried for Stephen, he was flung into the air, he was falling....

He woke and found that he was lying on the floor amongst the tumbled sheets and blankets. In the distance he could hear stifled laughter. The terror of that awful wakening was still upon him, and he thought for a moment that he would die because his heart would never beat again.

Then slowly he gathered his clothes together and tried to arrange them on the bed. He was dreadfully cold and his toes stuck out at the end of the bed. He could not cover them.

But, tired as he was, he dared not fall asleep again, lest there should come once more that dreadful wakening.

CHAPTER V

DAWSON'S, THE GATE INTO HELL

I

A letter from Peter to Stephen:

Dear, dear Steve,

There's a noise going on and boys are throwing paper and things and there's another boy jogging my elbows so that I can't hold my pen. Dear Steve, I hope that you are very, very happy as I am. I am very happy here. I am in the bottom form because my sums are so awful and my master beat me for them yesterday but he is nothing to father. I was top in the essay. I like football—I have a friend who is called Galion (I don't think that is the right way to spell it. He says that it is like a treasure-ship). He is a nice boy and Mrs. Trussit was his father's housekeeper once; his father writes stories. There is a boy I hate called Cheeseman, and one called Pollock. Please give my love to Mrs. Brant, the cows, Mollie and the pigs, Mr. and Mrs. Figgis, Mr. Tan and all my friends. Dear Steve, I love you very, very, very much. I am very happy.

Your loving friend,

Peter Westcott.

A letter from Stephen to Peter:

Dear Mr. Peter,

I have thought every day of you and I was mighty glad to get your bit of a letter fearing that, maybe, thiccy place in Devon might have driven your old friends out of your head. I am no hand with a pen and it is taking me a time to write this so I will just say that I'm right glad you're happy and that I'll greet the day I see you again, and that's it's poor trade here without you.

I am always, your friend,

Stephen Brant.

But Peter had lied in his letter. He was not in any way happy at all. He had lied because he knew that it would have hurt Stephen if he had told him the truth—and the truth was something that must be met with clenched teeth and shoulders set back.

Taking him at the end of the first week one finds simple bewilderment and also a conviction that silence is the best policy. He was placed in the lowest form because of his ignorance of Latin and Mathematics, and here every one was younger and weaker. During school hours there was comparative peace, and he sat with perplexed brow and inky fingers, or was sent down to the bottom for inattention. It was not inattention but rather a complete incapacity for grasping the system on which everything worked. Meanwhile in this first week he had earned a reputation and made three friends, and although he did not know it that was not a bad beginning.

On the day after his arrival Peter, after midday dinner, standing desolately in the playground and feeling certain that he ought to be playing football somewhere but completely ignorant as to the place where lists commonly hung, saw another new boy and hailed him. This boy he had noticed before—he was shapeless of body, with big, round, good-tempered eyes, and he moved more slowly than any one whom Peter had ever seen. Nothing stirred him; he did not mind it when his ears were pulled or his arms twisted, but only said slowly, "Oh, drop it!" To this wonderful boy Peter made approach.

"Can you tell me where the lists are for football? I ought to have been playing yesterday only I didn't know where to look."

The slow boy smiled. "I'm going to look myself," he said, "come on."

And then two things happened. First sauntering down the playground there came a boy whom Peter had noticed on that first morning in school—some one very little older than Peter and not very much bigger, but with a grace, a dignity, an air that was very wonderful indeed. He was a dark boy with his hair carelessly tossed over his forehead; he was very clean and he had beautiful hands. To Peter's rough and clumsy figure he seemed everything that a boy should be, and, in his mind, he had called him "Steerforth." As this boy approached there suddenly burst into view a discordant crowd with some one in their midst. They were shouting and laughing, and Peter could hear that some one was crying. The crowd separated and formed a ring and danced shouting round a very small and chubby boy who was standing crying quite desperately, with his head buried in his arm. Every now and then the infant was knocked by one boy in the ring into another boy's arms, and so was tossed from side to side.

The hopeless sound of the chubby one's crying caused Peter suddenly to go red hot somewhere inside his chest, and like a bullet from a gun he was into the middle of the circle. "You beasts! You beasts," he sobbed hysterically. He began to hit wildly, with his head down, at any one near him, and very soon there was a glorious mêlée. The crowd roared with laughter as they flung the two small boys against one another, then suddenly one of the circle got a wild blow in the eye from Peter's fist and went staggering back, another was kicked in the shins, a third was badly winded. Peter had lost all sense of place or time, of reason or sanity; he was wild with excitement, and the pent-up emotions of the last five days found magnificent overwhelming freedom. He did not know whether he were hit or no, once he was down and in an instant up again—once a face was close to his and he drove hard at the mouth—but he was small and his arms and legs were short. Indeed it would have gone badly with him had there not been heard, in all the roar of battle, the mystic whisper "Binns," and in an instant, as the snow flies before the sun, so had that gallant crowd disappeared. Only the small cause of the disturbance and Peter remained. The tall form of a master passed slowly down the playground, but it appeared that he had seen nothing, and he did not speak. The small boy was gazing at Peter with wide-opened eyes, large in a white face on which were many tear stains. Peter, who was conscious now that blood was pouring from a cut in his cheek, that one of his teeth was missing and that one of his eyes was fast closing, was about to speak to him when he was aware that his "Steerforth" had sprung from nowhere and was advancing gracefully to meet him. Peter's heart beat very fast.

The boy smiled at him and held out his hand.

"I say, shake hands. You've got pluck—my eye! I never saw such a rag!"

Peter shook hands and was speechless.

"What's your name?"

"Westcott."

"Mine's Cardillac. It isn't spelt as it's spoken, you know. C-a-r-d-i-l-l-a-c. I'm in White's—what do you say to places next each other at table?"

"Rather." Peter's face was crimson. "Thanks most awfully." He stammered in his eagerness.

"Right you are—see you after chapel." The boy moved away.

Peter said something to the infant whom he had delivered, and was considering where he might most unobtrusively wash when he was once more conscious of some one at his elbow. It was the slow boy who was smiling at him.

"I say, you're a sight. You'd better wash, you know."

"Yes, I was just thinking of that only I didn't quite know where to go."

"Come with me—I'll get round Mother Gill all right. She likes me. You've got some cheek. Prester and Banks Mi, and all sorts of fellows were in that crowd. You landed Prester nicely." He chuckled. "What's your name?"

"Westcott."

"Mine's Galleon."

"Galleon?" Peter's eyes shone. "I say, you didn't ever have a housekeeper called Mrs. Trussit?"

"Trussit? Yes, rather, of course I remember, when I was awfully small."

"Why, she's ours now! Then it must be your father who writes books!"

"Yes, rather. He's most awfully famous!"

Peter stopped still, his mouth open with excitement.

Of all the amazing things! What doesn't life give you if you trust it!

II

But before it became a question of individuals there is the place to be considered. This Dawson's of twenty years ago does not exist now nor, let us pray the Fates, are there others like it. It is not only with bitterness that a boy whom Dawson's had formed would look back on it but also with a dim, confused wonder that he had escaped with a straight soul and a straight body from that Place. There were many, very many indeed, who did not escape, and it would indeed have been better for them all had they died before they were old enough to test its hospitality. If any of those into whose hands this story of Peter may fall were, by the design of God, themselves trained by the place of which I speak, they will understand that all were not as fortunate as Peter—and for those others there should be sympathy....

To Peter indeed it all came very slowly because he had known so little before. He had not been a week in the place before there were very many things that he was told—there were other things that he saw for himself.

There is, for instance, at the end of the third week, the incident of Ferris, the Captain of the School. He was as a God in Peter's eyes, he was greater, more wonderful than Stephen, than any one in the world. His word was law....

One late afternoon Peter cleaned plates for him in his study, and Ferris watched him. Ferris was kind and talked about many things out of his great wisdom, and then he asked Peter whether he would always like to be his fag, and Peter, delighted, said "Yes."

Then Ferris smiled and spoke, dropping his voice. Three weeks earlier Peter would not have understood, but now he understood quite well and he went very white and broke from the room, leaving the plates where they were—and Cheeseman became Ferris' fag—

This was all very puzzling and perplexing to Peter.

But after that first evening when he had hidden his head in the greatcoat and cried, he had shown no sign of fear and he soon found that, on that side of Life, things became easy. He was speedily left alone, and indeed he must have been, in spite of his small size, something of a figure even then.

His head was so very firm on his shoulders, his grey eyes were so very straight, and his lip curled in a disagreeable way when he was displeased; he was something of the bulldog, and even at this early period the First and Second forms showed signs of meek surrender to his leadership. But he was, of course, not happy—he was entirely miserable. He would be happier later on when he had been able to arrange all these puzzling certainties so different from those dazzling imaginations that he had painted. How strange of him to have been so glad to leave Stephen and the others—even old Curtis! What could he have thought was coming!

He remembered as though it had been another life that Christmas Eve, the fight, the beating, the carols....

And yet, with it all, with the dreariness and greyness and fierceness and dirtiness of it all, he would not change it for those earlier things—this was growing, this was growing up!

He was certainly happier after his meeting with Cardillac—"Cards" as he was always called. Here was a hero indeed! Not to displace, of course, Stephen, who remained as a stained-glass window remains, to be looked at and treasured and remembered—but here was a living wonder! Every movement that Cards made was astounding, and not only Peter felt it. Even the masters seemed to suggest that he was different from the rest and watched him admiringly. Cards was only fourteen, but he had seen the world. He had been with his mother (his father was dead) about Europe, he knew London, he had been to the theatres; school, he gave them all to understand, was an interim in the social round. He took Peter's worship very easily and went for walks with him and talked in a wonderful way. He admired Peter's strength.

Peter found that Galleon—Bobby Galleon—was disappointing, not very interesting. He had never read his father's books, and he couldn't tell Peter very much about the great man; he was proud of him but rather reserved. He had not many ideas about anything and indeed when he went for a walk with Peter was usually very silent, although always in a good temper. Cards thought Galleon very dull and never spoke to him if he could avoid doing so, and Peter was sometimes quite angry with Galleon because he would "turn up so" when one might have had Cards to oneself.

Peter's main feeling about it all when half term arrived was that one must just stand with one's back to the wall if one was to avoid being hurt. He did not now plunge into broils to help other people; he found that it did not in reality help them and that it only meant that he got kicked as well as the other boy. One's life was a diligent watchfulness with the end in view of avoiding the enemy. The enemy was to be found in any shape and form; there was no security by night or day, but on the whole life was safer if one spoke as little as possible and stuck to the wall. There were Devils—most certainly Devils—roaming the world, and as he watched the Torture and the Terror and then the very dreadful submission, he vowed with clenched lips that he would never Submit...and so gradually he was learning the truth of that which Frosted Moses had spoken...

Cornwall, meanwhile—the Grey Hill, Scaw House, the hills above Truro—remained to him during these weeks, securely hidden.

III

There remains to be chronicled of that first term only the Comber Fight and, a little conversation, one windy day, with Galleon. The small boy, by name Beech Minimus, whom Peter had defended on that earlier occasion, had attached himself with unswerving fidelity to his preserver. He was round and fat, and on his arrival had had red cheeks and sparkling eyes—now he was pale and there were lines under his eyes; he started if any one spoke to him, and was always eager to hide when possible. Peter was very sorry for him, but, after a month of the term had passed he had, himself, acquired the indifference of those that stand with their backs to the wall. Beech would go on any kind of errand for him and would willingly have died for him had it been required of him—he did indeed during the hours that he was left in peace in his dormitory, picture to himself wonderful scenes in which he saved Peter from horrible deaths and for his own part perished.

It may have been that he clung to Peter partly because there was more safety in his neighbourhood, for amongst the lower school boys at any rate, very considerable fear of Peter was to be noticed, but Beech's large eyes raised to the other boy's face or his eager smile as he did something that Peter required of him, spoke devotion.

Beech Minimus was forced, however, for the good of his soul, to suffer especial torture between the hours of eight and nine in the evening. It was the custom that the Lower School should retire from preparation at eight o'clock, it being supposed that at that hour the Lower School went to bed. But Authority, blinded by trustful good nature and being engaged at that hour with its wine and dinner, left the issue to chance and the Gods, and human nature being what it is, the Lower School triumphed in freedom. There was a large, empty class room at the back of the building where much noise might safely be made, and in this place and at this hour followed the nightly torture of Beech and his minute companions—that torture named by the Gods, "Discipline," by the Authorities, "Boys will be Boys," by the Parent, "Learning to be a Man," and by the Lower School "A Rag." Beech and his companions had not as yet a name for it. Peter was, as a rule, left to his own thoughts and spent the hours amongst the greatcoats in the passage reading David Copperfield or talking in whispers to Bobby Galleon. But nevertheless he was not really indifferent, he was horribly conscious even in his sleep, of Beech's shrill "Oh! Comber, don't! Please, Comber, oh!" and Beech being in the same dormitory as himself he noticed, almost against his will, that shivering little mortal as he crept into bed and cowered beneath the sheets wondering whether before morning he would be tossed in sheets or would find his bed drenched in water or would be beaten with hair brushes. Peter's philosophy of standing it in silence and hitting back if he were himself attacked was scarcely satisfactory in Beech's case, and, again and again, his attention would be dragged away from his book to that other room where some small boys were learning lessons in life.

The head of this pleasant sport was one Comber, a large, pale-faced boy, some years older than his place in the school justified, but of a crass stupidity, a greedy stomach and a vicious cruelty. Peter had already met him in football and had annoyed him by collaring him violently on one occasion, it being the boy's habit, owing to his size and reputation, to run down the field in the Lower School game, unattacked. Peter's hatred of him grew more intense week by week; some days after Mid-Term, it had swollen into a passion. He finally told Bobby Galleon one day at luncheon that on that very evening he was going to defy this Comber. Galleon besought him not to do this, pointing out Comber's greater strength and the natural tendency of the Lower School to follow their leader blindly. Peter said nothing in reply but watched, when eight o'clock had struck and the Lower School had assembled in the class room, for his moment. It was a somewhat piteous spectacle. Comber and some half a dozen friends in the middle of the room, and forty boys ranging in years from eight to twelve, waiting with white faces and propitiatory smiles, eager to assist in the Torture if they only might themselves be spared.

"Now you chaps," this from Comber—"we'll have a Gauntlet. I votes we make young Beech run first."

"Rather! Come on, Beech—you've jolly well got to."

"Buck up, you funk!" from those relieved that they were themselves, for the instant, safe.

Peter was sitting on a bench at the back of the room—he stood on the bench and shouted, "You're a beast. Comber."

There was immediate silence—every one turned first to Comber, and then back to Peter. Comber paused in the preparation of the string whip that he was making, and his face was crimson.

"Oh, it's you, you young skunk, is it? Bring him here some of you fellows."

Eager movements were made in his direction, but Peter, still standing on his bench, shouted: "I claim a fight."

There was silence again—a silence now of incredulity and amazement. But there was nothing to be done; if any one claimed a fight, by all the rules and traditions of Dawson's he must have it. But that Westcott, a new boy and in the bottom form should challenge Comber! Slowly, and as it were against their will, hearts beat a little faster, faces brightened. Of course Westcott would be most hopelessly beaten, but might not this prove the beginning of the end of their tyrant?

Meanwhile, Comber between his teeth: "All right, you young devil, I'll give you such a hiding as you damned well won't forget. Then we'll treat you properly afterwards."

A ring was made, and there was silence, so that the prefects might not be attracted, because fighting in the Lower School was forbidden. Coats were taken off and Peter faced Comber with the sensation of attacking a mountain. Peter knew nothing about fighting at all, but Comber had long subsisted on an easy reputation and he was a coward at heart. There swung into Peter's brain the picture of The Bending

Mule, the crowding faces, the swinging lamp, Stephen with the sledge-hammer blow...it was the first time for weeks that he had thought of Treliss.

He was indifferent—he did not care; things could not be worse, and he did not mind what happened to him, and Comber minded very much indeed, and he had not been hit in the face for a long time. His arms went round like windmills, and the things that he would like to have done were to pull Peter's hair from its roots and to bite him on the arm. As the fight proceeded and he knew that his face was bleeding and that the end of his nose had no sensation in it at all he kicked with his feet and was conscious of cries that he was not playing the game. Infuriated that his recent supporters should so easily desert him, he now flung himself upon Peter, who at once gave way beneath the bigger boy's weight. Comber then began to bite and tear and scratch, uttering shrill screams of rage and kicking on the floor with his feet. He was at once pulled away, assured by those dearest friends who had so recently and merrily assisted him in his "rags" that he was not playing the game and was no sportsman. He was moreover a ludicrous sight, his trousers being torn, one blue-black eye staring from a confused outline of dust and blood, his hair amazingly on end.

There were also many cries of "Shame, Comber," "Dirty game," and even "Well played young Westcott!"

He knew as he wept bitter tears into his blood-stained hands that his reign was at an end.

There were indeed, for the time at any rate, no more "rags," and Peter might, an he would, have reigned magnificently over the Lower School. But he was as silent and aloof as ever, and was considered "a sidey devil, but jolly plucky, by Gad."

And for himself he got at any rate the more continued companionship of Cards, who languidly, and, perhaps a younger Sir Willoughby Patterne "with a leg," admired his muscle.

IV

Finally, towards the end of the term, Peter and Bobby Galleon may be seen sitting on a high hill. It is a Sunday afternoon in spring, and far away there is a thin line of faintly blue hills. Nearer to view there are grey heights more sharply outlined and rough, like drawing paper—painted with a green wood, a red-roofed farm, a black church spire, and a brown ploughed field. Immediately below them a green hedge hanging over a running stream that has caught the blue of the sky. Above them vast swollen clouds flooding slowly with the faint yellow of the coming sunset, hanging stationary above the stream and seeming to have flung to earth some patches of their colour in the first primroses below the hedge. A rabbit watches, his head out of his hole.

The boys' voices cut the air.

"I say, Bobby, don't you ever wonder about things—you never seem to want to ask questions."

"No, I don't suppose I do. I'm awfully stupid. Father says so."

"It's funny your being stupid when your father's so clever."

"Do you mind my being stupid?"

"No—only I'd like you to want to know things—things like what people are like inside—their thinking part I mean, not their real insides. People like Mother Gill and old Binns and Prester Ma: and then what one's going to do when one's grown up—you never want to know that."

"No, it'll just come I suppose. Of course, I shan't be clever like the governor."

"No, I don't think you will."

Once again: "Do you mind my being so stupid, Peter?"

"No—I'm awfully stupid too. But I like to wonder about things. There was once a man I met at home with rings and things who lived in London...." Peter stops, Galleon wouldn't be interested in that.

"Anyhow, you know, you've got Cards—he's an awfully clever chap."

"Yes, he's wonderful," Peter sighs, "and he's seen such a lot of things."

"Yes, but you know I don't think Cards really cares for you as much as I do." This is an approach to sentiment, and Peter brushes it hastily aside:

"I like you both awfully. But I say, won't it be splendid to be grown up in London?"

"I don't know—lots of fellows don't like it."

"That's nothing," Peter says slowly, "to do with its not being splendid!"

And the rabbit, tired of listening to such tiresome stuff, thinks that they must be very young boys indeed.

CHAPTER VI

A LOOKING-GLASS, A SILVER MATCH-BOX, A GLASS OF WHISKY, AND—VOX POPULI

I

Peter, thirteen to sixteen!—and left, so it appears, very much the same, as far as actual possessions go, at the end of it as at the poverty-struck commencement. Friendship, Honour, Glory—how these things came and went with him during these years might have a book to themselves were it not that our business is with a wider stage and more lasting issues—and there is but little room for a full-fledged chronicle. Though Dawson's—and to take the history of Miss Gill only—of her love affair with the curate, of her final desperate appeal to him and of his ultimate confession that he was married already—provides a story quite sufficient for three excellent volumes. Or there is the history of Benbow, that bucolic gentleman into whose study we led Peter a chapter or two ago, Head for this year or two of Dawson's—soon to be head of nothing but the dung-heap and there to crow only dismally—with a childlike Mrs. Benbow, led unwittingly to Dawson's as a lamb to the slaughter-house—later to flee, crying, back to her hearth and home, her life smashed to the tiniest pieces and no brain nor strength to put it together again. Or there is the natural and interesting progression, on the part of any child, behind whose back those iron gates of Dawson's have swung, from innocence to knowledge, from knowledge to practice, from practice to miserable Submission, Concealment, and a merry prospective Hell—this is a diverting study with which it would be easy to fill these pages....

But the theme is Peter's education, and Dawson's is only an incident to that history—an incident that may be taken by the percipient reader, for a most admirable Symbol—even an early rehearsal of a Comedy entitled "How to Learn to be a Man, or The World as a Prancing Ground."...

But with Peter, if you take him from that first asking Mrs. Trussit (swinging his short legs from the table and diving into the mixed biscuit tin). "Is it, Mrs. Trussit, like David Copperfield?"... to his meeting of her again, he still rather short-legged but no longer caring over much for mixed biscuits, in his sixteenth year, with Dawson's over and done with—"No, Mrs. Trussit, not in the least like," and grimly said in addition, the changes, alterations and general growing-up Development may be said to be inside him rather than out, and there they are vital enough.

With those three and a half years it is a case of Things sticking out, like hillocks in a flat country, and it is retrospection rather than impressions at the time that show what mattered and what did not. But, on the whole, the vital things at Dawson's are pretty plain to the eye and must be squeezed into a chapter as best they can.

Treliss, as it appeared in the holidays, seemed to Peter to change very little. His relations with his father were curiously passive during this time, and suggested, in their hint of future developments, something ominous and uneasy. They scarcely ever spoke to one another, and it was Peter's object to avoid the house as often as possible, but in his father's silence now (Peter himself being older and intuitively sharper as to the reason of things) he saw active dislike, and even, at times, a suggested fear. Outwardly they—his father, his grandfather, his aunt, Mrs. Trussit—had changed not at all; his grandfather the same old creature of grey hairs and cushions and rugs, his father broad and square and white in the face with his black hair carefully brushed, his aunt with her mittens and trembling hands and silly voice, Mrs. Trussit with her black silk gown and stout prosperous face—Oh! they were all there, but he fancied—and this might easily be imagination—that they, like the portraits of the old Westcotts about the walls, watched him, as he grew, knowing that ever, as the months passed, the day came nearer when father and son must come to terms. And beyond this he had, even at this early time, a consciousness that it was round his mother's room that the whole matter hung—his mother whom he saw once or twice a week for a very little time in the morning, when that old terror of the white silent room would creep upon him and hold him tongue-tied.

And yet, with it all, he knew, as every holiday came, more clearly, that again and again they, his mother and himself, were on the verge of speech or action. He could see it in her eyes, her beautiful grey eyes that moved him so curiously. There were days when he was on the edge of a rush of questions, and then something held him back—perhaps the unconscious certainty that his mother's answers would precipitate his relations with his father—and he was not, as yet, ready.

Anyhow a grim place, Scaw House, grimmer with every return to it, and not a brightly coloured interlude to Dawson's, grim enough in its own conditions. The silence that was gradually growing with Peter—the fixed assurance, whether at home or at school, that life was easier if one said nothing—might have found an outlet in Stephen's company, but here again there was no cheerful chronicle.

Each holiday showed Peter less of Stephen than the last had done, and he was afraid to ask himself why this was. Perhaps in reality he did not know, but at any rate he was sure that the change was in Stephen. He cared for Stephen as devotedly as ever, and, indeed, in that perhaps he needed him more than ever and saw him so little, his affection was even stronger than it had been. But Stephen had changed, not, Peter knew, in any affection towards himself, but in his own habits and person. Burstead—his old enemy—had taken a farm near his own farm, in order, so they said at The Bending Mule, that he might flaunt Mrs. Burstead (once Stephen's sweetheart) in Stephen's face.

They also said that Burstead beat his wife and ill-used her horribly, and that she would give all her soul now that she was Stephen Brant's wife, but that she was a weak, silly young woman, poor thing. They said that Stephen knew all this, and that he could hear her crying at nights, and that it was sending him off his head—and that he was drinking. And they shook their heads, down at The Bending Mule, and foreboded ill. Moreover, that old lady, Mrs. Brant, had died during Peter's first year at Dawson's, and Stephen was alone now. He had changed in his appearance, his beard tangled and untidy, his clothes unbrushed and his eyes wild and bloodshot, and once Peter had ventured up to Stephen's farm and had climbed the stairs and had opened the door and had seen Stephen (although it was early evening) sitting all naked on his bed, very drunk and shouting wildly—and he had not recognised Peter. But the boy knew when he met him again, sober this time, by the sad look in his eyes, that Stephen must go his way alone now, lead him where it would.... A boy of fifteen could not help.

And so those holidays were more and more lonely, as the days passed and Peter's heart was very heavy. He did not go often to The Bending Mule now because Stephen was not there. He went once or twice to Zachary Tan's shop, but he did not see Mr. Zanti again nor any one who spoke of London. He had not, however, forgotten Mr. Zanti's talk of looking-glasses. As he grew and his mind distinguished more clearly between fact and fancy, he saw that it was foolish to suppose that one saw anything in looking-glasses but the immediate view. Tables and chairs, walls and windows, dust and fire-places, there was the furniture of a looking-glass. Nevertheless during his first year at school he had, on occasions, climbed to his dormitory, seen that he was alone and then gazed into his glass and thought of London ... London in his young brain, being a place of romantic fog, pantomime, oranges, fat, chivalrous old gentlemen, Queen Victoria and Punch and Judy. Nothing had happened—of course nothing had happened—it was only very cold and unpleasant up there all alone, and, at the end of it, a silly thing to do.

And then one night something did happen. He woke suddenly and heard in the distance beyond the deep breathing of twenty-four sleepers, a clock strike three. He turned and lay on his back; he was very sleepy and he did not know why he had wakened. The long high room was dark, but directly opposite him beyond the end of his bed, the light seemed to shine full on to the face of his looking-glass. As he sat up in bed and looked at it seemed to stand out like a sheet of silver.

He gripped the sides of the bed and stared. He rubbed his eyes. He could see no reflection in the glass at all but only this shining expanse, and then, as he looked at it, that too seemed to pass away, and in its place at first confusedly, like smoke across the face of the glass, and then, settling into shape and form, there appeared the interior of a room—a small low-roofed dark room. There was a large fire burning, and in front of it, kneeling on the floor, with their backs to Peter, were two men, and they were thrusting papers into the fire. The glass seemed to stretch and broaden out so that the whole of the room was visible, and suddenly Peter saw a little window high in the top of the wall, and behind that window was a face that watched the two men.

He wanted to warn them—he suddenly cried out aloud "Look out!" and with that he was wide awake and saw that his glass could be only dimly discerned in the grey of the advancing morning—and yet he had heard that clock strike three!... So much for confusing dreams, and so vivid was it that in the morning he remembered the face at the window and knew that he would recognise it again if he saw it.

II

But out of the three years there stand his relations with Cards and young Galleon, a symbol of so much that was to come to him later. As he grew in position in the school Cards saw him continually. Cards undoubtedly admired his stocky, determined strength, his grey eyes, his brusque speech, his ability at games. He did not pretend also that he was not flattered by Peter's attentions. Curiously, for so young a boy, he had a satirical irony that showed him the world very much in the light that he was always afterwards to see it. To Cards the world was a show, a Vanity Fair—a place where manner, savoir-faire, dignity, humour and ease, mattered everything; he saw also that there was nothing by which people are so easily deceived.

Peter had none of these things; he would always be rough, he would never be elegant, and afterwards, in life, Cards did not suppose that he would see very much of Peter, their lives would be along different paths; but now, more genuinely perhaps than ever again, Cards was to admire that honest bedrock of feeling, of sentiment, of criticism, of love and anger, that gave Peter his immense value.

"There is a fellow here," wrote Cards to his mother, "whom I like very much. He's got a most awful lot of stuff in him although he doesn't say much and he looks like nothing on earth sometimes. He's very good at football, although he's only been here a year. His name is Westcott—Peter Westcott. I expect I'll bring him back one holiday."

But, of course, he never did. Peter, when it came to actuality, wouldn't look right at home. It was during Peter's second year that these things were happening, and, all this time, Peter was climbing slowly to a very real popularity. Cards was leaving at the end of this second year—had he stayed until the end of the third his superficialities would have been most severely tested.

To him Peter gave all that whole-hearted love and devotion that only Stephen had known before. He gave it with a very considerable sense of humour and with no sentiment at all. He saw Cards quite clearly, he watched his poses and his elaborate pretences, and he laughed at him sometimes and called him names.

Cards' pride was, on several occasions, distinctly hurt by this laughter, but his certain conviction of his own superiority always comforted him. Nor was Peter ever sentimental in his attitude. He never told Cards that he cared for him, and he even hung back a little when Cards was in a demonstrative mood and wanted to be told that he was "wonderful." Cards sometimes wondered whether Peter cared for him at all and whether he wasn't really fonder of that "stupid ass Galleon" who never had a word to say for himself. Peter's grey eyes would have told Cards a great deal if he had cared to examine them, but he did not know anything about eyes. Peter noticed, a little against his will, that as he advanced up the school so Cards cared increasingly about him. He grasped this discovery philosophically; after all, there were many fellows who took their colour from the world's opinion, and it was natural enough that they should. He himself regarded his growing popularity as a thing of no importance whatever; it did not touch him anywhere at all because he despised and hated the place. "When the time does come," he said once to Cards, "and one is allowed to do things, I'll stop a lot of this filth."

"You'll have your work cut out," Cards told him. "What does it all matter to us? Let 'em wallow—and they'll only hate you."

Cards added this because he knew that Peter had a curious passion for being liked. Cards wanted to be admired, but to be liked!... what was the gain? But that second year was, in spite of it all, the best time that Peter had ever had. There was warmth of a kind in their appreciation of him. He was only fifteen and small for his age, but his uncompromising attitude about things, his silence, his football, gave him a surprising importance—but even now it was respect rather than popularity. He was growing more like a bull-dog than ever, his hair was stiff and short, rather shaggy eyebrows, a square jaw, his short legs rather far apart, a broad back and thick strong arms.

Now that Stephen had slipped so sadly into the background he built up his life about Cards. He put everything into that room—not the old room that had held Stephen, but a new shining place that gained some added brilliance from the fact that its guest realised so little the honour that was done him. He would lie awake at night and think about Cards, of the things that he would do for him, of the way that he would serve him, of the guardian that he would be.

And then, as that summer term, at the end of the second year, wore on the pain of Cards' departure grew daily more terrible. He didn't know, as the days advanced, how he would be able to bear that place without Cards. There would be no life, no interest, and all the disorganisation, the immorality, the cruelty would oppress him as they had never oppressed him before. Besides next year he would be a person of some importance—he would probably be Captain of the Football and a Monitor...everything would be terribly hard. Of course there was old Bobby Galleon, who was a very good chap and really fond of Peter, but there was no excitement about that relationship. Bobby was quite ready to play servant to Peter's master, and Peter could never respect any one very much who did that. Beside Cards, so brilliant, so handsome, with such an "air," old Bobby really didn't come off very well.

Bobby also at times was inclined to be a little sentimental. He used to ask Peter whether he liked him—whether he would miss him if he died—and he used to tell Peter that he would very gladly die for him. There were things that one didn't—if one had self-respect—say.

That year the summer was of a blazing heat. Every morning saw a sky of steely blue, the corn stood like a golden band about the hills, and little clouds like the softest feathers were blown by the Gods about the world. A mist clung about the distant hills and clothed them in purple grey. As the term grew to its close Peter felt that the world was a prison of coloured steel, and that Dawson's was a true Hell...he would escape from it with Cards. And then when he saw that such an escape would be running away and a confession of defeat—he turned back and held his will in command.

Cards looked upon his approaching departure as a great deliverance. He was to be a man immediately; not for him that absurdly dilatory condition of pimples and hobbledehoy boots that mark a transition period. Dawson's had been the most insignificant sojourn in the tent of the enemy, and the world, it was implied, had lamented his enforced absence. But, as the end of term flung its shadows in front of it in the form of examinations, and that especial quality of excited expectancy hovering about the corridors, Cards felt, for the first time in his existence, a genuine emotion. He minded, curiously, leaving Peter. He felt, although in this he wrongly anticipated the gods, that he would never see him again, and he calculated perhaps at the little piece of real affection and friendship that stood out from the Continental Tour that he wished Life to be, like a palm tree on the limitless desert. And yet it was characteristic of them both that on the last day when, seated under a hedge at the top of the playing fields, the school buildings a grey mist below them and the air tensely rigid with heat, they said good-bye to one another, it was Cards who found all the words.

Peter had nothing to say at all; he only clutched at tufts of grass, lugged them from the earth and flung them before him. But Cards, as usual, rose to the occasion.

"You know, Peter, it's been most splendid knowing you here. I don't think I'd ever have got through Dawson's if it hadn't been for you. It's a hell of a place and I suppose if the mater hadn't been abroad so much I should never have stayed on. But it's no use making a fuss. Besides, it's only for a little while— one will have forgotten all about it in a year's time."

Peter smiled. "You will, I shan't."

"Why, of course you will. And you must come and stay with us often. My mother's most awfully anxious to know you. Won't it be splendid going out to join her in Italy? It'll be a bit hot this time of year I expect."

Peter seemed to struggle with his words. "I say—Cards—you won't—altogether—forget me?"

"Forget you! Why, good Lord, I'll be always writing. I'll have such lots to tell you. I've never liked any one in all my life (this said with a great sense of age) as I've liked you!"

He stood up and fumbled in his coat. Peter always remembered him, his dark slim body against the sky, his hair tumbled about his forehead, the grace and ease with which his body was balanced, the trick that he had of swaying a little from the hips. He felt in his pocket.

"I say—I've got something for you. I bought it down in the town the other day and I made them put your name on it." He produced it, wrapped in tissue paper, out of his pocket, and Peter took it without a word. It was a silver match-box with "Peter Westcott from his friend Cardillac," and the month and the year printed on it.

"Thanks most awfully," Peter said gruffly. "Jolly decent of you. Good-bye old man."

They shook hands and avoided each other's eyes, and Cardillac had a sudden desire to fling the Grand Tour and the rest of it to the dogs and to come back for another year to Dawson's.

"Well, I must get back, got to be in library at four," he said.

"I'm going to stop here a bit," said Peter.

He watched Cards walk slowly down the hill and then he flung himself on his face and pursued with a vacant eye the efforts of an ant to climb a swaying blade of grass ... he was there for a long time.

III

And so he entered into his third year at Dawson's with a dogged determination to get through with it as well as possible and not to miss Cards more than he could help. He did, as an actual fact, miss Cards terribly. There were so many places, so many things that were connected with him, but he found, as a kind of reward, that Bobby Galleon was more of a friend than before. Now that Cards had departed Galleon came a little out of his shell. He anticipated, obviously with very considerable enjoyment, that year when he would have Peter all to himself. Bobby Galleon's virtue was, at any rate, that one was not conscious of him, and during the time of Peter's popularity he was useful without being in the very least evident. When that year was over and he had seen the last shining twinkle of Cards' charms and fascinations he looked at Peter a little wistfully, "Peter, old man, next year will be topping...." and Peter, the pleasant warmth of popularity about him, felt that there was a great deal to be said for Galleon after all.

But with the first week of that third year trouble began. Things lifted between the terms, into so different an air; at the end of the summer with Peter's authority in prospect and his splendid popularity (confined by no jailer-like insistence on rules) around him that immediate year seemed simple enough. But in the holidays that preceded the autumn term something had occurred; Peter returned in the mists and damp of September with every eye upon him. Although only fifteen and a half he was a Monitor and Captain of the Football ... far too young for both these posts, with fellows of a great size and a greater age in the school, but Barbour (his nose providing, daily, a more lively guide to his festal evenings) was seized by Peter's silence and imperturbability in the midst of danger, "That kid's got guts" (this a vinous confidence amongst friends) "and will pull the place up—gettin' a bit slack, yer know—Young? Lord bless yer, no—wonderful for his age and Captain of the Football—that's always popular."

So upon Peter the burden of "pulling things up" descended. How far Cards might have helped him here it is difficult to say. Cards had, in his apparently casual contempt of that school world, a remarkably competent sense of the direction in which straws were blowing. That most certainly Peter had not, being inclined, at this stage of things, to go straight for the thing that he saw and to leave the outskirts of the subject to look after themselves. And here Bobby Galleon was of no use to him, being as blundering and near-sighted and simple as a boy could very well be. Moreover his implicit trust in the perfection of that hero, Peter, did not help clarity of vision. He was never aware of the causes of things and only dimly noticed effects, but he was unflinchingly faithful.

"The primrose path" was, of course, open to Peter. He was popular enough, at the beginning of that Autumn term, to do anything, and, had he followed the "closed-eyes" policy of his predecessor, smiling pleasantly upon all crime and even gently with his own authority "lending a hand," all would have been well. There were boys with strangely simple names, simple for such criminals—Barton, Jerrard, Watson, West, Underbill—who were old-established hands at their own especial games, and they saw no reason at all for disturbance. "Young Westcott had better not come meddling here," they muttered darkly, having discerned already a tendency on his part to show disapproval. Nothing happened during the first term—no concrete incident—but Peter had stepped, by the end of it, from an exultant popularity to an actual distrust and suspicion. The football season had not been very successful and Peter had not the graces and charm of a leader. He distrusted the revelation of enthusiasm because he was himself so enthusiastic and his silence was mistaken for coldness. He hated the criminals with the simple names and showed them that he hated them and they in their turn, skilfully and with some very genuine humour, persuaded the school that he cut a very poor figure.

At the absurd concert that closed the Autumn term (Mr. Barbour, red-nosed and bulging shirt-front, hilariously in the chair) Peter knew that he had lost his throne. He had Bobby—there was no one else— and in a sudden bitterness and scorn at the fickle colour of that esteem that he had valued so highly he almost wished that he were altogether alone.... Bobby only accentuated things.

Nothing to go home to—nothing to come back to. The Christmas holidays over he returned to the Easter term with an eager determination to improve matters.

It was geniality that he lacked: he knew that that was the matter with him, and he felt a kind of despair about it because he seemed to return at the end of every holiday from Cornwall with that old conviction in his head that the easiest way to get through the world was to stand with your back to the wall and say nothing ... and if these fellows, who thought him so pleasant last year, thought him pleasant no longer, well, then he must put up with it. He had not changed—there he was, as ever.

But the Easter term was a chronicle of mistakes. He could not be genial to people who defied and mocked him; he found, dangerously, that they could all be afraid of him. When his face was white and his voice very quiet and his whole body tense like a bow, then they feared him—the biggest and strongest of those criminals obeyed. He was sixteen now and he could when he liked rule them all, and gradually, as the term advanced, he used his strength more and more and was more and more alone. Days would come when he would hate his loneliness and would rush out of it with friendly advances and always he would be beaten back into his reserve again. Had only Cards been there!... But what side would Cards have taken? Perhaps Peter was fortunate in that the test was not demanded. Poor Bobby simply did not understand it at all. Peter! the most splendid fellow in the world! What were they all up to? But that point of view did not help matters. No other monitor spoke to Peter now if he could help it, and even the masters, judging that where there was smoke there must be fire, passed him coldly. That Easter term, in the late winds and rains of March, closed hideously. The Easter holidays, although perhaps he did not realise it, were a deliberate backing for the ordeal that was, he knew, to come.

He faced it on his return almost humorously, prepared, with a self-consciousness that was unusual in him, for all the worst things, and it is true enough that they were as bad as they could be. Bobby Galleon shared in it all, of course, but he had never been a popular person and he did not miss anything so long as there was Peter. Once he said, as Cards had said before:

"Leave 'em alone, Peter. After all, we can't do anything. They're too many for us, and, most important thing of all, they aren't worth it."

"Not much," said Peter, "things have got to be different."

Things were not different. They were too many for him, but he struggled on. The more open bullying he stopped, and there were other things that he drove into dark corners. But they remained there—in those corners. There were so many dark places at Dawson's, and it began to get on his brain so that he heard whispers and suspicions and marked the trail of the beast at every minute of the day. He could find nothing now in the open—they were too clever for him. The Captain of the Citadel—Ellershaw— was as he knew the worst fellow in the school, but there was nothing to be done, nothing unless something were caught in the open. As the term advanced the whispers grew and he felt that there were plots in the air. He was obeyed, Ellershaw and some of the others were politer than they had ever been, and for many weeks now there had been no disturbance—then suddenly the storm broke.

One hot afternoon he was sitting in his study alone, trying to read. Things seemed to him that day at their very worst, there was no place to which he might turn. People were playing cricket beyond his window. Some fly buzzed on his window pane, the sunlight was golden about his room and little ladders of dust twisted and curved against the glare—the house was very still. Then suddenly, from a neighbouring study, there were sounds. At first they did not penetrate his day dream, then they caught his ear and he put his book down and listened. The sounds were muffled; there was laughter and then some one cried out.

He knew that it was Jerrard's study and he hated Jerrard more than any one in the school. The fellow was a huge stupid oaf, low down in the middle fourth, but the best bowler that the school had; yes, he hated him. He opened his study door and listened. The passage was deserted, and, for a moment, there was no sound save some one shouting down in the cricket field and the buzzing of the fly on the pane. Then he heard voices from behind Jerrard's door.

"No, I say—Jerrard—don't give me any more—please ... please don't."

"There I say—hold his mouth open; that's right, pour it down. We'll have him singing in a moment."

"Oh I say—" there were sounds of a struggle and then silence again. At last there began the most horrible laughter that Peter had ever known; weak, silly, giggling, and little excited cries.

Then Jerrard's voice: "There, that will do; he's merry enough now."

Peter waited for no more, but strode across the passage and flung open the door. Some chairs were overturned; Jerrard and a friend, hearing the door open, had turned round. Leaning against the table, very flushed, his eyes shining, his hair covered with dust, waving his arms and singing in a quivering voice, was a small boy, very drunk. A glass and a whisky bottle were on the table.

"You damned hound!" Peter was trembling from head to foot. "You shall get kicked out for this."

Peter closed the door quietly behind him, and went back to his study. Here at last was the moment for which he had been waiting. Jerrard should be expelled if he, Peter, died in the attempt. Jerrard was the school's best bowler; he was immensely popular ... it would, indeed, be a matter of life and death. On that same evening he called a meeting of the Monitors; they were bound to meet if one of their number had anything of sufficient importance to declare, but they came reluctantly and showed Peter that they resented his action. When they heard what Peter had to say their attitude was even more mutinous. Jerrard, the school's best bowler, was their one thought. The end of the term was at hand, and the great match of the year against Radford, a neighbouring school, approached. Without Jerrard Dawson's would be hopelessly defeated. If Barbour heard of the incident Jerrard would be expelled; Barbour might be reluctant to act, but act he must. They were not, by an absurd and ancient rule, allowed to punish any grave offence without reporting it to the head-master. If, therefore, they took any action at all, it must be reported, Jerrard would be expelled, a boon companion and the great cricket match of the year, would be lost. And all this through that interfering prig of a Westcott! Any ordinary fellow would have shut his eyes to the whole affair. After all what is there to make a fuss about in having a rag with a kid? What are kids for? Thus the conclave sourly regarding Peter who watched them in turn, and sat sternly, ominously militant. They approached him with courtesy; Ellershaw showed him what this might mean to the school were it persisted in. After all, Jerrard was, in all probability, sorry enough ... it was a rotten thing to do—he should apologise to them. No, Peter would have none of it, they must 'act; it must be reported to the Head. He would, if necessary, report it himself.

Then they turned and cursed him, asking him whom he thought that he was, warned him about the way that the school would take his interference when the school knew, advised him for his own good to drop the matter; Peter was unmoved.

Barbour was informed; Jerrard was expelled—the school was beaten in the cricket match by an innings.

Then the storm broke. Peter moved, with Bobby Galleon, through a cloud of enemies. It was a hostility that cut like a knife, silent, motionless, but so bitter that every boy from Ellershaw to the tiniest infant at the bottom of the first took it as the motif of his day. That beast Westcott was the song that rang through the last fortnight.

Bobby Galleon was cowed by it; he did not mind his own ostracism, and he was proud that he could give practical effect to his devotion for his friend, but deep down in his loyalty, there was an unconfessed suspicion as to whether Peter, after all, hadn't been a little unwise and interfering—what was the good of making all this trouble? He even wondered whether Peter didn't rather enjoy it?

And Peter, for the first time in his school life, was happy. There was something after all in being up against all these people. He was a general fighting against tremendous odds. He would show them next year that they must obey.

On the last afternoon of the term he sat alone in his study. Bobby was with the matron, packing. He was conscious, as he sat there, of the sound of many feet shuffling. There were many whispers beyond his door, and yet a great silence.

He waited for a little, and then he opened his door and looked out. As he did so the bell for roll-call rang through the building, and he knew that it was his roll.

Afternoon roll-call was always taken in the gymnasium, a large empty room beyond the study passage, and it was the custom for boys to come up as their name was about to be called and thus to pass on.

But to-day he saw that the whole of the school was gathered there, along the dusky passage and packed, in a silent motionless throng, into the gymnasium.

He knew that they were all there with a purpose, and suddenly as he realised the insult that they intended, that spirit of exultation came upon him again. Ah! it was worth while, this battle!

They made way in silence as he passed quietly to the other end of the gymnasium and stood, a little above them, on the steps that led to the gallery. He started the roll-call with the head of the school and the sixth form ... there was no answer to any name; only perfect silence and every eye fixed upon him. For a wild moment he wished to burst out upon them, to crash their heads together, to hurt—then his self-control returned. Very quietly and clearly he read through the school list, a faint smile on his lips. Bobby Galleon was the only boy, out of three hundred, who answered.

When he had finished he called out as was the custom, "Roll is over," then for a brief instant, with the list in his hand, smiling, he faced them all. Every eye was upon him—Ellershaw, West, Barton smiling a little, some faces nervous, some excited, all bitterly, intensely hostile ... and he must return next year!

He came down from the steps and walked very slowly to the door, and then as his fingers touched the handle there was a sound—a whisper, very soft and then louder; it grew about his ear like a shot ... the whole school, motionless as before, was hissing him.

There was no word spoken, and he closed the door behind him.

IV

That same night he walked, before chapel, with Bobby to the top of the playing fields. The night was dark and heavy, with no moon nor stars—but there was a cool wind that touched his cheek.

"Well, I've been a pretty good failure, Bobby. You've stuck to me like a brick. I shall never forget it.... But you know never in all my life have I been as happy as I was this afternoon. The devils! I'll have 'em under next year."

"That's not the way—" Bobby tried timorously to explain.

"Oh, yes, it is.... Anyhow it's my way. I wonder what there is about me that makes people hate me so."

"People don't."

"Yes, they do. At home, here—it's all the same. I'm always having to fight about something, always coming up against things."

"I suppose it's your destiny," said Bobby. "You always say it's to teach you pluck."

"That's what an old chap I knew in Cornwall said. But why can't I be let alone? How I loved that bit last year when the fellows liked me—only the decent things never last."

"It'll be all right later," Bobby answered, thinking that he had never seen anything finer than the way Peter had taken that afternoon. "In a way," he went on, "you fellows are lucky to get a chance of standing up against that sort of thing; it's damned good practice. Nobody ever thinks I'm worth while."

"Well," said Peter, throwing a clod of dark, scented earth into the air and losing sight of it in the black wall about him—"Here's to next year's battle!"

CHAPTER VII

PRIDE OF LIFE

I

Peter never saw Dawson's again. When the summer holidays had run some three weeks a letter arrived stating, quite simply and tersely, that, owing to the non-payment by evading parents of bills long overdue and to many other depressing and unavoidable circumstances Mr. Barbour and that House of Cards, his school, had fallen to pieces. There at any rate was an end to that disastrous accumulation of brick and mortar, and the harm that, living, it had wrought upon the souls and bodies of its victims its dying could not excuse. No tears were shed for Dawson's.

Peter, at the news, knew that now his battle never could be won. That battle at any rate must be left behind him with his defeat written large upon the plain of it, and this made in some unrealised way the penalty of the future months harder to bear. He had, behind him, defeat. Look at it as he might, he had been a failure at Dawson's—he had not done the things that he had been put there to do—and yet through the disaster he knew that in so far as he had refused to bend to the storm so far there had been victory; of that at any rate he was sure.

So he turned resolutely from the past and faced the future. It was as though suddenly Dawson's had never existed—a dream, a fantasy, a delirium—something that had left no external things behind it and had only in the effect that it had worked upon himself spiritually made its mark. He faced his House....

Scaw House had seemed to him, during these last three years, merely an interlude at Dawson's. There had been hurried holidays that had been spent in recovering from and preparing for the term and the House had scarcely, and only very quietly, raised its head to disturb him. He had not been disturbed—he had had other things to think about—and now he was very greatly disturbed indeed; that was the first difference that he consciously realised. The disturbance lay, of course, partly in the presence of his father and in the sense that he had had growing upon him, during the last two years, that their relationship, the one to the other, would, suddenly, one fine day, spring into acute emotion. They were approaching one another gradually as in a room whose walls were slowly closing. "Face to face—and then body to body—at last, soul to soul!"

He did not, he thought, actively hate his father; his father did not actively hate him, but hate might spring up at any moment between them, and Peter, although he was only sixteen, was no longer a child. But the feeling of apprehension that Scaw House gave him was caused by wider influences than his father. Three years at Dawson's had given Peter an acute sense of expecting things, it might be defined as "the glance over the shoulder to see who followed"—some one was always following at Scaw House. He saw in this how closely life was bound together, because every little moment at Dawson's contributed to his present active fear. Dawson's explained Scaw House to Peter. And yet this was all morbidity and Peter, square, broad-shouldered, had no scrap of morbidity in his clean body. He did not await the future with the shaking candle of the suddenly awakened coward, but rather with the planted feet and the bared teeth of the bull-dog....

He watched the faces of his father, his aunt and Mrs. Trussit. He observed the frightened dreams of his grandfather, the way that old Curtis the gardener would suddenly cease his fugitive digging and glance with furtive eyes at the windows of the house; about them were the dark shadows of the long passages, the sharp note of some banging door in a distant room, the wail of that endless wind beyond the walls. He felt too that Mrs. Trussit and his aunt were furtively watching him. He never caught them in anything tangible but he knew that, when his back was turned, their eyes followed him—questioning, wondering.

Something must be done or he could not answer for his control. If he were not to return to Dawson's, what then?

It was his seventeenth birthday one hot day towards the end of August, and at breakfast his father, without looking up from his paper, said:

"I have made arrangements for you with Mr. Aitchinson to enter his office next week. You'll have to work—you've been idling long enough."

The windows were wide open, the lawn was burning in the sun, bees carried the scent of the flowers with them into the air that hung like shining metal about the earth, a cart rattled as though it were a giant clattering his pleasure at the day down the road. It was a wonderful day and somewhere streams were flowing under dark protecting trees, and the grass was thick in cool hollows and the woods were so dense that no blue sky reached the moss, but only the softest twilight ... and old Aitchinson, the town's solicitor, with his nutcracker face, his snuffling nose, his false teeth—and the tightly-closed office, the piles of paper, the ink, the silly view from the dusty windows of Treliss High Street—and life always in the future to be like that until he died.

But Peter showed no emotion.

"Very well, father—What day do I go?"

"Monday—nine o'clock."

Nothing more was said. At any rate Aitchinson and his red tape and his moral dust would fill the day—no time then to dwell on these dark passages and Mrs. Trussit's frightened eyes and the startled jump of the marble clock in the dining-room just before it struck the hour....

II

And so for weeks it proved. Aitchinson demanded no serious consideration. He was a hideous little man with eyes like pins, shaggy eyebrows, a nose that swelled at the end and was pinched by the sharpest of pince-nez, cheeks that hung white and loose except when he was hungry or angry, and then they were tight and red, a little body rather dandily dressed with a flowered waistcoat, a white stock, a skirted coat and pepper-and-salt trousers—and last of all, tiny feet, of which he was inordinately proud and with which, like Agag, he always walked delicately. He had a high falsetto voice, fingers that were always picking, like eager hens, at the buttons on his waistcoat or the little waxed moustache above his mouth, and hair that occupied its time in covering a bald patch that always escaped every design upon it. So much for Mr. Aitchinson. Let him be flattered sufficiently and Peter saw that his way would be easy. The wizened little creature had, moreover, a certain admiration for Peter's strength and broad shoulders and used sometimes in the middle of the morning's work to ask Peter how much he weighed, whether he'd ever considered taking up prize-fighting as a profession, and how much he measured across the chest.

There were two other youths, articled like Peter, stupid sons of honest Treliss householders, with high collars, faces that shone with soap and hair that glistened with oil, languid voices and a perpetual fund of small talk about the ladies of the town, moral and otherwise. Peter did not like them and they did not like Peter. One day, because he was tired and unhappy, he knocked their heads together, and they plotted to destroy him, but they were afraid, and secretly admired what they called his coarse habits.

The Summer stole away and Autumn crept into its place, and at the end of October something occurred. Something suddenly happened at Scaw House that made action imperative, and filled his brain all day so that Aitchinson's office and his work there was only a dream and the people in it were shadows. He had heard his mother crying from behind her closed door....

He had been coming, on a wet autumnal afternoon, down the dark stairs from his attic and suddenly at the other end of the long passage there had been this sound, so sudden and so pitiful coming upon that dreary stillness that he had stopped with his hands clenched and his face white and his heart beating like a knock on a door. Instantly all those many little moments that he had had in that white room with that heavy-scented air crowded upon him and he remembered the smile that she had always given him and the way that her hair lay so tragically about the pillow. He had always been frightened and eager to escape; he felt suddenly so deeply ashamed that the crimson flooded his face there in the dark passage. She had wanted him all these years and he had allowed those other people to prevent him from going to her. What had been happening to her in that room? The sound of her crying came to him as though beseeching him to come and help her. He put his hands to his ears and went desperately into the dark wet garden. He knew now when he thought of it, that his behaviour to his mother had been, during these months since he had left Dawson's, an unconscious cowardice. Whilst he had been yet at school those little five minutes' visits to his mother's room might have been excused, but during these last months there had been, with regard to her, in his conscience, if he had cared to examine it, sharp accusation.

The defence that she did not really want to see him, that his presence might bring on some bad attack, might excite her, was no real defence. He had postponed an interview with her from day to day because he realised that that interview would strike into flame all the slumbering relations that that household held. It would fling them all, as though from a preconcerted signal, into war....

But now there could be only one thought in his mind. He must see his mother—if he could still help her he must be at her service. There was no one whom he could ask about her. Mrs. Trussit now never spoke to him (and indeed never spoke to any one if she could help it), and went up and down the stairs in her rustling black and flat white face and jingling keys as though she was no human being at all but only a walking automaton that you wound up in the morning and put away in the cupboard at night— Mrs. Trussit was of no use.

There remained Stephen, and this decided Peter to break through that barrier that there was between them and to find out why it had ever existed. He had not seen Stephen that summer at all—no one saw Stephen—only at The Bending Mule they shook their heads over him and spoke of the wild devil that had come upon him because the woman he loved was being tortured to death by her husband only a mile away. He was drinking, they said, and his farm was going to ruin, and he would speak to nobody— and they shook their heads. It was not through cowardice that Peter had avoided him, but since those three years at Dawson's he had been lonely and silent himself, and Stephen had never sent for him as he would have done, Peter thought, if he had wanted him. Now the time had come when he could stand alone no longer....

He slipped away one night after supper, leaving that quiet room with his aunt playing Patience at the table, his old grandfather mumbling in his sleep, his father like a stone, staring at his paper but not, Peter was sure, reading any of it.

Mrs. Trussit, silent before the fire in her room, his aunt not seeing the cards that she laid upon the table, his father not reading his paper—for what were they all listening?

It was a fierce night and the wind rushed up the high road as though it would tear Peter off his feet and fling him into the sea, but he walked sturdily, no cap on his head and the wind streaming through his hair. Some way along the road he found a child crying in a ditch. He loved children, and, picking the small boy up, he found that he had been sent for beer to the Cap and Feathers, at the turn of the road, and been blown by the wind into the ditch and was almost dead with terror. At first at the sight of Peter the child had cried out, but at the touch of his warm hand and at the sound of his laugh he had been suddenly comforted, and trotted down the road with his hand in Peter's and his tears dried.

Peter's way with the children of the place was sharp and entirely lacking in sentiment—"Little idiot, to fall into the ditch like that—not much of the man about you, young Thomas."

"Isn't Thomas," said the small boy with a chuckle, "I be Jan Proteroe, and I beant afeart only gert beast come out of hedge down along with eyes and a tail—gum!"

He would have told Peter a great deal more but he was suddenly frightened again by the dark hedges and began to whimper, so Peter picked him up and carried him to his cottage at the end of the road and kissed him and pushed him in at the lighted door. He was cheered by the little incident and felt less lonely. At the thought of making Stephen once more his friend his heart warmed. Stephen had been wanting him, perhaps, all this time to come to him but had been afraid that he might be interfering if he asked him—and how glad they would be to see one another!

After all, they needed one another. They had both had hard times, they were both lonely and no distance nor circumstances could lessen that early bond that there had been between them. Happier than he had been for many weeks, he struck off the road and started across the fields, stumbling over the rough soil and plunging sometimes into ditches and pools of water. The rain had begun to fall and the whispering hiss that it made as it struck the earth drowned the more distant noise of the sea that solemnly broke beyond the bending fields. Stephen's farm stood away from all other houses, and Peter as he pressed forward seemed to be leaving all civilisation behind him. He was cold and his boots were heavy with thick wet mud and his hair was soaked.

Beyond the fields was a wood through which he must pass before he reached Stephen's farm, and as the trees closed about him and he heard the rain driving through the bare branches the world seemed to be full of chattering noises. The confidence that he had had in Stephen's reception of him suddenly deserted him and a cold miserable unhappiness crept about him in this wet, heaving world of wind and rain and bare naked trees. Like a great cry there seemed to come suddenly to him through the wood his mother's voice appealing for help, so that he nearly turned, running back. It was a hard, cruel place this world—and all the little ditches and hollows of the wood were running with brown, stealthy water.

He broke through it at last and saw at the bottom of the hill Stephen's house, and he saw that there were no lights in the windows. He stood on the breast of the little hill for a moment and thought that he would turn back, but it was raining now with great heaviness and the wind at his back seemed to beat him down the hill. Suddenly seized with terror at the wood behind him, he ran stumbling down the slope. He undid the gate and pitched into the yard, plunging into great pools of water and seeing on every side of him the uncertain shapes of the barns and sheds and opposite him the great dark front of the house, so black in its unfriendliness, sharing in the night's rough hostility.

He shouted "Stephen," but his voice was drowned by the storm and the gate behind him, creaking on its hinges, answered him with shrill cries. He found the little wicket that led into the garden, and, stepping over the heavy wet grass, he banged loudly with the knocker on the door and called again "Stephen." The noise echoed through the house and then the silence seemed to be redoubled. Then pushing the great knocker, he found to his surprise that the door was unfastened and swung back before him. He felt his way into the dark hall and struck a match. He shouted "Stephen" once more and his voice came echoing back to him. The place seemed to be entirely deserted—the walls were wet with damp, there were no carpets on the floor, a window at the end of the passage showed its uncurtained square.

He passed into the kitchen, and here he found two candles and lighted them. Here also he found signs of life. On the bare deal table was a half-finished meal—a loaf of bread, cheese, butter, an empty whisky bottle lying on its side. Near these things there was a table, and on the floor, beside an overturned chair, there was a gun. Peter picked it up and saw that it was unloaded. There was something terribly desolate about these things; the room was very bare, a grandfather clock ticked solemnly in the corner, there were a few plates and cups on the dresser, an old calendar hung from a dusty nail and, blown by the wind from the cracked window, tip-tapped like a stealthy footstep against the wall. But Peter felt curiously certain that Stephen was going to return; something held him in his chair and he sat there, with his hands on the deal table, facing the clock and listening. The wind howled beyond the house, the rain lashed the panes, and suddenly—so suddenly that his heart leapt to his mouth—there was a scratching on the door. He went to the door and opened it and found outside a wretched sheep-dog, so starved that the bones showed through the skin, and so weak that he could scarcely drag himself along. Peter let him in and the animal came up to him and looked up in his eyes and, very faintly, wagged his tail. Peter gave him the bread, which the dog devoured, and then they both remained silent, without moving, the dog's head between Peter's knees.

The boy must have slept, because he woke suddenly to all the clocks in the house striking midnight, and in the silence the house seemed to be full of clocks. They came running down the stairs and up and down the passages and then, with a whir and a clatter, ceased as instantly as they had begun.

The house was silent again—the storm had died down—and then the dog that had been sleeping suddenly raised its head and barked. Somewhere in the distance a door was banged to, and then Peter heard a voice, a tremendous voice, singing.

There were heavy steps along the passage, then the kitchen door was banged open and Stephen stood in the doorway. Stephen's shirt was open at the neck, his hair waved wildly over his forehead, he stood, enormous, with his legs apart, his eyes shining, blood coming from a cut in his cheek, and in one of his hands was a thick cudgel. Standing there in the doorway, he might have been some ancient Hercules, some mighty Achilles.

He saw Peter, recognised him, but continued a kind of triumphal hymn that he was singing.

"Ho, Master Peter, I've beat him! I've battered his bloody carcass! I came along and I looked in at the winder and I saw 'im a ill-treatin' of 'er.

"I left the winder, I broke the glass, I was down upon 'im, the dirty 'ound, and"—(chorus)—"I've battered 'is bloody carcass! Praise be the Lord, I got 'im one between the eyes—"

"Praise be, I 'it him square in the jaw and the blood came a-pourin' out of his mouth and down 'e went, and—

(Chorus) "I've battered 'is bloody carcass—

"There she was, cryin' in the corner of the room, my lovely girl, and there 'e was, blast 'is bones, with 'is 'and on her lovely 'air, and—

(Chorus) "I've battered 'is bloody carcass.

"I got 'im one on the neck and I got 'im one between 'is lovely eyes and I got 'im one on 'is lovely nose, and 'e went down straight afore me, and—

(Chorus) "I've battered 'is bloody carcass!"

Peter knew that it must be Mr. Samuel Burstead to whom Stephen was referring, and he too, as he listened, was suddenly filled with a sense of glory and exultation. Here after all was a way out of all trouble, all this half-seen, half-imagined terror of the past weeks. Here too was an end to all Stephen's morbid condition, sitting alone by himself, drinking, seeing no one—now that he'd got Burstead between the eyes life would be a vigorous, decent thing once more.

Stephen stopped his hymn and came and put his arm round Peter's neck. "Well, boy, to think of you coming round this evening. All these months I've been sittin' 'ere thinking of you—but I've been in a nasty, black state, Master Peter, doing nothing but just brood. And the devils got thicker and thicker about me and I was just going off my head thinking of my girl in the 'ands of that beast up along. At last to-night I suddenly says, 'Stephen, my fine feller, you've 'ad enough of this,' I says. 'You go up and 'ave a good knock at 'im,' I says, 'and to-morrer marnin' you just go off to another bit o' country and start doin' something different.' Up I got and I caught hold of this stick here and out up along I walked. Sure enough there 'e was, through the winder, bullyin' her and she crying. So I just jumped through the winder and was up on to 'im. Lord, you should 'ave seen 'im jump.

"'Fair fight, Sam Burstead,' I says.

"'Yer bloody pirate!' says 'e.

"'Pirate, is it?' says I, landing him one—and at that first feel of my 'and along o' 'is cheek all these devils that I've been sufferin' from just turned tail and fled.

"Lord, I give it 'im! Lord, I give it 'im!

"He's living, I reckon, but that's about all 'e is doing. And then, without a word to 'er, I come away, and here I am, a free man ... and to-morrer marning I go out to tramp the world a bit—and to come back one day when she wants me."

And then in Peter there suddenly leapt to life a sense of battle, of glorious combat and conflict.

As he stood there in the bare kitchen—he and Stephen there under the light of the jumping candle—with the rain beating on the panes, the trees of the wood bending to the wind, he was seized, exalted, transformed with a sense of the vigour, the adventure, the surprising energy of life.

"Stephen! Stephen!" he cried. "It's glorious! By God! I wish I'd been there!"

Stephen caught him by the arm and held him. The old dog came from under the table and wagged his tail.

"Bless my soul," said Stephen, looking at him, "all these weeks I've been forgetting him. I've been in a kind of dream, boy—a kind o' dream. Why didn't I 'it 'im before? Lord, why didn't I 'it 'im before!"

Peter at the word thought of his mother.

"Yes," he thought, with clenched teeth, "I'll go for them!"

CHAPTER VIII

PETER AND HIS MOTHER

I

He had returned over the heavy fields, singing to a round-faced moon. In the morning, when he woke after a night of glorious fantastic dreams, and saw the sun beating very brightly across his carpet and birds singing beyond his window, he felt still that same exultation.

It seemed to him, as he sat on his bed, with the sun striking his face, that last night he had been brought into touch with a vigour that challenged all the mists and vapours by which he had felt himself surrounded. That was the way that now he would face them.

Looking back afterwards, he was to see that that evening with Stephen flung him on to all the events that so rapidly followed.

Moreover, above all the sensation of the evening there was also a triumphant recognition of the fact that Stephen had now been restored to him. He might never see him again, but they were friends once more, he could not be lonely now as he had been....

And then, coming out of the town into the dark street and the starlight, he thought that he recognised a square form walking before him. He puzzled his brain to recall the connection and then, as he passed Zachary Tan's shop, the figure turned in and showed, for a moment, his face.

It was that strange man from London, Mr. Emilio Zanti....

II

It seemed to Peter that now at Scaw House the sense of expectation that had been with them all during the last weeks was charged with suspense—at supper that night his aunt burst suddenly into tears and left the room. Shortly afterwards his father also, without a word, got up from the table and went upstairs....

Peter was left alone with his grandfather. The old man, sunk beneath his pile of cushions, his brown skinny hand clenching and unclenching above the rugs, was muttering to himself. In Peter himself, as he stood there by the fire, looking down on the old man, there was tremendous pity. He had never felt so tenderly towards his grandfather before; it was, perhaps, because he had himself grown up all in a day. Last night had proved that one was grown up indeed, although one was but seventeen. But it proved to him still more that the time had come for him to deal with the situation all about him, to discover the thing that was occupying them all so deeply.

Peter bent down to the cushions.

"Grandfather, what's the matter with the house?"

He could hear, faintly, beneath the rugs something about "hell" and "fire" and "poor old man."

"Grandfather, what's the matter with the house?" but still only "Poor old man ... poor old man ... nobody loves him ... nobody loves him ... to hell with the lot of 'em ... let 'em grizzle in hell fire ... oh! such nasty pains for a poor old man."

"Grandfather, what's the matter with the house?"

The old brown hand suddenly stopped clenching and unclenching, and out from the cushions the old brown head with its few hairs and its parchment face poked like a withered jack-in-the-box.

"Hullo, boy, you here?"

"Grandfather, what's the matter with the house?"

The old man's fingers, sharp like pins, drew Peter close to him.

"Boy, I'm terribly frightened. I've been having such dreams. I thought I was dead—in a coffin...."

But Peter whispered in his ear:

"Grandfather—tell me—what's the matter with every one here?"

The old man's eyes were suddenly sharp, like needles.

"Ah, he wants to know that, does he? He's found out something at last, has he? I know what they were about. They've been at it in here, boy, too. Oh, yes! for weeks and weeks—killing your mother, that's what my son's been doing ... frightening her to death.... He's cruel, my son. I had the Devil once, and now he's got hold of me and that's why I'm here. Mind you, boy," and the old man's ringers clutched him very tightly—"if you don't get the better of the Devil you'll be just like me one of these days. So'll he be, my son, one day. Just like me—and then it'll be your turn, my boy. Oh, they Westcotts!... Oh! my pains! Oh! my pains!... Oh! I'm a poor old man!—poor old man!"

His head sunk beneath the cushions again and his muttering died away like a kettle when the lid has been put on to it.

Peter had been kneeling so as to catch his grandfather's words. Now he drew himself up and with frowning brows faced the room. Had he but known it he was at that moment exactly like his father.

He went slowly up to his attic.

His little book-case had gained in the last two years—there were now three of Henry Galleon's novels there. Bobby had given him one, "Henry Lessingham," shining bravely in its red and gold; he had bought another, "The Downs," second hand, and it was rather tattered and well thumbed. Another, "The Roads," was a shilling paper copy. He had read these three again and again until he knew them by heart, almost word by word. He took down "Henry Lessingham" now and opened it at a page that was turned down. It is Book III, chapter VI, and there is this passage:

But, concerning the Traveller who would enter the House of Courage there are many lands that must be passed on the road before he rest there. There is, first, the Land of Lacking All Things—that is hard to cross. There is, Secondly, the Land of Having All Things. There is the Traveller's Fortitude most hardly tested. There is, Thirdly, The Land of Losing All Those Things that One Hath Possessed. That is a hard country indeed for the memory of the pleasantness of those earlier joys redoubleth the agony of lacking them. But at the end there is a Land of ice and snow that few travellers have compassed, and that is the Land of Knowing What One Hath Missed.... The Bird was in the hand and one let it go ... that is the hardest agony of all the journey ... but if these lands be encountered and surpassed then doth the Traveller at length possess his soul and is master of it ... this is the Meaning and Purpose of Life.

Peter read on through those pages where Lessingham, having found these words in some old book, takes courage after his many misadventures and starts again life—an old man, seventy years of age, but full of hope ... and then there is his wonderful death in the Plague City, closing it all like a Triumph.

The night had come down upon the house. Over the moor some twinkling light broke the black darkness and his candle blew in the wind. Everything was very still and as he clutched his book in his hand he knew that he was frightened. His grandfather's words had filled him with terror. He felt not only that his father was cruel and had been torturing his mother for many years because he loved to hurt, but he felt also that it was something in the blood, and that it would come upon him also, in later years, and that he might not be able to beat it down. He could understand definite things when they were tangible before his eyes but here was something that one could not catch hold of, something....

After all, he was very young—But he remembered, with bated breath, times at school when he had suddenly wanted to twist arms, to break things, to hurt, when suddenly a fierce hot pleasure had come upon him, when a boy had had his leg broken at football.

Dropping the book, shuddering, he fell upon his knees and prayed to what God he knew not.... "Then doth the Traveller at length possess his soul and is master of it ... this is the meaning and purpose of life."

At last he rose from his knees, physically tired, as though it had been some physical struggle. But he was quiet again ... the terror had left him, but he knew now with what beasts he had got to wrestle....

At supper that night he watched his father. Curiously, after his struggle of the afternoon, all terror had left him and he felt as though he was of his father's age and strength.

In the middle of the meal he spoke:

"How is mother to-night, father?"

He had never asked about his mother before, but his voice was quite even and steady. His aunt dropped her knife clattering on to her plate.

His father answered him:

"Why do you wish to know?"

"It is natural, isn't it? I am afraid that she is not so well."

"She is as well as can be expected."

They said no more, but once his father suddenly looked at him, as though he had noticed some new note in his voice.

III

On the next afternoon his father went into Truro. A doctor came occasionally to the house—a little man like a beaver—but Peter felt that he was under his father's hand and he despised him.

It was a clear Autumn afternoon with a scent of burning leaves in the air and heavy massive white clouds were piled in ramparts beyond the brown hills. It was so still a day that the sea seemed to be murmuring just beyond the garden-wall. The house was very silent; Mrs. Trussit was in the housekeeper's room, his grandfather was sleeping in the dining-room. The voices of some children laughing in the road came to him so clearly that it seemed to Peter impossible that his father ... and, at that, he knew instantly that his chance had come. He must see his mother now—there might not be another opportunity for many weeks.

He left his room and stood at the head of the stairs listening. There was no sound.

He stole down very softly and then waited again at the end of the long passage. The ticking of the grandfather clock in the hall drove him down the passage. He listened again outside his mother's door—there was no sound from within and very slowly he turned the handle.

As the door opened his senses were invaded by that air of medicine and flowers that he had remembered as a very small boy—he seemed to be surrounded by it and great white vases on the mantelpiece filled his eyes, and the white curtains at the window blew in the breeze of the opening door.

His aunt was sitting, with her eternal sewing, by the fire and she rose as he entered. She gave a little startled cry, like a twittering bird, as she saw that it was he and she came towards him with her hand out. He did not look at the bed at all, but bent his eyes gravely upon his aunt.

"Please, aunt—you must leave us—I want to speak to my mother."

"No—Peter—how could you? I daren't—I mustn't—your father—your mother is asleep," and then, from behind them, there came a very soft voice—

"No—let us be alone—please, Jessie."

Peter did not, even then, turn round to the bed, but fixed his eyes on his aunt.

"The doctor—" she gasped, and then, with frightened eyes, she picked up her sewing and crept out.

Then he turned round and faced the bed, and was suddenly smitten with great shyness at the sight of that white, tired face, and the black hair about the pillow.

"Well, mother," he said, stupidly.

But she smiled back at him, and although her voice was very small and faint, she spoke cheerfully and as though this were an ordinary event.

"Well, you've come to see me at last, Peter," she said.

"I mustn't stay long," he answered, gruffly, as he moved awkwardly towards the bed.

"Bring your chair close up to the bed—so—like that. You have never come to sit in here before. Peter, do you know that?"

"Yes, mother." He turned his eyes away and looked on to the floor.

"You have come in before because you have been told to. To-day you were not told—why did you come?"

"I don't know.... Father's in Truro."

"Yes, I know." He thought he caught, for an instant, a strange note in her voice. "But he will not be back yet."

There was a pause—a vast golden cloud hung like some mountain boulder beyond the window and some of its golden light seemed to steal over the white room.

"Is it bad for you talking to me?" at last he said, gruffly, "ought I to go away?"

Suddenly she clutched his strong brown hand with her thin wasted fingers, with so convulsive a grasp that his heart began to beat furiously.

"No—don't go—not until it is time for your father to come back. Isn't it strange that after all these years this is the first time that we should have a talk. Oh! so many times I've wanted you to come—and when you did come—when you were very little—you were always so frightened that you would not let me touch you—"

"They frightened me...."

"Yes—I know—but now, at last, we've got a little time together—and we must talk—quickly. I want you to tell me everything—everything—everything.... First, let me look at you...."

She took his head between her pale, slender hands and looked at him. "Oh, you are like him!—your father—wonderfully like." She lay back on the pillows with a little sigh. "You are very strong."

"Yes, I am going to be strong for you now. I am going to look after you. They shan't keep us apart any more."

"Oh, Peter, dear," she shook her head almost gaily at him. "It's too late."

"Too late?"

"Yes, I'm dying—at last it's come, after all these years when I've wanted it so much. But now I'm not sorry—now that we've had this talk—at last. Oh! Peter dear, I've wanted you so dreadfully and I was never strong enough to say that you must come ... and they said that you were noisy and it would be bad for me. But I believe if you had come earlier I might have lived."

"But you mustn't die—you mustn't die—I'll see that they have another doctor from Truro. This silly old fool here doesn't know what he's about—I'll go myself."

"Oh! how strong your hands are, Peter! How splendidly strong! No, no one can do anything now. But oh! I am happy at last..." She stroked his cheek with her hand—the golden light from the great cloud filled the room and touched the white vases with its colour.

"But quick, quick—tell me. There are so many things and there is so little time. I want to know everything—your school? Here when you were little?—all of it—"

But he was gripping the bed with his hands, his chest was heaving. Suddenly he broke down and burying his head in the bed-clothes began to sob as though his heart would break. "Oh! now ... after all this time ... you've wanted me ... and I never came ... and now to find you like this!"

She stroked his hair very softly and waited until the sobs ceased. He sat up and fiercely brushed his eyes.

"I won't be a fool—any more. It shan't be too late. I'll make you live. We'll never leave one another again."

"Dear boy, it can't be like that. Think how splendid it is that we have had this time now. Think what it might have been if I had gone and we had never known one another. But tell me, Peter, what are you going to do with your life afterwards—what are you going to be?"

"I want to write books"—he stared at the golden cloud—"to be a novelist. I daresay I can't—I don't know—but I'd rather do that than anything.... Father wants me to be a solicitor. I'm with Aitchinson now—I shall never be a good one."

Then he turned almost fiercely away from the window.

"But never mind about me, mother. It's you I want to hear about. I'm going to take this on now. It's my responsibility. I want to know about you."

"There's nothing to know, dear. I've been ill for a great many years now. It's more nerves than anything, I suppose. I think I've never had the courage to stand up against it—a stronger woman would have got the better of it, I expect. But I wasn't always like this," she added laughing a little far away ghost of a laugh—"Go and look in that drawer—there, in that cupboard—amongst my handkerchiefs—there where those old fans are—you'll find some old programmes there—Those old yellow papers...."

He brought them to her, three old yellow programmes of a "Concert Given at the Town Hall, Truro." "There, do you see? Miss Minnie Trenowth, In the Gloaming—There, I sang in those days. Oh! Truro was fun when I was a girl! There was always something going on! You see I wasn't always on my back!"

He crushed the papers in his hand.

"But, mother! If you were like that then—what's made you like this now?"

"It's nerves, dear—I've been stupid about it."

"And father, how has he treated you these years?"

"Your father has always been very kind."

"Mother, tell me the truth! I must know. Has he been kind to you?"

"Yes, dear—always."

But her voice was very faint and that look that Peter had noticed before was again in her eyes.

"Mother—you must tell me. That's not true."

"Yes, Peter. He's done his best. I have been annoying, sometimes—foolish."

"Mother, I know. I know because I know father and I know myself. I'm like him—I've just found it out. I've got those same things in me, and they'll do for me if I don't get the better of them. Grandfather told me—he was the same. All the Westcotts—"

He bent over the bed and took her hand and kissed it.

"Mother, dear—I know—father has been frightening you all this time—terrifying you. And you were all alone. If only I had been there—if only there had been some one—"

Her voice was very faint. "Yes ... he has frightened me all these years. At first I used to think that he didn't mean it. I was a bright, merry sort of a girl then—careless and knowing nothing about the world. And then I began to see—that he liked it—that it gave him pleasure to have something there that he could hurt. And then I began to be frightened. It was very lonely here for a girl who had had a gay time, and he usen't to like my going to Truro—and at last he even stopped my seeing people in Treliss. And then I began to be really frightened—and used to wake in the night and see him standing by the door watching me. Then I thought that when you were born that would draw us together, but it didn't, and I was always ill after that. He would do things—Oh!" her hand pressed her mouth. "Peter, dear, you mustn't think about it, only when I am dead I don't want you to think that I was quite a fool—if they tell you so. I don't want you to think it was all his fault either because it wasn't—I was silly and didn't understand sometimes ... but it's killed me, that dreadful waiting for him to do something, I never knew what it would be, and sometimes it was nothing ... but I knew that he liked to hurt ... and it was the expectation."

In that white room, now flaming with the fires of the setting sun, Peter caught his mother to his breast and held her there and her white hands clutched his knees.

Then his eyes, softened and he turned to her and arranged her head on the pillow and drew the sheets closely about her.

"I must go now. It has been bad for you this talking, but it had to be. I'm never, never going to leave you again—you shall not be alone any more—"

"Oh, Peter! I'm so happy! I have never been so happy... but it all comes of being a coward. If I had only been brave—never be afraid of anybody or anything. Promise me, Peter—"

"Except of myself," he answered, kissing her.

"Kiss me again.... And again..."

"To-morrow..." he looked back at her, smiling. He saw her, for an instant, as he left the room, with her cheek against the pillow and her black hair like a cloud about her; the twilight was already in the room.

An hour later, as he stood in the dining-room, the door opened and his father came in.

"You have been with your mother?"

"Yes."

"You have done her much harm. She is dying."

"I know everything," Peter answered, looking him in the face.

IV

He would never, until his own end had come, forget that evening. The golden sunset gave place to a cold and windy night, and the dark clouds rolled up along the grey sky, hiding and then revealing the thin and pallid moon.

Peter stayed there in the dining-room, waiting. His grandfather slept in his chair. Once his aunt came crying into the room and wandered aimlessly about.

"Aunt, how is she?"

"Oh, dear! oh, dear! Whatever shall I do? She is going ... she is going.... I can do nothing!"

Her thin body in the dusk flitted like a ghost about the room and then she was gone. The doctor's pony cart came rattling up to the door. The fussy little man got out and stamped in the hall, and then disappeared upstairs. There was a long pause during which there was no sound.

Then the door was opened and his aunt was there.

"You must come at once ... she wants you."

The doctor, his father, and Mrs. Trussit were there in the room, but he was only conscious of the great white bed with the candles about it and the white vases, like eyes, watching him.

As he entered the room there was a faint cry, "Peter." He had crossed to her, and her arms were about his shoulders and her mouth was pressed against his; she fell back, with a little sigh, dead.

V

In the darkened dining-room, later, his father stood in the doorway with a candle in his hand, and above it his white face and short black hair shone as though carved from marble.

Peter came from the window towards him. His father said: "You killed her by going to her."

Peter answered: "All these years you have been killing her!"

CHAPTER IX

THE THREE WESTCOTTS

I

The day crept, strangely and mysteriously, to its close. Peter, dulled by misery, sat opposite his grandfather in the dining-room without moving, conscious of the heavy twilight that the dark blinds flung about the room, feeling the silence that was only accentuated by the old man's uneasy "clack-clack" in his sleep and the clock's regular ticking. The unhappiness that had been gradually growing about him since his last term at Dawson's, was now all about him with the strength and horrible appearance of some unholy giant. It was indeed with some consciousness of Things that were flinging their shadows on the horizon and were not as yet fully visible to him that he sat there. That evening at Stephen's farm, realised only faintly at the time, hung before him now as a vivid induction or prologue to the later terrors. He was doomed—so he felt in that darkened and mysterious room—to a terrible time and horrors were creeping upon him from every side. "Clack-clack" went his grandfather beneath the rugs, as the cactus plant rattled in the window and the silence through the stairs and passages of the house crept in folds about the room.

Peter shivered; the coals fell from a dull gold into grey and crumbling ashes. He shut everything in the surrounding world from his mind and thought of his dead mother. There indeed there was strangeness enough, for it seemed now that that wonderful afternoon had filled also all the earlier years of his life. It seemed to him now that there had never been a time when he had not known her and talked with her, and yet with this was also a consciousness of all the joys that he had missed because he had not known her before. As he thought of it the hard irretrievable fact of those earlier empty years struck him physically with a sharp agonising pain—toothache, and no possible way of healing it. The irony of her proximity, of her desire for him as he, all unwittingly, had in reality desired her, hit him like a blow. The picture of her waiting, told that he did not wish to come, looking so sadly and lonely in that white room, whilst he, on the other side of that door, had not the courage to burst through those others and go to her, broke suddenly the hard dry passivity that had held him during so many weeks.

He was very young, he was very tired, he was very lonely. He sobbed with his hands pressed against his eyes.

Then his tears were quickly dried. There was this other thing to be considered—his father. He hated his father. He was terrified, as he sat there, at the fury with which he hated him. The sudden assurance of his hatred reminded him of the thing that his grandfather had said about the Westcotts ... was that true? and was this intensity of emotion that filled all the veins in his body a sign that he too was a Westcott? and were his father and grandfather mirrors of his own future years?... He did not know. That was another question....

He wondered what they were about in the room where his mother lay and it was curious that the house could remain silent during so many long hours. It seemed held by the command of some strong power, and his mind, overstrained and abnormal, waited for some outbreak of noise—many noises, clattering, banging, whistling through the house. But his grandfather slept on, no step was on the stairs, the room was very dark and evening fell beyond the long windows and over the sea.

His youth made of a day eternity—there was no end nor term to his love, to his hatred, to his loneliness, to his utter misery ... and also he was afraid. He would have given his world for Stephen, but Stephen was already off on his travels.

Very softly and stealthily the door opened and, holding a quivering candle, with her finger to her mouth, there appeared his aunt. He looked at her coldly as she came across the room towards him. He had never felt any affection for her because she had always seemed to him weak and useless—a frightened, miserable, vacillating, negative person—even when he had been a very small boy he had despised her. Her eyes were red and swollen with crying, her grey and scanty hair had fallen about her collar, her old black blouse was unbuttoned at the top showing her bony neck and her thin crooked hands were trembling in the candle-light. Her eyes were large and frightened and her back was bent as though she was cowering from a blow. She had never taken very much notice of her nephew—of late she had been afraid of him; he was surprised now that she should come to speak to him.

"Peter," she said in a whisper, looking back over her shoulder at the door.

"Yes," he answered, staring at her.

"Oh, Peter!" she said again and began to cry—a whimpering noise and her hands shaking so that the candle rocked in its stick.

"Well," he said more softly, "you'd better put that candle down."

She put it on the table and then stood beside him, crying pitifully, jerking out little sentences—"I can't bear it.... I don't know what to do.... I can't bear it."

He got up from his chair and made her sit down on it and then he stood by her and waited until she should recover a little. He felt suddenly strangely tender towards her; she was his mother's sister, she had known his mother all her life and perhaps in her weak silly way she had loved her.

"No, aunt, don't cry.... It will be all right. I too am very unhappy. I have missed so much. If I had only known earlier—"

The poor woman flung little distracted glances at the old man asleep on the other side of the fire-place—

"Oh, dear, I had to come and talk to some one.... I was so frightened upstairs. Your father's there with your mother. He sits looking at her ... and she was always so quiet and good and never did him any harm or indeed any one ... and now he sits looking at her—but she's happy now—he will be coming downstairs at any moment and I am afraid of what he'll do if he sees me talking to you like this. But I feel as though I must talk a little ... it's so quiet."

"It's all right, aunt. There's no one to be frightened of. I am very unhappy too. I'd like to talk about her to you."

"No, no—your poor mother—I mustn't say anything. They'll be down upon me if I say anything. They're very sharp. He's sitting up with her now."

Peter drew another chair up close to her and took her thin hand in his. She allowed him to do what he would and seemed to have no active knowledge of her surroundings.

"We'll talk about her," he said, "often. You shall tell me all about her early life. I want to know everything."

"Oh, no. I'm going away. Directly after the funeral. Directly after the funeral I'm going away."

Suddenly this frightened him. Was he to be left here entirely alone with his father and grandfather?

"You're going away?" he said.

"Oh, yes—your Uncle Jeremy will come for the funeral. I shall go away with him afterwards. I don't like your Aunt Agatha, but they always said I could come to them when your mother died. I don't like your Aunt Agatha but she means to be kind. Oh! I couldn't stay here after all that has happened. I was only staying for your mother's sake and I'm sure I've never gone to bed without wondering what would happen before the morning—Oh, yes, your Uncle Jeremy's coming and I shall go away with him after the funeral. I don't like your Aunt Agatha but I couldn't stay after all that has happened."

All this was said in a hurried frightened whisper. The poor lady shook from head to foot and the little bracelets on her trembling wrists jangled together.

"Then I shall be all alone here," Peter said suddenly, staring at the candle that was guttering in the breeze that came from behind the heavy blinds.

"Oh, dear," said his aunt, "I'm sure Uncle Jeremy will be kind if you have to leave here, you know."

"Why should I have to leave here?" asked Peter.

His aunt sunk her voice very low indeed—so low that it seemed to come from the heart of the cactus plant by the window.

"He hasn't got your mother now, you know. He'll want to have somebody...."

But she said nothing more—only gazed at the old man opposite her with staring eyes, and cried in a little desolate whimper and jangled her bracelets until at last Peter crept softly, miserably to bed.

II

The day of the funeral was a day of high wind and a furious sea. The Westcotts lived in the parish of the strange wild clergyman whose church looked over the sea; strange and wild in the eyes of Treliss because he was a giant in size and had a long flowing beard, because he kept a perfect menagerie of animals in his little house by the church, and because he talked in such an odd wild way about God being in the sea and the earth rather than in the hearts of the Treliss citizens—all these things odd enough and sometimes, early in the morning, he might be seen, mother-naked, going down the path to the sea to bathe, which was hardly decent considering his great size and the immediate neighbourhood of the high road. To those who remonstrated he had said that he was not ashamed of his body and that God was worshipped the better for there being no clothing to keep the wind away ... all mad enough, and there were never many parishioners in the little hill church of a Sunday. However, it was in the little windy churchyard that Mrs. Westcott was buried and it was up the steep and stony road to the little church that the hearse and its nodding plumes, followed by the two old and decrepit hackney carriages, slowly climbed.

Peter's impressions of the day were vague and uncertain. There were things that always remained in his memory but strangely his general conviction was that his mother had had nothing to do with it. The black coffin conveyed nothing to him of her presence: he saw her as he had seen her on that day when he had talked to her, and now she was, as Stephen was, somewhere away. That was his impression, that she had escaped....

Putting on his black clothes in the morning brought Dawson's back to his mind, and especially Bobby Galleon and Cards. He had not thought of them since the day of his return—first Stephen and then his mother had driven them from his mind. But now, with the old school black clothing upon him, he stood for a long time by his window, wondering, sorrowfully enough, where they were and what they were doing, whether they had forgotten him, whether he would ever see them again. He seemed to be surrounded by a wall of loneliness—some one was cutting everything off from him ... from maliciousness! For pleasure!... Oh! if one only knew about that God!

Meanwhile Uncle Jeremy and Aunt Agatha had arrived the night before. Uncle Jeremy was big and stout and he wore clothes that were very black and extremely bright. His face was crimson in colour and his eyes, large and bulging, wore a look of perpetual surprise. He was bald and an enormous gold watch chain crossed his stomach like a bridge. He had obviously never cared for either of his sisters and he always shouted when he spoke. Aunt Agatha was round and fat and comfortable, wore gold-rimmed spectacles and a black silk dress, and obviously considered that Uncle Jeremy had made the world.

Peter watched his father's attitude to these visitors. He realised that he had never seen his father with any stranger or visitor—no one came to the house and he had never been into the town with his father. With this realisation came a knowledge of other things—of things half heard at the office, of half looks in the street, of a deliberate avoidance of his father's name—the Westcotts of Scaw House! There were clouds about the name.

But his father, in contact with Uncle Jeremy and Aunt Agatha, was strangely impressive. His square, thick-set body clothed in black—his dark eyes, his short stiff hair, his high white forehead, his long beautiful hands—this was no ordinary man, moving so silently with a reserve that seemed nobly fitting on this sad occasion. The dark figure filled the house, touching in its restrained grief, admirable in its dignity, a fine spirit against the common clay of Uncle Jeremy and Aunt Agatha.

Mr. Westcott was courteous but sparing of words—a strong man, you would say, bowed down with a grief that demanded, in its intensity, silence.

Uncle Jeremy hated and feared his brother-in-law. His hatred he concealed with difficulty but his fear was betrayed by his loud and nervous laugh. He was obviously interested in Peter and stared at him, throughout breakfast, with his large, surprised eyes. Peter felt that this interest was a speculation as to his future and it made him uncomfortable ... he hated his uncle but the black suit that the stout gentleman wore on the day of the funeral was so black, so tight and so shiny that he was an occasion for laughter rather than hatred.

The black coffin was brought down the long stairs, through the hall and into the desolate garden. The sight of it roused no emotion in Peter—that was not his mother. The two aunts, Uncle Jeremy and his father rode in the first carriage; Peter and Mrs. Trussit in the second. Mrs. Trussit's bonnet and black silk dress were very fine and she wept bitterly throughout the journey.

Peter only dismally wished that he could arrange his knees so that they would not rub against her black silk. He did not think of his mother at all but only of the great age of the cab, of the furious wind that whistled about the road, and the roar that the sea, grey and furious far below them, flung against their windows.

He would have liked to talk to her but her sobbing seemed to surround her with a barrier. It was all inexpressibly dreary with the driving wind, the rustling of the black silk dress, the jolting and clattering of the old carriage. But he had no desire to cry—he was too miserable for that.

On the hill in the little churchyard, a tempest of wind swept across the graves. From the bending ground the cliff fell sheer to the sea and behold! it was a tossing, furious carpet of white and grey. The wind blew the spray up to the graveyard and stung the faces of the mourners and in the roar of the waves it was hard to hear the voice of the preacher. It was a picture that they made out there in the graveyard. Poor Aunt Jessie, trembling and shaking, Mrs. Trussit, stout and stiff with her handkerchief to her eyes, Uncle Jeremy with his legs apart, his face redder than ever, obviously wishing the thing over, Aunt Agatha concerned for her clothes in the streaming wind, Mr. Westcott unmoved by the storm, cold, stern, of a piece with the grey stone at the gravehead—all these figures interesting enough. But towering above them and dominating the scene was the clergyman—his great beard streaming, his surplice blowing behind him in a cloud, his great voice dominating the tumult, to Peter he was a part of the day—the storm, the earth, the flying, scudding clouds. All big things there, and somewhere sailing with those clouds, on the storm, the spirit of his mother ... that little black coffin standing, surely, for nothing that mattered.

But, strangely enough, when the black box had been lowered, at the sharp rattling of the sods upon the lid, his sorrow leapt to his eyes. Suddenly the sense of his loss drove down upon him. The place, the people were swept away—he could hear her voice again, see her thin white hands ... he wanted her so badly ... if he could only have his chance again ... he could have flung himself there upon the coffin, not caring whether he lived or died... his whole being, soul and body, ached for her....

He knew that it was all over; he broke away from them all and he never, afterwards, could tell where it was that he wandered during the rest of that day. At last, when it was dark, he crept back to the house, utterly, absolutely exhausted in every part of his body ... worn out.

III

On the following day Uncle Jeremy and Aunt Agatha departed and took Aunt Jessie with them. She had the air of being led away into captivity and seemed to be fastened to the buttons of Uncle Jeremy's tight black suit. She said nothing further to Peter and showed no sense of having, at any time, been confidential—she avoided him, he thought.

He of course returned to his office and tried to bury himself in the work that he found there—but his attention wandered; he was overstrung, excited abnormally, so that the whole world stood to him as a strange, unnatural picture, something seen dimly and in exaggerated shapes through coloured glass. That evening with Stephen shone upon him now with all the vigour of colour of a real fact in a multitude of vague shadows. The reality of that night was now of the utmost value.

Meanwhile there were changes at Scaw House. Mrs. Trussit had vanished a few days after the funeral, no one said anything about her departure and Peter did not see her go. He was vaguely sorry because she represented in his memory all the earlier years, and because her absence left the house even darker and more gloomy than it had been before. The cook, a stout and slatternly person, given, Peter thought, to excessive drinking, shared, with a small and noisy maid, the duties of the house—they were most inefficiently performed.

But, with this clearing of the platform, the hatred between Peter and his father became a definite and terrible thing. It expressed itself silently. At present they very rarely spoke and except on Sundays met only at breakfast and in the evening. But the air was charged with the violence of their relationship; the boy, growing in body so strangely like the man, expressed a sullen and dogged defiance in his every movement ... the man watched him as a snake might watch the bird held by its power. They stood, as wrestlers stand before the moment for their meeting has arrived. The house, always too large for their needs, seemed now to stretch into an infinity of echoing passages and empty rooms; the many windows gathered the dust thick upon their sills. The old grandfather stayed in his chair by the fire—only at night he was wheeled out into his dreary bedroom by the cook who, now, washed and tidied him with a vigour that called forth shrill screams and oaths from her victim. He hated this woman with the most bitter loathing and sometimes frightened her with the violence of his curses.

Christmas came and went and there followed a number of those wonderful crisp and shining days that a Cornish winter gives to its worshippers. Treliss sparkled and glittered—the stones of the market-place held the heat of the sun as though it had been midsummer and the Grey Tower lifted its old head proudly to the blue sky—the sea was so warm that bathing was possible and in the heart of the brown fields there was a whisper of early spring.

But all of this touched Scaw House not at all. Grey and hard in its bundle of dark trees it stood apart and refused the sun. Peter, in spite of himself, rejoiced in this brave weather. As the days slipped past, curiously aloof and reserved though he was, making no friends and seeking for none, nevertheless he began to look about him and considered the future.

All this had in it the element of suspense, of preparation. During these weeks one day slipped into another. No incidents marked their preparation—but up at Scaw House they were marching to no mean climax—every hour hurried the issue—and Peter, meanwhile, as February came whistling and storming upon the world, grew, with every chiming of the town clock, more morose, more sullen, more silent ... there were times when he thought of ending it all. An instant and he would be free of all his troubles—but after all that was the weakling's way; he had not altogether forgotten those words spoken so long ago by old Moses.... So much for the pause. Suddenly, one dark February afternoon the curtain was rung up outside Zachary Tan's shop and Peter was whirled into the centre of the stage.

Peter had not seen Zachary Tan for a long time. He had grown into a morbid way of avoiding everybody and would slink up side streets or go round on leaving the office by the sea road. When he did meet people who had once been kind to him he said as little as possible to them and left them abruptly.

But on this afternoon Zachary was not to be denied. He was standing at the door of his shop and shouted to Peter:

"Come away in, Mr. Peter. I haven't see you this long time. There's an old acquaintance of yours inside and a cup of tea for you."

The wind was whistling up the street, the first drops of a rain storm starred the pavement, and there was a pleasant glow behind Mr. Tan's window-panes. But there was something stronger yet that drove Peter into the shop. He knew with some strange knowledge who that old acquaintance was ... he felt no surprise when he saw in the little back room, laughing with all his white teeth shining in a row, the stout and cheerful figure of Mr. Emilio Zanti. Peter was a very different person now from that little boy who had once followed Stephen's broad figure into that little green room and stared at Mr. Zanti's cheerful countenance, but it all seemed a very little time ago. Outside in the shop there was the same suit of armour—on the shelves, the silver candlesticks, the old coins, the little Indian images, the pieces of tapestry—within the little room the same sense of mystery, the same intimate seclusion from the outer world.... On the other occasion of seeing him Mr. Zanti had been dimmed by a small boy's wonder. Now Peter was old enough to see him very clearly indeed.

Mr. Zanti seemed fat only because his clothes were so tight. He was bigly made and his legs and arms were round, bolster fashion—huge thighs and small ankles, thick arms and slender wrists. His clothes were so tight that they seemed in a jolly kind of way to protest. "Oh! come now, must you really put us on to anything quite so big? We shall burst in a minute—we really shall."

The face was large and flat and shining like a sun, with a small nose like a door knocker and a large mouth, the very essence of good-humoured surprise. The cheeks and the chin were soft and rounded and looked as though they might be very fat one day—a double chin just peeped round the corner.

He was a little bald on the top of his head and round this bald patch his black hair clustered protectingly. He gave you the impression that every part of his body was anxious that every other part of his body should have a good time. His suit was a very bright blue and his waistcoat had little brass buttons that met a friend with all the twinkling geniality of good wishes and numberless little hospitalities.

He had in his blue silk tie a pearl so large and so white that sophisticated citizens might have doubted that it was a pearl at all—but Peter swallowed Mr. Zanti whole, pearl and suit and all.

"Oh! it is ze little friend—my friend—'ow are you, young gentleman? It is a real delight to be with you again."

Mr. Zanti swung Peter's hand up and down as he would a pump handle and laughed as though it were all the best joke in the world. Curiously enough Peter did not resent this rapturous greeting. It moved him strongly. It was such a long time now since any one had shown any interest in him or expressed any pleasure at the sight of him that he was foolishly moved by Mr. Zanti's warmth.

He blushed and stammered something but his eyes were shining and his lip trembling.

Mr. Zanti fixed his gaze on the boy. "Oh! but you have grown—yes, indeed. You were a little slip before—but now—not so 'igh no—not 'igh—but broad, strong. Oh! ze arms and legs—there's a back!"

Zachary interrupted his enthusiasm with some general remark, and they had a pleasant little tea-party. Every now and again the shop bell tinkled and Zachary went out to attend to it, and then Mr. Zanti drew near to Peter as though he were going to confide in him but he never said anything, only laughed.

Once he mentioned Stephen.

"You know where he is?" Peter broke in with an eager whisper.

"Ah, ha—that would be telling," and Mr. Zanti winked his eye.

Peter's heart warmed under the friendliness of it all. There was very much of the boy still in him and he began to look back upon the days that he had spent with no other company than his own thoughts as cold and friendless. Zachary Tan had been always ready to receive him warmly. Why had he passed him so churlishly by and refused his outstretched hand? But there was more in it than that. Mr. Zanti attracted him most compellingly. The gaily-dressed genial man spoke to him of all the glitter and adventure of the outside world. Back, crowding upon him, came all those adventurous thoughts and desires that he had known before in Mr. Zanti's company—but tinged now by that grey threatening background of Scaw House and its melancholy inhabitants! What would he not give to escape? Perhaps Mr. Zanti!... The little green room began to extend its narrow walls and to include in its boundaries flashing rivers, shining cities, wide and bounteous plains. Beyond the shop—dark now with its treasures mysteriously gleaming—the steep little street held up its lamps to be transformed into yellow flame, and at its foot by the wooden jetty, as the night fell, the sea crept ever more secretly with its white fingers gleaming below the shingles of the beach.

Here was wonder and glory enough with the wind tearing and beating outside the windows, blowing the young flowers of the lamps up and down inside their glass houses and screaming down the chimneys for sheer zest of life.... But here it all had its centre in this little room "with Mr. Emilio Zanti's chuckling for no reason at all and spreading his broad fat hand over Peter Westcott's knee.

"Well, Mr. Peter, and 'ave you been to London in all these years? Or perhaps you 'ave forgotten that you ever wanted to go there?"

No, Peter was still of the same mind but Treliss and a few miles up and down the road were as much of the world as he'd had the pleasure of seeing—except for school in Devonshire—

"And you'd still go, my leetle friend?"

"Yes—I want to go—I hate being in an office here."

"And what is it zat you will do when you are there?"

Suddenly, in a flash, illuminating the little room, shining over the whole world, Peter knew what it was that he would do.

"I will write."

"Write what?"

"Stories."

With that word muttered, his head hanging, his cheeks flushing, as though it were something of which he was most mightily ashamed, he knew what it was he had been wanting all these months. The desire had been there, the impulse had been there ... now with the spoken word the blind faltering impulse was changed into definite certainty.

Mr. Zanti thought it a tremendous joke. He roared, shouted with riotous laughter. "Oh, ze boy—he will be the death of me—'I will write stories'—Oh yes, so easy, so very simple. 'I will write stories'—Oh yes."

But Peter was very solemn. He did not like his great intention to be laughed at.

"I mean it," he said rather gruffly.

"Oh yes, that's of course—but that is enough. Oh dear, yes ... well, my friend, I like you. You are very strong, you are brave I can see—you have a fine spirit. One thing you lack—with all you English it is the same."

He paused interrogatively but Peter did not seem to wish to know what this quality was.

"Yes, it is ze Humour—you do not see how funny life is—always—always funny. Death, murder, robberies, violences—always funny—you are. Oh! so solemn and per'aps you will be annoyed, think it tiresome, because I laugh—"

"No," said Peter gravely, "I like your laughing."

"Ah! That is well." Suddenly he jerked his body forward and stared into Peter's face.

"Well!... Will you come?"

Peter hung back, his face white. He was only conscious that Zachary, quiet and smiling in the background, watched him intently.

"What!... with you ... to London!"

"Yes ... wiz me—what of your father? Will he be furious, hey?"

"He won't like it—" Peter continued slowly. "But I don't care. I'll leave him—But I should have no money—nothing!"

"An', no matter—I will take you to London for nothing and then—if you like it—you may work for me. Two pounds a week—you would be useful."

"What should I do?"

"I have a bookshop—you would look after ze books and also ze customers." This seemed to amuse Mr. Zanti very much. "Two pounds a week is a lot of money for ze work—and you will have time—ho yes—much time for your stories."

Peter's eyes burned. London—a bookshop—freedom. Oh! wonderful world! His heart was beating so that words would not come.

"Oh!" he murmured. "Oh!"

"Ah, that's well!" Mr. Zanti clapped him on the shoulder. "There is no need for you to say now. On ze Wednesday in Easter week I go—before then you will tell me. We shall get on together, I know it. If you will 'ave a leetle more of ze Humour you will be a very pleasant boy—and useful—Ho, yes!"

To Peter then the shop was not visible—a mist hung about his eyes. "Much time for your stories"... said Mr. Zanti, and he shouted with laughter as his big form hung before Peter. The large white hand with the flashing rings enclosed Peter's.

For a moment the hands were on his shoulders and in his nostrils was the pungent scent of the hair-oil that Mr. Zanti affected—afterwards silence.

Peter said farewell to Zachary and promised to come soon and see him again. The little bell tinkled behind him and he was in the street. The great wind caught him and blew him along the cobbles. The flying mountains of cloud swept like galleons across the moor, and in Peter's heart was overwhelming triumph ... the lights of London lit the black darkness of the high sea road.

IV

The doors of Scaw House clanged behind him and at once he was aware that his father had to be faced. Supper was eaten in silence. Peter watched his father and his grandfather. Here were the three of them alone. What his grandfather was his father would one day be, what his father was, he ... yes, he must escape. He stared at the room's dreary furniture, he listened to the driving rain and he was conscious that, from the other side of the table, his father's eyes were upon him.

"Father," he said, "I want to go away." His heart was thumping.

Mr. Westcott got up from his place at the table and stood, with his legs a little apart, looking down at his son.

"Why?"

"I'm doing no good here. That office is no use to me. I shall never be a solicitor. I'm nearly eighteen and I shall never get on here. I remember things... my mother..." his voice choked.

His father smiled. "And where do you want to go?"

"To London."

"Oh! and what will you do there?"

"I have a friend—he has a bookshop there. He will give me two pounds a week at first so that I should be quite independent—"

"All very nice," Mr. Westcott was grave again. "And so you are tired of Treliss?"

"Not only Treliss—this house—everything. I hate it."

"You have no regret at leaving me?"

"You know—father—that..."

"Yes?"

Peter rose suddenly from the table—they faced one another.

"I want you to let me go. You have never cared in the least for me and you do not want me here. I shall go mad if I stay in this place. I must go."

"Oh, you must go? Well, that's plain enough at any rate—and when do you propose leaving us?"

"After Easter—the Wednesday after Easter," he said. "Oh, father, please. Give me a chance. I can do things in London—I feel it. Here I shall never do anything."

Peter raised his eyes to his father's and then dropped them. Mr. Westcott senior was not pleasant to look at.

"Let us have no more of this—you will stay here because I wish it. I like to have you here—father and son—father and son."

He placed his hand on the boy's shoulder—"Never mention this again for your own sake—you will stay here until I wish you to go."

But Peter broke free.

"I will go," he shouted—"I will go—you shall not keep me here. I have a right to my freedom—what have you ever done for me that I should obey you? I want to leave you and never see you again. I ..." And then his eyes fell—his legs were shaking. His father was watching him, no movement in his short thick body—Peter's voice faltered—"I will go," he said sullenly, his eyes on the ground.

His grandfather stirred in his sleep. "Oh, what a noise," he muttered, "with the rain and all."

But Mr. Westcott removed with a careful hand the melodrama that his young son had flung about the room.

"That's enough noise," he said, "you will not go to London—nor indeed anywhere else—and for your own peace of mind I should advise you not to mention the subject again. The hour is a little early but I recommend your bedroom."

Peter went. He was trembling from head to foot. Why? He undressed and prepared himself for battle. Battle it was to be, for the Wednesday in Easter week would find him in the London train—of that there was to be no question.

Meanwhile, with the candle blown out, and no moon across the floor, it was quite certain that courage would be necessary. He was fighting more than his father.

V

He woke suddenly. A little wind, blowing through the open door flickered the light of a candle that flung a dim circle about the floor. Within the circle was his father—black clothes and white face, he was looking with the candle held high, across the room to the bed.

He drew back the candle and closed the door softly behind him. His feet made no sound as they passed away down the passage.

Peter lay quaking, wide eyed in his bed, until full morning and time for getting up.

The opening, certainly, of a campaign.

CHAPTER X

SUNLIGHT, LIMELIGHT, DAYLIGHT

Easter fell early that year; the last days of March held its festival and the winds and rains of that blustering month attended the birth of its primroses.

Young Peter spent his days in preparation for the swift coming of Easter Wednesday and in varying moods of exultation, terror, industry and idleness. He did not see Mr. Zanti during this period—that gentleman was, he was informed, away on business—and it was characteristic of him that he asked Zachary Tan no questions whether of the mysterious bookshop, of London generally, or of any possible news about Stephen, the latter a secret that he was convinced the dark little curiosity shop somewhere contained.

But he had an amazing number of things to think about and the solicitor's office was the barest background for his chasing thoughts. He spoke to no one of his approaching freedom—but the thought of it hung in rich and burning colour ever at the back of his thoughts.

Meanwhile the changing developments at Scaw House were of a nature to frighten any boy who was compelled to share in them. It could not be denied that Mr. Westcott had altered very strangely since his wife's death. The grim place with its deserted garden had never seen many callers nor friendly faces but the man with the milk, the boy with the butcher's meat, the old postman with the letters stayed now as brief a time over their business as might be and hurried down the grass-grown paths with eager haste. Since the departure of the invaluable Mrs. Trussit a new order reigned—red-faced Mrs. Pascoe, her dress unfastened, her hair astray, her shoes at heel, her speech thick and uncertain, was queen of the kitchen, and indeed of other things had they but known all. But to Peter there was more in this than the arrival of Mrs. Pascoe. With every day his father was changing—changing so swiftly that when Peter's mother had been buried only a month, that earlier Mr. Westcott, cold, stern, reserved, terrible, seemed incredible; he was terrible now but with how different a terror.

To Peter this new figure was a thing of the utmost horror. He had known how to brace himself for that other authority—there had, at any rate, been consistency and even a kind of chiselled magnificence in that stiff brutality—now there was degradation, crawling devilry, things unmentionable....

This new terror broke upon him at supper two nights after he had first spoken about London. The meal had not been passed, as usual, in silence. His father had talked strangely to himself—his voice was thick, and uncertain—his hand shook as he cut the bread. Mrs. Pascoe had come, in the middle of the meal, to give food to the old grandfather who displayed his usual trembling greed. She stood with arms akimbo, watching them as they sat at table and smiling, her coarse face flushed.

"Pudding," said Mr. Westcott.

"Ye'll be 'aving the pudding when it's ready," says she.

"Damn" from Mr. Westcott but he sits still looking at the table-cloth and his hand shaking.

To Peter this new thing was beyond all possibility horrible. This new shaking creature—

"I didn't kill her, you know, Peter," Mr. Westcott says quite smoothly, when the cloth had been cleared and they are alone. And then suddenly, "Stay where you are—I have stories to tell you."

Peter, white to the lips, was held in his place. He could not move or speak. Then during the following two hours, his father, without moving from his place, poured forth a stream of stories—foul, filthy, horrible beyond all telling. He related them with no joy or humour or bestial gloating over their obscenities—only with a staring eye and his fingers twisting and untwisting on the table-cloth. At last Peter, his head hanging, his cheeks flaming, crept to his attic.

At breakfast his father was again that other man—stern, immovable, a rock-where was that trembling shadow of the night before?

And Mrs. Pascoe—once more in her red-faced way, submissive—in her place.

The most abiding impression with Peter, thinking of it afterwards in the dark lanes that run towards the sea, when the evening was creeping along the hill, was of a fiery eye gleaming from old grandfather Westcott's pile of rugs. Was it imagined or was there indeed a triumph there—a triumph that no age nor weakness could obscure?

And from the induction of that first terrible evening Peter stepped into a blind terror that gave the promised deliverance of that approaching Easter Wednesday an air of blind necessity. Also about the house the dust and neglect crept and increased as though it had been, in its menace and evil omen, a veritable beast of prey. Doors were off their hinges, windows screamed to their clanging shutters, the grime lay, like sand, about the sills and corners of the rooms. At night the house was astir with sound but with no human voices.

II

But it was only at night that Terror crept from its cupboard and leapt on to Peter's shoulders. He defied it even then with set lips and the beginning of a conception of the duties that Courage demands of its worshippers. He would fight it, let it develop as it would—but, during these weeks, in the sunlight, he thought nothing of it at all, but only with eager eyes watched his father.

His reading had, in these latter years, been slender enough. It was seldom that he had any money, there was no circulating library in Treliss at that time and he knew no one who could lend him books. He fell back, perforce, on the few that he had and especially on the three "Henry Galleons." But he had in his head—and he had known it without putting it into words, for a very long time—"The Thousand and One Nights of Peter Westcott, Esq."—stories that would go on night after night before he went to sleep, stories that were concerned with enormous families whose genealogies had to be worked out on paper (here was incipient Realism)—or again, stories concerning Treasure and Masses of it—banks of diamonds, mountains of pearls, columns of rubies, white marble temples, processions of white elephants, cloth of gold (here was incipient Romance). Never, be it noticed, at this time, incipient Humour; life had been too heavy a thing for that.

But these stories, formerly racing through his brain because they must, because indeed they were there against his own will or any one else's, had now a most definite place and purpose in their existence. They were there now because they were to be trained, to be educated, to be developed, until they were fit to appear in public. He had, even in these early days, no false idea of the agonies and tortures of this gift of his. Was it not in "Henry Lessingham"?... "and so with this task before him he knew that words were of many orders and regiments and armies, and those that were hard of purchase and difficult of discipline were the possessions of value, for nothing that is light and easy in its production is of any duration or lasting merit."

And so, during these weeks, when he should have attended to the duties of a solicitor his mind was hunting far away in those forests where very many had hunted before him. And, behold, he was out for Fame....

Spring was blown across the country by the wildest storms that the sea-coast had known for very many years. For days the seas rose against the rocks in a cursing fury—the battle of rock and wave gave pretty spectacle to the surrounding country and suddenly the warriors, having proved the mettle of their hardihood, turned once again to good fellowship. But the wind and the rain had done their work. In the week before Easter, with the first broadening sweep of the sun across the rich brown earth and down into the depths of the twisting lanes the spring was there—there in the sweet smell of the roots as they stirred towards the light, there in the watery gleam of the grass as it caught diamonds from the sun, but there, above all, in the primrose clump hidden in the clefts of the little Cornish woods—so with a cry of delight Spring had leapt from the shoulders of that roaring wind and danced across the Cornish hills.

On Good Friday there was an incident. Peter was free of the office for the day and had walked towards Truro. There was a little hill that stood above the town. It was marked by a tree clump black against the blue sky—at its side was a chalk pit, naked white—beyond was Truro huddled, with the Fal a silver ribbon in the sun. Peter stood and watched and sat down because he liked the view. He had walked a very long way and was tired and it was an afternoon as hot as Summer.

Suddenly there was a cry: "Help, please—oh—help to get Crumpet."

He looked up and saw standing in front of him a little girl in a black hat and a short black frock—she had red hair that the sun was transforming into gold. Her face was white with terror, and tears were making muddy marks on it and her hands were black with dirt. She was a very little girl. She appealed to him between her sobs, and he understood that Crumpet was a dog, that it had fallen some way down the chalk-pit and that "Miss Jackson was reading her Bible under a tree."

He jumped up immediately and went to find Crumpet. A little way down the chalk-pit a fox-terrier puppy was balancing its fat body on a ledge of chalk and looking piteously up and down. Peter clambered down, caught the little struggling animal in his arms, and restored it to its mistress. And now followed an immense deal of kissing and embracing. The dog was buried in red hair and only once and again a wriggling paw might be observed—also these exclamations—"Oh, the umpty-rumpty—was it nearly falling down the great horrid pit, the darling—oh, the little darling, and was it scratched, the pet? But it was a wicked little dog—yes, it was, to go down that nasty place when it was told not to"—more murmurings, and then the back was straightened, the red, gold hair flung back, and a flushed face turned to the rather awkward Peter who stood at attention.

"Thank you—thanks, most awfully—oh, you darling" (this to the puppy). "You see, Miss Jackson was reading her Bible aloud to herself, and I can't stand that, neither can Crumpet, and she always forgets all about us, and so we go away by ourselves—and reading the Bible makes her sleep—she's asleep now— and then Crumpet wouldn't stay at heel although I was telling him ever so hard, and he would go over the cliff—and if you hadn't been there..." at the thought of the awful disaster the puppy was again embraced. Apparently Crumpet was no sentimentalist, and had had enough of feminine emotion—he wriggled out of his mistress' arms, flopped to the ground, shook himself, and, advancing to Peter, smelt his boots.

"He likes you. I'm so glad—he only does that to people he likes, and he's very particular." The small girl flung her hair back, smiled at Peter, and sat down on the grass.

"It may be rather damp," Peter said, feeling very old and cautious and thinking that she really was the oddest child he'd even seen in his life. "It's only March you know."

"It's nothing to do with months, it's whether it's rained or not—and it hasn't—sit down with me. Old Jackson won't be here for ages."

Peter sat down. The puppy was a charming specimen of its kind—it had enormous ears, huge flat feet, and a round fat body like a very small barrel. It was very fond of Peter, and licked his cheek and his hands, and finally dragged off his cap, imagined it a rabbit, and bit it with a great deal of savagery and good-humour.

There followed conversation.

"I like you most awfully. I like your neck and your eyes and your hair—it's stiff, like my father's. My name is Clare Elizabeth Rossiter. What's yours?"

"Peter Westcott."

"Do you live here?"

"No—a good long way away—by the sea."

"Oh, I'm staying at Kenwyn—my uncle lives at Kenwyn, but I live in London with father and mother and Aunt Grace—it's nice here. I think you're such a nice boy. Will you come and see father and mother in London?"

Peter smiled. It would not be the thing for some one in a bookshop to go and call on the parents of any one who could afford Crumpet and Miss Jackson, but the thought of London, the very name of it, sent his blood tingling to his face.

"Perhaps we shall meet," he said. "I'm going to London soon."

"Oh! are you? Oh! How nice! Then, of course, you will come to tea. Every one comes to tea."

Crumpet, tired of the rabbit, worn out with adventure and peril, struggled into Peter's lap and slumbered with one ear lying back across his eyes. The sun slipped down upon the town and touched the black cathedral with flame, and turned the silver of the river into burning gold. On the bend of the hill against the sky came a black gaunt figure.

"Miss Jackson!" Clare Elizabeth Rossiter leapt to her feet, clutched Crumpet, held him upside down, and turned to go.

But for an instant she stayed, and Peter was rewarded with a very wonderful smile.

"I am so glad you were here—she generally sleeps longer, but perhaps it was New Testament to-day, and that's more exciting. It is a pity, because there were such lots of things—I like you most awfully."

She gave him a very dirty hand, and then her black stockings vanished over the hill.

Peter turned, through a flaming sunset, towards his home ... the end of the incident.

III

But he came home, on that Good Friday evening with an idea that that afternoon on the hill had given him. It was an idea that came to him from the little piece of superstition that he carried about with him—every Cornishman carries it. Treliss was always a place of many customs, and, although now these ceremonies drag themselves along with all the mercenary self-consciousness that America and cheap trips from Manchester have given to the place, at this stage of Peter's history they were genuine and honest enough. To see from the top of the Grey Hill, the rising of the sun on Easter morning was one of them—a charm that brought the most infallible good luck until next Easter Day came round again, and, good for you, if you could watch that sunrise with the lad or lass of your choice, for to pass round the Giant's Finger as the beams caught the stone made the success of your union beyond all question. There was risk about it, for if mists veiled the light or if clouds dimmed the rising then were your prospects but gloomy—but a fine Easter morning had decided many a wedding in Treliss.

Peter had known of this for many years, but, in earlier times, he had not been at liberty, and of late there had been other things to think about. But here was a fine chance! Was he not flinging himself into the world under the very hazardous patronage of Mr. Zanti on Easter Wednesday, and would he not therefore need every blessing that he could get? And who knew, after all, whether these things were such nonsense? They were old enough, these customs, and many wise people believed in them. Moreover, one had not been brought up in the company of Frosted Moses and Dicky the Fool without catching some of their fever! "There was a little star rolling down hill like a button," says Dicky, with his eyes staring....' Well, and why not?

And indeed here was Peter at this stage of things, a mad I bundle of contradictions—old as a judge when up against the Realities, young as Crumpet the puppy when staring at Romance. Give him bread and you have him of cast-iron—stern, cold, hard of muscle, grim frown, stiff back, no smiles. Give him jam and you have credulity, simplicity, longing for friendship, tenderness, devotion to a small girl in a black frock, a heart big as the world. See him on Good Friday afternoon, laughing, eagerly questioning, a boy—see him on Good Friday night, grim, legs stiff, eyes cold as stones, a man—no easy thing for Mrs. Pascoe's blowzy thunderings to conquer, but something vastly amusing apparently to grandfather Westcott to watch.

He discovered that the sun rose about six o'clock, and therefore five o'clock on Easter morning found him shivering, in the desolate garden with his nose pressed to the little wooden gate. The High Road crossed the moor at no great distance from him, but the faint grey light that hung like gauze about him was not yet strong enough to reveal it. He would hear them as they passed and they must all go up that road on the way to the hill. In the garden there was darkness, and beyond it in the high shadow of the house and the surrounding trees, blackness. He could smell the soil, and his cheeks were wet with beads of moisture; very faintly the recurrent boom of the sea came through the mist, dimmed as though by thick folds of hanging carpet.

Suddenly the dark trees by the house, moved by a secret wind, would shudder. The little black gate slowly revealed its bars against the sky as the grey shadows lightened. Then there were voices, coming through the dark shut off, like the sea, by the mist—strange voices, not human, but sharing with the soil and the trees the mysterious quality of the night. The voices passed up the road—silence and then more voices.

Peter unlatched the gate and stole out to the road, stumbling over the rough moorland path and clambering across the ditch to safer ground. Figures were moving like shadows and voices fell echoing and re-echoing like notes of music—this was dissociated from all human feeling, and the mists curled up like smoke and faded into the air. Peter, in silence, followed these shadows and knew that there were other shadows behind him. It would not take long to climb the Grey Hill—they would be at the top by half-past five.

There was a voice in his ear:

"Hallo! You—Westcott! Why, who would have thought it?"

He turned round and found at his side the peaked face of Willie Daffoll, now a young man of eighteen, with an affection for bright ties and socks, once the small child who had fought with Peter at old Parlow's years ago. Peter had not seen very much of him during those years. They had met in the streets of Treliss, had spoken a word or two, but no friendship or intimacy. But this early hour, this mysterious dawn, bred confidence, and Peter having grown, under the approaching glitter of London, more human, during the last few weeks than he had been in all his life before, was glad to talk to him.

"Oh, I've often wanted to go," he said. "It brings good luck, you know."

"Well, fancy your believing that. I never thought you'd believe in rot like that."

"Why are you going, then?"

The young man of ties and waistcoats dropped his voice. "Oh—a girl. She's here somewhere—she said she'd come—thinks there's something in it. Anyhow she wants it—she's stunning...."

A girl! Peter's mind flew absurdly back to a small child in a short black frock. "Oh! Crumpet!" ... A girl! Young Daffoll had spoken as though it were indeed something to get up at four in the morning for! Peter wanted to hear more. Young Daffoll was quite ready to tell him. No names, of course, but they were going to be married one day. His governor would be furious, of course, and they might have to run away, but she was game for anything. No, he'd only known her a fortnight, but it had been a matter of love at first sight—extraordinary thing—he'd thought he'd been head over ears before, but never anything like this—yes, as a matter of fact she was in a flower-shop—Trunter's in the High Street—her people had come down in the world—and so the golden picture unfolded as the gauze curtains were drawn back from the world, and the shoulder of the Grey Hill rose, like a cloud, before them.

Peter's heart beat faster as he listened to this story. Here was one of his dreams translated into actual fact. Would he one day also have some one for whom he would be ready to run to the end of the world, if furious parents demanded it? She would have, he was sure, red-gold hair and a wonderful smile.

They climbed the Grey Hill. There was with them now quite a company of persons—still shadow-shapes, for the mists were thick about the road, but soon all the butchers and bakers of the world—and, let it be remembered, all the lovers, would be revealed. Now, as they climbed the hill, silence fell—even young Daffoll was quiet; that, too, it seemed, was part of the ceremony.

The hill top was swiftly gained. The Giant's Finger, black and straight, like a needle, stood through the shadows. Beyond there would be the sea, and that was where the sun would rise, at present darkness. They all sat down on the stones that covered the summit—on either side of Peter there were figures, but Daffoll had vanished—it seemed that he had discovered his lady.

Peter, sitting meditating on the story that he had heard and feeling, suddenly, lonely and deserted, was conscious of a small shoe that touched his boot. It was, beyond argument, a friendly shoe—he could feel that in the inviting tap that it gave to him. He was aware also that his shoulder was touching another shoulder, and that that shoulder was soft and warm. Finally his hand touched another hand—fingers were intertwined.

There was much conversation out of the mist:

"Law, chrisy! Well, it's the last Easter morning for me—thiccy sun hides himself right enough—it's poor trade sitting shivering your toes."

"Not that I care for the woman, mind ye, Mr. Tregothan, sir—with her haverings talking—all I'm saying is that if she's to come wastin' my time—

"Thiccy man sitting there stormin' like an old owl in a tree."

"Oh, get along with ye—No, I won't be sitting by ye—There's—"

Now the sea, like a young web stretched at the foot of the hill, stole out of the darkness. On the horizon a thin line of dull yellow—wouldn't it be a fine sunrise?—the figures on the hill were gathering shape and form, and many of them now were standing, their bodies sharp against the grey sky.

Peter had not turned; his eyes were staring out to sea, but his body was pressed closely against the girl at his side. He did not turn nor look at her—she was staring at him with wonder in her eyes and a smile on her lips. She was a very common girl with black hair and over-red cheeks, and she was one of the dairymaids from Tregothan Farm. She did not know whom this strange young man might be, and it was not yet light enough to see. She did not care—such things had happened often enough before, and she leant her fat body against his shoulder. She could feel his heart thumping and his hands were very hot, but she thought that it was strange that he did not turn and look at her....

There was a stir and murmur among the crowd on the hill for behold it would be a fine sunrise! The dull yellow had brightened to gold and was speeding like a herald across the grey. Black on the hill, gold on the sky, a trembling whispering blue across the sea—in a moment there would be the sun! What gods were there hiding, at that instant, on the hill, watching, with scornful eyes this crowd of moderns?

Hidden there behind the stones, what mysteries? Screening with their delicate bodies the faint colours of the true dawn, playing on their pipes tunes that these citizens with their coarse voices and dull hearing could not understand, what ancient watchers of the hill pass and repass!

Behold the butchers and bakers! Behold Mr. Winneren, hosier and outfitter, young Robert Trefusis, farmer, Miss Bessie Waddell from the sweet-shop!... These others fade away as the sun rises—the grey mists pass with them.

The sun is about to leap above the rim of the sea. Peter turns and crushes the poor dairymaid in his arms and stifles the little scream with the first kiss of his life. His whole body burns in that kiss—and then, as the sun streams across the sea he has sprung to his feet and vanishes over the brow of the hill.

The dairymaid wipes her lips with the back of her hand. They have joined hands and are already dancing round the Giant's Finger. It is black now, but in a moment the flames of the sun will leap upon it, and good omens will send them all singing down the hill.

IV

On Tuesday evening Peter slipped for a moment into Zachary Tan's shop and told Mr. Zanti that he would be on the station platform at half-past seven on the following morning. He could scarcely speak for excitement. He was also filled with a penetrating sadness. Above all, he wished only to exchange the briefest word with his future master. He did not understand altogether but it was perhaps because Mr. Zanti and all his world belonged to to-morrow.... Mr. Zanti's fat, jolly body, his laugh, his huge soft hands ... Peter could not do more to this gentleman than remember that he meant so much that he would be overwhelmed by him if he did not leave him alone. So he darted in and gave his message and darted out again. The little street was shining in the sun and the gentlest waves were lapping the wooden jetty— Oh, this dear town! These houses, these cobbles—all the smells and colours of the place—he was leaving it all so easily on so perilous an adventure. Poor Peter was moved by so many things that he could only gulp the tears back and hurry home. There was at any rate work to be done there about which there could be no uncertain intention.

His father had been drinking all the afternoon. Mrs. Pascoe with red arms akimbo, watched them as they ate their supper.

When the meal was finished Peter, standing by his father, his face very white, said:

"I am going to London to-morrow."

Mr. Westcott had aged a great deal during the last month. His hair was touched with grey, there were dark lines under his eyes, his cheeks were sunken, his lip trembled. He was looking moodily at the cloth, crumbling his bread. He did not hear Peter's remark, but continued his argument with Mrs. Pascoe:

"It wasn't cooked, I tell you—you're growing as slack as Hell."

"Your precious son 'as got something as 'e would like to say to yer," remarked that pleasant woman grimly.

Peter repeated his remark. His father grasped it but slowly—at last he said:

"Damn you, what are you talking about?"

"I'm leaving here and going to London to-morrow."

Mr. Westcott turned his bloodshot eyes in the direction of the fire-place—"Curse it, I can't see straight. You young devil—I'll do for you—" all this said rather sullenly and as though he were speaking to himself.

Peter, having delivered his news, passed Mrs. Pascoe's broad body, and moved to the doorway. He turned with his hand on the door.

"I'm glad I'm going," he said, "you've always bullied me, and I've always hated you. You killed my mother and she was a good woman. You can have this house to yourself—you and grandfather—and that woman—" he nodded contemptuously at Mrs. Pascoe, who was staring at him fiercely. His grandfather was fast asleep beneath the cushions.

"Damn you," said Mr. Westcott very quietly. "You've always been ungrateful—I didn't kill your mother, but she was always a tiresome, crying woman."

He stopped crumbling the bread and suddenly picked up a table knife and hurled it at Peter. His hand was trembling, and the knife quivering, was fastened to the door.

Mrs. Pascoe gasped, "Gawd 'elp us!"

Peter quietly closed the door behind him and went up to his room.

He was in no way disturbed by this interview. His relations with his father were not of the things that now mattered. They had mattered before his mother died. They had mattered whilst his father had been somebody strong and terrible. Even at the funeral how splendid he had seemed! But this trembling creature who drank whisky with the cook was some one who concerned Peter not at all—something like the house, to be left behind.

There was an old black bag that had held his things in the Dawson's days—it held his things now. Not a vast number—only the black suit beside the blue serge one that he was going to wear, some under-linen, a sponge, and a toothbrush, the books and an old faded photograph of his mother as a girl. Nothing like that white face that he had seen, this photograph, old, yellow, and faded, but a girl laughing and beautiful—after all, his most precious possession.

Then, when the bag was packed, he sat on the bed, swung his legs, and thought about everything. He was nearly eighteen, nearly a man, and as hard as rock. He could feel the muscles swelling, there was no fat about him, he was sound all over.

He looked back and saw the things that stood out like hills above the plain—that night, years ago, when he was whipped, the day that he first met Mr. Zanti, the first day at school, the day when he said good-bye to Cards, the hour, at the end of it all, when they hissed him, that last evening with Stephen, the day with his mother ... and then, quite lately, that afternoon when Mr. Zanti asked him to go to London, the little girl with the black frock on the hill ... last of all, that kiss (never mind with whom) on Easter morning—all these things had made him what he was—yes, and all the people—Frosted Moses, Stephen, his father, his mother, Bobby Galleon, Cards, Mr. Zanti, the little girl. As he swung his legs he knew that everything that he did afterwards would be, in some way, attached to these earlier things and these earlier people.

He had brave hopes and brave ambitions and a warm heart as he flung himself into bed; it speaks well for him that, on the night before he set out on his adventure, he slept like the child that he really was.

But he knew that he would wake at six o'clock. He had determined that it should be so, and the clocks were striking as he opened his eyes. It was very dark and the cocks crowed beyond his open window, and the misty morning swept in and blew his lighted candle up and down. He dressed in the blue serge suit with a blue tie fastened in a sailor's knot. He leaned out of his window and tried to imagine, out of the darkness, the beloved moor—then he took his black bag and crept downstairs; it was striking half-past six as he came softly into the hall.

There he saw that the gas was flaring and that his father was standing in his night-shirt.

"I think I'm in front of you," he said, smiling.

"Let me go, father," Peter said, very white, and putting down the bag.

"Be damned to you," said his father. "You don't get through this door."

It was all so ludicrous, so utterly absurd, that his father should be standing, in his night-shirt, on this very cold morning, under the flaring gas. It occurred to Peter that as he wanted to laugh at this Mr. Zanti could not have been right about his lack of humour. Peter walked up to his father, and his father caught him by the throat. Mr. Westcott was still, in spite of recent excesses, sufficiently strong.

"I very much want to choke you," he said.

Peter, however, was stronger.

His father dropped the hold of his throat, and had him, by the waist, but his hands slipped amongst his clothes. For a moment they swayed together, and Peter could feel the heat of his father's body beneath the night-shirt and the violent beating of his heart. It was immensely ludicrous; moreover there now appeared on the stairs Mrs. Pascoe, in a flannel jacket over a night-gown, and untidy hair about her ample shoulders.

"The Lord be kind!" she cried, and stood, staring. Mr. Westcott was breathing very heavily in Peter's face, and their eyes were so close together that Peter could notice how bloodshot his father's were.

"God damn you!" said his father and slipped, and they came down on to the wood floor together. Peter rose, but his father lay there, breathing heavily.

"God damn you," he said again, but he did not move.

"You'd better look after him," Peter said, turning to the astounded Mrs. Pascoe. As he moved he saw a surprising sight, his grandfather's door was opened and his grandfather (who had not been on his feet for a great many years) was standing in the middle of it, cackling with laughter, dressed in a very ugly yellow dressing-gown, his old knotted hands clutching the sides of the door, his shrivelled body shaking, and his feet in large red slippers.

"Dear me, that was a nasty knock," he chattered.

And so Peter left them.

The high road was cool and fresh and dark. The sea sung somewhere below amongst the rocks, and Peter immediately was aware that he was leaving Cornwall.

Now he had no other thought. The streets of the town were deserted, clean, smelling of the fields, hay-carts, and primroses, with the darkness broken by dim lamps, and a very slender moon. His heart was full, his throat burning. He crossed the market-place and suddenly bent down and kissed the worn stones of the Tower. There was no one to see.

He was in the station at twenty minutes past seven. The platform was long and cold and deserted, but in the waiting-room was Mr. Zanti enveloped in an enormous black coat.

"Ah, my dear boy, this is indeed splendid. And 'ave you said farewell to your father?"

"Yes, I've said good-bye to every one," he answered slowly. Suddenly he would have given all the wide world and his prospects in it not to be going. The terrors of Scaw House were as nothing beside that little grey town with the waves breaking on the jetty, the Grey Hill above it, the twisted cobbled streets.

The morning wind blew up the platform, the train rolled in; there were porters, but Mr. Zanti had only a big brown bag which he kept with him.

Soon they were in corners facing one another. As the train swept past the Tower the grey dawn was breaking into blue over the houses that rose, tier by tier, to the sky over the grey rolling breakers, over the hills beyond ... Cornwall!

Poor Peter stared with passionate eyes as the vision passed.

"London soon," said Mr. Zanti, gaily.

CHAPTER XI

ALL KINDS OF FOG IN THE CHARING CROSS ROAD

I

Towards the middle of the dim afternoon as the first straight pale houses began to close in upon the train, a lady and gentleman on the opposite side to Peter were discovered by him, as he awoke from a long sleep, to be talking:

"Well, my dear Lucy, how we are ever to get on if you want to do these absurd things I don't know. In London one must do as London does. In the country of course..."

He was short, breathless and a little bald. The lady was young and very upset.

"But, Henry, what does it matter?"

"What does it matter? My dear Lucy, in London everything matters—"

She was excited. "In Kensington perhaps, but in London—"

"Allow me, my dear Lucy, to decide for you. When you are my age—"

Peter went to sleep again.

II

The vast iron-girdled station was very dark and Mr. Zanti explained that this was because, outside, there was a Fog—

"The Fog," he added, as though it had been a huge and ferocious animal, "is very yellow and has eaten up London. It will take us a very long time to find our home."

To Peter, short and square, in his rough suit shouldering his bag, this was all as the infernal regions. The vast place towered high, into misty distances above him. Trains, like huge beasts, stretched their limbs into infinity; screams, piercing and angry, broke suddenly the voices and busy movement that flooded the place with sounds. He was jostled and pushed aside and people turned and swore at him and a heated porter ran a truck into his legs. And through it and above it all the yellow fog came twisting in coils from the dark street beyond and every one coughed and choked and cursed England.

Mr. Zanti, after five minutes' angry pursuit, caught a reluctant and very shabby four-wheeler, and they both climbed into its cavernous depths and Peter's nose was filled with something that had leather and oranges and paper bags and whisky in it; he felt exactly as though Mr. Zanti (looking very like an ogre in the mysterious yellow light with his bowler on the back of his head and mopping his face with a huge crimson handkerchief) were decoying him away to some terrible fastness where it was always dark and smelly.

And indeed that first vision of London, seen through the grimy windows of the cab, was terrible enough. The cab moved a little, stopped, moved again; it seemed that they would be there for ever and they exchanged no word. There were no buildings to be seen; a vast wall of darkness surrounded him and ever and again, out of the heart of it, a great cauldron of fire flamed and by the side of it there were wild, agitated faces—and again darkness. On every side of the stumbling cab there was noise—voices shouting, women screaming, the rumbling of wheels, the plunging of horses' hoofs; sometimes things brushed against their cab—once Peter thought that they were down because they were jerked right forward against the opposite seats. And then suddenly, in the most wonderful way, they would plunge into silence, a silence so deep and cavernous that it was more fearful than those other noises had been, and the yellow darkness seemed to crowd upon them with a closer eagerness and it was as though they were driving over the edge of the world. Then the noises returned, for a moment the fog lifted showing houses, rising like rocks from the sea sheer about them on every side, then darkness again and the cab stopped with a jerk.

"Ah, good," said Mr. Zanti, rolling his red handkerchief into a ball. "'Ere we are, my young friend—Mr. Peter, after you, please."

Before him a light faintly glimmered and towards this, after stumbling on the slippery pavement, he made his way. He found himself in a bookshop lighted with gas that hissed and spit like an angry cat; the shop was low and stuffy but its walls were covered with books that stretched into misty fog near the ceiling. Behind a dingy counter a man was sitting. This man struck Peter's attention at once because of the enormous size of his head and the amount of hair that covered it—starting out of the mist and obscurity of the shop, this head looked like some strange fungus, and from the heart of it there glittered two very bright eyes.

Peter, standing awkwardly in the middle of the shop, gazed at this head and was speechless.

Outside, Mr. Zanti could be heard disputing with the cabman.

"You can go and be damned—ze bags were not on ze outside—Zat is plenty for your pay and you be damned—"

The shop door closed with a bang shutting out the fog and Mr. Zanti filled the little bookshop. He seemed taller and larger than he had been in Cornwall and his voice was sharper. The head removed itself from the counter and Peter saw that it belonged to a small man with a hump who came forward to Mr. Zanti very humbly.

"Ah, Gottfried," said Zanti, "you well?"

"Very, sir," answered the little man, bowing a little and smiling; his voice was guttural with a very slight accent.

"This is Mr. Peter Westcott. 'E will work here and 'elp you with ze books. 'E is a friend of mine and you will be kind to him. Mr. Peter, zis is Herr Gottfried Hanz—I owe 'im much—ver' clever man."

They shook hands and Peter liked the pair of eyes that gazed into his.

Then Mr. Zanti said, "Come, I will show you ze rest of ze place. It is not a mansion, you will find."

Indeed it was not. Behind the shop there was a room, brown and green, with two windows that looked on to a yard, so Mr. Zanti said. There was no furniture in it save a table and some chairs; a woman was spreading a cloth on the table as they came in. This woman had grey hair that escaped its pins and fell untidily about her shoulders. She was very pale, tall and thin and her most striking features were her piercing black eyes and with these she stared at Peter.

"Zis is Mrs. Dantzig," said Mr. Zanti, "an old friend—Mr. Peter Westcott, Mrs. Dantzig. 'E will work wiz us."

The woman said nothing but nodded her head and continued her work. They passed out of the room. Stairs ran both up and down.

"What is down there?" asked Peter.

"Ah, zat is ze kitchen," said Mr. Zanti, laughing. Upstairs there was a clean and neat bedroom with a large bed in it, an old sofa and two chairs.

"Zis is where I sleep," said Mr. Zanti. "For a night or two until you 'ave discovered a lodging you shall sleep on zat sofa. Zay will make it whilst we 'ave supper."

It was now late and Peter was very very tired. Downstairs there was much bread and butter and bacon and eggs, and beer. The woman waited upon them but they were all very silent and Peter was too sleepy to be hungry.

The table was cleared and Mr. Zanti sat smoking his pipe and talking to the woman. Peter sat there, nodding, and he thought that their conversation was in a foreign tongue and he thought that they looked at him and that the woman was angry about something—but the sleep always gained upon him—he could not keep it away.

At last a hand was upon his shoulder and he was led up to bed.

He tumbled out of his clothes and his last impression was of Mr. Zanti standing in front of him, looking vast and very solemn in a blue cotton night-shirt.

"Peter," Mr. Zanti seemed to be saying, "you see in me, one, two, a hundred men.... All my life I seek adventure—fun—and I find it—but there 'as not been room for ze affections. Then I find you—I love you as my son and I say 'Come to my bookshop'—But only ze bookshop mind you—you are there for ze books and because I care for you—I care for you ver' much, Peter, and zere 'as not been room in my life for ze affections ... but I will be a ver' good friend to you—and you shall only be in ze shop—with ze books—I will be a good friend—"

Then it seemed that Mr. Zanti kissed Peter on both cheeks, blew out the candle, and climbed into his huge bed; soon he was snoring.

But Peter could not be sure of these things because he was so very tired that he did not know whether he were standing on his head or his heels and he was asleep on his sofa and dreaming about the strangest and most confused events in less than no time at all.

III

And then how wonderful to discover, on waking up the next morning, that it was a beautiful day, as beautiful a day as any that Cornwall could give him. It was indeed odd, after the great darkness of the afternoon before to find now a burning blue sky, bright shining pavements and the pieces of iron and metal on the cabs glittering as they rolled along. The streets were doubtless delightful but Peter was not, on this day at any rate, to see very much of them; he was handed over to the care of Herr Gottfried Hanz, who had obviously not brushed his hair when he got up in the morning; he also wore large blue slippers that were too big for his feet and clattered behind him as he walked. Whatever light there might be in the street outside only chinks of it found their way into the shop and the gas-jet hissed and flared as it had done on the day before. The books seemed mistier and dustier than ever and Peter wondered, in a kind of despair, how in the world if any one did come in and ask for anything he was going to tell them whether it were there or not.

But here Herr Gottfried came to the rescue. "See you," he said with an air of pride, "it is thus that they are arranged. Here you have the Novel—Brontë, Bulwer, Bunyan ("The Pilgrim's Progress," that is not a novel but it is near enough). Here you have History, and here the Poets, and here Philosophy and here Travel—it will all be simple in time—"

Peter's eyes spun dizzily to the heights.

"There is a little ladder," said Herr Gottfried.

"And," at last said Peter timidly, "May I—read—when there is no one here?"

Herr Gottfried looked at him with a new interest. "You like reading?"

"Like!" Peter's voice was an ecstasy.

"Why of course, often." Herr Gottfried smiled. "And then see! (he opened the shop door) there is a small boy, James, who is supposed to look after these (these were the 1d., 2d. and 3d. boxes outside the window, on the pavement) but he is an idle boy and often enough he is not there and then we must have the door open and you must watch them. Often enough (this seemed a favourite phrase of his) these gentlemen (this with great scorn) will turn the books over and over and they will look up the street once and they will look down the street once, and then into the pocket a book will go—often enough," he added, looking beyond the door savagely at a very tired and tattered lady who was turning the 1d. lot over and over.

Then, this introductory lesson concluded, Herr Gottfried suddenly withdrew into the tangles of his hair and retreated behind his counter. Through the open door there came the most entrancing sound and the bustle of the street was loud and startling—bells ringing, boys shouting, wheels rattling, and beyond these immediate notes a steady hum like the murmur of an orchestra heard through closed doors. All this was wonderful enough but it was nothing at all to the superlative fascination of that multitude of books. Peter found a hard little chair in a dark corner and sat down upon it. Here he was in the very heart of his kingdom! He could never read all the books in this place if he lived for two hundred years... and so he had better not try. He made a blind dash at the volumes nearest him (quietly lest he should disturb Herr Gottfried who seemed very busy at his counter) and secured something and read it as well as he could, for the light was very bad. It was called "The True and Faithful Experiences of the Reverend James Scott in the Other World Being a Veracious History of his Experiences of the Life after Death"— the dust rose from its pages in little clouds and tempted him to sneeze but he bit his lip and counted forty and saved the situation.

Herr Gottfried dealt with the customers that morning and Peter stood nervously watching him. The customers were not very many—an old lady who "wanted something to read" caused many volumes to be laid before her, and finally left the shop without buying anything—a young man with spectacles purchased some tattered science and a clergyman some Sermons. A thin and very hungry looking man entered, clutching a badly-tied paper parcel. These were books he wanted to sell. They were obviously treasured possessions because he touched them, when they were laid upon the counter, with a loving hand.

"They are very good books," he said plaintively.

"Three shillings," said Herr Gottfried.

The hungry man sighed.

"Five shillings," he said, "they are worth more."

"Three shillings for the lot," said Herr Gottfried.

"It is very little," said the hungry man, but he took the money and went out sadly.

Once their came a magnificent gentleman—that is, he looked magnificent in the distance away from the gas jet. He was tall with a high hat, a fine moustache and a tailcoat; he had melancholy eyes and a languid air. Peter was sorry to observe on a closer view that his tail-coat was frayed and his collar not very clean.

He gave Herr Gottfried a languid bow and passed through the shop into the room beyond.

"Guten Tag, Herr Signer," said Herr Gottfried with deference, but the gentleman had already disappeared.

Then, after a time, one o'clock struck and Peter understood that if he would place himself under Herr Gottfried's protection he should be led to an establishment where for a small sum meat-pies were to be had... all this very novel and delightful, and Peter laid down "The Experiences of the Reverend James Scott," which were not at present very thrilling and followed his guide into the street. Peter was still wondering where Herr Gottfried had put his blue slippers and whence had come the large flat boots and the brown and faded squash hat when he was suddenly in a little dark street with the houses hanging forward as though they were listening and any number of clothes dangling from the window sills and waving about as though their owners were still inside them and kicking vigorously. Although the street was dark it was full of noise, and a blaze of light at the other end of it proclaimed more civilised quarters (Trafalgar Square in fact) at no great distance.

"Gerade aus," said Herr Gottfried and pushed open a swinging door. Peter followed him into the most amazing babel of voices, a confusion and a roaring, an atmosphere thick with smoke and steam and a scent in the air as though ten thousand meat-pies were cooking there before his eyes. By the door a neat stout little woman, hung all over with lockets and medallions as though she were wearing all the prizes that the famous meat-pies had ever won, was sitting in a little box with a glass front to it.

"Bon jour, Monsieur Hanz."

"Tag, Meine Gnädige Frau."

All down the room, by the wall, ran long tables black with age and grime. Men of every age and nationality were eating, drinking, smoking and talking. Some of them knew Herr Gottfried, some did not.

"Wie gehts, Gottfried?"

And Herr Gottfried, planting his flat feet like dead weights in front of him, taking off his hat and running his fingers through his hair, smiled at some, spoke to others, and at last found a little corner at the end of the room, a corner comparatively quiet but most astoundingly smelly.

Peter sat down and recovered his breath. How far away now was Treliss with its cobbled street, and the Grey Hill with the Giant's Finger pointing solemnly to the sky.

"I have no money," he said.

"The Master has given me this for you," Herr Gottfried said, handing him two sovereigns, "he says it is in advance for the week."

The meat-pies, beer and bread were ordered and then for a time they sat in silence. Peter was turning in his mind a thousand questions that he would like to ask but he was still afraid of his strange companion and he felt a little as though he were some human volcano that might at any moment burst forth and cover him with furious disaster.

Then Herr Gottfried said:

"And so you care for reading?"

"Yes."

"What do you read?"

What had Peter read? He mentioned timidly "David Copperfield," "Don Quixote," and "Henry Lessingham."

"Ah, that's the way—novels, novels, novels—always sugar ... Greek, Latin?"

"No, just a little at school."

"Ah, yes, your schools. I know them. Homer?"

"No, I'm afraid not."

"Ah, well you shall read Homer. He is the greatest, he is the Master. There is Pope for a beginning. I will teach you Greek.... Goethe?"

"I—beg your pardon."

"Goethe, Goethe, Goethe—he has never heard of him—never. Ah, these schools—I know them. Teach them nonsense—often enough—but any wisdom—never—"

"I'm very sorry—" said Peter humbly.

"And music?"

"I've had no opportunity—"

"But you would love it? Yes, I see that you would love it—it is in your eyes. Beethoven? No—later perhaps—then often enough—but Schubert! Ah, Schubert!" (Here the meat-pies arrived but Herr Gottfried did not see them). "Ah, the Unfinished! He shall hear that and he will have a new soul—And the songs! Gott in Himmel, the songs! There is a man I know, he will sing them to you. Die Mullerlieder. It is always water, the Flowers, the Sun and all the roses in the world ... ach! 'Dir Spinnerin' 'Meersstille' ... 'Meersstille'—yah, Homer, Schubert—meat and drink—Homer the meat-pie, Schubert the beer, but not this beer—no, Helles, beautiful Helles with the sun in it...."

He had forgotten Peter and Peter did not understand anything that he said, but he sat there with his eyes wide open and felt assured that it was all very useful to him and very important. The inferno continued around them, the air grew thicker with smoke, a barrel-organ began to play at the door, draughts and dominoes rattled against the long wooden tables....

Ah! this was, indeed, London.

Peter was so greatly moved that his hunger left him and it was with difficulty that the meat-pie was finished.

IV

During the three days that followed Peter learnt a very great deal about the bookshop. At night he still slept in Mr. Zanti's bedroom, but it was only a temporary pitching of tents during these days whilst he was a stranger and baffled by the noise and confusion.

Already his immediate surroundings had ceased to be a mystery. He had as it were taken them to himself and seated himself in the midst of them with surprising ease. Treliss, Scaw House, his father, had slipped back into an unintelligible distance. He felt that they still mattered to him and that the time would most certainly come when they would matter to him even more, but they were not of immediate concern. The memory of his mother was closer to him....

But in this discovery of London he was amazingly happy—happier than he had ever been in all his life, and younger too. There were a great many things that he wished to know, a great many questions that he wished to ask—but for the moment he was content to rest and to grasp what he could see.

In a day he seemed to understand the way that the books went, and not only that but even the places where the individual books were lodged. He did not, of course, know anything about the contents of the books, but their titles gave them, in his mind, human existence so that he thought of them as actual persons living in different parts of the shop. There was, for instance, the triumph of "Lady Audley's Secret." An old lady with a trembling voice and a very sharp pair of eyes wished for a secondhand copy.

"I've very sorry, Madame," began Herr Gottfried, "but I'm afraid we haven't..."

"I think—" said Peter timidly, and he climbed the little ladder and brought the book down from a misty corner. Herr Gottfried was indeed amazed at him—he said very little but he was certainly amazed. Indeed, with the exception of the "meat-pie" interval he scarcely spoke throughout the day. Peter began to look forward to one o'clock for then the German, in the midst of the babel and the smoke, continued the educating progress, and even read Goethe's poetry aloud (translating it into the strangest English) and developed Peter's conception of Homer into an alluring and fascinating picture.

Of London itself during these days Peter saw nothing. At eight o'clock in the evening the shutters were put up by the disobedient James and the shop retired for the night. Herr Gottfried shuffled away to some hidden resting-place of his own and Peter found supper waiting for him in the room at the back. He ate this alone, for Mr. Zanti was not there and during these three days he was hardly visible at all. He was up in the morning before Peter was and he came to bed when Peter was already asleep. The boy was not, however, certain that his master was always away when he seemed to be. He appeared suddenly at the most surprising moments, smiling and cheerful as ever and with no sign of hurry about him. He always gave Peter a nod and a kind word and asked him how the books were going and patted him on the shoulder, but he was away almost as soon as he was there.

One strange thing was the number of people that came into the bookshop with no intention whatever of having anything to do with the books. Indeed they paid no heed to the bookshop, and after flinging a word at Herr Gottfried, they would pass straight into the room beyond and as far as Peter could see, never came out again.

The magnificently-dressed gentleman, called by Herr Gottfried "Herr Signor," was one of these persons.

However, Peter, happy enough in the excitement of the present, asking no questions and only at night, before he fell asleep, lying on his sofa, listening to the sounds in the street below him, watching the reflections of the gas light flung up by the street lamps on to the walls of his room, he would wonder ... and, so wondering, he was asleep.

And then, on the fourth day, something happened.

It was growing late, and Peter underneath the gas jet was buried in Mr. Pope's Homer. A knock on the door and the postman entered with the letters. As a rule Herr Gottfried took them, but on this afternoon he had left the shop in Peter's hands for half an hour whilst he went out to see a friend. Peter took the letters and immediately the letter on the top of the pile (Mr. Zanti's post was always a large one) set his heart thumping. The handwriting was the handwriting of Stephen. There could be no doubt about it, no possible doubt. Peter had seen that writing many times and he had always kept the letter that Stephen had written to him when he first went to Dawson's. To other eyes it might seem an ordinary enough hand—rough and uneducated and sprawling—anybody's hand, but Peter knew that there could be no mistake.

The sight of the letter as it lay there on the counter swept away the shop, the books, London—he sat looking at it with a longing, stronger than any longing that he had ever known, to see the writer again. He lived once more through that night on the farm—perhaps at that moment he felt suddenly his loneliness, here in this huge and tempestuous London, here in this dark bookshop with so many people going in or out. He rubbed the sleeves of his blue serge suit because they made him feel like Treliss, and he sat, with eyes staring into the dark, thinking of Stephen.

That evening, just as he was going up to bed, Mr. Zanti came in and greeted him with his accustomed cheerfulness.

"Going to bed, Peter? Ah, good boy."

Peter stopped, hesitating, by the door.

"Oh, I wonder—" he said and stopped.

"Yes?" said Mr. Zanti, looking at him.

"Oh—well—it's nothing—" Then he blurted out—"I saw a letter—I couldn't help it—a letter from Stephen this afternoon. They came when Herr Gottfried was out—and I wanted—I want dreadfully—to hear about him—if you could tell me—"

For an instant Mr. Zanti's large eyes closed until they seemed to be no larger than pin-points—then they opened again.

"Stephen—Stephen? Stephen what? What is it that the boy talks of?"

"You know—Stephen Brant—the man who first brought me to see you when I was quite a kid. I was—I always have been very fond of him. I should be so very glad—"

"Surely the boy is mad—what has come to you? Stephen Brant—yes I remember the man—but I have heard nothing for years and years—no, nothing. See, here are my afternoon's letters."

He took a bundle of letters out of his pocket and showed them to Peter. The boy found the one in Stephen's handwriting.

"You may read it," said Mr. Zanti smiling. Peter read it. He could not understand it and it was signed "John Simmons" ... but it was certainly in Stephen's handwriting.

"Thank you," said Peter in rather a quivering voice and he turned away, gulping down his disappointment.

Mr. Zanti patted him on the shoulder.

"That's right, my boy. Ah, I expect you miss your friend. You will be lonely here, yes? Well—see—now that you have been here a few days perhaps it is time for you to find a place to live—and I have talked wiz a friend of mine, a ver' good friend who 'as lived for many years in a 'ouse where 'e says there is a room that will just do for you—cheap, pleasant people ... yes? To-morrow 'e will show you the place. There you will 'ave friends—"

Peter smiled, thanked Mr. Zanti and went to bed. But his dreams were confused that night. It seemed to him that London was a huge room with closing walls, and that ever they came closer and closer and that he screamed for Stephen and they would not let Stephen come to him.

And bells were ringing, and Mr. Zanti, with a lighted candle in his hands, was creeping down those dark stairs that led to the kitchen, and he might have stopped those closing walls but he would not. Then suddenly Peter was running down the Sea Road above Treliss and the waves were sounding furiously below him—his father was there waiting for him sternly, at the road's end and Herr Gottfried with a Homer in one hand and his blue shoes in the other sat watching them out of his bright eyes. His father was waiting to kill him and Mrs. Pascoe was at his elbow. Peter screamed, the sweat was pouring off his forehead, his throat was tight with agony when suddenly by his side was old Frosted Moses, with his flowing beard. "It isn't life that matters," he was whispering in his old cracked voice, "but the courage that you bring to it."

The figures faded, the light grew broader and broader, and Peter woke to find Mr. Zanti, by the aid of a candle, climbing into bed.

But some time passed before he had courage to fall asleep again.

CHAPTER XII

BROCKETTS: ITS CHARACTER, AND ESPECIALLY MRS. BROCKETT

I

On the next afternoon about six o'clock, Mr. Zanti, accompanied by the languid and shabby gentleman whom Peter had noticed before, appeared in the shop.

"Signor Rastelli," said Mr. Zanti, and the languid gentleman shook hands with Peter as though he were conferring a great benefit upon him and he hoped Peter wouldn't forget it.

"Zis," said Mr. Zanti, "is my young friend, Peter Westcott, whom I love as if 'e were my own son—Signor Rastelli," he continued, turning to Peter, "I've known him for very many years and I can only say zat ze longer I 'ave known him ze more admirable I 'ave thought 'im."

The gentleman took off his tall hat, stroked it, put it on again and looked, with his languid eyes, at Peter.

"And," continued Mr. Zanti, cheerfully, conscious perhaps that he was carrying all the conversation on his own shoulders, "'e will take you to a 'ouse where 'e has been for—'ow many years, Signor?"

"Ten," said that gentleman.

"For ten years—every comfort. Zere's a little room 'e tells me where you will be 'appy—and all your food and friendship for one pound a week. There!" he ended triumphantly.

"Thank you very much," said Peter, but he did not altogether like the look of the seedily dressed gentleman, and would much rather have stayed with Mr. Zanti.

He had packed his black bag in readiness, and now he fetched it and, after promising to be in the shop at half-past eight the next morning, started off with his melancholy guide.

The lamps were coming out, and a silence that often falls upon London just before sunset had come down upon the traffic and the people. Windows caught the departing flame, held it for an instant, and sank into grey twilight.

"I know what you're thinking about me," Peter's companion suddenly said (he was walking very fast as though trying to catch something), "I know you don't like me. I could see it at once—I never make a mistake about those things. You were saying to yourself: 'What does that horrible, over-dressed stranger want to come interfering with me for?'"

"Indeed, I wasn't," said Peter, breathlessly, because the bag was so heavy and they were walking so fast.

"Oh, yes, you were. Never mind. I'm not a popular man, and when you know me better you'll like me still less. That's always the way I affect people. And always with the best intentions. And you were thinking, too, that you never saw anything less Italian than I am, and you're sure my name's Brown or Smith, and indeed it's true that I was born in Clapham, but my parents were Italians—refugees, you know, although I'm sure I don't know what from—and every one calls me the Signor, and so there you are—and I don't see how I'm to help it. But that's just me all over—always fighting against the tide but I don't complain, I'm sure." All this said very rapidly and in a melancholy way as though tears were not very far off. Then he suddenly added:

"Let me carry your bag for you."

"No, thank you," said Peter, laughing, "I can manage it."

"Ah, well, you look strong," said the Signor appreciatively. "I envy you, I'm sure—never had a day's health myself—but I don't complain."

By this time they had passed the British Museum and were entering into the shadows of Bloomsbury. At this hour, when the lamps and the stars are coming out, and the sun is going in, Bloomsbury has an air of melancholy that is peculiarly its own. The dark grey houses stand as a perpetual witness of those people that have found life too hard for them and have been compelled to give in. The streets of those melancholy squares seen beneath flickering lamp light and a wan moon protest against all gaiety of spirit and urge resignation and a mournful acquiescence. Bloomsbury is Life on Thirty Shillings a week without the drama of starvation or the tragedy of the Embankment, but with all the ignominy of making ends meet under the stern and relentless eye of a boarding-house keeper.

But of all the sad and unhappy squares in Bloomsbury the saddest is Bennett Square. It is shut in by all the other Bloomsbury Squares and is further than any of them from the lights and traffic of popular streets. There are only four lamp posts there—one at each corner—and between these patches of light everything is darkness and desolation.

Every house in Bennett Square is a boarding-house, and No. 72 is Brockett's.

"Mrs. Brockett is a very terrifying but lovable woman," said the Signor darkly, and Peter, whose spirits had sunk lower and ever lower as he stumbled through the dark streets, felt, at the sound of this threatening prophecy, entirely miserable.

No. 72 is certainly the grimiest of the houses in Bennett Square. It is tall and built of that grey stone that takes the mind of the observer back to those school precincts of his youth. It is a thin house, not broad and fat and comfortably bulging, but rather flinging a spiteful glance at the house that squeezed it in on either side. It is like a soured, elderly caustic old maid, unhappy in its own experiences and determined to make every one else unhappy in theirs. Peter, of course, did not see these things, because it was very dark, but he wished he had not come.

The Signor had a key of his own and Peter was soon inside a hall that smelt of oilcloth and the cooking of beef; the gas was burning, but the only things that really benefited from its light were a long row of mournful black coats that hung against the wall.

Peter sneezed, and was suddenly conscious of an enormous woman whom he knew by instinct to be Mrs. Brockett. She was truly enormous—she stood facing him like some avenging Fate. She had the body of a man—flat, straight, broad. Her black hair, carefully parted down the middle, was brushed back and bound into hard black coils low down over the neck. She stood there, looking down on them, her arms akimbo, her legs apart. Her eyes were black and deep set, her cheek bones very prominent, her nose thin and sharp; her black dress caught in a little at the waist, fell otherwise in straight folds to her feet. There was a faint moustache on her upper lip, her hands, with long white slender fingers, were beautiful, lying straight by her side, against the stuff of her dress.

"Well?" she said—and her voice was deep like a man's. "Good evening, Signor."

"Good evening, Madame." He took off his hat and gave her a deep bow. "This is the young gentleman, Mr. Westcott, of whom I spoke to you this morning."

"Well—how are you, Mr. Westcott?" Her words were sharply clipped and had the resonance of coins as they rang in the air.

"Quite well, thank you," said Peter, and he noticed, in spite of his dismay at her appearance, that the clasp of her hand was strong and friendly.

"Florence will show you your room, Mr. Westcott. It is a pound a week including your meals and attendance and the use of the general sitting-room. If you do not like it you must tell me and we will wish one another good evening. If you do like it I shall do my best to make you comfortable."

Peter found afterwards that this was her invariable manner of addressing a new-comer. It could scarcely be called a warm welcome. She turned and called, "Florence!" and a maid-servant, diminutive in size but spotless in appearance, suddenly appeared from nowhere at all, as it seemed to Peter.

He followed this girl up many flights of stairs. On every side of him were doors and, once and again, gas flared above him. It was all very cold, and gusts of wind passed up and down, whisking in and out of the oilcloth, and Peter thought that he had never seen so many closed doors in his life.

At last they came to an end of the stairs and there with a skylight covering the passage outside was his room. It was certainly small and the window looked out on a dismal little piece of garden far below and a great number of roofs and chimneys and at last a high dome rising like a black cloud in the farther distance. It was spotlessly clean.

"I think it will do very well, thank you," said Peter and he put down his black bag.

"Do you?" said the maid. "There's a bell," she said, pointing, "and the meal's at seving sharp." She disappeared.

He spent the time, very cheerfully, taking the things out of the black bag and arranging them. He had suddenly, as was natural in him, forgotten the dismal approach to the house, the overwhelming appearance of Mrs. Brockett, his recent loneliness. Here, at last, was a little spot that he could, for a time, at any rate, call his own. He could come, at any time of the evening and shut his door, and be alone here, master of everything that he surveyed. Perhaps—and the thought sent the blood to his cheeks—it was here that he would write! He looked about the room lovingly. It was quite bare except for the bed, the washing stand and a chair, and there was no fire-place. But he arranged the books, David Copperfield, Don Quixote, Henry Lessingham, The Roads, The Downs, on the window sill, and the little faded photograph of his mother on the ledge above the washing basin. He had scarcely finished doing these things when there was a tap on his door. He opened it, and found the Signor, no longer in a tail-coat, but in a short, faded blue jacket that made him look shabbier than ever.

"Excuse—not intruding, I hope?" He looked gloomily round the room. "Everything all right?"

"Very nice," said Peter.

"Ah, you'll like it at first—but never mind. Wonderful woman, Mrs. Brockett. I expect you were alarmed just now."

"I was, a little," admitted Peter.

"Ah, well, we all are at first. But you'll get over that, you'll love her—every one loves her. By the way," he pushed his hand through his hair, "what I came about was to tell you that we all foregather—as you might say—in the sitting-room before dinner—yes—and I'd like to introduce you to my wife, the Signora—not Italian, you know—but you'll like her better than me—every one's agreed that hers is a nicer character."

Peter, trembling a little at the thought of more strangers, followed the Signer downstairs and found, in the middle of one of the dark landings, looking as though she had been left there by some one and completely forgotten, a little wisp of a woman with bright yellow hair and a straw coloured dress, and this was the Signora. This lady shook hands with him in a frightened tearful way and made choking noises all the way downstairs, and this distressed Peter very much until he discovered that she had a passion for cough drops, which she kept in her pocket in a little tin box and sucked perpetually. The Signor drove his wife and Peter before him into the sitting-room. This was a very brightly-coloured room with any number of brilliant purple vases on the mantelpiece, a pink wall-paper, a great number of shining pictures in the most splendid gilt frames, and in the middle of the room a bright green settee with red cushions on it. On this settee, which was round, with a space in the middle of it, like a circus, several persons were seated, but there was apparently no conversation. They all looked up at the opening of the door, and Peter was so dazzled by the bright colour of the room that it was some time before he could collect his thoughts.

But the Signor beckoned to him, and he followed.

"Allow me, Mrs. Monogue," said the Signor, "to introduce to you Mr. Peter Westcott." The lady in question was stout, red-faced, and muffled in shawls. She extended him a haughty finger.

There followed then Miss Norah Monogue, a girl with a pleasant smile and untidy hair, Miss Dall, a lady with a very stiff back, a face like an interrogation mark, because her eyebrows went up in a point and a very tight black dress, Mr. Herbert Crumley, and Mr. Peter Crumley, two short, thin gentlemen with wizened and anxious faces (they were obviously brothers, because they were exactly alike), and Mrs. and Mr. Tressiter, two pleasant-faced, cheerful people, who sat very close together as though they were cold.

All these people shook hands agreeably with Peter, but made no remarks, and he stood awkwardly looking at the purple vases and wishing that something would happen.

Something did happen. The door was very softly and slowly opened, and a little woman came hurrying in. She had white hair, and glasses were dangling on the end of her nose, and she wore a very old and shabby black silk dress. She looked round with an agitated air.

"I don't know why it is," she said, with a little chirrup, like a bird's, "but I'm always late—always!"

Then she did an amazing thing. She walked to the green settee and sat down between Miss Dall, the lady with the tight dress, and Mrs. Monogue. She then took out of one pocket an orange and out of another a piece of newspaper.

"I must have my orange, you know," she said, looking gaily round on every one.

She spread the newspaper on her knee, and then peeled the orange very slowly and with great care. The silence was maintained—no one spoke. Then suddenly the Signor darted forward: "Oh, Mrs. Lazarus I must introduce you to Madame's new guest, Mr. Westcott."

"How do you do?" the old lady chirruped. "Oh! but my fingers are all over orange—never mind, we'll smile at one another. I hope you'll like the place, I'm sure. I always have an orange before dinner. They've got used to me, you know. We've all got our little habits."

Peter did not know what to say, and was wondering whether he ought to relieve the old lady of her orange peel (at which she was gazing rather helplessly), when a bell rang and Florence appeared at the door.

"Dinner!" she said, laconically.

A procession was formed, Mrs. Monogue, with her shawls sweeping behind her, sailed in front, and Peter brought up the rear. Mrs. Lazarus put the orange peel into the newspaper and placed it all carefully in her pocket.

Mrs. Brockett was sitting, more like a soldier than ever, at the head of the table. Mutton was in front of her, and there seemed to be nothing on the table cloth but cruets and three dusty and melancholic palms. Peter found that he was sitting between Mrs. Lazarus and Miss Dall, and that he was not expected to talk. It was apparent indeed that the regularity with which every one met every one at this hour of the day, during months and months of the year negatived any polite necessity of cordiality or genial spirits. When any one spoke it was crossly and in considerable irritation, and although the food was consumed with great eagerness on everybody's part, the faces of the company were obviously anxious to express the fact that the food was worse than ever, and they wouldn't stand it another minute. They all did stand it, however, and Peter thought that they were all, secretly, rather happy and contented. During most of the meal no one spoke to him, and as he was very hungry this did not matter. Opposite him, all down the side of the room, were dusty grey pillars, and between these pillars heavy dark green curtains were hanging. This had the effect of muffling and crushing the conversation and quite forbidding anybody to be cheerful in any circumstances. Mrs. Lazarus indeed chirruped along comfortably and happily for the most part to herself—as, for instance, "I am orangy, but then I was late and couldn't finish it. Dear me, it's mutton again. I really must tell Madame about it and there's nothing so nice as beef and Yorkshire pudding, is there? Dear me, would you mind, young man, just asking Dear Miss Dall to pass the salt spoon. She's left that behind. I have the salt-cellar, thank you."

She also hummed to herself at times and made her bread into little hard pellets, which she flicked across the table with her thumb at no one in particular and in sheer absence of mind. The two Mr. Crumleys were sitting opposite to her, and they accepted the little charge of shot with all the placid equanimity bred of ancient custom.

Peter noticed other things. He noticed that Mrs. Monogue was an exceedingly ill-tempered and selfish woman, and that she bullied the pleasant girl with the untidy hair throughout the meal, and that the girl took it all in the easiest possible way. He noticed that Mrs. Brockett dealt with each of her company in turn—one remark apiece, and always in that stern, deep voice with the strangely beautiful musical note in it. To himself she said: "Well, Mr. Westcott, I'm pleased, I'm sure, that everything is to your satisfaction," and listened gravely to his assurance. To Miss Dall: "Well, Miss Ball, I looked at the book you lent me and couldn't find any sense in it, I'm afraid." To Mrs. Tressiter: "I had little Minnie with me for half an hour this evening, and I'm sure a better behaved child never breathed" ... and so on.

Once Miss Dall turned upon him sharply with: "I suppose you never go and hear the Rev. Mr. M. J. Valdwell?" and Peter had to confess ignorance.

"Really! Well, it 'ud do you young men a world of good."

He assured her that he would go.

"I will lend you a volume of his sermons if you would care to read them."

Peter said that he would be delighted. The meal was soon over, and every one returned to the sitting-room. They sat about in a desolate way, and Peter discovered afterwards that Mrs. Brockett liked every one to be there together for half an hour to encourage friendly relations. That object could scarcely be said to be achieved, because there was very little conversation and many anxious glances were flung at the clocks. Mrs. Brockett, however, sat sternly in a chair and sewed, and no one ventured to leave the room.

One pleasant thing happened. Peter was standing by the window turning over some fashion papers of an ancient date, when he saw that Miss Monogue was at his elbow. Now that she was close to him he observed that she looked thin and delicate; her dress was worn and old-fashioned, she looked as though she ought to be wrapped up warmly and taken care of—but her eyes were large and soft and grey, and although her wrists looked strangely white and sharp through her black dress her hands were beautiful. Her voice was soft with an Irish brogue lingering pleasantly amongst her words:

"I hope that you will like being here."

"I'm sure I shall," he said, smiling. He felt grateful to her for talking to him.

"You're very fortunate to have come to Mrs. Brockett's straight away. You mayn't think so now, because Mrs. Brockett is alarming at first, and we none of us—" she looked round her with a little laugh—"can strike the on-looker as very cheerful company. But really Madame has a heart of gold—you'll find that out in time. She's had a terribly hard time of it herself, and I believe it's a great struggle to keep things going now. But she's helped all kinds of people in her time."

Peter looked, with new eyes, at the lady so sternly sewing.

"You don't know," Miss Monogue went on in her soft, pleasant voice, "how horrible these boarding-houses can be. Mother and I have tried a good many. But here people stay for ever—a pretty good testimony to it, I think ... and then, you know, she never lets any one stay here if she doesn't like them—so that prevents scoundrels. There've been one or two, but she's always found them out ... and I believe she keeps old Mrs. Lazarus quite free of charge."

She paused, and then she added:

"And there's no one here who hasn't found life pretty hard. That gives us a kind of freemasonry, you know. The Tressiters, for instance, they have three children, and he has been out of work for months—sometimes there's such a frightened look in her eyes ... but you mustn't think that we're melancholy here," she went on more happily. "We get a lot of happiness out of it all."

He looked at her, and remembering Mrs. Monogue at dinner and seeing now how delicate the girl looked, thought that she must have a very considerable amount of pluck on her own account.

"And you?" she said. "Have you only just come up to London?"

"Yes," he answered, "I'm in a bookseller's shop—a second-hand bookseller's. I've only been in London a few days—it's all very exciting for me—and a little confusing at present."

"I'm sure you'll get on," she said. "You look so strong and confident and happy. I envy you your strength—one can do so much if one's got that."

He felt almost ashamed of his rough suit, his ragged build. "Well, I've always been in the country," he said, a little apologetically. "I expect London will change that."

Then there came across the room Mrs. Monogue's sharp voice. "Norah! Norah! I want you."

She left him.

That night in his little room, he looked from his window at the sea of black roofs that stretched into the sky and found in their ultimate distance the wonderful sweep of stars that domed them; a great moon, full-rounded, dull gold, staring like a huge eye, above them. His heart was full. A God there must be somewhere to have given him all this splendour—a splendour surely for him to work upon. He felt as a craftsman feels, when some new and wonderful tools have been given to him; as a woman feels the child in her womb, stirring mysteriously, moving her to deep and glad thankfulness, so now, with the night wind blowing about him, and all London lying, dark and motionless, below him, he felt the first stirring of his power. This was his to work with, this was his to praise and glorify and make beautiful—now crude and formless—a seed dark and without form or colour—one day to make one more flower in that garden that God has given his servants to work in.

He did not, at this instant, doubt that some God was there, crying to him, and that he must answer. Of that moon, of those stars, of that mighty city, he would make one little stone that might be added to that Eternal Temple of Beauty....

He turned from his window and thought of other things. He thought of his father and Scaw House, of the windy day when his mother was buried, of Mr. Zanti and Stephen's letter, of Herr Gottfried and his blue slippers, of this house and its people, of the friendly girl and her grey eyes ... finally, for a little, of himself—of his temper and his ambitions and his selfishness. Here, indeed, suddenly jumping out at him, was the truth.

He felt, as he got into bed, that he would have to change a great deal if he were to write that great book that he thought of: "Little Peter Westcott," London seemed to say, "there's lots to be done to you first before you're worth anything ... I'll batter at you."

Well, let it, he thought, sleepily. There was nothing that he would like better. He tumbled into sleep, with London after him, and Fame in front of him, and a soft and resonant murmur, as of a slumbering giant, rising to his open window.

BOOK II — THE BOOKSHOP

CHAPTER I

"REUBEN HALLARD"

I

There is a story in an early volume of Henry Galleon's about a man who caught—as he may have caught other sicknesses in his time—the disease of the Terror of London. Eating his breakfast cheerfully in his luxurious chambers in Mayfair, in the act of pouring his coffee out of his handsome silver coffee-pot, he paused. It was the very slightest thing that held his attention—the noise of the rumbling of the traffic down Piccadilly—but he was startled and, on that morning, he left his breakfast unfinished. He had, of course, heard that rumbling traffic on many other occasions—it may be said to have been the musical accompaniment to his breakfast for many years past. But on this morning it was different; as one has a headache before scarlet fever so did this young man hear the rumble of the traffic down Piccadilly. He listened to it very attentively, and it was, he told himself, very like the noise of some huge animal breathing in its sleep. There was a regularity, a monotony about it ... and also perhaps a sense of great force, quiescent now and held in restraint. He was a very normal, well-balanced young man and thoughts of this kind were unlike him.

Then he heard other things—the trees rustling in the park, bells ringing on every side of him, builders knocking and hammering, windows rattling, doors opening and shutting. In the Club one evening he confided in a friend. "I say, it's damned funny—but what would you say to this old place being alive, taking on a regular existence of its own, don't you know? You might draw it—a great beast like some old alligator, all curled up, with its teeth and things—making a noise a bit as it moves about ... and then, one day when it's got us nicely all on top of it, down it will bring us all, houses and the rest. Damned funny idea, what? Do for a cartoon-fellow or some one—"

The disease developed; he had it very badly, but at first his friends did not know. He lay awake at night hearing things—one heard much more at night—sometimes he fancied that the ground shook under his feet—but most terrible of all was it when there was perfect silence. The traffic ceased, the trees and windows and doors were still ... the Creature was listening. Sometimes he read in papers that buildings had suddenly collapsed. He smiled to himself. "When we are all nicely gathered together," he said, "when there are enough people ... then—"

His friends said that he had a nervous breakdown; they sent him to a rest-cure. He came back. The Creature was fascinating—he was terrified, but he could not leave it.

He knew more and more about it; he knew now what it was like, and he saw its eyes and he sometimes could picture its grey scaly back with churches and theatres and government buildings and the little houses of Mr. Smith and Mr. Jones perched upon it—and the noises that it made now were so many and so threatening that he never slept at all. Then he began to run, shouting, down Piccadilly, so they put him—very reluctantly—into a nice Private Asylum, and there he died, screaming. This story is a prologue to Peter's life in London.... The story struck his fancy; he thought of it sometimes.

II

On a late stormy afternoon in November, 1895, Peter finished his book, "Reuben Hallard." It had been raining all day, and now the windows were blurred and the sea of shining roofs that stretched into the mist emphasised the dark and gloom of the heavy overhanging sky.

Peter's little room was very cold, but his body was burning—he was in a state of overpowering excitement; his hands trembled so that he could scarcely hold his pen ... "So died Reuben Hallard, a fool and a gentleman"—and then "Finis" with a hard straight line underneath it.... He had been working at it for three years, and he had been in London seven.

He walked up and down his little room, he was so hot that he flung up his window and leaned out and let the rain, that was coming down fiercely now, lash his face. Mud! London was full of mud. He could see it, he fancied, gathering in thick brown layers upon the pavement, shining and glistening as it mounted, slipping in streams into the gutter, sweeping about the foundations of the houses, climbing perhaps, one day, to the very windows. That was London. And yet he loved it, London and its dirt and darkness. Had he not written "Reuben Hallard" here! Had the place not taken him into its arms, given him books and leisure out of its hospitality, treated him kindly during these years so that they had fled like an instant of time, and here he was, Peter Westcott, aged twenty-five, with a book written, four friends made, and the best health possible to man. The book was "Reuben Hallard," the friends were

Mrs. Brockett, Mr. Zanti, Herr Gottfried, and Norah Monogue, and for his health one had only to look at him!

"So died Reuben Hallard, a fool and a gentleman!" His excitement was tremendous; his cheeks were flaming, his eyes glittering, his heart beating. Here was a book written!—so many pages covered with so much writing, his claim to be somebody, to have done something, justified and, most wonderful of all, live, exciting people created by him, Peter Westcott. He did not think now of publication, of money, of fame—only, after sharing for three years in the trials and adventures of dear, beloved souls, now, suddenly, he emerged cold, breathless ... alone ... into the world again.

Exciting! Why, furiously, of course. He could have sung and shouted and walked, right over the tops of the roofs, with the rain beating and cooling his body, out into the mist of the horizon. His book, "Reuben Hallard!" London was swimming in thick brown mud, and the four lamps coming out in Bennett Square in a dim, sickly fashion and he, Peter Westcott, had written a book....

The Signor—the same Signor, some seven years older, a little shabbier, but nevertheless the same Signor—came to summon him to supper.

"I have finished it!"

"What! The book?"

"Yes!"

Their voices were awed whispers. The whole house had during the last three years shared in the fortunes of the book. Peter had come to dinner with a cloud upon his brow—the book therefore has gone badly—even Mrs. Brockett is disturbed and Mrs. Lazarus is less chirpy than usual. Peter comes to dinner with a smile—the book therefore has gone well and even Mrs. Monogue is a little less selfish than ordinary. The Signor now gazed round the little room as though he might find there the secret of so great an achievement. On Peter's dressing-table the manuscript was piled—"You'll miss it," the Signor said, gloomily. "You'll miss it very much—you're bound to. You'll have to get it typewritten, and that'll cost money."

"Never mind, it's done," said Peter, shaking his head as a dog shakes himself when he leaves the water. "There they are, those people—and now I'm going to wash."

He stripped to the waist, and the Signor watched his broad back and strong arms with a sigh for his own feeble proportions. He wondered how it was that being in a stuffy bookshop for seven years had done Peter no harm, he wondered how he could keep the back of his neck so brown as that in London and his cheeks as healthy a colour and his eyes as clear.

"I'm amazingly unpleasant to look at," the Signor said at last. "I often wonder why my wife married me. I'm not surprised that every one finds me uninteresting. I am uninteresting."

"Well, you are not uninteresting to me, I can tell you," said Peter. He had put on a soft white shirt, a black tie, and a black coat and trousers, the last of these a little shiny perhaps in places, but neat and well brushed, and you would really not guess when you saw him, that he only possessed two suits in the wide world.

"I think you're absorbing," Peter said, a little patronisingly perhaps.

"Ah, that proves nothing," the Signer retorted. "You only care for fools and children—Mrs. Brockett always says so."

They went downstairs—Peter was, of course, not hungry at all, but the conventions had to be observed. In the sitting-room, round about the green settee, the company was waiting as it had waited seven years ago; there were one or two unimportant additions and Mrs. Monogue had died the year before and Mrs. Lazarus was now very old and trembling, but in effect there was very little change.

"He has finished it," the Signor announced in a wondering whisper. A little buzz rose, filled the air for a moment and then sank into silence again. Mrs. Lazarus was without her orange because she had to wear mittens now, and that made peeling the thing difficult. "I'm sure," she said, in a voice like that of a very excited cricket, "that Mr. Westcott will feel better after he's had something to eat. I always do."

This remark left conversation at a standstill. The rain drove against the panes, the mud rose ever higher against the walls, and dinner was announced. Mrs. Brockett made her remarks to each member of the company in turn as usual. To Peter she said:

"I hear that you have finished your book, Mr. Westcott. We shall all watch eagerly for its appearance, I'm sure."

He felt his excitement slipping away from him as the moments passed. Suddenly he was tired. Instead of elation there was wonder, doubt. What if, after all, the book should be very bad? During all these years in London he had thought of it, during all these years he had known that it was going to succeed. What, if now he should discover suddenly that it was bad?... Could he endure it? The people of his book seemed now to stand very far away from him—they were unreal—he could remember scenes, things that they had said and done, absurd, ignorant things.

He began to feel panic. Why should he imagine that he was able to write? Of course it was all crude, worthless stuff. He looked at the dingy white pillars and heavy green curtains with a kind of despair ... of course it was all bad. He had been hypnotised by the thing for the time being. Then he caught Norah Monogue's eyes and smiled. He would show it to her, and she would tell him what it was worth.

Poor Mrs. Tressiter's baby had died last week and now, suddenly, she burst out crying and had to leave the room. There was a little twitter of sympathy. How good they all were to one another, these people, stupid and odd perhaps in some ways, but so brave for themselves and so generous to one another. It was no mean gathering of souls that Mrs. Brockett's dingy gas illuminated.

Every now and again the heavy curtains blew forward in the wind and the gas flared. There was no conversation, and the wind could be heard driving the rain past the windows.

III

Peter, that evening, took the manuscript of "Reuben Hallard" into Miss Monogue's room. Since her mother died Norah Monogue had had a bed sitting-room to herself. The bed was hidden by a high screen, the wall paper was a dark green, and low bookshelves, painted white, ran round the room. There were no pictures (she always said that until she could have good ones she wouldn't have any at all). There were some brown pots and vases on the shelves and a writing-table with a typewriter by the window.

When Peter came in, Norah Monogue was sitting in a low chair over a rather miserable fire; a little pool of light above her head came from two candles on the mantelpiece—otherwise the room was in darkness.

"Shall I turn on the gas?" she said, when she saw who it was.

"No, leave it as it is, I like it." He sat down in a chair near her and put a pile of manuscript on the floor beside him. "I've brought it for you to read," he said, "I'm frightened about it. I suddenly think it is the most rotten thing that ever was written." He had become very intimate with her during these seven years. At first he had admired her because she behaved so splendidly to her abominable mother—then she had obviously been interested in him, had talked about the things that he was reading and his life at the bookshop. They had speedily become the very best of friends, and she understood friendship he thought in the right way—as though she had herself been a man. And yet she was with that completely feminine, a woman who had known struggle from the beginning and would know it to the end; but her personality—humorous, pathetic, understanding—was felt in her presence so strongly that no one ever forgot her after meeting her. Some one once said of her, "She's the nicest ugly woman to look at I've ever seen."

She cared immensely about her appearance. She saved, through blood and tears, to buy clothes and then always bought the wrong ones. She had perfect taste about everything except herself, and as soon as it touched her it was villainous. She was untidy; her hair—streaked already with grey—was never in its place; her dress was generally undone at the back, her gloves had holes.

Her mother's death had left her some fifty pounds a year and she earned another fifty pounds by typewriting. Untidy in everything else, in her work she was scrupulously neat. She had had a story taken by The Green Volume. Her friends belonged (as indeed just at this time so many people belonged) to the Cult of the Lily, repeated the witticisms of Oscar Wilde and treasured the art of Mr. Aubrey Beardsley. Miss Monogue believed in the movement and rejected the affectations. In 1895, when the reaction began, she defended her old giants, but looked forward eagerly to new ones. She worked too hard to have very many friends, and Peter saved her from hours of loneliness. To him she was the last word in Criticism, in Literature. He would have liked to have fashioned "Reuben Hallard" after the manner of The Green Volume, but now thought sadly that it was as unlike that manner as possible; that is why he was afraid to bring it to her.

"You won't like it," he said. "I thought for a moment I had done something fine when I finished it this afternoon, but now I know that it's bad. It's all rough and crude. It's terribly disappointing."

"That's all right," she answered quietly. "We won't say any more about it until I have read it—then we'll talk."

They were silent for a little. He was feeling unhappy and, curiously enough, frightened. He would have liked to jump up suddenly and shout, "Well, what's going to happen now?"—not only to Norah Monogue, but to London, to all the world. The work at the book had, during these years, upheld him with a sense of purpose and aim. Now, feeling that that work was bad, his aim seemed wasted, his purpose gone. Here were seven years gone and he had done nothing—seen nothing, become nothing. What was his future to be? Where was he to go? What to do? He had reasoned blindly to himself during these years, that "Reuben Hallard" would make his fortune—now that seemed the very last thing it would do.

"I knew what you're feeling," she said, "now that the book's done, you're wondering what's coming next."

"It's more than that. I've been in London seven years. Instead of writing a novel that no one will want to read I might have been getting my foot in. I might at any rate have been learning London, finding my way about. Why," he went on, excitedly, "do you know that, except for a walk or two and going into the gallery at Covent Garden once or twice and the Proms sometimes and meeting some people at Herr Gottfried's once or twice I've spent the whole of my seven years between here and the bookshop—"

"You mustn't worry about that. It was quite the right thing to do. You must remember that there are two ways of learning things. First through all that every one has written, then through all that every one is doing. Up to now you've been studying the first of those two. Now you're ready to take part in all the hurly-burly, and you will. London will fling you into it as soon as you're ready, you can be sure."

"I've been awfully happy all this time," he went on, reflectively. "Too happy I expect. I never thought about anything except reading and writing the book, and talking to you and Gottfried. Now things will begin I suppose."

"What kind of things?"

"Oh, well, it isn't likely that I'm going to be let alone for ever. I've never told you, have I, about my life before I came up to London?"

She hesitated a little before she answered. "No, you've never told me anything. I could see, of course, that it hadn't been easy."

"How could you see that?"

"Well, it hadn't been easy for either of us. That made us friends. And then you don't look like a person who would take things easily—ever. Tell me about your early life before you came here," Norah Monogue said.

She watched his face as he told her. She had found him exceedingly good company during the seven years that she had known him. They had slipped into their friendship so easily and so naturally that she had never taken herself to task about it in any way; it existed as a very delightful accompaniment to the day's worries and disappointments. She suddenly realised now with a little surprised shock how bitterly she would miss it all were it to cease. In the darkened room, with the storm blowing outside, she felt her loneliness with an acute wave of emotion and self-pity that was very unlike her. If Peter were to go, she felt, she could scarcely endure to live on in the dreary building.

Part of his charm from the beginning had been that he was so astoundingly young, part of his interest that he could be, at times, so amazingly old. She felt that she herself could be equal neither to his youth nor his age. She was herself so ordinary a person, but watching him made the most fascinating occupation, and speculating over his future made the most wonderful dreams. That he was a personality, that he might do anything, she had always believed, but there had, until now, been no proof of it in any work that he had done ... he had had nothing to show ... now at last there lay there, with her in the room, the evidence of her belief—his book.

But the book seemed now, at this moment, of small account and, as she watched him, with the candle-light and the last flicker of the fire-light upon his face, she saw that he had forgotten her and was back again, soul and spirit, amongst the things of which he was speaking.

His voice was low and monotonous, his eyes staring straight in front of him, his hands, spread on his knees, gripped the cloth of his trousers. She would not admit to herself that she was frightened, but her heart was beating very fast and it was as though some stranger were with her in the room. It may have been the effect of the candlelight, blowing now in the wind that came through the cracks in the window panes, but it seemed to her that Peter's face was changed. His face had lines that had not been there before, his mouth was thinner and harder and his eyes were old and tired ... she had never seen the man before, that was her impression.

But she had never known anything so vivid. Quietly, as though he were reciting the story to himself and were not sure whether he were telling it aloud or no, he began. As he continued she could see the place as though it was there with her in the room, the little Inn that ran out into the water, the high-cobbled street, the sea road, the grim stone house standing back amongst its belt of trees, the Grey Hill, the coast, the fields ... and then the story—the night of the fight, the beating, the school-days, that day with his mother (here he gave her actual dialogue as though there was no word of it that he had forgotten), the funeral—and then at last, gradually, climbing to its climax breathlessly, the relation of father and son, its hatred, then its degradation, and last of all that ludicrous scene in the early morning ... he told her everything.

When he had finished, there was a long silence between them: the fire was out and the room very cold. The storm had fallen now in a fury about the house, and the rain lashed the windows and then fell in gurgling stuttering torrents through the pipes and along the leads. Miss Monogue could not move; the scene, the place, the incidents were slowly fading away, and the room slowly coming back again. The face opposite her, also, gradually seemed to drop, as though it had been a mask, the expression that it had worn. Peter Westcott, the Peter that she knew, sat before her again; she could have believed as she looked at him, that the impressions of the last half-hour had been entirely false. And yet the things that he had told her were not altogether a surprise; she had not known him for seven years without seeing signs of some other temper and spirit—controlled indeed, but nevertheless there, and very different from the pleasant, happy Peter who played with the Tressiter children and dared to chaff Mrs. Brockett.

"You've paid me a great compliment, telling me this," she said at last. "Remember we're friends; you've proved that we are by coming like this to-night. I shan't forget it. At any rate," she added, softly, "it's all right now, Peter—it's all over now."

"Over! No, indeed," he answered her. "Do you suppose that one can grow up like that and then shake it off? Sometimes I think ... I'm afraid ..." he stopped, abruptly biting his lips. "Oh, well," he went on suddenly in a brighter tone, "there's no need to bother you with all that. It's nothing. I'm a bit done up over this book, I expect. But that's really why I told you that little piece of autobiography—because it will help you to understand the book. The book's come out of all that, and you mightn't have believed that it was me at all—unless I'd told you these things."

He stood facing her and a sudden awkwardness came over both of them. The fire was dead (save for one red coal), and the windows rattled like pistol-shots. He was feeling perhaps that he had told her too much, and the reserve of his age, the fear of being indiscreet, had come upon him. And with her there was the difficulty of not knowing exactly what comfort it was that he wanted, or whether, indeed, any kind of comfort would not be an insult to him. And, with all that awkwardness, there was also a knowledge that they had never been so near together before, an intimacy had been established that night that would never again be broken.

Into their silence there came a knock on the door. When Miss Monogue opened it the stern figure of Mrs. Brockett confronted her.

"I beg your pardon, Miss Monogue, but is Mr. Westcott here?"

Peter stepped forward.

"Oh, I'm sure I'm sorry to have to disturb you, Mr. Westcott, but there's a man outside on the steps who insists on seeing you."

"Seeing me?"

"Yes—he won't come in or go away. He won't move until he's seen you. Very obstinate I'm sure—and such a night! Rather late, too—"

Mrs. Brockett was obviously displeased. Her tall black figure was drawn up outside the door, as a sentry might guard Buckingham Palace. There was a confusion of regality, displeasure, and grim humour in her attitude. But Peter was a favourite of hers. With a hurried goodnight to Miss Monogue he left the two women standing on the stairs and went to the hall-door.

When he opened it the wind was blowing up the steps so furiously that it flung him back into the hall again. Outside in the square the world was a wild tempestuous black, only, a little to the right, the feeble glow of the lamp blew hither and thither in the wind. The rain had stopped but all the pipes and funnels of the city were roaring with water. The noise was that of a thousand chattering voices, and very faintly through the tumult the bells of St. Matthews in Euston Square tinkled the hour.

On the steps a figure was standing bending beneath the wind. The light from the hall shone out on to the black slabs of stone, bright with the shining rain, but his cape covered the man's head. Nevertheless Peter knew at once who it was.

"Stephen," he said, quietly.

The hall door was flung to with a crash; the wind hurled Peter against Stephen's body.

"At last! Oh, Stephen! Why didn't you come before?"

"I couldn't, Master Peter. I oughtn't to of come now, but I 'ad to see yer face a minute. Not more than a minute though—"

"But you must come in now, and get dry things on at once. I'll see Mrs. Brockett, she'll get you a room. I'm not going to let you go now that—"

"No, Master Peter, I can't stop. I mustn't. I 'aven't been so far away all this time as you might have thought. But I mustn't see yer unless I can be of use to yer. And that's what I've come about."

He pressed close up to Peter, held both his hands in his and said: "Look 'ere, Peter boy, yer may be wanting me soon—no, I can't say more than that. But I want yer—to be on the look-out. Down there at the bookshop be ready, and then if any sort o' thing should 'appen down along—why I'm there, d'ye see? I'll be with yer when you want me—"

"Well, but Stephen, what do you mean? What could happen? Anyhow you mustn't go now, like this. I won't let you go—"

"Ah, but I must now—I must. Maybe we shall be meeting soon enough. Only I'm there, boy, if yer wants me. And—keep yer eye open—"

In an instant that warm pressure of the hand was gone; the darker black of Stephen's body no longer silhouetted against the lighter black of the night sky.

Still in Peter's nose there was that scent of wet clothes and the deep, husky voice was in his ears. But, save for the faint yellow flickering lamp, struggling against the tempest, he was alone in the square.

The rain had begun to fall again.

CHAPTER II

THE MAN ON THE LION

I

After the storm, the Fog.

It came, a yellow, shrouded witch down upon the town, clinging, choking, writhing, and bringing in its train a thousand mysteries, a thousand visions. It was many years since so dense and cruel a fog had startled London—in his seven years' experience of the place Peter had known nothing like it, and his mind flew back to that afternoon of his arrival, seven years before, and it seemed to him that he was now moving straight on from that point and that there had been no intervening period at all. The Signer saw in a fog as a cat sees in the dark, and he led Peter to the bookshop without hesitation. He saw a good many other things beside his immediate direction and became comparatively cheerful and happy.

"It is such a good thing that people can't see me," he said. "It relieves one of a lot of responsibility if one's plain to look at—one can act more freely." Certainly the Signor acted with very considerable freedom, darting off suddenly into the fog, apparently with the intention of speaking to some one, and leaving Peter perfectly helpless and then suddenly darting back again, catching Peter in tow and tugging him forward once more.

To the bookshop itself the fog made very little difference. There were always the gas-jets burning over the two dark corners and the top shelves even in the brightest of weather, were mistily shrouded by dust and distance. The fog indeed seemed to bring the books out and, whilst the world outside was so dark, the little shop flickered away under the gas-jets with little spasmodic leaps into light and colour when the door opened and blew the quivering flame.

It was not of the books that Peter was thinking this morning. He sat at a little desk in one dark corner under one of the gas-jets, and Herr Gottfried, huddled up as usual, with his hair sticking out above the desk like a mop, sat under the other; an old brass clock, perched on a heap of books, ticked away the minutes. Otherwise there was silence save when a customer entered, bringing with him a trail of fog, or some one who was not a customer passed solemnly, seriously through to the rooms beyond. The shop was, of course, full of fog, and the books seemed to form into lines and rows and curves in and out amongst the shelves of their own accord.

Peter meanwhile was most intently thinking. He knew as though he had seen it written down in large black letters in front of him, that a period was shortly to be put to his present occupation, but he could not have said how it was that he knew. The finishing of his book left the way clear for a number of things to attack his mind. Here in this misty shop he was beset with questions. Why was he here at all? Had he during these seven years been of such value, that the shop could not get on without him?... To that second question he must certainly answer, no. Why then had Mr. Zanti kept him all this time? Surely because Mr. Zanti was fond of him. Yes, that undoubtedly was a part of the reason. The relationship, all this time, had grown very strong and it was only now, when he set himself seriously to think about it, that he realised how glad he always was when Mr. Zanti returned from his travels and how happy he had been when it had been possible for them to spend an afternoon together. Yes, Mr. Zanti was attached to him; he had often said that he looked upon him as a son, and sometimes it seemed to Peter that the strange man was about to make some declaration, something that would clear the air, and explain the world—but he never did.

Peter had discovered strangely little about him. He knew now that Mr. Zanti's connection with the bookshop was of the very slenderest, that that was indeed entirely Herr Gottfried's affair, and that it was used by the large and smiling gentleman as a cloak and a covering. As a cloak and a covering to what? Well, at any rate, to some large and complicated game that a great number of gentlemen were engaged in playing. Peter knew a good many of them now by sight—untidy, dirty, many, foreigners most, all it seemed to Peter, with an air of attempting something that they could never hope to accomplish. Anything that they might do he was quite sure that they would bungle and, with the hearts of children, the dirty tatters of foreign countries, and the imaginations of exuberant story-tellers, he could see them go, ignorantly, to dreadful catastrophes.

Peter was even conscious that the shop was tolerantly watched by inspectors, detectives, and policemen, and that it was all too childish—whatever it was—for any one to take it in the least seriously. But nevertheless there were elements of very real danger in all those blundering mysteries that had been going on now for so many years, and it was at any rate of the greatest importance to Peter, because he earned his living by it, because of his love for Stephen and his affection for Mr. Zanti, and because if once anything were to happen his one resting-place in this wild sea of London would be swept away and he would be utterly resourceless and destitute.

This last fact bit him, as he sat there in the shop, with sudden and acute sharpness. What a fool he had been, all this time, to let things slide! He should have been making connections, having irons in the fire, bustling about—how could he have sat down thus happily and easily for seven years, as though such a condition of things could continue for ever? He had had wild ideas of "Reuben Hallard" making his fortune!... that showed his ignorance of the world. Let him begin to bustle. He would not lose another moment. There were two things for him now to do, to beard editors (those mythical creatures!) in their caves and to find out where Stephen lived ... both these things as soon as possible.

In the afternoon the fog became of an impenetrable thickness, and beyond the shop it seemed that there was pandemonium. Some fire, blazing at some street corner, flared as though it were the beating heart of all that darkness, and the cries of men and the slow, clumsy passing of the traffic filled the bookshop with sound.

No customers came; Herr Gottfried worked away at his desk, the brass clock ticked, Peter sat listening, waiting.

Herr Gottfried broke the silence once with: "Peter, my friend, at ten o'clock to-night there will be a little music in my room. Herr Dettzolter and his 'cello—a little Brahms—if the fog is not too much for you."

Peter accepted. He loved the low-roofed attic, the clouds of tobacco, the dark corner where he sat and listened to Herr Gottfried's friends (German exiles like Herr Gottfried playing their beloved music). It was his only luxury.

Once two men whom Peter knew very well by sight came into the shop. They were, he believed, Russians—one of them was called Oblotzky—a tall, bearded fierce-looking creature who could speak no English.

Then suddenly, just as Peter was thinking of finding his way home to the boarding-house, Mr. Zanti appeared. He had been away for the last two months, but there he was, his huge body filling the shop, the fog circling his beard like a halo, beaming, calm, and unflustered as though he had just come from the next street.

"Damned fog," he said, and then he went and put his hand on Peter's shoulder and looked down at him smiling.

"Well, 'ow goes the shop?" he said.

"Oh, well enough," said Peter.

"What 'ave you been doing, boy? Finished the book?"

"Yes."

"Ah, good. You'll be ze great man, Peter." He looked down at him proudly as a father might look upon his son.

"Ze damnedest fog—" he began, then suddenly he stopped and Peter felt his hand on his shoulder tighten. "Ze damnedest—" Mr. Zanti said slowly.

Peter looked up into his face. He was listening. Herr Gottfried, standing in the middle of the shop, was also listening.

For a moment there was an intense breathless silence. The noise from the street seemed also, for the instant, to be hushed.

Very slowly, very quietly, Mr. Zanti went to the street door and opened it. A cloud of yellow fog blew into the shop.

"Ze damnedest fog ..." repeated Mr. Zanti, still very slowly, as though he were thinking.

"Any one been?" he said at last to Herr Gottfried.

"Oblotzky."

Mr. Zanti, after flinging a strange, half-affectionate, half-inquisitive look at Peter, went through into the room beyond.

"What ..." said Peter.

"Often enough," interrupted Herr Gottfried, shuffling back to his seat, "young boys want to know—too much ... often enough."

II

The Tressiter children, of whom there were eight, loved Peter with a devotion that was in fact idolatry. They loved him because he understood them so completely and from Anne Susan, aged one and a half, to Rupert Bernard, aged nine, there was no member of the family who did not repose complete trust and confidence in Peter's opinions, and rejoice in his wonderful grasp of the things in the world that really mattered. Other persons might be seen shifting, slowly and laboriously, their estimates and standards in order to bring them into line with the youthful Tressiter estimates and standards.... Peter had his ready without any shifting.

First of all the family did Robin Tressiter, aged four, adore Peter. He was a fat, round child with brown eyes and brown hair, and an immense and overwhelming interest in the world and everything contained therein. He was a silent child, with a delightful fat chuckle when really amused and pleased, and he never cried. His interest in the world led him into strange and terrible catastrophes, and Mrs. Tressiter was always far too busy and too helpless to be of any real assistance. On this foggy afternoon, Peter, arriving at Brockett's after much difficulty and hesitation, found Robin Tressiter, on Miss Monogue's landing, with his head fastened between the railings that overlooked the hall below. He was stuck very fast indeed, but appeared to be perfectly unperturbed—only every now and again he kicked a little with his legs.

"I've sticked my neck in these silly things," he said, when he saw Peter. "You must pull at me."

Peter tried to wriggle the child through, but he found that he must have some one to help him. Urging Robin not to move he knocked at Miss Monogue's door. She opened it, and he stepped back with an apology when he saw that some one else was there.

"It's a friend of mine," Norah Monogue said, "Come in and be introduced, Peter."

"It's only," Peter explained, "that young Robin has got his head stuck in the banisters and I want some one to help me—"

Between them they pulled the boy through to safety. He chuckled.

"I'll do it again," he said.

"I'd rather you didn't," said Peter.

"Then I won't," said Robin. "I did it 'cause Rupert said I couldn't—Rupert's silly ass."

"You mustn't call your brother names or I won't come and see you in bed."

"You will come?" said Robin, very earnestly.

"I will," said Peter, "to-night, if you don't call your brother names."

"I think," said Robin, reflectively, "that now I will hunt for the lion and the tigers on the stairs—"

"Bring him into my room until his bedtime," said Miss Monogue, laughing. "It's safer. Mrs. Tressiter is busy and has quite enough children in with her already."

So Peter brought Robin into Miss Norah Monogue's room and was introduced, at once, to Clare Elizabeth Rossiter—so easily and simply do the furious events of life occur.

She was standing with her back to the window, and the light from Miss Monogue's candles fell on her black dress and her red-gold hair. As he came towards her he knew at once that she was the little girl who had talked to him on a hill-top one Good Friday afternoon. He could almost hear her now as she spoke to Crumpet—the candle-light glow was dim and sacred in the foggy room; the colour of her hair was filled more wonderfully with light and fire. Her hands were so delicate and fine as they moved against her black dress that they seemed to have some harmony of their own like a piece of music or a running stream. She wore blue feathers in her black hat. She did not know him at all when he came forward, but she smiled down at Robin, who was clinging on to Peter's trousers.

"This is a friend of mine, Mr. Westcott," Miss Monogue said.

She turned gravely and met him. They shook hands and then she sat down; suddenly she bent down and took Robin into her lap. He sat there sucking his thumb, and taking every now and again a sudden look at her hair and the light that the candles made on it, but he was very silent and quiet which was unlike him because he generally hated strangers.

Peter sat down and was filled with embarrassment; his heart also was beating very quickly.

"I have met you before," he said suddenly. "You don't remember."

"No—I'm afraid—"

"You had once, a great many years ago, a dog called Crumpet. Once in Cornwall ... one Good Friday, he tumbled into a lime-pit. A boy—"

"Why, of course," she broke in, "I remember you perfectly. Why of all the things! Norah, do you realise? Your friend and I have known each other for eight years. Isn't the world a small place! Why I remember perfectly now!"

She turned and talked to Norah Monogue, and whilst she talked he took her in. Although now she was grown up she was still strangely like that little girl in Cornwall. He realised that now, as he looked at her, he had still something of the same feeling about her as he had had then—that she was some one to be cared for, protected, something fragile that the world might break if she were not guarded.

She was porcelain but without anything of Meredith's "rogue." Because Peter was strong and burly the contrast of her appealing fragility attracted him all the more. Had she not been so perfectly proportioned her size would have been a defect; but now it was simple that her delicacy of colour and feature demanded that slightness and slenderness of build. Her hair was of so burning a red-gold that its colour gave her precisely the setting that she required. She seemed, as she sat there, a little helpless, and Peter fancied that she was wishing him to understand that she wanted friends who should assist her in rather a rough-and-tumble world. Just as she had once appealed to him to save Crumpet, so now she seemed to appeal for some far greater assistance. Ah! how he could protect her! Peter thought.

Something in Peter's steady gaze seemed suddenly to surprise her. She stopped—the colour mounted into her cheeks—she bent down over the boy.

They were both of them supremely conscious of one another. There was a moment.... Then, as men feel, when some music that has held them ceases, they came, with a sense of breathlessness, back to Norah Monogue and her dim room.

Peter was conscious that Robin had watched them both. He almost, Peter thought, chuckled to himself, in his fat solemn way.

"Miss Rossiter," Norah Monogue said—and her voice seemed a long way away—"has just come back from Germany and has brought some wonderful photographs with her. She was going to show them to me when you came in—"

"Let me see them too, please," said Peter.

Robin was put on to the floor and he went slowly and with ceremony to an old brown china Toby that had his place on a little shelf by the door. This Toby—his name was Nathaniel—was an old friend of Robin's. Robin sat on the floor in a corner and told Nathaniel the things about the world that he had noticed. Every now and again he paused for Nathaniel's reply; he was always waiting for him to speak, and the continued silence of a now ancient acquaintance had not shaken Robin's faith.... Robin forgot the rest of the company.

"Photographs?" said Peter.

"Yes. Germany. I have just been there." She looked up at him eagerly and then opened a portfolio that she had behind her chair and began to show them.

He bent gravely forward feeling that all of this was pretence of the most absurd kind and that she also knew that it was.

But they were very beautiful photographs—the most beautiful that he had ever seen, and as each, in its turn, was shown for a moment his eyes met hers and his mouth almost against his will, smiled. His hand too was very near the silk of her dress. If he moved it a very little more then they would touch. He felt that if that happened the room would immediately burst into flame, the air was so charged with the breathless tension; but he watched the little space of air between his fingers and the black silk and his hand did not move.

They were all very silent as she turned the photographs over and there were no sounds but the sharp crackling of the fire as it burst into little spurts of flame, the noise that her hand made on the silk of her dress as she turned each picture and the little mutterings of Robin in his corner as he talked to his Toby.

Peter had never seen anything like this photography. The man had used his medium as delicately as though he had drawn every line. Things stood out—castles, a hill, trees, running water, a shining road—and behind them there was darkness and mystery.

Suddenly Peter cried out:

"Oh! that!" he said. It was the photograph of a great statue standing on a hill that overlooked a river. That was all that could be seen—the background was dark and vague, it was the statue of a man who rode a lion. The lion was of enormous size and struggling to be free, but the man, naked, with his utmost energy, his back set, his arms stiff, had it in control, but only just in control ... his face was terrible in the agony of his struggle and that struggle had lasted for a great period of time ... but at length, when all but defeated, he had mastered his beast.

"Ah that!" Miss Rossiter held it up that Norah Monogue might see it better. "That is on a hill outside a little town in Bavaria. They put it up to a Herr Drexter who had done something, saved their town from riot I think. It's a fine thing, isn't it, and I think it so clever of them to have made him middle-aged with all the marks of the struggle about him—those scars, his face—so that you can see that it's all been tremendous—"

Peter spoke very slowly—"I'd give anything to see that!" he said.

"Well, it's in Bavaria; I wonder that it isn't better known. But funnily enough the people that were with me at the time didn't like it; it was only afterwards, when I showed them the photograph that they saw that there might have been ... aren't people funny?" she ended abruptly, appealing to him with a kind of freemasonry against the world.

But, still bending his brows upon it he said insistently—

"Tell me more about it—the place—everything—"

"There isn't really anything to tell; it's only a very ordinary, very beautiful, little German town. There are many orchards and this forest at the back of it and the river running through it—little cobbled streets and bridges over the river. And then, outside, this great statue on the hill—"

"Ah, but it's wonderful, that man's face—I'd like to go to that town—" He felt perhaps that he was taking it all too seriously for he turned round and said laughing: "The boy's daft on lions—Robin, come and look at this lion—here's an animal for you."

The boy put down the Toby and walked slowly and solemnly toward them. He climbed on to Peter's knee and looked at the photograph: "Oh! it is a lion!" he said at last, rubbing his fat finger on the surface of it to see of what material it was made. "Oh! for me!" he said at last in a shrill, excited voice and clutching on to it with one hand. "For me—to hang over my bed."

"No, old man," Peter answered, "it belongs to the lady here. She must take it away with her."

"Oh! but I want it!" his eyes began to fill with tears.

Miss Rossiter bent down and kissed him. He looked at her distrustfully. "I know now I'm not to have it," he said at last, eyeing her, "or you wouldn't have kissed me."

"Come on," said Peter, afraid of a scene, "the lady will show you the lion another day—meantime I think bed is the thing."

He mounted the boy on to his shoulder and turned round to Miss Rossiter to say "Good-bye." The photograph lay on the table between them—"I shan't forget that," he said.

"Oh! but you must come and see us one day. My mother will be delighted. There are a lot more photographs at home. You must bring him out one day, Norah," she said turning to Miss Monogue.

If he had been a primitive member of society in the Stone Age he would at this point, have placed Robin carefully on the floor and have picked Miss Rossiter up and she should never again have left his care.

As it was he said, "I shall be delighted to come one day."

"We will talk about Cornwall—"

"And Germany."

His hand was burning hot when he gave it her—he knew that she was looking at his eyes.

He was abruptly conscious of Miss Monogue's voice behind him.

"I've read a quarter of the book, Peter."

He wondered as he turned to her how it could be possible to regard two women so differently. To be so sternly critical of one—her hair that was nearly down, a little ink on her thumb, her blouse that was unbuttoned—and of the other to see her all in a glory so that her whole body, for colour and light and beautiful silence, had no equal amongst the possessions of the earth or the wonders of heaven. Here there was a button undone, there there was a flaming fire.

"I won't say anything," Miss Monogue said, "until I've read more, but it's going to be extraordinarily good I think." What did he care about "Reuben Hallard?" What did that matter when he had Claire Elizabeth Rossiter in front of him.

And then he pulled himself up. It must matter. How delighted an hour ago those words would have made him.

"Oh! you think there's something in it?" he said.

"We'll wait," she answered, but her smile and the sparkle in her eyes showed what she thought. What a brick she was!

He turned round back to Miss Rossiter.

"My first book," he said laughing. "Of course we're excited—"

And then he was out of the room in a moment with Robin clutching his hair. He did not want to look at her again ... he had so wonderful a picture!

And as he left Robin in the heart of his family he heard him say—

"Such a lion, Mother, a lady's got—with a man on it—a 'normous lion, and the man hasn't any clothes on, and his legs are all scratched...."

CHAPTER III

ROYAL PERSONAGES ARE COMING

I

Peter, sitting obscurely in a corner of Herr Gottfried's attic on the evening of this eventful day and listening to that string sextette that was written by Brahms when he was nineteen years of age (and it came straight from the heights of Olympus if any piece of music ever did), was conscious of the eyes of Herr Lutz.

Herr Lutz was Herr Gottfried's greatest friend and was notable for three things, his enormous size, his surpassing skill on the violoncello and his devoted attachment to the veriest shrew of a little sharp-boned wife that ever crossed from Germany into England. For all these things Peter loved him, but Herr Lutz was never very actively conscious of Peter because from the moment that he entered Herr Gottfried's attic to the moment he left it his soul was wrapped in the music and in nothing else whatever. To-night as usual he was absorbed and after the second movement of the sextette had come to a most rapturous conclusion he was violently dissatisfied and pulled them back over it again, because they had been ragged and their enthusiasm had got the better of their time and they were altogether disgraceful villains, but through all of this his grey eyes were upon Peter.

Peter, watching from his dark corner even felt that the 'cello was being played especially for his benefit and that Herr Lutz was talking all the time to him through the medium of his instrument. It may have been that he himself was in a state of most exalted emotion, and never until the end of all things mortal and possibly all things eternal will he forget that sextette by Brahms; he may perhaps have put more into Herr Lutz than was really there, but it is certain that he was conscious of the German's attention.

As is common to all persons of his age and condition he was amazed at the glorified vision of everyday things. In Herr Gottfried's flat there was a model of Beethoven in plaster of Paris, a bed, and a tin wash-hand stand, a tiny bookshelf containing some tattered volumes of Reclame's Universal Bibliothek, a piano and six cane-bottomed chairs covered at the moment by the stout bodies of the six musicians—nothing here to light the world with wonder!—and yet to-night, Peter, sitting on a cushion in a dark corner watched the glories of Olympus; the music of heaven was in his ear and before him, laughing at him, smiling, vanishing only to reappear more rapturous and beautiful than ever was the lady, the wonderful and only lady.

His cheeks were hot and his heart was beating so loudly that it was surely no wonder that Herr Lutz had discovered his malady. The sextette came to an end and the six musicians sat, for a moment, silent on their chairs whilst they dragged themselves into the world that they had for a moment forsaken. That was a great instant of silence when every one in the room was concerned entirely with their souls and had forgotten that they so much as had bodies at all. Then Herr Lutz gathered his huge frame together, stuck his hand into his beard and cried aloud for drink.

Beer was provided—conversation was, for the next two hours, volcanic. When twelve o'clock struck in the church round the corner the meeting was broken up.

Herr Lutz said to Peter, "There is still the 'verdammte' fog. Together we will go part of the way."

So they went together. But on the top of the dark and crooked staircase Herr Gottfried stopped Peter.

"Boy," he said and he rubbed his nose with his finger as he always did when he was nervous and embarrassed, "I shouldn't go to the shop for a week or two if I were you."

"Not go?" said Peter astonished.

"No—for reason why—well—who knows? The days come and they go, and again it will be all right for you. I should rub up the Editors, I should—"

"Rub up the Editors?" repeated Peter still confused.

"Yes—have other irons, you know—often enough other irons are handy—"

"Did Zanti tell you to say this to me?"

"No, he says nothing. It is only I—as a friend, you understand—"

"Well, thank you very much," said Peter at last. Herr Gottfried, he reflected, must think that he, Peter, had mints of money if he could so lightly and on so slender a warning propose his abandoning his precious two pounds a week. Moreover there was loyalty to Mr. Zanti to be considered.... Anyway, what did it all mean?

"I can't go," he said at last, "unless Zanti says something to me. But what are they all up to?"

"Seven years," said Herr Gottfried darkly, "has the Boy been in the shop—of so little enquiring a mind is he."

And he would say nothing further. Peter followed Herr Lutz' huge body into the street. They took arms when they encountered the fog and went stumbling along together.

"You are in lof," said Herr Lutz, breathlessly avoiding a lamp post.

"Yes," said Peter, "I am."

"Ah," said Herr Lutz giving Peter's arm a squeeze. "It is the only thing—The—Only—Thing.... However it may be for you—bad or ill—whether she scold or smile, it is a most blessed state."

He spoke when under stress of emotion, in capitals with a pause before the important word.

"It won't come to anything," said Peter. "It can't possibly. I haven't got anything to offer anybody—an uncertain two pounds a week."

"You have a—Career," said Herr Lutz solemnly, "I know—I have often watched you. You have written a—Book. Karl Gottfried has told me. But all that does not matter," he went on impetuously. "It does not matter what you get—It is—Being—in—Love—The—divine— never—to—be—equalled—State—"

The enormous German stopped on an island in the middle of the road and waved his arms. On every side of him through the darkness the traffic rolled and thundered. He waved his arms and exulted because he had been married to a shrew of a wife for thirty years. During that time she had never given him a kind word, not a loving look, but Peter knew that out of all the fog and obscurity that life might bring to him that Word, sprung though it might be out of Teutonic sentiment and Heller's beer, that word, at any rate, was true.

II

London, in the morning, recovered from the fog and prepared to receive Foreign Personages. They were not to arrive for another week, but it was some while since anything of the kind had occurred and London meant to carry it out well. The newspapers were crowded with details; personal anecdotes about the Personages abounded—a Procession was to take place, stands began to climb into the air and the Queen and her visitors were to have addresses presented to them at intervals during the Progress.

To Peter this all seemed supremely unimportant. At the same moment, to confuse little things with big ones, Mrs. Lazarus suddenly decided to die. She had been unwell for many months and her brain had been very clouded and temper uncertain—but now suddenly she felt perfectly well, her intelligence was as sharp and bright as it had ever been and the doctor gave her a week at the utmost. She would like, she said, to have seen the dear Queen ride through the streets amidst the plaudits of the populace, but she supposed it was not to be. So with a lace cap on her head and her nose sharp and shiny she sat up in bed, flicked imaginary bread pellets along the counterpane, talked happily to the boarding-house and made ready to die.

The boarding-house was immensely moved, and Peter, during these days came back early from the bookshop in order to sit with her. He was surprised that he cared as he did. The old lady had been for so long a part of his daily background that he could no more believe in her departure than he could in the sudden disappearance of the dark green curtains and the marble pillars in the dining-room. She had had, from the first, a great liking for Peter. He had never known how much of that affection was an incoherent madness and he had never in any way analysed his own feeling for her, but now he was surprised at the acute sharpness of his regret.

On a bright evening of sunshine, about six o'clock, she died—Mrs. Brockett, the Tressiters, Norah Monogue also were with her at the time. Peter had been with her alone during the earlier afternoon and although she had been very weak she had talked to him in her trembling voice (it was like the noise that two needles knocking against one another would make), and she had told him how she believed in him.

She made him ashamed with the things that she said about him. He had paid her little enough attention, he thought, during these seven years. There were so many things that he might have done. As the afternoon sun streamed into the room and the old lady, her hands like ivory upon the counterpane, fell into a quiet sleep he wondered—Was he bad or good? Was he strong or weak? These things that people said, the affection that people gave him ... he deserved none of it. Surely never were two so opposite presences bound together in one body—he was profoundly selfish, profoundly unselfish, loving, hard, kind, cruel, proud, humble, generous, mean, completely possessed, entirely uncontrolled, old beyond his years, young beyond belief—

As he sat there beside the sleeping old lady he felt a contempt of himself that was beyond all expression, and also he felt a pride at the things that he knew that he might do, a pride that brought the blood to his cheeks.

The Man on the Lion? The Man under the Lion's Paw?... The years would show. A quiet happy serenity passed over Mrs. Lazarus' face and he called the others into the room.

Stern Mrs. Brockett was crying. Mrs. Lazarus woke for a moment and smiled upon them all. She took Peter's hand.

"Be good to old people," she breathed very faintly—then she closed her eyes and so died.

Below in the street a boy was calling the evening papers. "Arrival of the Prince and Princess of Schloss.... Arrival of the Prince and—"

They closed the windows and pulled down the blinds.

II

Thursday was to be the day of Royal Processions, and on Friday old Mrs. Lazarus was to be buried.

To Peter, Wednesday was a day of extravagant confusion—extravagant because it was a day on which nothing was done. Customers were not served in the shop. Editors were not attacked in their lairs. Nothing was done, every one hung about.

Peter could not name any one as directly responsible for this state of things, nor could he define his own condition of mind; only he knew that he could not leave the shop. About its doors and passages there fell all day an air of suspense. Mr. Zanti was himself a little responsible for this; it was so unusual for that large and smiling gentleman to waste the day idly; and yet there he was, starting every now and again for the door, looking into the empty yard from the windows at the back of the house, disappearing sometimes into the rooms above, reappearing suddenly with an air of unconcern a little too elaborately contrived.

Peter felt that Mr. Zanti had a great deal that he would like to say to him, and once or twice he came to him and began "Oh, I say, boy," and then stopped with an air of confusion as though he had recollected something, suddenly.

There was a Russian girl, too, who was about the shop, uneasily on this day. She was thin, slight, very dark; fierce eyes and hands that seemed to be always curving. Her name was Maria Notroska and she was engaged to the big Russian, Oblotzky, whom Peter had seen, on other days up and down through the shop. She spoke to no one. She knew but little English—but she would stand for hours at the door looking out into the street. It was a long uneasy day and Peter was glad when the evening, in slow straight lines of golden light, came in through the black door. The evening too seemed to bring forward a renewed hope of seeing Stephen again—enquiries could bring nothing from either Zanti or Herr Gottfried; they had never heard of the man, oh no!... Stephen Brant? Stephen ...? No! Never—

That sudden springing out of the darkness had meant something however. Peter could still feel his wet clothes and see his shining beard. Yes, if there were any trouble Stephen would be there. What were they all about? Peter closed the shutters of the shop that night without having any explanation to offer. Mr. Zanti was indeed a strange man; when Peter turned to go he stopped him with his hand on his shoulder: "Peter, boy," he said, whispering, "come upstairs—I have something to tell you."

Peter was about to follow him back into the shop when suddenly the man shook his head. "No, not to-night," he said and almost pushed him into the street.

Peter, looking back, saw that he was talking to the Russian girl.

But the day was not over with that. Wondering about Mr. Zanti, thinking that the boarding-house would be gloomy now after Mrs. Lazarus' death, recalling, above all, to himself every slightest incident of his meeting with Miss Rossiter, Peter, crossing Oxford Street, flung his broad body against a fat and soft one. There was nearly a collapse.

The other man and Peter grasped arms to steady themselves, and then behold! the fat body was Bobby Galleon's. Bobby Galleon, after all these years! But there could be no possible doubt about it. There he stood, standing back a little from the shock, his bowler hat knocked to one side of his head, a deprecating, apologetic smile on his dear fat face! A man of course now, but very little altered in spite of all the years; a little fatter perhaps, his body seemed rather shapeless—but those same kind eyes, that large mouth and the clear straight look in all his face that spoke him to all the world for what he was.

Peter felt exactly as though, after a long and tiring journey, he had tumbled at last into a large arm-chair. He was excited, he waved his arms:

"Bobby, Bobby," he cried, so loudly that two old women in bonnets, crossing the road like a couple of hens turned to look at him.

"I'm sorry—" Bobby said vaguely, and then slowly recognition came into his eyes.

"Peter!" he said in a voice lost in amazement, the colour flooding his cheeks.

It was all absurdly moving; they were quite ridiculously stirred, both of them. The lamps were coming out down Oxford Street, a pale saffron sky outlined the dark bulk of the Church that is opposite Mudie's shop and stands back from the street, a little as though it wondered at all the noise and clamour, a limpid and watery blue still lingered, wavering, in the evening sky.

They turned into an A.B.C. shop and ordered glasses of milk and they sat and looked at one another. They had altered remarkably little and to both of them, although the roar of the Oxford Street traffic was outside the window, it might have been, easily enough, that a clanging bell would soon summon them back to ink-stained desks and Latin exercises.

"Why, in heaven's name, did you ever get out of my sight so completely? I wrote to Treliss again and again but I don't suppose anything was forwarded."

"They don't know where I am."

"But why did you never write to me?"

"Why should I? I wanted to do something first—to show you-"

"What rot! Is that friendship? I call that the most selfish thing I've ever known." No, obviously enough, Bobby could never understand that kind of thing. With him, once a friend always a friend, that is what life is for. With Peter, once an adventure always an adventure—that is what life is for—but as soon as a friend ceases to be an adventure, why then—

But Bobby had not ceased to be an adventure. He was, as he sat there, more of one than he had ever been before.

"What have you been doing all these years?"

"Been in a bookshop."

"In a bookshop?"

"Yes, selling second-hand books."

"What else?"

"Oh reading a lot... seeing one or two people... and some music." Peter was vague; what after all had he been doing?

Bobby looked at him tenderly and affectionately. "You want seeing after—you look fierce, as you used to when you'd been having a bad time at school. The day they all hissed you."

"But I haven't been having a bad time. I've had a jolly good one. By the way," Peter leant forward, "have you seen or heard anything of Cards?"

Bobby coloured a little. "No, not for a long time. His mother died. He's a great swell now with heaps of money, I believe. I'm not his sort a bit."

They drank milk and beamed upon one another. Peter wanted to tell Bobby everything. That was one of his invaluable qualities, that one did like telling him everything. Talking to him eagerly now, Peter wondered how it could be that he'd ever managed to get through these many years without him. Bobby simply existed to help his friends and that was the kind of person that Peter had so often wanted.

But in it all—in their talking, their laughing together, their remembering certain catchwords that they had used together, there was nothing more remarkable than their finding each other exactly as they had been during those years before at Dawson's. Not even Bobby's tremendous statement could alter that.

"I'm married," he said.

"Married?"

Bobby blushed. "Yes—two years now—got a baby. She's quite splendid!"

"Oh!" Peter was a little blank. Somehow this did remove Bobby a little—it also made him, suddenly, strangely old.

"But it doesn't make any difference," Bobby said, leaning forward eagerly and putting his hand on Peter's arm—"not the least difference. You two will simply get on famously. I've so often told her about you and we've always been hoping that you'd turn up again—and now she'll be simply delighted."

But it made a difference to Peter, nevertheless. He went back a little into his shell; Bobby with a home and a wife and a baby couldn't spare time, of course, for ordinary friends. But even here his conscience pricked him. Did he not know Bobby well enough to be assured that he was as firm and solid as a rock, that nothing at all could move or change him? And after all, was not he, Peter, wishing to be engaged and married and the father of a family and the owner of a respectable mansion?

Clare Elizabeth Rossiter! How glorious for an instant were the thin, sharp-faced waitresses, the little marble-topped tables, the glass windows filled with sponge-cakes and hard-boiled eggs!

Peter came out of his shell again. "I shall just love to come and see her," he said.

"Well, just as soon as you can. By Jove, old man, I'll never let you go again. Now tell me, everything—all that you have done since I saw you."

Peter told him a great deal—not quite everything. He told him nothing, for instance, about meeting a certain young lady on a Good Friday afternoon and he passed over some of the Scaw House incidents as speedily as possible.

"And since I came up to London," he went on, "the whole of my time has been spent either in the bookshop or the boarding-house. They're awfully good sorts at both, but it's all very uncertain of course and instead of writing a novel that no one will want to read I ought to have been getting on to editors. I've a kind of feeling that the bookshop's going to end very shortly."

"Let me see the book," said Bobby.

"Yes, certainly," said Peter.

"Anyhow, we go on together from this time forth—72 Cheyne Walk is my little house. When will you come—to-morrow?"

"Oh! To-morrow! I don't think I can. There are these Processions and things—I think I ought to be in the shop. But I'll come very soon. This is the name of my boarding-house—"

Bobby, as he saw his friend, broad-shouldered, swinging along, pass down the street with the orange lamps throwing chains of light about him, was confronted again by that old elusive spirit that he had known so well at school. Peter liked him, Peter was glad to see him again, but there were so many other Peters, so many doors closed against intruders.... Bobby would always, to the end, be for Peter, outside these doors. He knew it quite certainly, a little sadly, as he climbed on to his bus. What was there about Peter? Something hard, fierce, wildly hostile ... a devil, a God. Something that Bobby going quietly home to his comfortable dinner, might watch and guard and even love but something that he could never share.

Now, in the cool and quiet of the Chelsea Embankment as he walked to his door, Bobby sighed a little because life was so comfortable.

CHAPTER IV

A LITTLE DUST

I

That night Peter had one of his old dreams. In all the seven years that he had been in London the visions that had so often made his nights at Scaw House terrible had never come to him. Now, after so long an interval they returned.

He thought that he was once more back on the sea-road above Treliss, that the wind was blowing in a tempest and that the sea below him was foaming on to the rocks. He could see those rocks like sharp black teeth, stretching up to him—a grey sky was above his head and to his right stretched the grey and undulating moor.

Round the bend of the road, beyond the point that he could see, he thought that Clare Rossiter was waiting for him. He must get there before it struck eleven or something terrible would happen to him. Only a few minutes remained to him, and only a little stretch of the thin white road, but two things prevented his progress; first, the wind blew so fiercely in his face that it drove him back and for every step that he took forward, although his head was bent and his teeth set, he seemed to lose two. Also, across the moor voices cried to him and they seemed to him like the voices of Stephen and Bobby Galleon, and they were pleading to him to stop; he paused to listen but the cries mingled softly with the wind and he could hear bells from the town below the road begin to strike eleven. The sweat was pouring from him—she was waiting for him, and if he did not reach her all would be lost. He would never see her again; he began to cry, to beat against the wind with his hands. The voices grew louder, the wind more vehement, the jagged edges of the rocks sharper in their outline; the bells were still striking, but as, at last, breathless, a sharp terror at his heart, he turned the corner there fell suddenly a silence. At last he was there—only a few trees blowing a little, a little white dust curling over the road, as though there had been no rain, and then suddenly the laughing face of Cards, no longer now a boy, but a man, more handsome than ever, laughing at him as he battled round the corner.

Cards shouted something to him, suddenly the road was gone and Peter was in the water, fighting for his life. He felt all the breathless terror of approaching death—he was sinking—black, silent water rose above and around him. For an instant he caught once more the sight of sky and land. Cards was still on the road and beside him was a woman whose face Peter could not see. Cards was still laughing. Then in the darkening light the Grey Hill was visible against the horizon and instead of the Giant's Finger there was that figure of the rider on the lion.... The waters closed.... Peter woke to a grey, stormy morning. The sweat was pouring down his face, his body was burning hot and his hands were trembling.

II

When he came down to breakfast his head was aching and heavy and Mrs. Brockett's boiled egg and hard crackling toast were impossible. Miss Monogue had things to tell him about the book—it was wonderful, tremendous ... beyond everything that she had believed possible. But strangely enough, he was scarcely interested. He was pleased of course, but he was weighted with the sense of overhanging catastrophe. The green bulging curtains, the row of black beads about Mrs. Brockett's thin neck, the untidy egg-shells—everything depressed him.

"I have had a rotten night," he said, "nightmares. I suppose I ate something—anyhow it's a gloomy day."

"Yes," said Miss Monogue, pinning some of her hair in at the wrong place and unpinning other parts of it that happened by accident to be right. "I'm afraid it's a poor sort of day for the Procession. But Miss Black and I are going to do our best to see it. It may clear up later." He had forgotten about the Procession and he wished that she would keep her hair tidier.

He wanted to ask her whether she had seen Miss Rossiter but had not the courage. A little misty rain made feathery noises against the window-pane.

"Well, I must go down to the shop," he said, finding his umbrella in the hall.

"I think it's superb," she said, referring back to the book. "You won't be having to go down to the shop much longer."

It was really surprising that he cared so little. He banged the door behind him and did not see her eyes as she watched him go.

Processions be damned! He wished that the wet, shining street were not so strangely like the sea-road at Treliss, and that the omnibuses at a distance did not murmur like the sea. People, black and funereal, were filling stands down Oxford Street; soldiers were already lining the way, the music of bands could be heard some streets away.

He was in a thoroughly bad temper and scowled at the people who passed him. He hated Royal Processions, he hated the bookshop, he hated all his friends and he wished that he were dead. Here he had been seven years, he reflected, and nothing had been done. Where was his city paved with gold? Where his Fame, where his Glory?

He even found himself envying those old Treliss days. There at any rate things had happened. There had been an air, a spirit. Fighting his father—or at any rate, escaping from his father—had been something vital. And here he was now, an ill-tempered, useless youth, earning two pounds a week, in love with some one who was scarcely conscious of his existence. He cursed the futility of it all.

And so fuming, he crossed the threshold of the bookshop, and, unwitting, heedless, left for ever behind him the first period of his history.

"Programme of the Royal Procession," a man was shouting—"Coloured 'Andkerchief with Programme of Royal Procession—"

Peter, stepping into the dark shop, was conscious of Mr. Zanti's white face and that behind him was standing Stephen.

III

At the sight of their faces, of their motionless bodies and at the solemn odd expression of their eyes as they looked past him into the dark expanse of the door through which he had entered, he knew that something was very wrong.

He had known it, plainly enough, by the fact of Stephen's presence there, but it seemed to him that he had known it from his first awakening that morning and that he was only waiting to change into hard outline the misty shapelessness of his earlier fears. But, there and then, he was to know nothing—

Stephen greeted him with a great hand-shake as though he had met him only the day before, and Mr. Zanti with a smile gave him his accustomed greeting. In the doorway at the other end of the shop the Russian girl was standing, one arm on the door-post, staring, with her dark eyes, straight through into the gloomy street.

"What are you all waiting for?" Peter said to the motionless figures. With his words they seemed at once to spring to life. Mr. Zanti rolled his big body casually to the door and looked down the street, Stephen, smiling at Peter said:

"I was just passing, so I thought to myself I'd just look in," his voice came from his beard like the roll of the sea from a cave. "Just for an hour, maybe. It's a long day since we've 'ad a bit of a chat, Mr. Peter."

Peter could not take it on that casual scale. Here was Stephen vanished during all those years, returned now suddenly and with as little fuss as possible, as though indeed he had only been hiding no farther than behind the door of the shop and waiting merely to walk out when the right moment should have arrived. If he had been no farther than that then it was unkind of him—he might have known how badly Peter had wanted him; if, on the other hand, he had been farther afield, then he should show more excitement at his return.

But, Peter thought, it was impossible to recognise in the grave reserved figure at his side that Stephen who had once given him the most glorious evening of his life. The connection was there somewhere but many things must have happened between those years.

"Shall we go and have luncheon together?" Peter asked.

Stephen appeared to fling a troubled look in the direction of Mr. Zanti's broad back. He hesitated. "Well," he said awkwardly, "I don't rightly know. I've got to be going out for an hour or two—I can't rightly say as I'll be back. This afternoon, maybe—"

Peter did not press it any farther. They must settle these things for themselves, but what was the matter with them all this morning was more than he could pretend to discover.

Stephen, still troubled, went out.

Fortunately there was this morning a good deal of work for Peter to do. A large number of second-hand books had arrived during the day before and they must be catalogued and arranged. Moreover there were several customers. A young lady wanted "something about Wagner, just a description of the plays, you know."

"Of the Operas," Peter corrected.

"Oh, well, the stories—that's what I want—something about two shillings, have you? I don't think it's really worth more—but so that one will know where one is, you know."

She was bright and confidential. She had thought that everything would be closed because of the Procession... so lucky—

A short red-faced woman, dressed in bright colours, and carrying innumerable little parcels wanted "Under Two Flags," by Mrs. Henry Wood.

"It's by Ouida, Madam," Peter told her.

"Nonsense, don't tell me. As if I didn't know."

Peter produced the volume and showed it to her. She dropped some of her parcels—they both went to pick them up.

Red in the face, she glared at him. "Really it's too provoking, I know it was Mrs. Henry Wood I wanted."

"Perhaps 'East Lynne,' or 'The Channings'—"

"Nonsense—don't tell me—it was 'Under Two Flags.'"

Finally the woman put both "Under Two Flags" and "East Lynne" into her bag and departed. A silence fell upon the shop. Herr Gottfried was at his desk, Mr. Zanti at the street door, the girl at the door of the inner room, they were all motionless. Beyond the shop the murmur of the gathering crowd was like the confused, blundering hum of bees; a band was playing stridently in Oxford Street.

Once Peter said: "It passes about three-thirty, doesn't it? I think I'll just go out and have a look later. It'll be fine if only the sun comes."

Mr. Zanti turned slowly round.

"I'm afraid, boy," he said, "you'll be wanted in ze shop. At two Herr Gottfried must be going out for some business—zere will be no one—I am zo zorry."

They wanted to keep him there, that was evident. Or, at any rate, they didn't want him to see the Procession.

"Very well," he said cheerfully, "I'll stay. There'll be plenty more Processions before I die." But why, why, why? What was there that they wanted him to avoid?

He went on arranging the piles of dusty books, the sense of weighty expectation growing on him with every instant. The clock struck one, but he did not go out to luncheon; the others were still motionless in their places.

Once Herr Gottfried spoke: "The people will have been waiting a much-more-than-necessary long time," he said. "The police doubtless have frightened them, but there is still room to walk in the streets and there have been some unfortunates, since early in the morning—"

The street beyond the shop was now deserted because soldiers guarded its approach into Oxford Street; the shop seemed to be left high and dry, beyond the noise and confusion of the street.

Then there came into the silence a sharp sound that made Peter amongst his books, jump to his feet: the Russian girl was crying.

She stood there, leaning her thin dark body against the side of the door, surely the most desolate figure in the world. Her hands were about her face, her body heaved with her sobbing and the little sad noise came into the dusty tangled room and hung amongst the old broken books as though they only could sympathise and give it shelter. The band in Oxford Street was blazing with sound but it did not hide her crying.

Mr. Zanti crossed to her and spoke to her but she suddenly let her hands fall from her face and turned upon him, furiously, wildly—"You ..." she said, "You ..." and then as though the words choked her she turned back into the inner room. Peter saw Mr. Zanti's face and it was puckered with distress like a child's. It was almost laughable in its helpless dismay.

Two o'clock struck. "They'll be starting in half an hour," Herr Gottfried said.

"Women," Mr. Zanti said, still looking distressfully about him, "they are, in truth, very difficult."

And now there was no pretence, any longer, of disguising the nervous tension that was with them in the room. They were all waiting for something—what it might be Peter did not know, but, with every tick of the old brass clock, some event crept more nearly towards them.

Then Stephen came back.

He came in very quietly as though he were trying to keep the note of agitation that he must have felt on every side of him as near the normal as possible.

His face above his beard was grey and streaky and his breath came rapidly as though he had been running. When he saw Mr. Zanti his hand went up suddenly in front of his face as though he would protect himself from the other's questioning.

"I've 'eard nothing—" he said almost sullenly and then he turned and looked at Peter.

"Why must 'e be 'ere?" he said sharply to Zanti.

"Why not? Where else?" the other answered and the two men watched each other with hostility across the floor.

"I wish we'd all bloomin' wull kept out of it," Stephen murmured to himself it seemed.

Peter's eyes were upon Mr. Zanti. That gentleman looked more like a naughty child than ever. In his eyes there was the piteous appeal of a small boy about to be punished for some grievous fault. In some strange way Peter was, it appeared, his court of appeal because he glanced towards him again and again and then looked away.

Peter could stand it no longer. He got up from the place where he was and faced them all.

"What is it? What have you all done? What is the matter with you all?"

The Russian girl had come back. Her face was white and her hair fell untidily about her eyes. She came forward fiercely as though she would have answered Peter, but Mr. Zanti motioned her back with his hand.

"No, no," he said almost imploringly, "let the boy be—what has he to do with all this? Leave him. He has nothing to do with it. He knows nothing."

"But I ought to know," Peter burst in. "Why have I been kept in the dark all this time? What right have you—"

He broke off suddenly. Absolute silence fell amongst them all and they stood looking at the door, motionless, in their places. There was a new note in the murmuring of the crowd, and the swift steady passing of it came up the street to the shop and in at the door. Voices could be heard rising above others, and then the eager passing of some piece of news from one to another.

No one in the shop spoke. Outside in the deserted street there was silence and then the bands, as though driven by some common wave of feeling, seemed at the same moment to burst into a blare of music. Some voice, from the crowd, started "God save the Queen" and immediately it was taken up and flung into the air by a thousand voices. They must give vent to their feelings, some news had passed down the crowds like a flame setting fire to a chain of beacons.

"What is it?" Peter pressed forwards to the door. And at once he was answered. Men were running past the shop, crying out; one stopped for an instant and, wild with excitement, his hands gesticulating, stammering, the words tumbling from his lips, he shouted at them—"They've bin flinging bombs ... dirty foreigners ... up there by the Marble Arch—flinging them at the Old Lady. But it's all right, by Gawd—only blew 'imself up, dirty foreigner—little bits of 'im and no one else 'urt and now the Old Lady's comin' down the street—she'll be 'ere in quarter of an 'our and won't we show 'er ... by Gawd ... flingin' their dirty bombs up there by the Marble Arch and killin' nobody but 'imself—Gawd save the Old Lady—" he rushed on.

So that was it. Peter, standing in the middle of the room, looked at them all and understood at last amongst whom he had been working these seven years. They were murderers, the lot of them—all of them—Gottfried, Zanti ... Stephen—Oh God! Stephen! He understood now for what they had been waiting.

He turned sick at the sudden realisation of it. It did not, at first, seem to touch himself in any way. At the first immediate knowledge of it he had been faced by its amazing incongruity. There by the Marble Arch, with bands flying, flags waving, in all the tumult of a Royal Progress some one had been blown into little pieces. Elsewhere there were people waiting, eating buns out of paper bags, and here in the shop the sun lighted the backs of rows of second-hand novels and down in Treliss the water was, very gently, lapping the little wooden jetty. Oh! the silly jumbling of things in this silly jumbling world!

And then he began to look more closely into it as it concerned himself. He saw with amazing clearness. He knew that it was Oblotzky the tall Russian who had been killed. He knew because Oblotzky was the lover of this Russian girl and he turned round to watch her, curiously, as one who was outside it all. She was standing with her back against the wall, her hands spread out flat, looking through the door into the bright street, seeing none of them. Then she turned and said something in Russian between her clenched teeth to Mr. Zanti. He would have answered her but very quietly and speaking now in English she flung at him, as though it had been a stone:

"God curse you! You drove him to it!" Then she turned round and left the room. But the tall man was blubbering like a child. He had turned round to them all, with his hands outstretched, appealing:

"But it's not true!" he cried between his sobs, "it's not true! I did all I could to stop them—I did not know that they would do things—not really—until now, this morning, when it was too late. It is the others, Sergius, Paslov, Odinsky—zey were always wild, desperate. But we, the rest of us, with us it was only tall words."

Little Herr Gottfried, who had been silent behind them, came forward now and spoke:

"It is too late," he said, "for this crying like a baby. We have no time—we must consider what must be done. If it is true, what that man says that Oblotzky has blown himself up and no other is touched then no harm is done. Why regret the Russian? He wanted a violent end and he has got it—and he has given it to no other. Often enough we are not so fortunate. He will have spoken to no one. We are safe." Then he turned to Peter:

"Poor boy," he said.

But Peter was not there to be pitied. He had only one thought, "Stephen, tell me—tell me. You did not know? You had nothing to do with this?"

Stephen turned and faced him. "No, Peter boy, nothing. I did not know what they were at. They—Zanti there—'ad 'elped me when I was in trouble years ago. They've given me jobs before now, but they've always been bunglers and now, thank the Lord, they've bungled again. You come with me, Mr. Peter—come along from it all. We'll manage something. I've only been waiting until you wanted me."

Zanti turned furiously upon him but the words that he would have spoken were for the moment held. The Procession was passing. The roar of cheering came up against the walls of the shop like waves against the rocks; the windows shook. There she was, the little Old Lady in her black bonnet, sitting smiling and bowing, and somewhere behind her a little dust had been blown into the air, had hung for a moment about her and then had once more settled down into the other dust from which it had come.

That was all. In front of her were the Royal Personages, on every side of her her faithful subjects ... only a cloud of dust had given occasion for a surer sign of her people's devotion. That, at any rate, Oblotzky had done.

The carriage passed.

Mr. Zanti now faced Peter.

"Peter—Boy—you must believe me. I did not know, believe me, I did not. They had talked and I had listened but there is so much talk and never anything is done. Peter, you must not go, you must not leave me. You would break my 'eart—"

"All these years," Peter said, "you have let me be here while you have deceived me and blinded me. I am going now and I pray to God that I may never see you again."

"No, Boy, listen. You must not go like this. 'Ave I not been good to you? 'Ave I ever made you do anything wrong? 'Ave I not always kept you out of these things? You are the only person zat I 'ave ever loved. You 'ave become my son to me. I am not wicked. I was not one of these men—these anarchists—but it is only that all my life I 'ave wanted adventure, what you call Ro-mance. And I 'ave found it 'ere, there—'one place, anuzzer place. But it 'as never been wicked—I 'ave never 'armed a soul. What zat girl says it is not true—I would 'ave done all to stop it if I could. But you—if you leave me now, I am all alone. There is no one in the world for me—a poor old man—but if you will be with me I will show you wonderful things.

"See," he went on eagerly, almost breathlessly, "we 'ave been socialists 'ere, what you will. We 'ave talked and talked. It amuses me—to intrigue, to pretend, to 'ave games—one day it is Treason, another

Brigands, another Travel—what you will. But never, never, never danger to a soul. Now only this morning did I 'ear that they were going to do this. Always it had been words before—but this morning I got a rumour. But it was only rumour. I 'ad not enough to be sure of my news. Stephen here and I—we could do nozzing—we 'ad no time—I did not know where Oblotzky was—this girl 'ere did not know—I could do nozzing—Peter, believe me, believe me—"

The man was no scoundrel. It was plain enough as he stood there, his eyes simple as a child's, pleading still like a small boy.

A minute ago Peter had hated him, now he crossed over and put his hand on his shoulder.

"You have been wonderfully good to me," he said. "I owe you everything. But I must go—all this has only made sure what I have been knowing this long time that I ought to do. I can't—I mustn't—depend on your charity any longer—it has been too long as it is. I must be on my own and then one day, when I have proved myself, I will come back to you."

"No—Peter, Boy—come with me now. I will show you wonderful things all over Europe; we will have adventures. There is gold in Cornwall in a place I know. There is a place in Germany where there is treasure—ze world is full of ze most wonderful things that I know and you and I—we two—Oh! ze times we all 'ave—"

"No," ... Peter drew back. "That is not my way. I am going to make my living here, in London—or die for it."

"No—you must not. You will succeed—you will grow fat and sleepy and ze good things of the world and ze many friends will kill your soul. I know it ... but come with me, first and we will 'ave adventures ... and zen you shall write."

But Peter's face was set. The time for the new life had come. Up to this moment he had been passive, he had used his life as an instrument on which others might play. From henceforward his should be the active part.

The crowds were pouring up the street on their homeward way. Bands were playing the soldiers back to the barracks. Soon the streets would have only the paper bags left to them for company. The little bookshop hung, with its misty shelves about the three men.... Somewhere in another room, a girl was staring with white set face and burning eyes in front of her, for her lover was dead and the world had died with him.

After a little time amongst the second-hand novels Mr. Zanti sat, his great head buried in his hands, the tears trickling down through his fingers, and Herr Gottfried, motionless from behind his counter watched him in silent sympathy.

Peter and Stephen had gone together.

CHAPTER V

I

The bomb was, that evening, the dominant note of the occasion. Through the illuminated streets, the slowly surging crowds—inhuman in their abandon to the monotonous ebb and flow as of a sweeping river—the cries and laughter and shouting of songs, that note was above all. An eye-witness—a Mr. Frank Harris, butcher of 82 Cheapside—had his veracious account journalistically doctored.

"I was standing quite close to the man, a foreigner of course, with a dirty hanging black moustache—tall, big fellow, with coat up over his ears—I must say that I wasn't looking at him. I had Mrs. Harris with me and was trying to get her a place where she could see better, you understand. Then suddenly—before one was expecting it—the Procession began and I forgot the man, the foreigner, although he was quite up close against me. One was excited of course—a most moving sight—and then suddenly, when by the distant shouting we understood that the Queen was approaching, I saw the man break through. I was conscious of the man's vigour as he rushed past—he must have been immensely strong—because there he was, through the soldiers and everybody—out in the middle of the street. It all happened so quickly of course. I heard vaguely that some one was shouting and I think a policeman started forward, but anyhow the man raised his arm and in an instant there was the explosion. It went off before he was ready I suppose, but the ground rocked under one's feet. Two soldiers fell, unhurt, I have learnt since. There was a hideous dust, horses plunging and men shouting and then suddenly silence. The dust cleared and there was a hole in the ground, stones rooted up ... no sign of the man but some pieces of cloth and men had rushed forward and covered something up—a limb I suppose.... I was only anxious of course that my wife should see nothing ... she was considerably affected...."

So Mr. Harris of Cheapside, with the assistance of an eager and talented young journalist. But the fact remained in the heart of the crowd—blasted foreigner had had a shot at the Old Lady and missed her, therefore whatever gaiety may have been originally intended let it now be redoubled, shouted into frenzy—and frenzy it was.

"There was no clue," an evening paper added to the criminal's identity.... The police were blamed, of course.... Such a thing must never be allowed to occur again. It was reported that the Queen had in no way suffered from the shock—was in capital health.

Outside the bookshop Stephen and Peter had parted.

"I'll meet you about half-past ten, Trafalgar Square by the lion that faces Whitehall; I must go back to Brockett's, have supper and get my things, and say good-bye. Then I'll join you ... half-past ten."

"Peter boy, we'll have to rough it—"

"Oh! at last! Life's beginning. We'll soon get work, both of us—where do you mean to go?"

"There's a place I been before—down East End—not much of a place for your sort, but just for a bit...."

For a moment Peter's thoughts swept back to the shop.

"Poor Zanti!" He half turned. "After so many years ... the good old chap." Then he pulled himself up and set his shoulders. "Well, half-past ten—"

The streets were, at the instant, almost deserted. It was about five o'clock now and at seven o'clock they would be closed to all traffic. Then the surging crowds would come sweeping down.

Peter, furiously excited, hurried through the grimy deserts of Bloomsbury, to Brockett's. To his singing, beating heart the thin ribbon of the grey street with the faint dim blue of the evening sky was out of place, ill-judged as a setting to his exultations. He had swept in the tempestuous way that was natural to him, the shop and all that it had been to him, behind him. Even Brockett's must go with the rest. Of course he could not stay there now that the weekly two pounds had stopped. He quite savagely desired to be free from all business. These seven years had been well enough as a preparation; now at last he was to be flung, head foremost, into life.

He could have sung, he could have shouted. He burst through the heavy doors of Brockett's. But there, inside the quiet and solemn building, another mood seized him. He crept quietly, on tiptoe, up to his room because he did not want to see any of them before supper. After all, he was leaving the best friends that he had ever had, the only home that he had ever really known. Mrs. Brockett, Norah Monogue, Robin, the Signor.... Seven years is a long time and one gets fond of a place. He closed his bedroom door softly behind him. The little room had been very much to him during all these years, and that view over the London roofs would never be forgotten by him. But he wondered, as he looked at it, how he had ever been able to sit there so quietly and write "Reuben Hallard." Now, between his writing and himself, a thousand things were sweeping. Far away he saw it like the height of some inaccessible hill—his emotions, his adventures, the excitement of life made his thoughts, his ideas, thinner than smoke. He even, standing there in his little room and looking over the London roofs, despised the writer's inaction.... Often again he was to know that rivalry.

A quarter of an hour before supper he went down to say good-bye to Miss Monogue. She was sitting quietly reading and he thought suddenly, as he came upon her, there under the light of her candles in the grey room, that she did not look well. He had never during their seven years' friendship, noticed anything before, and now he could not have said what it was that he saw except perhaps that her cheeks were flushed and that there were heavy dark lines beneath her eyes. But she seemed to him, as he took her, thus unprepared, with her untidy hair and her white cheap evening dress that showed her thin fragile arms, to be something that he was leaving to face the world alone, something very delicate that he ought not to leave.

Then she looked up and saw him and put her book down and smiled at him and was the old cheerful Norah Monogue whom he had always known.

He stood with his legs apart facing her and told her:

"I've come to say good-bye."

"Good-bye?"

"Yes—I'm going to-night. What I've been expecting for so long has happened at last. There's been a blow up at the bookshop and I've got to go."

For an instant the colour left her face; her book fell to the ground and she put her hand back on the arm of the chair to steady herself.

"Oh! how silly of me ... never mind picking it up.... Oh thank you, Peter. You gave me quite a shock, telling me like that. We shall all miss you dreadfully."

His affection for her was strong enough to break in upon the great overwhelming excited exultation that had held him all the evening. He was dreadfully sorry to leave her!... dear Norah Monogue, what a pal she'd been!

"I shall miss you horribly," he said with that note in his voice that showed that, above all things, he wished to avoid a scene. "We've been such tremendous pals all this time—you've been such a brick—I don't know what I should have done...." He pulled himself up. "But it's got to be. I've felt it coming you know and it's time I really lashed out for myself."

"Where are you going?"

"Ah! I must keep that dark for a bit. There's been trouble at the bookshop. It'll be all right I expect but I don't want Mother Brockett to stand any chance of being mixed up in it. I shall just disappear for a week or two and then I'll be back again."

She smiled at him bravely: "Well, I won't ask what's happened, if you don't want to tell me, but of course—I shall miss you. After seven years it seems so abrupt. And, Peter, do take care of yourself."

"Oh, I shall be all right." He was very gruff. He felt now a furious angry reluctance at leaving her behind. He stormed at himself as a fool; one of the things that the strong man must learn of life is to be ruthless in these partings and breaking of relations. He stood further away from her and spoke as though he hated being there.

She understood him with wonderful tenderness.

"Well," she said cheerfully, "I daresay it will be better for you to try for a little and see what you can make of it all. And then if you want anything you'll come back to us, won't you?... You promise that?"

"Of course."

"And then there's the book. I know that man in Heriot and Lord's that I told you about. I'll send it to them right away, if you like."

"Aren't they rather tremendous people for me to begin with? Oughtn't I to begin with some one smaller?"

"Oh! there's no harm in starting at the top. They can't do more than refuse it. But I don't think they will. I believe in it. But how shall I let you know what they say?"

"Oh, I'll come in a week or two and see what's happening—I'll be on a paper by then probably. I say, I don't want the others to know. I'll have supper with them as usual and just tell Mother Brockett afterwards. I don't want to have to say good-bye lots of times. Well"—he moved off awkwardly towards the door—"You've been most tremendously good to me."

"Rot, Peter: Don't forget me!"

"Forget you! The best pal I've ever had." They clasped hands for a moment. There was a pause and then Peter said: "I say—there is a thing you can do if you like—"

"Yes?—anything—"

"Well—about Miss Rossiter—you'll be seeing her I suppose?"

"Oh yes, often—"

"Well, you might just keep her in mind of me. I know it sounds silly but—just a word or two, sometimes."

He felt that he was blushing—their hands separated. She moved back from him and pushed at her hair in the nervous way that she had.

"Why, of course—she was awfully interested. She won't forget you. Well, we'll meet at supper." She moved back with a last little nod at him and he went awkwardly out of the room with a curious little sense of sudden dismissal. Would she rather he didn't know Miss Rossiter, he vaguely wondered. Women were such queer creatures.

As he went downstairs he wondered with a sudden almost shameful confusion whether he was responsible in some way for the awkwardness that the scene had had. He had noticed lately that she had not been quite herself when he had been with her—that she would stop in the middle of a sentence, that she would be, for instance, vexed at something he said, that she would look at him sometimes as though ...

He pulled himself up. He was angry with himself for imagining such a thing—as though ... Well, women were strange creatures....

And then supper was more difficult than he had expected. They would show him, the silly things, that they were fond of him just when he would much rather have persuaded himself that they hated him. It was almost, as he told himself furiously, as though they knew that he was going; Norah Monogue was the only person who chattered and laughed in a natural way; he was rather relieved that after all she seemed to care so little.

He found that he couldn't eat. There was a silly lump in his throat and he looked at the marble pillars and the heavy curtains through a kind of mist.... Especially was there Robin....

Mrs. Tressiter told him that Robin had something very important to say to him and that he was going to stay awake until he, Peter, came up to him.

"I told him," she said, "that he must lie down and go to sleep like a good boy and that his father would punish him if he didn't. But there! What's the use of it? He isn't afraid of his father the slightest. He would go on—something about a lion...."

At any rate this gave Peter an excuse to escape from the table and it was, indeed, time, for they had all settled, like a clatter of hens, on to the subject of the bomb, and they all had a great deal to say about it and a great many questions to ask Peter.

"It's these Foreigners... of course our Police are entirely inadequate."

"Yes—that's what I say—the Police are really absurdly inadequate—"

"If they will allow these foreigners—"

"Yes, what can you expect—and the Police really can't—"

Peter escaped to Robin. He glowered down at the child who was sitting up in his cot counting the flowers on the old wall-paper to keep himself awake.

"I always am so muddled after fourteen," he said. "Never mind, I'm not sleeping—"

Peter frowned at him. "You ought to have been asleep long ago," he said. He wished the boy hadn't got his hair tousled in that absurdly fascinating way and that his cheeks weren't flushed so beautiful a red— also his nightgown had lost a button at the top and showed a very white little neck. Peter blinked his eyes—"Look here, kid, you must go to sleep right away at once. What do you want?"

"It's that lion—the one the lady had—I want it."

"You can't have it—the lady's got it."

"Well—take me to see them—the real ones—there are lots somewhere Mother says." Robin inserted his very small hand into Peter's large one.

"All right, one day—we'll go to the 'Zoo."

Robin sighed with satisfaction—he lay down and murmured sleepily to himself, "I love Mister Peter and lions and Mother and God," and was suddenly asleep.

Peter bent down over the cot and kissed him. He felt miserably wretched. He had known nothing like it since that day when he had said good-bye to his mother. He wondered that he could ever have felt any exultation; he wondered that writing and glory and ambition could ever have seemed worth anything to him at all. Could he have had his prayer granted he would have prayed that he might always stay in Brockett's, always have these same friends, watch over Robin as he grew up, talk to Norah Monogue— and then all the others ... and Mr. Zanti. He felt fourteen years old ... more miserable than he had ever been.

He kissed Robin again—then he went down to find Mrs. Brockett. Here, too, he was faced with an unexpected difficulty. The good lady, listening to him sternly in her grim little sitting-room, refused to hear of his departure. She sat upright in her stiff chair, her thin black dress in folds about her, the gas-light shining on her neatly parted hair.

"You see, Mrs. Brockett," he explained to her, "I'm no longer in the same position. I can't be sure of my two pounds a week any more and so it wouldn't be right for me to live in a place like this."

"If it's expense that you're thinking about," she answered him grimly, "you're perfectly welcome to stay on here and pay me when you can. I'm sure that one day with so clever a young man—"

"That's awfully good of you, Mrs. Brockett, but of course I couldn't hear of anything like that." For the third time that evening he had to fight against a disposition to blow his nose and be absurd. They were, both of them, increasingly grim with every word that they spoke and any outside observer would have supposed that they were the deadliest of enemies.

"Of course," she began again, "there's a room that I could let you have at the back of the house that's only four shillings a week and really you'd be doing me a kindness in taking it off my hands. I'm sure—"

"No, there's more in it than that," he answered. "I've got to go away—right away. It's time I had a change of scene. It's good for me to get along a bit by myself. You've all been too kind to me, spoilt me—"

She stood up and faced him sternly. "In all my years," she said, "I've never spoilt anybody yet and I'm not likely to be going to begin now. Spoilt you! Bah!" She almost snorted at him—but there were tears in her eyes.

"I'm not a philanthropist," she went on more dryly than ever, "but I like to have you about the house—you keep the lodgers contented and the babies quiet. I'm sure," and the little break in her voice was the first sign of submission, "that we've been very good friends these seven years and it isn't everywhere that one can pick up friends for the asking—"

"You've been splendid to me," he answered. "But it isn't as though I were going away altogether—you'll see me back in a week or two. And—and—I say I shall make a fool of myself if I go on talking like this—"

He suddenly gripped her hand and wrung it again and again—then he burst away from her, leaving her standing there in the middle of the room.

The old black bag was very soon packed, his possessions had not greatly increased during these seven years, and soon he was creeping down the stairs softly so that no one should hear.

The hall was empty. He gave it one last friendly look, the door had closed behind him and he was in the street.

II

In its exuberance and high spirits and general lack of self-control London was similar to a small child taken to the Drury Lane Pantomime for the first time. Of the numbers of young men who, with hats on the back of their heads, passed arm-in-arm down the main thoroughfares announcing it as their definite opinion that "Britons never shall be slaves," of the numbers of young women who, armed with feathers and the sharpest of tongues, showed conclusively the superiority of their sex and personal attractions, of the numbers of old men and old women who had no right whatever to be out on a night like this but couldn't help themselves, and enjoyed it just as much as their sons and daughters did, there is here no room to tell. The houses were ablaze with light, the very lamp-posts seemed to rock up and down with delight at the spirit of the whole affair and the Feast of the Glorification of the Bomb that Didn't Come Off was being celebrated with all the honours.

Peter was very soon in the thick of it. The grey silences of Bennett Square and Bloomsbury were left behind and with them the emotions of those tender partings. After all, it would only be a very few weeks before he would be back again among them all, telling them of his success on some paper and going back perhaps to live with them all when his income was assured.

And, anyhow, here he was, out to seek his fortune and with Stephen to help him! He battled with the crowd dragging the black bag with him and shouting sometimes in sheer excitement and good spirits. Young women tickled him with feathers, once some one linked arms with him and dragged him along, always he was surrounded with this sea of shouting, exultant humanity—this was life!

By the lion Stephen was waiting for him, standing huge and solemn as the crowd surged past. He pressed Peter's arm to show that he was pleased to see him and then, without speaking, they pushed through, past Charing Cross station, and down the hill to the Underground.

Here, once again, there was startling silence. No one seemed to be using the trains at all.

"I'm afraid it ain't much of a place that I'm taking yer to," Stephen said. "We can't pick and choose yer know and I was there before and she's a good woman."

A chill seemed to come with them into the carriage. Suddenly to Peter the comforts of Brockett's stretched out alluring arms, then he pulled himself together.

"I'm sure it will be splendid," he said, "and it will be just lovely being with you after all this time."

They got out and plunged into a city of black night. Around them, on every side there was silence—even the broad central thoroughfare seemed to be deserted and on either side of it, to right and left, black grim roads like open mouths, lay waiting for the unwary traveller.

Down one of these they plunged; Peter was conscious of faces watching them. "Bucket Lane" was the street's title to fame. Windows showed dim candles, in the distance a sharp cry broke the silence and then fell away again. The street was very narrow and from the running gutters there stole into the air the odour of stale cabbage.

"This is the 'ouse." Stephen stopped. Somewhere, above their heads, a child was crying.

CHAPTER VI

THE WORLD AND BUCKET LANE

A light flashed in the upper windows, stayed for a moment, and disappeared. There was a pause and then the door slowly opened and a woman's head protruded.

She stared at them without speaking.

"Mr. Brant," Stephen said. "I'm come back, Mrs. Williams 'oping you might 'ave that same room me and my friend might use if it's agreeable."

She stepped forward then and looked at them more carefully. She was a stout red-faced woman, her hair hanging about her face, her dirty bodice drawn tightly over her enormous bosom and her skirt pulled up in front and hanging, draggled behind her. Her long, dirty fingers went up to her face continually; she had a way of pushing at her teeth with them.

She seemed, however, pleased to see Stephen.

"Well, Mr. Brant," she said, "come in. It's a surprise I must say but Lord! as I'm always telling Mrs. Griggs oo's on the bottom floor when she can afford 'er rent which 'asn't been often lately, poor thing, owing to 'aving 'er tenth only three weeks back, quite unexpected, and 'er man being turned off 'is 'ouse-painting business what 'e's been at this ten year and more—well come along in, I'm sure—"

They were in by this time having been urged by their hostess into the very narrowest, darkest and smelliest passage that Peter had ever encountered. Somewhere behind the walls, the world was moving. On every side of him above and below, children were crying, voices swearing, murmuring, complaining, arguing; Peter could feel Mrs. Williams' breath hot against his cheek. Up the wheezy stairs she panted, they following her. Peter had never heard such loquacity. It poured from her as though she meant nothing whatever by it and was scarcely aware indeed of the things that she was saying. "And it's a long time, Mr. Brant, since we 'ad the pleasure of seeing you. My last 'usband's left me since yer was 'ere—indeed 'e 'av—all along of a fight 'e 'ad with old Colly Moles down Three Barrer walk—penal servitude, poor feller and all along of 'is nasty temper as I was always tellin' 'im. Why the very morning before it 'appened I remember sayin' to 'im when 'e up and threw a knife at me for contradictin' 'is words I remember sayin' to 'im that 'is temper would be the settlin' of me but 'e wouldn't listen, not 'e. Obstinate! Lord! that simply isn't the word for it ... but 'ere's the room and nobody been in it since Sairy Grace and she was always bringin' men along with 'er, dirty slut and that's a month since she's been and gone and I always like 'aving yer, Mr. Brant, for you're quiet enough and no trouble at all—and your friend looks pleasant I must say."

The room was, indeed, remarkably respectable—not blessed with much furniture in addition to two beds and two chairs but roomy and with a large and moderately clean window.

"Now what about terms for me and my friend?" said Stephen.

Now followed friendly argument in which the lady and Stephen seemed perfectly to understand one another. After asserting that under no circumstances whatever could she possibly take less than at least double the price that Stephen offered her she suddenly, at the sound of a child's shrill crying from below, shrugged her shoulders with: "There's young 'Lisbeth Anne again ... well, Mr. Brant, 'ave it your own way—I'm contented enough I'm sure," and vanished.

But the little discussion had brought Peter to a sharp realisation of the immediate business of ways and means. Sitting on one of the beds afterwards with Stephen beside him he inquired—

"How much have we got, Stephen? I've got thirty bob."

"Never you mind, Peter. We'll soon be gettin' work."

"Why, of course. I'll force 'em to take me. That's all you want in these things—to look fierce and say you won't go until they give you something—a trial anyhow."

And sitting there on the bed with Stephen beside him he felt immensely confident. There was nothing that he could not do. With one swift movement he seemed to have flung from him all the things that were beginning to crowd in between him and his work. He must never, never allow that to happen again—how could one ever be expected to work if one were always thinking of other people, interested in them and their doings, involved with anarchists and bombs and romantic adventures. Why here he was with nothing in the world to hold him or to interfere and no one except dear old Stephen with whom he must talk. Ambition crept very close to him that night—ambition with its glittering, shining rewards, its music and colours—close to him as he sat in that bare, naked room.

"I'd rather be with you than any one in the world—we'll have such times, you and I."

Perhaps Stephen knew more about the world; perhaps during the years that he had been tumbled and knocked about he had realised that the world was no easy nut to crack and that loaves and fishes don't come to the hungry for the asking. But Peter that night was to be appalled by nothing.

They sat up into the early morning, talking. The noises in the house and in the streets about them rose and fell. Some distant cry would climb into the silence and draw from it other cries set like notes of music to tumble back into a common scheme together.

"Steve, tell me about Zanti. Is he really a scoundrel?"

"A scoundrel? No, poor feller. Why, Mr. Peter, you ought to know better than that. 'E ain't got a spark of malice in him but 'e's always after adventure. 'E knows all the queer people in Europe—and more'n Europe too. There's nothin' 'e don't put 'is nose into in a clumsy, childish way but always, you understand, Mr. Peter, because 'e's after 'is romantic fancies. It was when 'e was after gold down in Cornwall—some old treasure story—that I came across 'im and 'e was kind to me.... 'E was a kind-'earted man, Mr. Zanti, and never meant 'arm to a soul. And 'e's very fond of you, Mr. Peter."

"Yes, I know." Peter was vaguely troubled. "I hope I haven't been unkind about him. I suppose it was the shock of the whole thing. But it was time I went anyway. But tell me, Stephen, what you've been doing all these years. And why you let me be all that time without seeing you—"

"Well, Mr. Peter, I didn't think it would be good for you—I was knowing lots o' strange people time and again and then you might have been mixed up with me. I'm safe enough now, I'm thinking, and I'd have been safe enough all the time the way Cornwall was then and every one sympathising with me—"

"But what have you been doing all the time?"

"I was in America a bit and there are few things I haven't worked at in my time—always waiting for 'er to come—and she will come some time—it's only patience that's wanted."

"Have you ever heard from her?"

"There was a line once—just a line—she's all right." His great body seemed to glow with confidence.

Peter would like then to have spoken about Clare Rossiter. But no—some shyness held him—one day he would tell Stephen.

He unpacked his few possessions carefully and then, on a very hard bed, dreaming of bombs, of Mrs. Brockett dressed as a ballet dancer, of Mr. Zanti digging for treasure beneath the grey flags of Bennett Square, of Clare Elizabeth Rossiter riding down Oxford Street amidst the shouts of the populace, of the world as a coloured globe on which he, Peter Westcott, the author of that masterpiece, "Reuben Hallard," had set his foot ... so, triumphant, he slept.

II

On the next morning the Attack on London began. The house in Bucket Lane was dark and grim when he left it—the street was hidden from the light and hung like a strip of black ribbon between the sunshine of the broader highways that lay at each end of it. It was a Jewish quarter-notices in Yiddish were in all the little grimy shop windows, in the bakers and the sweetshops and the laundries. But it was not, this Bucket Lane, a street without its dignity and its own personal little cleanliness. It had its attempts at such things. His own room and Mrs. Williams' tea and bread and butter had been clean.

But as he came down out of these strange murmuring places with their sense of hiding from the world at large the things that they were occupied in doing, Bucket Lane stuck in his head as a dark little quarry into which he must at the day's end, whatever gorgeous places he had meanwhile encountered, creep. "Creeping" was the only way to get into such a place.

Meanwhile he had put on his best, had blackened his shoes until they shone like little mirrors, had brushed his bowler hat again and again and looked finally like a sailor on shore for a holiday. Seven years in Charing Cross Road had not taken the brown from his cheeks, nor bent his broad shoulders.

At the Mansion House he climbed on to the top of a lumbering omnibus and sailed down through the City. It was now that he discovered how seldom during his seven years he had ventured beyond his little square of country. Below him, on either side of him, black swarms stirred and moved, now forming ahead of him patterns, squares, circles, then suddenly rising it appeared like insects and in a cloud surging against the high stone buildings. All men—men moving with eyes straight ahead of them, bent furiously upon some business, but assembling, retreating, advancing, it seemed, by the order of some giant hand that in the air above them played a game. Imagine that, in some moment of boredom, the Hand were to brush the little pieces aside, were to close the board and put it away, then, with what ignominy and feeble helplessness would these little black figures topple clumsily into heaps.

Down through the midst of them the omnibus, like a man with an impediment in his speech, surrounded by the chatter of cabs and carts and bicycles, stammered its way. The streets opened and shut, shouts came up to them and fell away. Peter's heart danced—London was here at last and the silence of

Bennett Square, the dark omens of Bucket Lane and the clamour of the city had together been the key for the unlocking of its gates.

Ludgate Hill caught them into its heart, held them for an instant, and then flung them down in the confusion of Fleet Street.

Here it was at last then with its typewriters and its telephones and its printing machines hurling with a whir and clatter the news of the world into the air, and above it brooding, like an immense brain—the God of its restless activity—the Dome of St. Paul's.

Peter climbed down from his omnibus because he saw on his right a Public Reading Room. Here in tattered and anxious company, he studied the papers and took down addresses in a note book. He was frightened for an instant by the feet that shuffled up and down the floor from paper to paper. There was something most hopeless in the sound of that shuffle.

"'Ave yer a cigarette on yer, Mister, that yer wouldn't mind—"

He turned round and at once, like blows, two fierce gaunt eyes struck him in the face. Two eyes staring from some dirty brown pieces of cloth on end, it seemed, by reason of their own pathetic striving for notice, rather than because of any life inside them.

Peter murmured something and hurried away. Supposing that editors ... but no, this was not the proper beginning of a successful day. But the place, down steps under the earth, with its miserable shadows was not pleasant to remember.

His first visit was to the office of The Morning World. He remembered his remark to Stephen about self-assertion, but his heart sank as he entered the large high room with its railed counter running round the centre of it—a barrier cold, impassable. Already several people were sitting on chairs that were ranged along the wall.

Peter went up boldly to the counter and a very thin young man with a stone hatchet instead of a face and his hair very wonderfully parted in the middle—so accurately parted that Peter could think of nothing else—watched him coldly over the barrier.

"What can I do for you?" he said.

"I want to see the Editor."

"Have you an appointment?"

"No."

"Oh, I'm afraid that it would be impossible without an appointment."

"Is there any one whom I could see?"

"If you could tell me your business, perhaps—"

Peter began to be infuriated with this young man with the hatchet face.

"I want to know if there's any place for me on this paper. If I can—"

"Oh!" The voice was very cold indeed and the iron barrier seemed to multiply itself over and over again all round the room.

"I'm afraid in that case you had better write to the Editor and make an appointment. No, I'm afraid there is no one..."

Peter melted away. The faces on the chairs were all very glad. The stone building echoed with some voice that called some one a long way away. Peter was in the street. He stood outside the great offices of The Morning World and looked across the valley at the great dome that squatted above the moving threads of living figures. He was absurdly upset by this unfortunate interview. What could he have expected? Of what use was it that he should fling his insignificance against that kind of wall? Moreover he must try many times before his chance would be given him. It was absurd that he should mind that rebuff. But the hatchet-faced young man pursued him. He seemed to see now as he looked up and down the street, a hostility in the faces of those that passed him. Moreover he saw, here and there figures, wretched figures, moving in and out of the crowd, bending into the gutter for something that had been dropped—lean, haggard faces, burning eyes ... he began to see them as a chain that wound, up and down, amongst the people and the carriages along the street.

He pulled himself together—If he was feeling these things at the very beginning of his battle why then defeat was certain. He was ashamed and, looking at his paper, chose the offices of The Mascot, a very popular society journal that brightened the world with its cheerful good-tempered smile, every Friday morning. Here the room in which he found himself was small and cosy, it had a bright pink wall-paper, and behind a little shining table a shining young woman beamed upon him. The shining young woman was, however, very busy at her typewriter and Peter was examined by a tiny office boy who seemed to be made entirely of shining brass buttons and shining little boots and shining hair.

"And what can I do for you, sir?" he said.

"I should like to see the Editor," Peter explained.

"Your name?" said the Shining One.

Peter had no cards. He blamed himself for the omission and stammered in his reply.

The Boy gave the lady at the typewriter a very knowing look and disappeared. He swiftly returned and said that Mr. Boset could see Mr. Westcott for a few minutes, but for a few minutes only.

Mr. Boset sat resplendent in a room that was coloured a bright green. He was himself stout and red-faced and of a surpassing smartness, his light blue suit was very tight at the waist and very broad over the hips, his white spats gleamed, his pearl pin stared like an eye across the room, his neck bulged in red folds over his collar. Mr. Boset was eating chocolates out of a little cardboard box and his attention was continually held by the telephone that summoned him to its side at frequent intervals. He was however exceedingly pleasant. He begged Peter to take a chair.

"Just a minute, Mr. Westcott, will you? Yes—hullo—yes—This is 6140 Strand. Hullo! Hullo! Oh—is that you, Mrs. Wyman? Good morning—yes, splendid, thank you—never fitter—Very busy yes, of course—what—Lunch Thursday?... Oh, but delighted. Just let me look at my book a moment? Yes—quite free—Who? The Frasers and Pigots? Oh! delightful! 1.30, delightful!"

Mr. Boset, settled once more in his chair, was as charming as possible. You would suppose that the whole day was at Peter's service. He wanted to know a great many things. Peter's hopes ran high.

"Well—what have you got to show? What have you written?"

Peter had written a novel.

"Published?"

"No."

"Well ... got anything else?"

"No—not just at present."

"Oh well—must have something to show you know—"

"Yes." Peter's hopes were in his boots.

"Yes—must have something to show—" Mr. Boset's eyes were peering into the cardboard box on a voyage of selection.

"Yes—well—when you've written something send it along—"

"I suppose there isn't anything I can do—"

"Well, our staff, you know, is filled up to the eyes as it is—fellows waiting—lots of 'em—yes, you show us what you can do. Write an article or two. Buy The Mascot and see the kind of thing we like. Yes—Excuse me, the telephone—Yes—Yes 6140 Strand...."

Peter found himself once more in the outer room and then ushered forth by the Shining Boy he was in the street.

He was hungry now and sought an A.B.C. shop and there over the cold marble-topped tables consulted his list. The next attempt should be The Saturday Illustrated, one of the leading illustrated weeklies, and perhaps there he would be more successful. As he sat in the A.B.C. shop and watched the squares of street opposite the window he felt suddenly that no effort of his would enable him to struggle successfully against those indifferent crowds.

Above the houses in the patch of blue sky that filled the window-pane soft bundles of cloud streamed like flags before the wind. Into these soft grey meshes the sun was swept and with a cold shudder Fleet Street fell into shadow; beyond it and above it the great dome burned; a company of sandwich men, advertising on their stooping bodies the latest musical comedy, crept along the gutter.

III

At the offices of The Saturday Illustrated they told him that if he returned at four o'clock he would be able to see the Editor. He walked about and at last sat down on the Embankment and watched the barges slide down the river. The water was feathery and sometimes streamed into lines like spun silk reflecting many colours, and above the water the clouds turned and wheeled and changed against the limpid blue. The little slap that the motion of the river gave to the stone embankment reminded him of the wooden jetty at Treliss—the place was strangely sweet—the roar of the Strand was far away and muffled.

As he sat there listening there seemed to come up to him, straight out of the river, strange impersonal noises that had to do with no definite sounds. He was reminded of a story that he had once read, a story concerning a nice young man who caught the disease known as the Horror of London. Peter thought that in the air, coming from nowhere, intangible, floating between the river and the sky something stirred....

Big Ben struck quarter to four and he turned once more into the Strand.

The editor of The Saturday Illustrated was a very different person from Mr. Boset. At a desk piled with papers, stern, gaunt and sharp-chinned, his words rattled out of his mouth like peas onto a plate. But Peter saw that he had humorous twinkling eyes.

"Well, what can you do?"

"I've never tried anything—but I feel that I should learn—"

"Learn! Do you suppose this office is a nursery shop for teaching sucklings how to draw their milk? Are you ready for anything?"

"Anything—"

"Yes—they all say that. Journalism isn't any fun, you know."

"I'm not looking for fun."

"Well, it's the damnedest trade out. Anything's better. But you want to write?"

"I must."

"Yes—exactly. Well, I like the look of you. More blood and bones than most of the rotten puppies that come into this office. I've no job for you at the moment though. Go back to your digs and write something—anything you like—and send it along—leave me your address. Oh, ho! Bucket Lane—hard up?"

"I'm all right, thank you."

"All right, I wasn't offering you charity—no need to put your pride up. I shan't forget you ... but send me something."

The clouds had now enveloped the sun. As Peter, a little encouraged by this last experience but tired with a dull, listless fatigue, crept into the dark channels of Bucket Lane, the rain began to fall with heavy solemn drops.

CHAPTER VII

DEVIL'S MARCH

I

There could be nothing odder than the picture that Brockett's and Bennett Square presented from the vantage ground of Bucket Lane. How peaceful and happy those evenings (once considered a little dreary perhaps and monotonous) now seemed! Those mornings in the dusty bookshop, Mr. Zanti, Herr Gottfried, Mrs. Brockett, then Brockett's with its strange kind-hearted company—the dining-room, the marble pillars, the green curtains—Norah Monogue!

Not only did it seem another lifetime when he had been there but also inevitably, one was threatened with never getting back. Bucket Lane was another world—from its grimy windows one looked upon every tragedy that life had to offer. Into its back courts were born muddled indecent little lives, there blindly to wallow until the earth called them back to itself again.

But it was in the attitude of Bucket Lane to the Great Inevitable that the essential difference was to be observed. In Bennett Square things had been expected and, for the most part, obtained. Catastrophes came lumbering into their midst at times but rising in the morning one might decently expect to go to rest at night in safety. In Bucket Lane there was no safety but defiance—fierce, bitterly humorous, truculent defiance. Bucket Lane was a beleaguered army that stood behind the grime and dirty walls on guard. From the earliest moment there the faces of all the babies born into Bucket Lane caught the strain of cautious resistance that was always to remain with them. Life in Bucket Lane, for every one from the youngest infant to the oldest idiot, was War. War against Order and Civilised Force. War also against that great unseen Hand that might at any moment swoop down upon any one of them and bestow fire, death and imprisonment upon its victims. To the ladies and gentlemen from the Mission the citizens of Bucket Lane presented an amused and cynical tolerance. If those poor, meek, frightened creatures chose some faint-hearted attempts at flattery and submission before this abominable Deity— well, they did no harm.

Mrs. Williams said to Miss Connacher, a bright-faced young woman from St. Matthew's Mission—"And I'm sure we're always delighted to see you, Miss. But you can't 'ave us goin' and being grateful on our bended knees to the sort of person as according to your account of it gave me my first 'usband 'oo was a blackguard if ever there was one, and my last child wot 'ad rickets and so 'andsomely arranged me to go breakin' my leg one night coming back from a party and sliding on the stairs, and in losin' my little bit o' charin' and as near the workus as ever yer see—no—it ain't common sense."

To which Miss Connacher vaguely looking around for a list of Mrs. Williams' blessings and finding none to speak of, had no reply.

But the astonishing thing was that Peter seemed at once to be seized with the Bucket Lane position. He was now, he understood, in a world of earthquake—wise citizens lived from minute to minute and counted on no longer safety. He began also to eliminate everything that was not absolutely essential. At Brockett's he had never consciously done without anything that he wanted—in Bucket Lane he discarded to the last possible shred of possession.

He had returned from his first day's hunting with the resolve that before he ventured out again he would have something to show. With a precious sixpence he bought a copy of The Mascot and studied it—there was a short story entitled "Mrs. Adair's Co."—and an article on "What Society Drinks"—the remaining pages of the number were filled with pictures and "Chatter from Day to Day." This gaily-coloured production lying on one of the beds in the dark room in Bucket Lane seemed singularly out of place. Its pages fluttered in the breeze that came through the window cracks—"Maison Tep" it cried feebly to the screaming children in the court below, "is a very favourite place for supper just now, with Maitre Savori as its popular chef and its admirably stocked cellars...."

Peter gave himself a fortnight in which to produce something that he could "show." Stephen meanwhile had found work as a waiter in one of the small Soho restaurants; it was only a temporary engagement but he hoped to get something better within a week or two.

For the moment all was well. At the end of his fortnight, with four things written Peter meant to advance once more to the attack. Meanwhile he sat with a pen, a penny bottle of ink and an exercise book and did what he could. At the end of the fortnight he had written "The Sea Road," an essay for which Robert Louis Stevenson was largely responsible, "The Redgate Mill," a story of the fantastic, terrible kind, "Stones for Bread," moralising on Bucket Lane, and the "Red-Haired Boy," a somewhat bitter reminiscence of Dawson's. Of this the best was undoubtedly "The Sea Road," but in his heart of hearts Peter knew that there was something the matter with all of them. "Reuben Hallard" he had written because he had to write it, these four things he had written because he ought to write them ... difference sufficient. Nevertheless, he put them into halfpenny wrappes and sent them away.

In the struggle to produce these things he had not found that fortnight wearisome. Before him, every day, there was the evening when Stephen would return, to which he might look forward. Stephen was always very late—often it was two o'clock before he came in, but they had a talk before going to sleep. And here in these evenings Stephen developed in the most wonderful way, developed because Peter had really never known him before.

Stephen had never appeared to Peter as a character at all. In the early days Peter had been too young. Stephen had, at that time, been simply something to be worshipped, without any question or statement. Now that worshipping had gone and the space that it left had to be filled by some new relationship, something that could only come slowly, out of the close juxtaposition that living together in Bucket Lane had provided.

And it was Stephen who found, unconsciously and quite simply, the shape and colour of Peter's idea of him. Peter had in reality, nothing at all to do with it, and had Stephen been a whit more self-conscious the effect would have been spoiled.

In the first place Peter came quite freshly to the way that Stephen looked. Stephen expressed nothing, consciously, with his body; it was wonderful indeed considering its size and strength, the little that he managed to do with it. His eyes were mild and amiable, his face largely covered with a deep brown beard, once wildly flowing, now sharply pointed. He was at least six foot four in height, the breadth of shoulder was tremendous, but although he knew admirably what to do with it as a means of conveyance, of sheer physical habit, he had no conception of the possibilities that it held as the expression of his soul. That soul was to be found, by those who cared to look for it, glancing from his eyes, struggling sometimes through the swift friendliness of his smile—but he gave it no invitation. It all came, perhaps, from the fact that he treated himself—if anything so unconscious may be called treatment—as the very simplest creature alive. The word introspection meant nothing to him whatever, there were in life certain direct sharp motives and on these he acted. He never thought of himself or of any one else in terms of complexity; the body acted simply through certain clear and direct physical laws ... so the spirit. He loved the woman who had dominated his whole life and one day he would find her and marry her. He loved Peter as he would love a son of his own if he possessed one, and he would be at Peter's side so long as Peter needed him, and would rather be there than anywhere else. For the rest life was a matter of birth and death, of loving one man and hating another, of food and drink, and—but this last uncertainly—of some strange thrill that was stirred in him, at times, by certain sights and sounds.

He was glad to have been born ... he would be quite ready to die. He did not question the reason of the one state or the other. For the very fact that life was so simple and unentangled he clung, with the tenacity and dumb force of an animal to the things that he had. Peter felt, vaguely, from time to time, the strength with which Stephen held to him. It was never expressed in word nor in action but it came leaping sometimes, like fire, into the midst of their conversation—it was never tangible—always illusive.

To Peter's progress this simplicity of Stephen was of vast importance. The boy had now reached an age and a period where emotions, judgments, partialities, conclusions and surmises were fighting furiously for dominion. His seven years at Brockett's had been, introspectively, of little moment. He had been too busy discovering the things that other people had discovered and written down to think very much about himself.

Now released from the domination of books, he plunged into a whirlpool of surmise about himself. During the fortnight that he sat writing his articles in Bucket Lane he flew, he sank, according to his moods. It seemed to him that as soon as he had decided on one path and set out eagerly to follow it others crossed it and bewildered him.

He was now on that unwholesome, absorbing, thrilling, dangerous path of self-discovery. Opposed to this was the inarticulate, friendly soul of Stephen. Stephen understood nothing and at the same time understood everything. Against the testing of his few simple laws Peter's complexities often vanished ... but vanished only to recur again, unsatisfied, demanding a subtler answer. It was during those days, through all the trouble and even horror that so shortly came upon them both, that Stephen realised with a dull, unreasoned pain, like lead at the heart, that Peter was passing inevitably from him into a country whither Stephen could not follow—to deal with issues that Stephen could not, in any kind of way, understand. Stephen realised this many days before Peter even dimly perceived it, and the older man by the love that he had for the boy whom he had known from the very first period of his growth was enabled, although dimly, to see beyond, above all these complexities, to a day when Peter would once more, having learnt and suffered much in the meanwhile, come back to that first simplicity.

But that day was far distant.

On the evening of the day on which Peter finished the last of his five attempts to take the London journals by storm Stephen returned from his restaurant earlier than usual—so early indeed, that Peter, had he not been so bent on his own immediate affairs, must have noticed and questioned it. He might, too, have observed that Stephen, now and again, shot an anxious, troubled glance at him as though he were uneasy about something.

But Peter, since six o'clock that evening, at which moment he had written the concluding sentence of "The Sea Road," had been in deep and troubled thought concerning himself, and broke from that introspection, on Stephen's arrival, in a state of unhappy morbidity and entire self-absorption.

Their supper was beer, sardines and cheese.

"It's been pretty awful here this evening," Peter said. "Old Trubbit on the floor below's been beating his wife and she's been screaming like anything. I couldn't stand it, after a bit, and went down to see what I could do. The family was mopping her head with water and he was sitting on a chair, crying. Drunk again, of course, but he was turned off his job apparently this afternoon. They're closing down."

"'Ard luck," said Stephen, looking at the floor.

"Yes—it hasn't been altogether cheerful—and his getting the chuck like that set me thinking. It's awfully lucky you've got your job all right and of course now I've written these things and have got 'something to show,' I'll be all right." Peter paused for a moment a little uncertainly. "But it does, you know, make one a bit frightened, this place, seeing the way people get suddenly bowled over. There were the Gambits—a fortnight ago he was in work and they were as fit as anything ... they haven't had any food now for three days."

"There ain't anything to be frightened about," Stephen said slowly.

"No, I know. But Stephen, suppose I don't get work, after all. I've been so confident all this time, but I mightn't be able to do the job a bit.... I suppose this place is getting on my nerves but—I could get awfully frightened if I let myself."

"Oh, you'll be all right. Of course you'll be getting something—"

"Yes, but I hate spending your money like this. Do you know, Stephen, I'd almost rather you were out of work too. That sounds a rotten thing to say but I hate being given it all like this, especially when you haven't got much of your own either—"

"Between friends," said Stephen slowly, swinging his leg backwards and forwards and making the bed creak under his weight, "there aren't any giving or taking—it's just common."

"Oh, yes, I know," said Peter hurriedly, frightened lest he should have hurt his feelings, "of course it's all right between you and me. But all the same I'm rather eager to be earning part of it."

They were silent for a time. Bucket Lane too seemed silent and through their little window, between the black roofs and chimneys, a cluster of stars twinkled as though they had found their way, by accident, into a very dirty neighbourhood and were trying to get out of it again.

Peter was busy fishing for his thoughts; at last he caught one and held it out to Stephen's innocent gaze.

"It isn't," he said, "like anything so much as catching a disease from an infectious neighbourhood. I think if I lived here with five thousand a year I should still be frightened. It's in the air."

"Being frightened," said Stephen rather hurriedly and speaking with a kind of shame, as though he had done something to which he would rather not own up, "is a kind of 'abit. Very soon, Peter, you'll know what it's like and take it as it comes."

"Oh," said Peter, "if it's that kind of being frightened—seeing I mean quite clearly the things you're frightened of—why, that's pretty easy. One of the first books I ever read—'Henry Lessingham,' by Galleon, you know, I've talked about him to you—had a long bit about it—courage I mean. He made it a kind of parable, countries you'd got to go through before you'd learnt to be really brave; and the first, and by far the easiest courage is the sort that you want when you haven't got things—the sort the Gambits want—when you're starving or out of a job. Well, that's I suppose the easiest kind and yet I'm funking it. So what on earth am I going to do when the harder business comes along? ... Stephen, I'm beginning to have a secret and uncomfortable suspicion that your friend, Peter Westcott, is a poor creature."

"Thank the Lord," said Stephen furiously and kicking out with his leg as though he had got some especial enemy's back directly in front of him, "that you've finished them damned articles. You've been sittin' here thinkin' and writin' till you've given yerself blue devils—down-along, too, with all them poor creatures hittin' each other and drinkin'—I oughtn't to have left yer up here so much alone—"

"No—you couldn't help it, Stephen—it's nothing to do with you. It's all more than you can manage and nobody in the world can help me. It's seven years and a bit now since I left Cornwall, isn't it?"

"Yes," said Stephen, looking across at him.

"All that time I've never had a word nor a sign from any one there. Well, you might have thought that that would be long enough to break right away from it.... Well, it isn't—"

"Don't you go thinking about all that time. You've cleared it right away—"

"No, I haven't cleared it—that's just the point. I don't suppose one ever clears anything. All the time I was with Zanti I was reading so hard and living so safely that it was only at moments, when I was alone, that I thought about Treliss at all. But these last weeks it's been coming on me full tide."

"What's been coming on you?"

"Well, Scaw House, I suppose ... and my father and grandfather. My grandfather told me once that I couldn't escape from the family and I can't—it's the most extraordinary thing—"

Stephen saw that Peter was growing agitated; his hands were clenched and his face was white.

"Mind you, I've seen my grandfather and father both go under it. My father went down all in a moment. It isn't any one thing—you can call it drink if you like—but it's simply three parts of us aching to go to the bad ... aching, that's the word. Anything rotten—women or drink or anything you like—as long as we lose control and let the devil get the upper hand. Let him get it once—really get it—and we're really done—"

Peter paused for a moment and then went on hurriedly as though he were telling a story and had only a little time in which to tell it.

"But that isn't all—it's worse than that. I've been feeling these last weeks as though my father were sitting there in that beastly house with that filthy woman—and willing me—absolutely with all his might—to go under—"

"But what is it," said Stephen, going, as always, to the simplest aspect of the case, "that you exactly want to do?"

"Oh, I don't know ... just to let loose the whole thing—I did break out once at Brockett's—I've never told anybody, but I got badly drunk one night and then went back with some woman.... Oh! it was all filthy— but I was mad, wild, for hours ... insane—and that night, in the middle of it all, sitting there as plainly as you please, there in Scaw House, I saw my father—as plainly as I see you—"

"All young men," said Stephen, "'ave got to go through a bit of filth. You aren't the sort of fellow, Peter, that stays there. Your wanting not to shows that you'll come out of it all right."

Here was a case where Stephen's simplicities were obviously of little avail.

"Ah, but don't you see," said Peter impatiently, "it's not the thing itself that I feel matters so much, although that's rotten enough, but it's the beastly devil—real, personal—I tell you I saw him catch my grandfather as tight as though he'd been there in the room ... and my father, too. I tell you, this last week or two I've been almost mad ... wanting to chuck it all, this fighting and the rest and just go down and grovel..."

"I expect it's regular work you're wanting," said Stephen, "keeping your mind busy. It's bad to 'ave your sort of brain wandering round with nothing to feed on. It'll be all right, boy, in a day or two when you've got some work."

Peter's head dropped forward on to his hands. "I don't know—it's like going round in a circle. You see, Stephen, what makes it all so difficult is—well, I don't know ... why I haven't told you before ... but the fact is—I'm in love—"

"I knew it a while back," said Stephen quietly, "watching your face when you didn't know I was lookin'—"

"Well, it's all hopeless, of course. I don't suppose I shall ever see her again ... but that's what's made this looking for work so difficult—I've been wanting to get on—and every day seems to place her further away. And then when I get hopeless these other devils come round and say 'Oh well, you can't get her, you know. That's as impossible as anything—so you'd better have your fling while you can....' My God! I'm a beast!"

The cry broke from him with a bitterness that filled the bare little room.

Stephen, after a little, got up and put his hand on the boy's shoulder.

"Nobody ain't going to touch you while I'm here," he said simply as though he were challenging devils and men alike.

Peter looked up and smiled. "What an old brick you are," he said. "Do you remember that fight Christmas time, years ago? ... You're always like that.... I've been an ass to bother you with it all and while we've got each other things can't be so bad." He got up and stretched his arms.

"Well, it's bedtime, especially as you've got to be off early to that old restaurant—"

Stephen stepped back from him.

"I've been meaning to tell you," he said, "that's off. The place ain't paying and the boss shut four of us down to-night ... I'm not to go back ... Peter, boy," he finished, almost triumphantly. "We're up against it ... I've got a quid in my pocket and that's all there is to it."

They faced one another whilst the candle behind them guttered and blew in the window cracks, and the cluster of stars, still caught in the dirty roofs and chimneys of Bucket Lane, twinkled, desperately—in vain.

CHAPTER VIII

STEPHEN'S CHAPTER

I

No knight—the hero of any chronicle—ever went forward to his battle with a braver heart than did Peter now in his desperate adventure against the world. His morbidity, his introspection, his irritation with Stephen's simplicities fled from him... he was gay, filled with the glamour of showing what one could do... he did not doubt but that a fortnight would see him in a magnificent position. And then—the fortnight passed and he and Stephen had still their positions to discover—the money moreover was almost at an end... another fortnight would behold them penniless.

It was absurd—it was monstrous, incredible. Life was not like that—Peter bit his lip and set out again. Editors had not, on most occasions, vouchsafed him even an interview. Then had come no answer to the four halfpenny wrappers. The world, like a wall of shining steel, closed him in with impenetrable silence.

It was absurd—it was monstrous. Peter fought desperately, as a bird beats with its wings on the bars of its cage. They were having the worst of luck. On several occasions he had been just too late and some one had got the position before him. Stephen too found that the places where he had worked before had now no job for him. "It was the worst time in the world... a month ago now or possibly in a month's time...."

Stephen did not tell the boy that away from London there were many things that he could do—the boy was not up to tramping. Indeed, nothing was more remarkable than the way in which Peter's strength seemed to strain, like a flood, away. It was, perhaps, a matter of nerves as much as physical strength— the boy was burning with the anxiety of it, whereas to Stephen this was no new experience. Peter saw it in the light of some horrible disaster that belonged, in all the world's history, to him alone. He came back at the end of one of his days, white, his eyes almost closed, his fingers twitching, his head hanging a little ... very silent.

He seemed to feel bitterly the ignominy of it as though he were realising, for the first time, that nobody wanted him. He had come now to be ready to do anything, anything in the world, and he had the look of one who was ready to do anything. His blue coat was shiny, his boots had been patched by Stephen— there were deep black hollows under his eyes and his mouth had become thin and hard.

Stephen—having himself his own distresses to support—watched the boy with acute anxiety. He felt with increasing unhappiness, that here was an organism, a temperament, that was new to him, that was beyond his grasp. Peter saw things in it all—this position of a desperate cry for work—that he, Stephen, had never seen at all. Peter would sit in the evening, in his chair, staring in front of him, silent, and hearing nothing that Stephen said to him. With Stephen life was a case of having money or not having it—if one had not money one went without everything possible and waited until the money came again ... the tide was sure to turn. But, with Peter, this was all a fight against his father who sat, apparently, in the dark rooms at Scaw House, willing disaster. Now, as Stephen and all the sensible world knew, this was nonsense—

It was also, in some still stranger way, a fight against London itself—not London, a place of streets and houses, of Oxford Street and Piccadilly Circus but London, an animal—a kind of dragon as far as Stephen could make it out with scales and a tail—

Now what was one to make of this except that the boy's head was being turned and that he ought to see a doctor.

There was also the further question of an appeal to Brockett's or Mr. Zanti. Stephen knew that Herr Gottfried or Mr. Zanti would lend help eagerly did they but know, and he supposed, from the things that Peter had told him, that there were also warm friends at Brockett's; but the boy had made him swear, with the last order of solemnity, that he would send no word to either place. Peter had said that he would never speak to him again should he do such a thing. He had said that should he once obtain an independent position then he would go back ... but not before.

Stephen did not know what to do nor where to go. In another month's time the rent could not be paid and then they must go into the street and Peter was in no condition for that—he should rather be in bed. Mrs. Williams, it is true, would not be hard upon them, for she was a kind woman and had formed a great liking for Peter, but she had only enough herself to keep her family alive and she must, for her children's sake, let the room.

To Stephen, puzzling in vain and going round and round in a hopeless circle, it seemed as though Peter's brains were locked in an iron box and they could not find a key. For himself, well, it was natural enough! But Peter, with that genius, that no one should want him!

And yet through it all, at the back of the misery and distress of it, there was a wild pride, a fierce joy that he had the key with him, that he was all in the world to whom the boy might look, that to him and to him alone, in this wild, cold world Peter now belonged.

It was his moment....

II

At the end of a terrible day of disastrous rejections Peter, stumbling down the Strand, was conscious of a little public-house, with a neat bow-window, that stood back from the street. At the bottom of his trouser pocket a tiny threepenny piece that Stephen had, that morning, thrust upon him, turned round and round in his fingers. He had not spent it—he had intended to restore it to Stephen in the evening. He had meant, too, to walk back all the way to Bucket Lane but now he felt that he could not do that unless he were first to take something. This little inn with its bow-windows.... Down the Strand in the light of the setting sun, he saw again that which he had often seen during these last weeks—that chain of gaunt figures that moved with bending backs and twisted fingers, on and out of the crowds and the carriages—The beggars!... He felt, already, that they knew that he was soon to be one of their number, that every day, every hour brought him nearer to their ranks. An old man, dirty, in rags, stepped with an eager eye past him and stooped for a moment into the gutter. He rose again, slipping something into his pocket of his tattered coat. He gave Peter a glance—to the boy it seemed a glance of triumphant recognition and then he had slipped away.

Peter had had very little to eat during these last days and to-night, for the first time, things began to take an uncertain shape. As he stood on the kerb and looked, it seemed to him that the Strand was the sea-road at Treliss, that the roar of the traffic was the noise that the sea made, far below them. If one could see round the corner, there where the sun flung a patch of red light, one would come upon Scaw House in its dark clump of trees—and through the window of that front room, Peter could see his father and that old woman, one on each side of the fire-place, drinking.

But the sea-road was stormy to-night, its noise was loud in Peter's ears. And then the way that people brushed against him as they passed recalled him to himself and he slipped back almost into the bow-window of the little inn. He was feeling very unwell and there was a burning pain in his chest that hurt him when he drew a deep breath ... and then too he was very cold and his teeth chattered in fits as though he had suddenly lost control of them and they had become some other person's teeth.

Well, why not go into the little inn and have a drink? Then he would go back to Bucket Lane and lie down and never wake again. For he was so tired that he had never known before what it was to be tired at all—only Stephen would not let him sleep.... Stephen was cruel and would not let him alone. No one would let him alone—the world had treated him very evilly—what did he owe the world?

He would go now and surrender to these things, these things that were stronger than he ... he would drink and he would sleep and that should be the end of everything ... the blessed end.

He swayed a little on his feet and he put his hand to his forehead in order that he might think more clearly.

Some one had said once to him a great many years ago—"It is not life that matters but the Courage that you bring to it." Well, that was untrue. He would like to tell the man who had said that that he was a liar. No Courage could be enough if life chose to be hard. No Courage—

Nevertheless, the thought of somewhere a long time ago when some one had said that to him, slowly filled his tired brain with a distaste for the little inn with the bow-windows. He would not go there yet, just a little while and then he would go.

Almost dreaming—certainly seeing nothing about him that he recognised—he stumbled confusedly down to the Embankment. Here there was at any rate air, he drew his shabby blue coat more closely about him and sat down on a wooden bench, in company with a lady who wore a large damaged feather in her hat and a red stained blouse with torn lace upon it and a skirt of a bright and tarnished blue.

The lady gave him a nod.

"Cheer, chucky," she said.

Peter made no reply.

"Down on your uppers? My word, you look bad—Poor Kid! Well, never say die—strike me blimy but there's a good day coming—"

"I sat here once before," said Peter, leaning forward and addressing her very earnestly, "and it was the first time that I ever heard the noise that London makes. If you listen you can hear it now—London's a beast you know—"

But the lady had paid very little attention. "Men are beasts, beasts," she said, scowling at a gap in the side of her boots, "beasts, that's what they are. 'Aven't 'ad any luck the last few nights. Suppose I'm losin' my looks sittin' out 'ere in the mud and rain. There was a time, young feller, my lad, when I 'ad my carriage, not 'arf!" She spat in front of her—"'E was a good sort, 'e was—give me no end of a time ... but the lot of men I've been meetin' lately ain't fit to be called men—they ain't—mean devils—leavin' me like this, curse 'em!" She coughed. The sun had set now and the lights were coming out, like glass beads on a string on the other side of the river. "Stoppin' out all night, ducky? Stayin' 'ere? 'Cause I got a bit of a cough!—disturbs fellers a bit ... last feller said as 'ow 'e couldn't get a bit o' sleep because of it—damned rot I call it. 'Owever it isn't out of doors you ought to be sittin', chucky. Feelin' bad?"

Peter looked at her out of his half-closed eyes.

"I can't bother any more," he said to her sleepily. "They're so cruel—they won't let me go to sleep. I've got a pain here—in my chest you know. Have you got a pain in your chest?"

"My leg's sore," she answered, "where a chap kicked me last week—just because—oh well," she paused modestly and spat again—"It's comin' on cold."

A cold little wind was coming up the river, ruffling the tips of the trees and turning the leaves of the plane-trees back as though it wanted to clean the other sides of them.

Peter got up unsteadily. "I'm going home to sleep," he said, "I'm dreadfully tired. Good-night."

"So long, chucky," the lady with the damaged feather said to him. He left her eyeing discontentedly the hole in her boot and trying to fasten, with confused fingers, the buttons of the red blouse.

Peter mechanically, as one walking in a dream, crept into an omnibus. Mechanically he left it and mechanically climbed the stairs of the house in Bucket Lane. There were two fixed thoughts in his brain—one was that no one in the world had ever before been as thirsty as he was, and that he would willingly commit murder or any violence if thereby he might obtain drink, and the other thought was that Stephen was his enemy, that he hated Stephen because Stephen never left him alone and would not let him sleep—also in the back of his mind distantly, as though it concerned some one else, that he was very unhappy....

Stephen was sitting on one of the beds, looking in front of him. Peter moved forward heavily and sat on the other bed. They looked at one another.

"No luck," said Stephen, "Armstrong's hadn't room for a man. Ricroft wouldn't see me. Peter, I'm thinking we'll have to take to the roads—"

Peter made no answer.

"Yer not lookin' a bit well, lad. I doubt if yer can stand much more of it."

Peter looked across at him sullenly.

"Why can't you leave me alone?" he said. "You're always worrying—"

A slow flush mounted into Stephen's cheeks but he said nothing.

"Well, why don't you say something? Nothing to say—it isn't bad enough that you've brought me into this—"

"Come, Mr. Peter," Stephen answered slowly. "That ain't fair. I never brought you into this. I've done my best."

"Oh, blame me, of course. That's natural enough. If it hadn't been for you—"

Stephen came into the middle of the floor.

"Come, Peter boy, yer tired. Yer don't know what yer saying. Best go to bed. Don't be saying anything that yer'd be regretting afterwards—"

Peter's eyes that had been closed, suddenly opened, blazing. "Oh, damn you and your talk—I hate you. I wish I'd never seen you—a rotten kind of friendship—" his voice died off into muttering.

Stephen went back to his bed. "This ain't fair, Mr. Peter," he said in a low voice. "You'll be sorry afterwards. I ain't 'ad any very 'appy time myself these last weeks and now—"

Their nerves were like hot, jangling wires. Suddenly into the midst of that bare room there had sprung between them hatred. They faced each other ... they could have leapt at one another's throats and fought....

Suddenly Peter gave a little cry that seemed to fill the room. His head fell forward—

"Oh, Stephen, Stephen, I'm so damned ill, I'm so damnably ill."

He caught for a moment at his chest as though he would tear his shirt open. Then he stumbled from the bed and lay in a heap on the floor with his hands spread out—

Stephen picked him up in his arms and carried him on to his bed.

III

The little doctor who attended to the wants of Bucket Lane was discovered at his supper. He was a dirty little man, with large dusty spectacles, a red nose and a bald head. He wore an old, faded velveteen jacket out of the pockets of which stuck innumerable papers. He was very often drunk and had a shrew of a wife who made the sober parts of his life a misery, but he was kind-hearted and generous and had a very real knowledge of his business.

Mrs. Williams volubly could not conceal her concern at Peter's condition—"and 'im such a nice-spoken young genelman as I was saying only yesterday tea-time, there's nothin' I said, as I wouldn't be willin' to do for that there poor Mr. Westcott and that there poor Mr. Brant 'oo are as like two 'elpless children in their fightin' the world as ever I see and 'ow ever can I help 'em I said—"

"Well, my good woman," the little doctor finally interrupted, "you can help here and now by getting some hot water and the other things I've put down here."

When she was gone he turned slowly to Stephen who stood, the picture of despair, looking down upon Peter.

"'E's goin' to die?" he asked.

"That depends," the little doctor answered. "The boy's been starved—ought never to have been allowed to get into this condition. Both of you hard up, I suppose?"

"As 'ard up as we very well could be—" Stephen answered grimly.

"Well—has he no friends?"

There—the question at last. Stephen took it as he would have taken a blow between the eyes. He saw very clearly that the end of his reign had come. He had done what he could and he had failed. But in him was the fierce furious desire to fight for the boy. Why should he give him up, now, when they had spent all these weeks together, when they had struggled for their very existence side by side. What right had any of these others to Peter compared with his right? He knew very well that if he gave him up now the boy would never be his again. He might see him—yes—but that passing of Peter that he had already begun to realise would be accomplished. He might look at him but only as a wanderer may look from the valley up to the hill. The doctor broke in upon him as he stood hesitating there—

"Come," he said roughly, "we have not much time. The boy may die. Has he no friends?"

Stephen turned his back to Peter. "Yes," he said, "I know where they are. I will fetch them myself."

The doctor had not lived in Bucket Lane all these years for nothing. He put his hand on Stephen's arm and said: "You're a good fellow, by God. It'll be all right."

Stephen went.

On his way to Bennett Square a thousand thoughts filled his mind. He knew, as though he had been told it by some higher power, that Peter was leaving him now never to return. He had done what he could for Peter—now the boy must pass on to others who might be able, more fittingly, to help him. He cursed the Gods that they had not allowed him to obtain work during these weeks, for then Peter and he might have gone on, working, prospering and the parting might have been far distant.

But he felt also that Peter's destiny was something higher and larger than anything that he could ever compass—it must be Peter's life that he should always be leaving people behind him—stages on his road—until he had attained his place. But for Stephen, a loneliness swept down upon him that seemed to turn the world to stone. Never, in all the years of his wandering, had he known anything like this. It is very hard that a man should care for only two creatures in the world and that he should be held, by God's hand, from reaching either of them.

The door of Brockett's was opened to him by a servant and he asked for Mrs. Brockett. In the cold and dark hall the lady sternly awaited him, but the sternness fell from her like a cloak when he told her the reason of his coming—

"Dear me, and the poor boy so ill," she said. "We have all been very anxious indeed about poor Mr. Peter. We had tried every clue but could hear nothing of him. We were especially eager to find him because Miss Monogue had some good news for him about his book. There is a gentleman—a friend of Mr. Peter's—who has been doing everything to find him—who is with Miss Monogue now. He will be delighted. Perhaps you will go up."

Stephen can have looked no agreeable object at this time, worn out by the struggle of the last weeks, haggard and gaunt, his beard unkempt—but Norah Monogue came forward to him with both her hands outstretched.

"Oh, you know something of Peter—tell us, please," she said.

A stout, pleasant-faced gentleman behind her was introduced as Mr. Galleon.

Stephen explained. "But why, why," said the gentleman, "didn't you let us know before, my good fellow?"

Stephen's brow darkened. "Peter didn't wish it," he said.

But Norah Monogue came forward and put her hand on his arm. "You must be the Mr. Brant about whom he has so often talked," she said. "I am so glad to meet you at last. Peter owes so much to you. We have been trying everywhere to get word of him because some publishers have taken his novel and think very well of it indeed. But come—do let us go at once. There is no time to lose—"

So they had taken his novel, had they? All these days—all these terrible hours—that starving, that ghastly anxiety, the boy's terror—all these things had been unnecessary. Had they only known, this separation now might have been avoided.

He could not trust himself to speak to Bobby Galleon and Norah Monogue. These were the people who were going to take Peter away.

He turned and went, in silence, down the stairs.

At Bucket Lane Bobby Galleon took affairs into his own hands. At once Peter should be removed to his house in Chelsea—it would not apparently harm him to be moved that night.

Peter was still unconscious. Stephen stood in the back of the room and watched them make their preparations. They had all forgotten him. For a moment as they passed down the stairs Stephen had his last glimpse of Peter. He saw the high white forehead, the long black eyelashes, the white drawn cheeks.... At this parting Peter had no eye for him.

Bobby Galleon and Miss Monogue both spoke to Stephen pleasantly before they went away. Stephen did not hear what they said. Bobby took Stephen's name down on a piece of paper.... Then they were gone. They were all gone.

Mrs. Williams looked through the door at him for a moment but something in the man's face drove her away. Very slowly he put his few clothes together. He must tramp the roads again—the hard roads, the glaring sun, cold moon—always going on, always alone—

He shouldered his bag and went out....

BOOK III — THE ROUNDABOUT

CHAPTER I

NO. 72, CHEYNE WALK

I

Burnished clouds—swollen with golden light and soft and changing in their outline—were sailing, against a pale green autumn evening sky, over Chelsea.

It was nearly six o'clock and at the Knightsbridge end of Sloane Street a cloud of black towers quivered against the pale green.

The yellow light that the golden clouds shed upon the earth bathed the neat and demure houses of Sloane Street in a brief bewildered unreality. Sloane Street, not accustomed to unreality, regretted amiably and with its gentle smile that Nature should insist, once every day, for some half-hour or so, on these mists and enchantments. The neat little houses called their masters and mistresses within doors and advised them to rest before dressing for dinner and so insured these many comfortable souls that they should not be disturbed by any unwelcome violence on their emotions. Soon, before looking-glasses and tables shining with silver hair-brushes bodies would be tied and twisted and faces would be powdered and painted—meanwhile, for that dying moment, Sloane Street was lifted into the hearts of those burnished clouds and held for an instant in glory. Then to the relief of the neat and shining houses the electric lights came out, one by one, and the world was itself again....

Beyond Sloane Square, however, the King's Road chattered and rattled and minded not at all whether the sky were yellow or blue. This was the hour when shopping must be done and barrows shone beneath their flaring gas, and many ladies, with the appearance of having left their homes for the merest minute, hurried from stall to stall. The King's Road stands like a noisy Cheap Jack outside the sanctities of Chelsea. Behind its chatter are the quietest streets in the world, streets that are silent because they prefer rest to noise and not at all because they have nothing to say. The King's Road has been hired by Chelsea to keep foreigners away, and the faint smile that the streets wear is a smile of relief because that noisy road so admirably achieves its purpose. In this mellow evening light the little houses glow, through the river mists, across the cobbles. The stranger, on leaving the King's Road behind him, is swept into a quiet intimacy that has nothing of any town about it; he is refreshed as he might be were he to leave the noisy train behind him and plunge into the dark, scented hedge-rows and see before him the twinkling lights of some friendly inn. As the burnished clouds fade from the sky on the dark surface of the river the black barges hang their lights and in Cheyne Row and Glebe Place, down Oakley Street, and along the wide spaces of Cheyne Walk, lamps burn mildly in a hundred windows. Guarded on one side by the sweeping murmur of the river, on the other by the loud grimaces of the King's Road Chelsea sinks, with a sound like a whisper of its own name, into evening....

As the last trailing fingers of the golden clouds die before the approaching army of the stars, as the yellow above the horizon gives way to a cold and iron blue, lights come out in that house with the green door and the white stone steps—No. 72, Cheyne Walk—that is now Peter Westcott's home.

II

Peter had, on the very afternoon of that beautiful evening, returned from the sea; there, during the last three weeks, he had passed his convalescence and now, once again, he faced the world. Mrs. Galleon and the Galleon baby had been with him and Bobby had come down to them for the week-ends. In this manner Peter had had an opportunity of getting to know Mrs. Galleon with a certainty and speed that nothing else could have given him. During the first weeks after his removal from Bucket Lane, he had been too ill to take any account of his neighbours or surroundings. He had been sent down to the sea as soon as it was possible and it was here, watching her quietly or listening to her as she read to him, walking a little with her, playing with her baby, that he grew to know her and to love her. She had been a Miss Alice du Cane, at first an intelligent, cynical and rather trivial person. Then suddenly, for no very sure reason that any one could discover, her character changed. She had known Bobby during many years and had always laughed at him for a solemn, rather-priggish young man—then she fell in love with him and, to his own wild and delirious surprise, married him. The companions of her earlier girlhood missed her cynicism and complained that brilliance had given way to commonplace but you could not find, in the whole of London, a happier marriage.

To Peter she was something entirely new. Norah Monogue was the only woman with whom, as yet, he had come into any close contact, and she, by her very humility, had allowed him to assume to her a superior, rather patronising attitude. The brief vision of Clare Rossiter had been altogether of the opposite kind, partaking too furiously of heaven to have any earthly quality. But here in Alice Galleon he discovered a woman who gave him something—companionship, a lively and critical intelligence, some indefinable quality of charm—that was entirely new to him.

She chaffed him, criticised him, admired him, absorbed him and nattered him in a breath. She told him that he had a "degree" of talent, that he was the youngest and most ignorant person for his age that she had ever met, that he was conceited, that he was rough and he had no manners, that he was too humble, that he was a "flopper" because he was so anxious to please, that he was a boy and an old man at the same time and finally that the Galleon baby—a solemn child—had taken to him as it had never taken to any one during the eventful three years of its life.

Behind these contradictory criticisms Peter knew that there was a friend, and he was sensible enough also to realise that many of the things that she said to him were perfectly true and that he would do well to take them to heart. At first she had made him angry and that had delighted her, so he had been angry no longer; it seemed to him, during these days of convalescence, that the solemn melodramatic young man of Bucket Lane was an incredibility.

And yet, although he felt that that episode had been definitely closed—shut off as it were by wide doors that held back at a distance, every sound, the noise, the confusion, the terror, was nevertheless there, but for the moment, the doors were closed. Only in his dreams they rolled back and, night after night he awoke, screaming, bathed in sweat, trembling from head to foot. Sometimes he thought that he saw an army of rats advancing across the floor of their Bucket Lane room and Stephen and he beat them off, but ever they returned....

Once he thought that their room was invaded by a number of old toothless hags who came in at the door and the window, and these creatures, with taloned fingers fought, screeching and rolling their eyes....

Twice he dreamt that he saw on a hill, high uplifted against a stormy sky, the statue of the Man on the Lion, gigantic. He struggled to see the Rider's face and it seemed to him that multitudes of other persons—men and women—were pleading, with hands uplifted, that they too might see the face. But always it was denied them, and Peter woke with a strange oppression of crushing disappointment. Sometimes he dreamt of Scaw House and it was always the same dream. He saw the old room with the marble clock and the cactus plant, but about it all now there was dust and neglect. In the arm-chair, by the fire, facing the window, his father, old now and bent, was sitting, listening and waiting. The wind howled about the place, old boards creaked, casements rattled and his father never moved but leaning forward in his chair, watched, waited, eagerly, passionately, for some news....

III

They were having dinner now—Bobby, Mrs. Galleon and Peter—in the studio of the Cheyne Walk House. Outside, a sheet of stars, a dark river and the pale lamps of the street. The curtains of the studio were still undrawn and the glow from the night beyond fell softly along the gleaming black boards of the floor that stretched into shadow by the farther wall, over the round mahogany table—without a cloth and shining with its own colour—deep and liquid brown,—and out to the pictures that hung in their dull gold frames along the wall.

About Peter was a sense of ease and rest, of space that was as new to him as America was to Columbus. He was not even now completely recovered from his Bucket Lane experiences and there was still about him that uncertainty of life—when one sees it as though through gauze curtains—that gives reality to the quality of dreams. Life was behind him, Life was ahead of him, but meantime let him rest in this uncertain and beautiful country until it was time for him to go forward again. This intangibility—walking as it were in a fog round and round the Nelson monument, knowing it was there but never seeing it— remained with him even when practical matters were discussed. For instance, "Reuben Hallard" was to be published in a week's time and Peter was to receive fifty pounds in advance on the day of publication (unusually good terms for a first novel Bobby assured him); also Bobby, through his father, thought that he could secure Peter regular reviewing. The intention then was that Peter should remain with the Galleons as a kind of paying guest, and so his pride would not be hurt and they could have an eye upon him during this launching of him into London. It was fortunate, perhaps, that Alice Galleon had liked him down there at the sea, because she was a lady who had her own way at No. 72, and she by no means liked every one. But perhaps the Galleon baby had had more to do with everything than any one knew, and Mrs. Galleon assured her friends that the baby's heart would most certainly be broken if "the wild young guest" as she called Peter, were carried off.

And wild he was—of that seeing him now at dinner there in the studio there could be no doubt. He was wearing Bobby's clothes and there was still a look of suffering in his eyes and around his mouth, but the difference—his difference from the things about him—went deeper than that. The large high windows of the studio with the expanse of wild and burning stars between their black frames answered Peter's eyes as he faced them. Mrs. Galleon, as she watched him, was reminded of other things, of other persons, of other events, that had marked his earlier life. She glanced from Peter's eyes to Bobby's. She smiled, for on an earlier day, she had seen that same antithesis—the gulf that is fixed between Imagination and Reality—and had known its meaning.

But for Peter, all he asked now was that he might be allowed to rest in the midst of this glorious comfort. His evil dreams were very far away from him to-night. The food, the colour—the fruit piled high in the silver dishes, the glittering of the great silver candelabra that stood on the middle of the table, the deep red of the roses in the bowl at his side, the deeper red of the Port that shone in front of Bobby and then, beneath all this, as though the table were a coloured ship sailing on a solemn sea, the dark, deep shining floor that faded into shadow—all this excited him so that his hands trembled.

He spoke to Mrs. Galleon:

"I wonder if you will do me a favour," he said very earnestly.

"Anything in reason," she answered, laughing back at his gravity.

"Well, don't call me Mr. Westcott any more. Because I'm going to live here and because I'm too old a friend of Bobby's and because, finally, I hate being called Mr. Westcott by anybody, might it be Peter?"

"Joseph calls him Peter as it is," said Bobby quite earnestly looking at his wife.

They were both so grave about it that Alice Galleon couldn't be anything but grave too. She knew that it was really a definite appeal on behalf of both of them that she should here and now, solemnly put her sign of approval on Peter. It was almost in the way that they waited for her to answer, a ceremony. She was even, as she looked at them, surprised into a sudden burst of tenderness towards them both. Bobby so solemn, such a dear, really quite an age and yet as young as any infant in arms. Peter with forces and impulses that might lead to anything or wreck him altogether, and yet, through it all younger even than Bobby. Oh! what an age she, Alice Galleon, seemed to muster at the sight of their innocent trust! Did every woman feel as old, as protecting, as tenderly indulgent, towards every man?...

"Why, of course," she answered quietly, "Peter it shall be—"

Bobby raised his port. "Here's to Peter—to Peter and 'Reuben Hallard'—overwhelming success to both of them."

Emotion, for an instant, held them. Then quietly, they stepped back again. It was almost too good to be true that, after all the turnings and twistings, life should have brought Peter to this. He did not look very far ahead, he did not ask himself whether the book were likely to be a success, whether his career would justify this beginning. If only they would let him alone.... He did not, even to himself, name those powers. He was wrapped about with comfort, he had friends, above all (and this he had discovered at the sea) the Galleons knew Miss Rossiter ... this last thought seemed, by the glorious clamour of it, to draw that sheet of stars down through the window into the room, the air crackled with their splendour.

He was drawn back, down into the world again, by hearing Bobby's voice:

"The evening post and a letter for you. Peter."

He looked down and, with a sudden pang of accusing shame because he had forgotten so easily, with also a sure knowledge that that easy escape from his other life was already forbidden him, saw that the letter was from Stephen. He felt that their eyes were upon him as he took the letter up and he also felt that in Alice Galleon's gaze there was a wise and tender understanding of the things that he must be feeling. The roughness of the envelope, the rudeness of the hand-writing, a stain in one corner that might be beer, the stamp set crookedly—these things seemed to him like so many voices that called him back. Five minutes ago those days in Bucket Lane had belonged to another life, now he was still there and to-morrow he must tramp out again, to-morrow....

The letter said:

Writing here dear Peter at twelve o'clock noon, the Red Crown Inn, Druttledge, on the road to Exeter, a little house where thiccy bandy-legged man you've heard me tell about is Keeper and a good fellow and there's queer enough company in kitchen now to please you. A rough lot of fellows: and a storm coming up black over high woods that'll make walkin' no easy matter on a slimy road, and, dear boy, I've been thinkin' strange about you and 'ow you'll pull along with your kind friends. That nice gentleman sent a telegram as he promised to and says you pull finely along. Hopin' you really are better. But dear boy, if you find you can give me just a word on paper sayin' that hear there is no course for worryin' about your health, then I'm happy because, dear boy, you'm always in my thoughts and I love you fine and wish to

God I could have made everything easier up along in thiccy Bucket Lane. I go from hear by road to Cornwall and Treliss. I'm expecting to find work there. Dear boy, don't forget me and see me again one day and write a letter. They are getting too much into their bellies and making the devil's own noise. There is Thunder coming the air is that still over the roof of the barn and the road's dead white. Dear Boy, I am your friend,

STEPHEN BRANT.

The candles blew a little in the breeze from the open window and the lighted shadows ran flickering in silver lines, along the dark floor. Peter stood holding the letter in his hand, looking out on to the black square of sky; the lights of the barges swung down the river and he could hear, very faintly, the straining of ropes and the turning of some mysterious wheel.

He saw Stephen—the great head, the flowing beard, the huge body—and then the inn with the thunder coming over the hill, and then, beyond that Treliss gleaming with its tiers of lights, above the breast of the sea. And from here, from this wide Embankment, down to that sea, there stretched, riding over hills, bending into valleys, always white and hard and stony, the road....

For an instant he felt as though the studio, the lights, the comforts were holding him like a prison—

"It's a letter from Stephen Brant," he said, turning back from the window. "He seems well and happy—"

"Where is he?"

"Eating bread and cheese at an inn somewhere—on the road down to Cornwall."

IV

On the following Tuesday "Reuben Hallard" was published and on the Thursday afternoon Henry Galleon and Clare Rossiter were to come to tea. "Reuben Hallard" arrived in a dark red cover with a white paper label. The six copies lay on the table and looked at Peter as though he had had nothing whatever to do with their existence. He looked down upon them, opened one of them very tenderly, read half a page and felt that it was the best stuff he'd ever seen. He read the rest of the page and thought that the author, whoever the creature might be, deserved, imprisonment for writing such nonsense.

The feeling of strangeness towards it all was increased by the fact that Bobby had, with the exception of the final proofs—these Peter had read down by the sea—done most of the proof-correcting. It was a task for which his practical common sense and lack of all imagination admirably fitted him. There, at any rate, "Reuben Hallard" was, ready to face all the world, to go, perhaps, to the farthest Hebrides, to be lost in all probability, utterly lost, in the turgid flood of contemporary fiction.

There was a dedication "To Stephen"... How surprised Stephen would be! He looked at the chapter headings—An Old Man with a Lantern—the Road at Night.... Sun on the Western Moor—Stevenson—Tushery all of it! How they'd tear it to bits, those papers!

He laughed to himself to think that there had once been a day when he had thought that the thing would make his fortune! And yet—he turned the pages over tenderly—there might be something to be said for it, Miss Monogue had thought well of it. These publishers, blasé, cynical fellows, surely believed in it.

It was fat and red and comfortable. It had a worldly, prosperous look. "Reuben Hallard and His Adventures" ... Good Lord! What cheek.

There were five copies to give away. One between Bobby and Mrs. Galleon, one for Stephen, one for Miss Monogue, one for Mrs. Brockett and one for Mr. Zanti. "Reuben Hallard and His Adventures," by Peter Westcott. They would be getting it now at the newspaper offices. The Mascot would have a copy and the fat little chocolate consumer. It would stand with a heap of others, and be ticked off with a heap of others, for some youth to exercise his wit upon. As to any one buying the book? Who ever saw any one buying a six-shilling novel? It was only within the last year or so that the old three volumes with their thirty-one-and-six had departed this life. The publishers had assured Peter that this new six-shilling form was the thing. "Please have you got 'Reuben Hallard' by Peter Westcott?... Thank you, I'll take it with me."

No, it was inconceivable.

There poor Reuben would lie—deserted, still-born, ever dustier and dustier whilst other stories came pouring, pouring from endless presses, covering, crowding it down, stamping upon it, burying it.... "Here lies 'Reuben Hallard.'..."

Poor Peter!

On Thursday, however, there was the tea-party—a Thursday never to be forgotten whilst Peter was alive. Bobby had told him the day before that his father might be coming. "The rest of the family will turn up for certain. They want to see you. They're always all agog for any new thing—one of them's always playing Cabot to somebody else's Columbus. But father's uncertain. He gets something into his head and then nothing whatever will draw him out—but I expect he'll turn up."

The other visitor was announced to Peter on the very day.

"By the way, Peter, somebody's coming to tea this afternoon who's met you before—met you at that odd boarding-house of yours—a Miss Rossiter. Clare's an old friend of ours. I told you down at the sea about her and you said you remembered meeting her."

"Remembered meeting her!" Did Dante remember meeting Beatrice—did Petrarch remember Laura? Did Keats forget his Fanny Brawne? Did Richard Feverel forget his Lucy?

On a level with these high-thinking gentlemen was Peter, disguising his emotions from Alice's sharp eyes but silent, breathless, wanting some other place than that high studio in which to breathe. "Yes—she came to tea once with a Miss Monogue there—I liked her...."

He was not there, but rather on some height alone with her and their hands touched over a photograph. "The Man on the Lion." There was something worthy of his feeling for her!

Meanwhile, for the first part of the afternoon one must put up with the Galleon family. Had Peter been sufficiently calm and sensible these appendages to a great author would have been worth his attention.

Behold them in relation to "Henry Lessingham," soaked in the works, bearing on their backs the whole Edition de Luxe, decking themselves with the little odds and ends of literary finery that they had picked up, bursting with the good-nature of assured self-consequence—harmless, foolish, comfortable. Mrs. Galleon was massive with a large flat face that jumped suddenly into expression when one least expected it. There was a great deal of silk about her, much leisurely movement and her tactics were silence and a slow, significant smile—these she always contributed to any conversation that was really beyond her. Had she not, during many years of her life, been married to a genius she would have been an intensely slow-moving but adequate housekeeper—as it was, her size and her silence enabled her to keep her place at many literary dinners. Peter, watching her, was consumed with wonder that Henry Galleon could ever have married her and understood that Bobby was the child of both his parents. Bobby had a brother and sister—Percival and Millicent. Percival was twenty-five and had written two novels that were considered promising by those who did not know that he was the son of his father. He was slim and dark with a black thread of a moustache and rather fine white fingers. His clothes were very well cut but his appearance was a little too elaborately simple. His sister, a girl of about eighteen, was slim and dark also; she had the eager appearance of one who has heard just enough to make her very anxious to hear a great deal more.

One felt that she did not want to miss anything, but probably her determination to be her father's daughter would prevent her from becoming very valuable or intelligent.

Finally it was strange that Bobby had so completely escaped the shadow of his father's mantle. These people were intended, of course, to be the background of Peter's afternoon and it was therefore more than annoying that that was the very last thing that they were. Millicent and Percival made a ball and then flung it backwards and forwards throughout the affair. Their mother watched them with appreciation and Alice Galleon, who knew them, gave them tea and cake and let them have their way. Into the midst of this Henry Galleon came—a little, round, fat man with a face like a map, the body of Napoleon and a trot round the room like a very amiable pony, eyes that saw everything, understood everything, and forgave everything, a brown buff waistcoat with gilt buttons, white spats and a voice that rolled and roared ... he was the tenderest, most alarming person in any kind of a world. He was so gentle that any sparrow would trust him implicitly and so terrific that an army would most certainly fly from before him. He ate tea-cake, smiled and shook hands with Peter, listened for half an hour to the spirited conversation of his two children and trotted away again, leaving behind him an atmosphere of gentle politeness and an amazing savoir-faire that one saw his children struggling to catch. They finally gave it up about half-past five and retreated, pressing Peter to pay them a call at the earliest opportunity.

This was positively all that Peter saw, on this occasion, of Henry Galleon. It was quite enough to give him a great deal to think about, but it could scarcely be called a meeting.

At quarter to six when Peter was in despair and Alice Galleon had ordered the tea-things to be taken away Clare Rossiter rushed in. She stood a whirlwind of flying colours in the middle of the Studio now sinking into twilight. "Alice dear, I am most terribly sorry but mother would stay. I couldn't get her to leave and it was all so awkward. How do you do, Mr. Westcott? Do you remember—we met at Treliss—and now I must rush back this very minute. We are dining at seven before the Opera, and father wants that music you promised him—the Brahms thing. Oh! is it upstairs? Well, if you don't mind...."

Alice Galleon left them together. Peter could say nothing at all. He stood there, shifting from foot to foot, white, absolutely tongue-tied.

She felt his embarrassment and struggled.

"I hear that you've been very ill, Mr. Westcott. I'm so dreadfully sorry and I do hope that you're better?"

He muttered something.

"Your book is out, isn't it? 'Reuben Hallard' is the name. I must get father to put it down on his list. One's first books must be so dreadfully exciting—and so alarming ... the reviews and everything—what is it about?"

He murmured "Cornwall."

"Cornwall? How delightful! I was only there once. Mullion. Do you know Mullion?" She struggled along. The pain that had begun in his heart was now at his throat—his throat was full of spiders' webs. He could scarcely see her in the dark but her pale blue dress and her dark eyes and her beautiful white hands—her little figure danced against the dark, shining floor like a fairy's.

He heard her sigh of relief at Alice Galleon's return.

"Oh! thank you, dear, so much. Good-bye, Mr. Westcott—I shall read the book."

She was gone.

"Lights! Lights!" cried Alice Galleon. "How provoking of her not to come to tea properly. Well, Peter? How was it all?"

He was guilty of abominable rudeness.

He burst from the room without a word and banged, desperately, the door behind him.

CHAPTER II

A CHAPTER ABOUT SUCCESS I HOW TO WIN IT, HOW TO KEEP IT—WITH A NOTE AT THE END FROM HENRY GALLEON

I

The shout of applause with which "Reuben Hallard" was greeted still remains one of the interesting cases in modern literary history. At this time of day it all seems ancient and distant enough; the book has been praised, blamed, lifted up, hurled down a thousand times, and has finally been discovered to be a book of promise, of natural talent, with a great deal of crudity and melodrama and a little beauty. It does not stand of course in comparison with Peter Westcott's later period and yet it has a note that his hand never captured afterwards. How incredibly bad it is in places, the Datchett incidents, with their flames and screams and murder in the dark, sufficiently betray: how fine it can be such a delight as The Cherry Orchard chapter shows, and perhaps the very badness of the crudities helped in its popularity, for there was nothing more remarkable about it than the fashion in which it captured every class of reader. But its success, in reality, was a result of the exact moment of its appearance. Had Peter waited a thousand years he could not possibly have chosen a time more favourable. It was that moment in literary history, when the world had had enough of lilies and was turning, with relief, to artichokes. There was a periodical of this time entitled The Green Volume. This appeared somewhere about 1890 and it brought with it a band of young men and women who were exceedingly clever, saw the quaintness of life before its reality and stood on tiptoe in order to observe things that were really growing quite close to the ground. This quarterly produced some very admirable work; its contributors were all, for a year or two, as clever as they were—young and as cynical as either. The world was dressed in a powder puff and danced beneath Chinese lanterns and was as wicked as it could be in artificial rose-gardens. It was all great fun for a year or two....

Then The Green Volume died, people began to whisper about slums and drainage, and Swedish drill for ten minutes every morning was considered an admirable thing. On the edge of this new wave came "Reuben Hallard," combining as it did a certain amount of affectation with a good deal of naked truth, and having the rocks of Cornwall as well as its primroses for its background. It also told a story with a beginning to it and an end to it, and it contained the beautiful character of Mrs. Poveret, a character that was undoubtedly inspired by that afternoon that Peter had with his mother..

In addition to all this it must be remembered that the world was entirely unprepared for the book's arrival. It had been in no fashion heralded and until a long review appeared in The Daily Globe no one noticed it in any way. Then the thing really began. The reviewers were glad to find something in a dead season, about which a column or two might possibly be written; the general public was delighted to discover a novel that was considered by good judges to be literature and that, nevertheless, had as good a story as though it weren't—its faults were many and some of its virtues accidental, but it certainly deserved success as thoroughly as did most of its contemporaries. Edition followed edition and "Reuben Hallard" was the novel of the spring of 1896.

The effect of all this upon Peter may easily be imagined. It came to him first, with those early reviews and an encouraging letter from the publishers, as something that did not belong to him at all, then after a month or so it belonged to him so completely that he felt as though he had been used to it all his life. Then slowly, as the weeks passed and the success continued, he knew that the publication of this book had changed the course of his life. Letters from agents and publishers asking for his next novel, letters from America, letters from unknown readers, all these things showed him that he could look now towards countries that had not, hitherto, been enclosed by his horizon. He breathed another air.

And yet he was astonishingly simple about it all—very young and very naive. The two things that he felt about it were, first, that it would please very much his friends—Bobby and his wife, Mrs. Brockett, Norah Monogue, Mr. Zanti, Herr Gottfried and, above all, Stephen; and secondly, that all those early years in Cornwall—the beatings, his mother, Scaw House, even Dawson's—had been of use to him. One remembers those extraordinary chapters concerning Reuben and his father—here Peter had, for the first time, allowed some expression of his attitude to it all to escape him.

He felt indeed as though the success of the book placed for a moment all that other life in the background—really away from him. For the first time since he left Brockett's he was free from a strange feeling of apprehension.... Scaw House was hidden.

He gave himself up to glorious life. He plunged into it....

He stepped, at first timidly, into literary London. It was, at first sight, alarming enough because it seemed to consist, so largely and so stridently, of the opposite sex. Bobby would have had Peter avoid it altogether. "There are some young idiots," he said, "who go about to these literary tea-parties. They've just written a line or two somewhere or other, and they go curving and bending all over the place. Young Tony Gale and young Robin Trojan and my young ass of a brother ... don't want you to join that lot, Peter, my boy. The women like to have 'em of course, they're useful for handing the cake about but that's all there is to it ... keep out of it."

But Peter had not had so many friends during the early part of his life that he could afford to do without possible ones now. He wanted indeed just as many as he could grasp. The comfort and happiness of his life with Bobby, the success of the book, the opening of a career in front of him, these things had made of him another creature. He had grown ten years younger; his cheeks were bright, his eye clear, his step buoyant. He moved now as though he loved his fellow creatures. One felt, on his entrance into a room, that the air was clearer, and that one was in the company of a human being who found the world, quite honestly and naturally, a delightful place. This was the first effect that success had upon Peter.

And indeed they met him—all of them—with open arms. They saw in him that burning flame that those who have been for the first time admitted into the freemasonry of their Art must ever show. Afterwards he would be accustomed to that country, would know its roads and hills and cities and would be perhaps disappointed that they were neither as holy nor as eternal as he had once imagined them to be—now he stood on the hill's edge and looked down into a golden landscape whose bounds he could not discern. But they met him too on the personal side. The fact that he had been found starving in a London garret was of itself a wonderful thing—then he had in his manner a rough, awkward charm that flattered them with his youth and inexperience. He was impetuous and confidential and then suddenly reserved and constrained. But, above it all, it was evident that he wanted friendliness and good fellowship. He took every one at the value that they offered to him. He first encouraged them to be at their most human and then convinced them that that was their natural character. He lighted every one's lamp at the flame of his own implicit faith.

These ladies and gentlemen put very plainly before him the business side of his profession. Their conversation was all of agents, publishers, the sums that one of their number obtained and how lucky to get so much so soon, and the sums that another of their number did not obtain and what a shame it was that such good work was rewarded by so little. It was all—this conversation—in the most generous strain. Jealousy never raised its head. They read—these precious people—the works of one another with an eager praise and a tender condemnation delightful to see. It was a warm bustling society that received Peter.

These tea-parties and fireside discussions had not, perhaps, been always so friendly and large-hearted but in the time when Peter first encountered them they were influenced and moulded by a very remarkable woman—a woman who succeeded in combining humour, common sense and imagination in admirably adjusted qualities. Her humour made her tolerant, her common sense made her wise, and her imagination made her tender—her name was Mrs. Launce.

She was short and broad, with large blue eyes that always, if one watched them, showed her thoughts and dispositions. Some people make of their faces a disguise, others use them as a revelation—the result to the observer is very much the same in either case. But with Mrs. Launce there was no definite attempt at either one thing or the other—she was so busily engaged in the matter in hand, so absorbed and interested, that the things that her face might be doing never occurred to her. Her hair was drawn back and parted down the middle. She liked to wear little straw coal-scuttle bonnets; she was very fond of blue silk, and her frocks had an inclination to trail. On her mother's side she was French and on her father's English; from her mother she got the technique of her stories, the light-hearted boldness of her conversation and her extraordinary devotion to her family. She was always something of a puzzle to English women because she was a great deal more domestic than most of them and yet bristled with theories about morals and life in general that had nothing whatever in common with domesticity. Some one once said of her that "she was a hot water bottle playing at being a bomb...."

She belonged to all the London worlds, although she found perhaps especial pleasure in the society of her fellow writers. This was largely because she loved, beyond everything else, the business side of her profession. There was nothing at all that she did not know about the publishing and distribution of a novel. Her capacity for remembering other people's prices was prodigious and she managed her agent and her publisher with a deftness that left them gasping. There were very few persons in her world who had not, at one time or another, poured their troubles into her ear. She had that gift, valuable in life beyond all others, of giving herself up entirely to the person with whom she was talking. When the time came to give advice the combination of her common sense and her tenderness made her invaluable. There was no crime black enough, no desertion, no cruelty horrible enough to outspeed her pity. She hated and understood the sin and loved and comforted the sinner. With a wide and accurate knowledge of humanity she combined a deep spiritual belief in the goodness of God.

Everything, however horrible, interested her ... she adored life.

This little person in the straw bonnet and the blue dress gave Peter something that he had never known before—she mothered him. He sat next to her at some dinner-party and she asked him to come and have tea with her. She lived in a little street in Westminster in a tiny house that had her children on the top floor, a beautiful copy of the Mona Lisa and a very untidy writing-table on the second, and a little round hall and a tiny dining-room on the ground floor. Her husband and her family—including an adorable child of two—were all as amiable as possible.

Peter told her most things on the first day that he had tea with her and everything on the second. He told her about his boyhood—Treliss, Scaw House, his father, Stephen. He told her about Brockett's and Bucket Lane. He told her, finally, about Clare Rossiter.

He always remembered one thing that she said at this time. They were sitting at her open window looking down into the blue evening that is in Westminster quieter even than it is at Chelsea. Behind the faint green cloud of trees the Abbey's huge black pile soared into space.

"You think you've made a tremendous break?" she said.

"Yes—this is an entirely new life—new in every way. I seem too to be set amongst an entirely new crowd of people. The division seems to me sharper every day. I believe I've left it all behind."

She looked at him sharply. "You're afraid of all that earlier time," she said.

"Yes, I am."

"It made you write 'Reuben Hallard.' Perhaps this life here in London..."

"It's safer," he caught her up.

"Don't," she answered him very gravely, "play for safety. It's the most dangerous thing in the world." She paused for a moment and then added: "But probably they won't let you alone."

"I hope to God they will," he cried.

III

He saw Clare Rossiter twice during this time and, on each occasion, it seemed to him that she was trying to make up to him for his awkwardness at their first meeting. On the first of these two occasions she had only a few words with him, but there was a note in her voice that he fancied, wildly, unreasonably, was different from the tone that she used to other people. She looked so beautiful with her golden hair coiled above her head. It was the most wonderful gold that he had ever seen. He could only, in his excitement, think of marmalade and that was a sticky comparison. "The Lady with the Marmalade Hair"—how monstrous! but that did convey the colour. Her eyes seemed darker now than they had been before and her cheeks whiter. The curve of her neck was so wonderful that it hurt him physically. He wanted so terribly to kiss her just beneath her ear. He saw how he would do it, and that he would have to move away some of the shiny hair that strayed like sunlight across the white skin.

She did not seem to him quite so tiny when she smiled; it was exactly as water ripples when the sun suddenly bursts dark clouds. He had a thousand comparisons for her, and then sometimes she would be, as it were, caught up into a cloud and he would only see a general radiance and be blinded by the light.

He wished very much that he could think of something else—something other than marmalade—that had that quality of gold. He often imagined what it would be like when she let it all down—like a forest of autumn trees—no, that spoke of decay—like the sunlight on sand towards evening—like the fires of Walhalla in the last act of Gotterdämmerung—like the lights of some harbour seen from the farther shore—like clouds that are ready to burst with evening sunlight. Perhaps, after all, amber was the nearest....

"Peter, ask Miss Rossiter if she will have some more tea...." Oh! What a fool he is! What an absolute ass!

On the second of these two meetings she had read "Reuben Hallard." She loved it! She thought it astounding! The most wonderful first novel she had ever read. How had he been able to make one feel Cornwall so? She had been once to Cornwall, to Mullion and it had been just like that! Those rocks! it was like a poem! And then so exciting!

She had not been able to put it down for a single minute. "Mother was furious with me because there I sat until I don't know how early in the morning reading it! Oh! Mr. Westcott, how wonderful to write like that!"

Her praise inflamed him like wine. He looked at her with exultation.

"Oh! you feel like that!" he said, drawing a great breath, "I did want you to like it so!" He was enraptured—the world was heaven! He did not realise that some young woman at a tea-party the day before had said precisely these same things and he had said: "Of all the affected idiots!"...

IV

This might all be termed a period of preparation—that period was fixed for Peter with its sign and seal on a certain evening of spring when an enormous orange moon was in the sky, scents were in all the Chelsea gardens, and the Chelsea streets were like glass in the silver luminous light.

Peter was walking home after a party at the Rossiters'. It was the first time that he had been invited to their house and it had been a great success. Dr. Rossiter was a little round fat man with snow-white hair, red cheeks and twinkling eyes. He cured his patients and irritated his relations by his good temper. Mrs. Rossiter, Peter thought, had a great resemblance to Bobby's mother, Mrs. Galleon, senior. They were, both of them, massive and phlegmatic. They had both acquired that solemn dignity that comes of living up to one's husband's reputation. They both looked on their families—Mrs. Rossiter on Clare and Mrs. Galleon on Millicent, Percival and Bobby—with curiosity, tolerance and a mild soft of wonder. They were both massively happy and completely unimaginative. They were, indeed, old friends, having been at school together, they were Emma and Jane to one another and Mrs. Rossiter could never forget that Mrs. Galleon came to school two years after herself and was therefore junior still; whilst Mrs. Galleon had stayed two years longer than Mrs. Rossiter, and was a power there when Mrs. Rossiter was completely forgotten; they were fond of each other as long as they were allowed to patronise one another.

Peter had spent a delicious evening. He had had half an hour in the garden with Clare. They had spoken in an undertone. He had told her his ambitions, she had told him her aspirations. Some one had sung in the garden and there had been one wonderful moment when Peter had touched her hand and she had not taken it away. At last they were both silent and the garden flowed about them, on every side of them, with the notes and threads that can only be heard at night.

Mrs. Rossiter, heavily and solemnly, brought her daughter a shawl. There was some one to whom she would like to introduce Mr. Westcott. Would he mind? Eden was robbed of its glories....

But he had had enough. He thought at one moment that already she was beginning to care for him, and at another, that a lover's fancy made signs out of the wind and portents out of the running water.

But he was happy with a mighty exultation, and then, as he turned down on to the Embankment and felt the breeze from the river as it came towards him, he met Henry Galleon.

The old man, in an enormous hat that was like a top hat only round at the brim and brown in colour, was trotting home. He saw Peter and stopped. He spoke to him in his slow tremendous voice and the words seemed to go on after they had left him, rolling along the Embankment.

"I am glad to see you, Mr. Westcott. I have thought that I would like to have a chat with you. I have just finished your book."

This was indeed tremendous—that Henry Galleon should have read "Reuben Hallard." Peter trembled all over.

"I wonder whether you would care to come and have a chat with me. I have some things you might care to see. What time like the present? It is early hours yet and you will be doing an old man who sleeps only poorly a kindness."

What a night of nights! Peter, trembling with excitement, felt Henry Galleon put his arm in his, felt the weight of the great man's body. They walked slowly along and the moon and the stars and the lights on the river and the early little leaves in the trees and the stones of the houses and the little "tish-tish" of the water against the Embankment seemed to say—"Oh! Peter Westcott's going to have a chat with Henry Galleon! Did you ever hear such a thing!"

Peter was sorry that his Embankment was deserted and that there was no one to see them go into the house together. He drew a great breath as the door closed behind them. The house was large and dark and mysterious. The rest of the family were still out at some party. Henry Galleon drew Peter into his own especial quarters and soon they were sitting in a lofty library, its walls covered with books that stretched to the ceiling. Peter meanwhile buried in a huge arm-chair and feeling that Henry Galleon's eyes were piercing him through and through.

The old man talked for some time about other things—talked wonderfully about the great ones of the earth whom he had known, the great things that he had seen. It was amazing to Peter to hear the gods of his world alluded to as "poor old S—— poor fellow!... Yes, indeed. I remember his coming into breakfast one day..." or "You were asking about T—— Old Wallie, as we used to call him—poor fellow, poor fellow—we lived together in rooms for some time. That was before I married—and perilously, dangerously—I might almost say magnificently near starvation we were too...."

Peter already inflamed with that earlier half-hour in the garden now breathed a portentous air. He was with the Gods ... there on the Olympian heights he drank with them, he sang songs with them, with mighty voices they applauded "Reuben Hallard." He drank in his excitement many whiskies and sodas and soon the white room with its books was like the inside of a golden shell. The old man opposite him grew in size—his face was ever larger and larger, his shirt front bulged and bulged—his hand raised to emphasise some point was tremendous as the hand of a God. Peter felt that he himself was growing smaller and smaller, would soon, in the depths of that mighty arm-chair disappear altogether but that opposite him two mighty burning eyes held him. And always like thunder the voice rolled on.... "My son tells me that this book of yours is a success ... that they are emptying their purses to fill yours. That may be a dangerous thing for you. I have read your book, it has many faults; it is not written at all—it is loose and lacking in all construction. You know nothing, as yet, about life—you do not know what to use or what to reject. But the Spirit is there, the right Spirit. It is a little flame—it will be very easily quenched and nothing can kill it so easily as success—guard it, my son, guard it."

Peter felt as Siegfried must have felt when confronted by Wotan.

His poor little book was dwindling now before his eyes. He was conscious of a great despair. How useless of him to attempt so impossible a task....

The voice rolled on:

"I am an old man now and only twice before in my time nave I seen that spirit in a young man's eyes. You may remember now an old man's words—for I would urge you, I would implore you to keep nothing before you but the one thing that can bring Life into Art. I will not speak to you of the sacredness of your calling. Many will laugh at you and tell you that it is pretentious to name it so. Others will come to you and will advise how this is to be done and that is to be done. Others will talk to you of schools, they will tell you that once it was in that manner and that now it is in this manner. Some will tell you that you have no style—others will tell you that you have too much. Some again will tempt you with money and money is not to be despised. Again you will be tested with photographs and paragraphs, with lectures and public dinners.... Worst of all there will come to you terrible hours when you yourself know of a sure certainty that your work is worthless. In your middle age a great barrenness will come upon you. You have been a little teller of little tales, and on every side of you there will be others who have striven for other prizes and have won them. Sitting alone in your room with your poor strands of coloured silk that had once been intended to make so beautiful a pattern, poor boy, you will know that you have failed. That will be a very dreadful hour—the only power that can meet it is a blind and deaf courage. Courage is the only thing that we are here to show ... the hour will pass."

The old man paused. There was a silence. Then he said very slowly as though he were drawing in front of him the earliest histories of his own past life....

"Against all these temptations, against these voices of the World and the Flesh, against the glory of power and the swinging hammer of success, you, sitting quietly in your room, must remember that a great charge has been given you, that you are here for one thing and one thing only ... to listen. The whole duty of Art is listening for the voice of God.

"I am not speaking in phrases. I am not pressing upon you any sensational discoveries, but here at the end of my long life, I, with all the things that I meant to do and have failed to do heavy upon me, can give you only this one word. I have hurried, I have scrambled, I have fought and cursed and striven, but as an Artist only those hours that I have spent listening, waiting, have been my real life.

"So it must be with you. You are here to listen. Never mind if they tell you that story-telling is a cheap thing, a popular thing, a mean thing. It is the instrument that is given to you and if, when you come to die you know that, for brief moments, you have heard, and that what you have heard you have written, Life has been justified.

"Nothing else can console you, nothing else can comfort you. There must be restraint, austerity, discipline—words must come to you easily but only because life has come to you with so great a pain ... the Artist's life is the harshest that God can give to a man. Make no mistake about that. Fortitude is the artist's only weapon of defence...."

Henry Galleon came over to Peter's chair and put his hand upon the boy's arm.

"I am at the end of my work. I have done what I can. You are at the beginning of yours. You will do what you can. I wish you good fortune."

A vision came to Peter. Through the open window, against the sheet of stars, gigantic, was the Rider on the Lion.

He could not see the Rider's face.

A great exultation inflamed him.

At that instant he was stripped bare. His history, the people whom he knew, the things that he had done, they were all as though they had never been.

His soul was, for that great moment, naked and alone before God.

"The whole duty of Art is listening for the voice of God...."

A sound, as though it came to him from another world, broke into the room.

There were voices and steps on the stairs.

"Ah, they are back from their party," Henry Galleon said, trotting happily to the door. "Come up and have a chat with my wife, Westcott, before going to bed."

CHAPTER III

THE ENCOUNTER

I

Peter was now the young man of the moment. He took this elevation with frank delight, was encouraged by it, gave it all rather more, perhaps, than its actual value, began a new novel, "The Stone House," started weekly reviewing on The Interpreter and yielded himself up entirely to Clare Rossiter.

He had been in love with her ever since that first day at Norah Monogue's, but the way that she gradually now absorbed him was like nothing so much as the slow covering of the rocks and the sand by the incoming tide. At first, in those days at Brockett's, she had seemed to him something mysterious, intangible, holy. But after that meeting in Cheyne Walk he knew her for a prize that some fortunate man might, one day, win. He did not, for an instant, suppose that he could ever be that one, but the mere imagined picture of what some other would one day have, sent the blood rushing through him. Her holiness for him was still intact but for another there would be human, earthly wonders.

Then, curiously, as he met her more often and knew her better there came a certain easy, almost casual, intercourse. One Clare Rossiter still reigned amongst the clouds, but there was now too another easy, fascinating, humorous creature who treated him almost like Alice Galleon herself—laughed at him, teased him, provoked him ... suddenly, like a shadow across a screen, would slip away; and he be on his knees again before something that was only to be worshipped.

These two shapes of her crossed and were confused and again were parted. His thoughts were first worshipping in heaven, then dwelling with delight on witty, charming things that she had said.

For that man, when he came, there would be a most wonderful treasure.

Peter now lost his appetite. He could not sleep at night. He would slip out of his room, cross the silent Chelsea streets and watch her dark window. He cultivated Mrs. Rossiter and that massive and complacent lady took it entirely to herself. Indeed, nothing, at this time was more remarkable than the little stir that Peter's devotion caused. It was perhaps that Clare had always had a cloud of young men about her, perhaps that Peter was thought to be having too wonderful a time, just now, to be falling in love as well—that would be piling Life on to Life! ... no one could live under it.

Besides Mrs. Rossiter liked him ... he was amazing, you see ... people said....

And the next stage arrived.

One May evening, at the Galleons' house, when some one was playing the piano and all the world seemed to be sitting in corners Clare's hand lay suddenly against his. The smooth outer curve of his hand lay against her palm. Their little fingers touched. Sheets of fire rose, inflamed him and fell ... rose again and fell. His hand began to shake, her hand began to shake. He heard, a thousand miles away, some one singing about "the morn."

Their hands parted. She rose and slowly, her white dress and red-gold hair flung against a background that seemed to him black and infinite, crossed the room.

That trembling of her hand had maddened him. It suddenly showed him that he—as well as another—might run the race for her. Everything that he had ever done or been—his sentiments, his grossnesses, his restraints and his rebellions—were now concerned in this pursuit. No other human being—Stephen, Norah Monogue, Bobby, Alice—now had any interest for him. His reviews were written he knew not how, the editions of "Reuben Hallard" might run into the gross for all he cared, "The Stone House" lay neglected.

And he avoided seeing her. He was afraid to spoil that moment when her hand had shaken at the touch of his, and yet he was tormented by the longing for a new meeting that might provide some new amazement. Perhaps he would hold her hand and feel the shadow of her body bending towards his own! And his heart stopped beating; and he was suddenly cold with a splendid terror.

Then he did meet her again and had nothing to say. It seemed to him that she was frightened. He came home that day in a cold fog of miserable despair. A letter from his publishers informing him of a tenth edition was of ironical unimportance. He lay awake all night restlessly unhappy.

For the first time for many months the old shadows stole out into the room—the black bulk of Scaw House—the trees, the windows, his father....

And to him, tossing on his bed there came thoughts of a certain house in the town. He could get up and dress now—a cab would soon take him there ... in the early morning he could slink back.

Clare did not want him! A fool to fancy that she had ever cared.

He, Peter Westcott, nobody! Why then should he not have his adventures, he still so young and vigorous? He would go to that house....

And then, almost reluctantly, as he sat up in bed and watched the grey, shadowy walls, Stephen seemed to be visible to him—Stephen, walking the road, starting early in the fresh air when the light was breaking and the scent of the grass was cool and filled with dew.

He would write to Stephen in the morning—he lay down and went to sleep.

By this time, meanwhile, Alice and Bobby had noticed. Alice, indeed, had a number of young men over whose emotions she kept guard and Peter had become, during these weeks, very valuable to her....

She did not want him to marry anybody—especially she did not want him to marry Clare. At breakfast, past Peter's ears, as though he were not concerned at all, she talked to Bobby—

"Really, Dr. Rossiter spoils Clare beyond all bounds—"

"Um?"

"He's taking her with him up to Glasgow to that Congress thing. He knows perfectly well that she ought to stay with Mrs. Rossiter—and so does she."

"Well, it's no business of ours—" Bobby's usual tolerant complacency.

"It is. Clare might be a fine creature if she didn't let herself be spoiled in this way. She's perpetually selfish and she ought to be told so."

"We're all perpetually selfish," said Bobby who began to be sorry for Peter.

"Oh! no, we're not. I'm very fond of Clare but I don't envy the man who marries her. There's no one in the world more delightful when she has her own way and things go smoothly, but they've wrapped her up in cotton wool to such an extent that she simply doesn't know how to live out of it. She's positively terrified of Life."

This, as Alice had intended, was too much for Peter. He burst out—

"I think Miss Rossiter's the pluckiest girl I've ever met. She's afraid of nothing."

"Except of being uncomfortable," Alice retorted. "That frightens her into fits. Make her uncomfortable, Peter, and you'll see—"

And, red in the face, Peter answered—"I don't think you ought to talk of any one who's so fond of you behind her back in that way—"

"Oh! I say just the same to her face. I'm always telling her these things and she always agrees and then's just as selfish as ever. That absurd little father of hers has spoilt her!"

Spoilt! Clare spoilt! Peter smiled darkly. Alice Galleon—delightful woman though she was, of course couldn't endure that another woman should receive such praise—Jealousy! Ah!...

And the aged and weighty author of "Reuben Hallard," to whom the world was naturally an open book, and life known to its foundations, nodded to himself. How people, intelligent enough in other ways, could be so short-sighted!

Afterwards, when they were alone, Bobby took him in hand—

"You're in love with Clare Rossiter, Peter," he said.

"Yes, I am," Peter answered defiantly.

"But you've known her so short a time!"

"What's that to do with it?"

"Oh, nothing, of course. But do you think you're the sort of people likely to get on?"

"Really, Bobby, I don't—"

"I know—none of my business—quite true. But you see I've known Clare pretty well all my life and you're the best friend I've got, so you might allow me to take an interest."

"Well, say what you like."

"Nothing to say except that Clare isn't altogether an easy problem. You're like all the other fellows I know—think because Clare's got red hair and laughs easily she's a goddess—she isn't, not a bit! She's got magnificent qualities and one day perhaps, when she's had a thoroughly bad time, she'll show one the kind of things she's made of. But she's an only child, she's been spoilt all her life and the moment she begins to be unhappy she's impossible."

"She shan't ever be unhappy if I can help it!" muttered Peter fiercely.

Bobby laughed. "You'll do your best of course, but are you the sort of man for her? She wants some one who'll give her every kind of comfort, moral, physical and intellectual. She wants somebody who'll accept her enthusiasms as genuine intelligence. You'll find her out intellectually in a week. Then she wants some one who'll give her his whole attention. You think now that you will but you won't—you can't—you're not made that way. By temperament and trade you're an artist. She thinks, at the moment, that an artist would suit her very well; but, in reality, my boy, he's the very last sort of person she ought to marry."

Peter caught at Bobby's words. "Do you really think she cares about me?"

"She's interested. Clare spends her days in successive enthusiasms. She's always being enthusiastic— dreadful disillusions in between the heights. Mind you, there's another side of Clare—a splendid side, but it wants very careful management and I don't know, Peter, that you're exactly the sort of person—"

"Thanks very much," said Peter grimly.

"No, but you're not—you don't, in the least, see her as she is, and she doesn't see you as you are— hence these misguided attempts on my part to show you one another."

But Peter had not been listening.

"Do you really think," he muttered, "that she cares about me?"

Bobby looked at him, laughed and shrugged his shoulders in despair.

"Ah! I see—it's no use," he said, "poor dear Peter—well, I wish you luck!"

And that was the end as far as Alice and Bobby were concerned. They never alluded to it again and indeed now seemed to favour meetings between Clare and Peter.

And now, through these wonderful Spring weeks, these two were continually together. The Galleons had, at first, been inclined to consider Clare's obvious preference for Peter as the simplest desire to be part of a general rather heady enthusiasm. "Clare loves little movements...." And Peter, throughout this Spring was a little movement. The weeks went on, and Clare was not herself—silent, absorbed, almost morose. One day she asked Alice Galleon a number of questions about Peter, and, after that, resolutely avoided speaking of him. "Of course," Alice said to Bobby—"Dr. Rossiter will let her marry any one she likes. She'll have plenty of money and Peter's going to have a great career. After all it may be the best thing."

Bobby shook his head. "They're both egoists," he said. "Peter because he's never had anything he wanted and Clare because she's always had everything ... it won't do."

But, after all, when May gave place to burning June, Bobby and Alice were inevitably drawn into that romance. They yielded to an atmosphere that both, by temperament, were too sentimental to resist.

Nearer and nearer was coming that intoxicating moment of Peter's final plunge, and Clare—beautiful, these weeks, with all the excitement of the wonderful episode—saw him as a young god who had leapt upon a submissive London and conquered it.

Mrs. Rossiter and Mrs. Galleon played waiting chorus. Mrs. Launce from her little house in Westminster, was, as usual, glowing with a piece of other people's happiness. Bobby and Alice had surrendered to the atmosphere. All were, of course, silent—until the word is spoken no movement must be made—the little god is so easily alarmed.

At last towards the close of this hot June, Mrs. Launce proposed to Clare a week-end at her Sussex cottage by the sea. She also told Peter that she could put him up if he chose to come down at the same time. What could be more delightful in this weather?

"Dear Clare, only the tiniest cottage as you know—no one else unless Peter Westcott happens to come down—I suggested it, and you can see the sea from your window and there's a common and a donkey, and you can roll in the sand—" Mrs. Launce, when she was very happy betrayed her French descent by the delightful way that she rolled her r's.

"Not a soul anywhere near—we can bathe all day."

Clare would love to come so strangely enough would Peter—"The 5.30 train then—Saturday...." Dear Mrs. Launce in her bonnet and blue silk! Clare had never thought her so entirely delightful!

Peter, of course, plainly understood the things that dear Mrs. Launce intended. His confidence in her had been, in no way, misplaced—she loved a wedding and was the only person in the world who could bring to its making so fine a compound of sentiment and common sense. She frankly loved it all and though, at the moment, occupied with the work of at least a dozen women, and with a family that needed her most earnest care, she hastened to assist the Idyll.

Peter's own feelings were curiously confused. He was going to propose to Clare; and now he seemed to face, suddenly, the change that this must mean to him. Those earlier months, when it had been pursuit with no certainty of capture had only shown him one thing desirable—Clare. But now that he was face to face with it he was frightened—what did he know of women?...

On the morning they were to go down, he sat in his room, this terrible question confronting him. No, he knew nothing about women! He had left his heroine very much alone in "Reuben Hallard" and those occasions when he had been obliged to bring her on the stage had not been too successful. He knew nothing about women!

There would be things—a great many—as a married man, he would have to change. Sometimes he was moody for days together and wanted to see no one. Sometimes he was so completely absorbed by his work that the real people around him were shadows and wraiths. These moods must vanish. Clare must always find him ready and cheerful and happy.

A dreadful sense of inadequacy weighed upon Peter. And then at the concrete fact of her actual presence, at the thought of her standing there, waiting for him, wanting him, his doubts left him and he was wildly, madly happy.

And yet, before he left the room, his glance fell on his writing-table. White against its shining surface lay a paper and on the top sheet, written: "The Stone House"; a Novel; Chapter II. Months ago—he had not touched it all these last weeks, and, at this moment he felt he would never write anything again. He turned away with a little movement of irritation....

That morning he went formally to Dr. Rossiter. The little man received him, smiling.

"I want to marry your daughter, sir," said Peter.

"You're very young," said the Doctor.

"Twenty-six," said Peter.

"Well, if she'll have you I won't stand in your way—"

Peter took the 5.30 train....

II

Mrs. Launce, on Sunday afternoon, from the door of her cottage, watched them both strike across the common towards the sea—Peter, "stocky," walking as though no force on earth could upset his self-possession and sturdy balance, Clare with her little body and easy movement meant for this air and sea and springing turf. Mrs. Launce having three magnificent children of her own believed in the science of

Eugenics heart and soul. Here, before her eyes, was the right and proper Union—talk about souls and spirit and temperament—important enough for the immediate Two—but give Nature flesh and bones, with cleanliness and a good straight stock to work on, and see what She will do!

Mrs. Launce went into the cottage again and prepared herself for an announcement at tea-time. She wiped her eyes before she settled down to her work. Loving both of them the thought of their happiness hung about her all the afternoon and made her very tender and forgiving when the little parlourmaid arrived with a piece of the blue and white china smashed to atoms. "I can't think 'ow it 'appened, Mum. I was just standing...."

Peter and Clare, crossing the common, beheld the sea at their feet. It was a hot misty afternoon and only the thin white line of tiny curling waves crept out of the haze on to the gleaming yellow sand. Behind them, on every side was common and the only habitation, a small cottage nearly hidden by a black belt of trees, on their right. These black, painted trees lay like a blot of ink against the blue sky.

Sitting down on the edge of the common they looked on to the yellow sand. The air was remorselessly still as though the world were cased in iron; somewhere deep within its silence, its heart might yet be beating, but the depths hid its reverberation.

Peter lay flat on his back and instantly his world was full of clamour. All about him insects were stirring, the thin stiff blades of grass were very faintly rustling, a tiny blue butterfly flew up from the soil into the bright air—some creature sang a little song that sounded like the faint melody of a spinet.

"All praising the Lord, I suppose—" Peter listened. "Hymn and glory songs and all the rest—" Then, clashing, out of the heart of the sky, the thought followed. "There must be a God"—the tinkling insect told him so.

He gazed into the great sheet of blue above him, so remote, so cruel ... and yet the tiny blue butterfly flew, without fear, into its very heart.

Peter's soul was drawn up. He swung, he flew, he fled.... Down below, there on the hard, brown soil his body lay—dust to the dust—there, dead amongst the singing insects.... He looked down, from his great heights and saw his body, with its red face and its suit of blue and its up-turned boots, and here, in freedom his Soul exulted!

"Of course there is a God!"

They are praising him down there—the ground is covered with creatures that are praising Him. Peter buried his eyes and instantly his soul came swinging down to him, found his body again, filled once more his veins with life and sound. After a vast silence he could hear, once more, the life amongst the grass, the faint rustle of the thin line of foam beneath him, and could smell the earth and the scent of the seaweed borne up to them from the sand.

"It's so still," he said suddenly, "that it's almost like thunder. There'll be a storm later. On a day like this in Cornwall you would hear the sound of the Mining Stamps for miles—"

"Well," she answered, "I am glad we're not in Cornwall—I hate it."

"Hate it!"

"Yes. That sounds horrible to you, I suppose, and I'm quite ready to admit that it's my cowardice. Cornwall frightens me. When I was there as a tiny girl it was just the same. I always hated it."

"I don't believe you're ever frightened at anything."

"I am. I'm under such a disadvantage, you see. If I'd been white-faced and haggard every one would have thought it quite natural that I should scream if I were left in the dark or hate being left alone with those horrible black rocks that Cornwall's so full of, but just because I'm healthy and was taught to hold my back up at school I have to pretend to a bravery that simply doesn't exist—" He rejected, for the moment the last part of her sentence. "Oh, but I understand perfectly what you mean by your fear of Cornwall. Of course I understand it although I love the place with all my soul and body. But it is terrifying—almost the only terrifying place that civilisation has left to us—Central Africa is nothing to it—"

"Are you afraid of it?" she said, looking at him intently.

"Tremendously—because I suppose it won't let me alone. It's difficult to put into words, but I think what I mean is that I want to go on now in London, writing and seeing people and being happy and it's pulling at me all the time."

"What way pulling at you?"

"I can't get out of my head all the things I did when I was a boy there. I wasn't very happy, you know. I've told you something about it.... I want to go back.... I want to go back. I mustn't, but I want to go back— and it hurts—"

He seemed to have forgotten her—he stared out to sea, his hands holding the grass on either side of him.

She moved and the sound suddenly brought him back. He turned to her laughing.

"Sorry. I was thinking about things. That cottage over there with the black trees reminded me of Scaw House a little.... But it's all right really. I suppose every fellow has the wild side and the sober side, and I've had such a rum life and been civilised so short a time...."

She said slowly: "I think I know what you mean, though. I know enough of it to be frightened of it—I don't want life to be like that. I don't suppose I've got imagination. I want it to be orderly and easy and no one to be hurt or damaged. Oh!"—her voice was suddenly like a cry—"Why can't we just go through life without any one being frightened or made miserable? I believe in cities and walls and fires and regulated emotions—all those other things can only hurt."

"They teach courage," Peter answered gravely. "And that's about the only thing we're here to learn, I expect. My mother died because she wasn't brave enough and I want ... I want...."

He broke off—"There's only one thing I want and that's you, Clare. You must have known all these weeks that I love you. I've loved you ever since I met you that Good Friday afternoon years ago. Let me take care of you, see that no one hurts you—love you ... love you—"

"Do you really want me, Peter?"

He didn't speak but his whole body turned towards her, answered her question.

"Because I am yours entirely. I became yours that day when your hand touched mine. I wasn't sure before—I knew then—"

He looked at her. He saw her, he thought for the first time. She sat with her hands pressing on the grass, her body bent back a little.

The curve from her neck to her feet was like the shadow of some colour against the brown earth because he saw her only dimly. Her hair burnt against the blue sky but her eyes—her eyes! His gaze caught hers and he surrendered himself to that tenderness, that mystery, that passion that she flung about him. In her eyes he saw what only a lover can see—the terror and the splendour of a soul surprised for the first time into love. She was caught, she was trapped, she was gorgeously delivered. In her eyes he saw that he had her in the hollow of his hand and that she was glad to be there.

But even now they had not touched—they had not moved from their places. They were urged towards one another by some fierce power but also some great suspense still restrained them.

Then Clare spoke, hurriedly, almost pleadingly.

"But Peter, listen—before I say any more—you must know me better. I think that it is just because I love you so much that I see myself clearly to-day as I have never seen myself before—although I have, I suppose really known ... things ... but I have denied them to myself. But now I know that all that I say is true—"

"I am ready," he said, smiling. But she did not smile back at him, she was intensely serious, she spoke without moving her eyes from his face.

"It is not altogether my fault. I have been an only child and everything that I have wanted I have always had. I have despised my mother and even my father because they have given in to me—that is not a pleasant thing to know. And now comfort, happiness, an absence of all misery, these things are essential—"

"I will look after you," said Peter. It was almost with irritation that she brushed aside his assurance.

"Yes, yes, I know, but you must understand that it's more than that. If I am unhappy I am another creature you haven't seen ... you don't know.... If I am frightened—"

"But Clare, dear, we're all like that—"

"No, it's sheer wickedness with me. Oh! Peter I love you so much that you must listen. You mustn't think afterwards, ah, if I'd only known—"

"Aren't you making too much of it all? We've all got these things and it's just because we can help each other that we marry. We give each the courage—"

"I've always been frightened," she said slowly, "always when anything big comes along—always. And this is the biggest thing I've ever met. If only it had been some ordinary man ... but you, Peter, that I should hurt you."

"You won't hurt me," he answered her, "and I'd rather be hurt by you than helped by some one else— let's leave all this. If you love me, there's nothing else to say.... Do you love me, Clare?"

"Yes, Peter."

Then suddenly before he could move towards her a storm that had been creeping upon them, burst over their heads. Five minutes ago there had been no sign of anything but the finest weather, but, in a moment the black clouds had rolled up and the thunder broke, clashing upon the world. The sea had vanished.

"We must run for it," cried Peter, raising his voice against the storm. "That cottage over there—it's the only place."

They ran. The common was black now—the rain drove hissing, against the soil, the air was hot with the faint sulphur smell.

Peter flung himself upon the cottage door and Clare followed him in. For a moment they stood, breathless. Then Peter, conscious only that Clare was beside him, wild with the excitement of the storm, caught her, held her for a moment away from him, breathed the thunder that was about them all, and then kissed her mouth, wet with the rain.

She clung to him, white, breathless, her head on his shoulder.

"Why, you're not frightened?" The sense of her helplessness filled him with a delicious vigour. The way that her hand pressed in upon his shoulder exalted him. Her wet golden hair brushed his cheek. Then he remembered that they had invaded the cottage. For the first time it occurred to him that their first embrace might have been observed; he turned around.

The room was filthy, a huge black fire-place occupied most of it, the floor was littered with pieces of paper, of vegetables and a disagreeable smell protested against the closed and dirty windows. At first it seemed that this place was empty and then, with a start, he was aware that two eyes were watching them. The thunder pealed above them, the rain lashed the roof and ran streaming from the eaves; the cottage was dark; but he saw in a chair, a bundle of rags from which those eyes were staring.

Clare gave a little cry; an old woman with a fallen chin and a face like yellow parchment sat huddled in the chair.

Peter spoke to her. "I hope you don't mind our taking shelter here, whilst the storm passes." She had seen them embrace; it made him uncomfortable, but the storm was passing away, already the thunder was more distant.

The old woman made no reply, only her eyes glared at them. Peter put his hand in Clare's—"It's all right; I think the old thing's deaf and dumb and blind—look, the storm's passing—there's a bit of blue sky. Isn't it odd an old thing like that..."

Clare, shuddered a little. "I don't like it—she's horrid—this place is so dirty. I believe the rain's stopped."

They opened the door and the earth met them, good and sweet, after the shower. The sky was breaking, the mists were leaving the sea and as the storm vanished, the sun, dipping towards the horizon flung upon the blue a fleet of tiny golden clouds.

Peter bent down to the old woman.

"Thank you," he said, "for giving us shelter." He placed a shilling on her lap.

"She's quite deaf and blind," he said. "Poor old thing!"

They closed the door behind them and passed down a little path to the seashore. Here wonders met them. The sand, wet with the recent storm catching all the colours of the sky shone with mother of pearl—here a pool of blue, there the fleet of golden clouds.

It stretched on every side of them, blazing with colour. Behind them the common, sinking now into the dull light of evening.

They stood, little pigmies, on that vast painted floor. Before them the breeze, blowing back the waves into the sun again turned the spray to gold.

Tiny figures, in all this glory, they embraced. In all the world they seemed the only living thing....

III

They had their witness. The old woman who lived in the heart of those black trees, was deaf and dumb indeed, but her eyes were alive in her fading and wrinkled body.

When the door had closed she rose slowly from her chair, and her face was wrinkled with the passion of the hatred that her old soul was feeling.

What did they mean, those two, coming there and haunting her with their youth and strength and love. Kissing there before her as though she were already dead—she to whom kisses were only bitter memories.

Her face worked with fury—she hobbled, painfully, to the door and opened it.

Below her, on a floor of gold, two black figures stood together.

Gazing at them she raised her thin and trembling hand; she flung with a passionate, furious gesture, something from her.

A small silver coin glittered in the air, whistled for a moment and fell.

CHAPTER IV

THE ROUNDABOUT

I

Mrs. Rossiter and Mrs. Galleon sat solemnly, with the majesty of spreading skirts and Sunday Best hats, in the little drawing-room of The Roundabout, awaiting the return from the honeymoon.

The Roundabout is the name that Peter has given to the little house in Dorset Street, Chelsea, that he has chosen to live in with his bride. High spirits lead to nicknames and Peter was in the very highest of spirits when he took the house. The name alluded both to the shape—round bow-windowed like—fat bulging little walls, lemon-coloured, and to the kind of life that Peter intended to lead. All was to be Happiness. Life is challenged with all the high spirits of a truly happy ceremony.

It is indeed a tiny house—tiny hall, tiny stairs, tiny rooms but quaint with a little tumble-down orchard behind it and that strange painted house that old mad Miss Anderson lives in on the other side of the orchard. Such a quiet little street too ... a line of the gravest trees, cobbles with only the most occasional cart and a little church with a sleepy bell at the farthest end ... all was to be Happiness.

Wedding presents—there had been six hundred or so—filled the rooms. People had, on the whole, been sensible, had given the right thing. The little drawing-room with its grey wall-paper, roses in blue jars, its two pictures—Velasquez' Maria Theresa in an old silver frame and Rembrandt's Night Watch—was pleasant, but overwhelmed now by the presence of these two enormous ladies. The evening sun, flooding it all with yellow light, was impertinent enough to blind the eyes of Mrs. Rossiter. She rose and moved slowly to draw down the blinds. A little silver clock struck half-past four.

"They must soon be here," said Mrs. Galleon gloomily. Her gloom was happy and comfortable. She was making the very most of a pleasant business with the greatest satisfaction in the world. She had done exactly the same at Bobby's wedding, and, in her heavy, determined way she would do the same again before she died. Alice Galleon would be there in a moment, meantime the two ladies, without moving in their chairs, flung sentences across at one another and smoothed their silk skirts with their white plump hands.

"It's not really a healthy house—"

"No—with the orchard—and it's much too small—"

"Poor dears, hope they'll be happy. But one can't help feeling, Jane dear, that it was a little rash of you ... your only girl ... and one knows so little about Mr. Westcott, really—"

"Well, your own Bobby vouched for him. He'd known him at school after all, and we all know how cautious Bobby is about people—besides, Emma, no one could have received him more warmly—"

"Yes—Oh! of course ... but still, having no family—coming out of nowhere, so to speak—"

"Well, it's to be hoped they'll get on. I must say that Clare will miss her home terribly. It takes a lot to make up for that—And her father so devoted too...."

"Yes, we must make the best of it."

The sun's light faded from the room—the clock and the pictures stood out sharply against the gathering dusk. Two ladies filled the room with their shadows and the little fire clicked and rattled behind the murmuring voices.

II

Alice Galleon burst in upon them. "What! Not arrived yet! the train must be dreadfully late. Lights! Lights! No, don't you move, mother!"

She returned with lamps and flooded the room with light. The ladies displayed a feeble protest against her exultant happiness.

"I'm sure, my dear, I hope that nothing has happened."

"My dear mother, what could happen?"

"Well, you never know with these trains—and a honeymoon, too, is always rather a dangerous time. I remember—"

"I hear them!" Alice cried and there indeed they were to be heard bumping and banging in the little hall. The door opened and Peter and Clare, radiant with happiness, appeared.

They stood in the doorway, side by side, Clare in a little white hat and grey travelling dress and Peter browner and stronger and squarer than ever.

All these people filled the little room. There was a crackling fire of conversation.

"Oh! but we've had a splendid time—"

"No, I don't think Clare's in the least tired—"

"Yes, isn't the house a duck?"

"Don't we just love being back!"

"... hoping you hadn't caught colds—"

"... besides we had the easiest crossing—"

"... How's Bobby?"

"... were so afraid that something must have happened—"

Mrs. Rossiter took Clare upstairs to help her to take her hat off.

Mother and daughter faced one another—Clare flung herself into her mother's arms.

"Oh! Mother dear, he's wonderful, wonderful!"

Downstairs Alice watched Peter critically. She had not realised until this marriage, how fond she had grown of Peter. She had, for him, very much the feeling that Bobby had—a sense of tolerance and even indulgence for all tempers and morosities and morbidities. She had seen him, on a day, like a boy of eighteen, loving the world and everything in it, having, too, a curious inexperience of the things that life might mean to people, unable, apparently, to see the sterner side of life at all—and then suddenly that had gone and given place to a mood in which no one could help him, nothing could cheer him... like Saul, he was possessed with Spirits.

Now, as he stood there, he looked not a day more than eighteen. Happiness filled him with colour—his eyes were shining—his mouth smiling.

"Alice, old girl—she's splendid. I couldn't have believed that life could be so good—"

A curious weight was lifted from her at his words. She did not know what it was that she had dreaded. Perhaps it had been merely a sense that Clare was too young and inexperienced to manage so difficult a temperament as Peter's—and now, after all, it seemed that she had managed it. But in realising the relief that she felt she realised too the love that she had for Peter. When he was young and happy the risks that he ran seemed just as heavy as when he was old and miserable.

"Oh, Peter! I'm so glad—I know she's splendid—Oh! I believe you are going to be happy—"

"Yes!" he answered her confidently, "I believe we are—"

The ladies—Mrs. Galleon, Mrs. Rossiter and Alice—retired. Later on Clare and Peter were coming into Bobby's for a short time.

Left alone in their little house, he drew her to the window that overlooked the orchard and silently they gazed out at the old, friendly, gnarled and knotted tree, and the old thick garden-wall that stretched sharply against the night-sky.

Behind them the fire crackled and the lamps shed their pleasant glow and that dear child with the great stiff dress that Velasquez painted smiled at them from the wall.

Peter gave a deep sigh of happiness.

"Our House..." he said and drew her very close to him. The two of them, as they stood there outlined against the window were so young and so pleasant that surely the Gods would have pity!

III

In the days that followed he watched it all with incredulity. So swiftly had he been tossed, it seemed, from fate to fate, and so easily, also, did he leave behind him the things that had weighed him down. No sign now of that Peter—evident enough in the Brockett days—morose, silent, sometimes oppressed by a sense of unreasoned catastrophe, stepping into his bookshop and out again as though all the world were his enemy.

Peter knew now that he was loved. He had felt that precious quality on the day that his mother died, he had felt it sometimes when he had been in Stephen's company, but against these isolated emotions what a world of hate and bitterness.

Now he felt Clare's affection on every side of him. They had already in so short a time a store of precious memories, intimacies, that they shared. They had been through wild, passionate wonders together and standing now, two human beings with casual words and laughing eyes, yet they knew that perfect holy secrets bound them together.

He stood sometimes in the little house and wondered for an instant whether it was all true. Where were all those half cloudy dreams, those impulses, those dread inheritances that once he had known so well? Where that other Peter Westcott? Not here in this dear delicious little house, with Love and Home and great raging happiness in his heart.

He wrote to Stephen, to Mr. Zanti, to Norah Monogue and told them. He received no answers—no word from the outer world had come to him. That other life seemed cut off, separated—closed. Perhaps it had left him for ever! Perhaps, as Clare said, walls and fires were better than wind and loneliness—comfort more than danger.... Meanwhile, in his study at the top of the house, "The Stone House" was still lying, waiting, at Chapter II—

But it was Clare who was the eternal wonder. He could not think of her, create her, pile up the offerings before her altar, sufficiently. That he should have had the good fortune... It never ceased to amaze him.

As the weeks and months passed his life centred more and more round Clare and the house that they shared together. He knew now many people in London; they were invited continually to dinners, parties, theatres, dances. Clare's set in London had been very different from Peter's literary world, and they were therefore acclaimed citizens of two very different circles. Peter, too, had his reviewing articles in many papers—the whole whirligig of Fleet Street. (How little a time, by the way, since that dreadful day when he had sat on that seat on the Embankment and talked to the lady with the Hat!)

His days during this first year of married life were full, varied, exciting as they could be—and yet, through it all, his eye was always upon that little house, upon the moment when the door might be closed, the fire blazing and they two were alone, alone—

He was, indeed, during this year, a charming Peter. He loved her with the hero worship of a boy, but also with a humour, a consciousness of success, a happy freedom that denied all mawkish sham sentiment. He studied only to please her. He found that, after all, she did not care very greatly for literature or music or pictures. Her enthusiasm for these things was the enthusiasm of a child who is bathed in an atmosphere of appreciation and would return it on to any object that she could find.

He discovered that she loved compliments, that she cared about dress, that she loved to have crowds of friends about her, and that parties excited her as though these were the first that she had ever known.

But he found, too, that in those half-hours when she was alone with him she showed her love for him with a passion and emphasis that was almost terrifying. Sometimes when she clung to him it was as though she was afraid that it was not going to last. He discovered in the very beginning that below all her happy easy life, an undercurrent of apprehension, sometimes only vaguely felt, sometimes springing into sight like the eyes of some beast in the dark, kept company with her.

It was always the future—a perfectly vague, indefinite future that terrified her. Every moment of her life had been sheltered and happy and, by reason of that very shelter, her fears had grown upon her. He remembered one evening when they had been present at some party and she had been radiant, beautiful, in his eyes divine. Her little body had been strung to its utmost energy, she had whirled through the evening and at last as they returned in the cab, she had laid her head on his shoulder and suddenly flung her arms about him and kissed him—his eyes, his cheeks, his mouth—again and again. "Oh! I'm so safe with you, Peter dear," she had cried to him.

He loved those evenings when they were alone and she would sit on the floor with her head on his knee and her hand against his. Then suddenly she would lean back and pull his head down and kiss his eyes, and then very slowly let him go. And the fierceness, the passion of her love for him roused in him a strength of devotion that all the years of unhappiness had been storing. He was still only a boy—the first married year brought his twenty-seventh birthday—but his love for Clare had the depth and reserve that belongs to a man.

Mrs. Launce, watching them both, was sometimes frightened. "God help them both if anything interferes," she said once to her husband. "I've seen that boy look at Clare with a devotion that hurts. Peter's no ordinary mortal—I wonder, now and again, whether Clare's worth it all."

But this year seemed to silence all her fears. The happiness of that little house shone through Chelsea. "Oh, we're dining with the Westcotts to-night—they'll cheer us up—they're always so happy"—"Oh! did you see Clare Westcott? I never saw any one so radiant."

And once Bobby said to Alice: "We made a mistake, old girl, about that marriage. It's made another man of Peter. He's joy personified."

"If only," Alice had answered, "destiny or whatever it is will let them alone. I feel as though they were two precious pieces of china that a housemaid might sweep off the chimney piece at any moment. If only nobody will touch them—"

Meanwhile Peter had forgotten, utterly forgotten, the rest of the world. Walls and fires—for a year they had held him. The Roundabout versus the World.... What of old Frosted Moses, of the Sea Road, of Stephen, of Mr. Zanti? What of those desperate days in Bucket Lane? All gone for nothing?

Clare, perhaps, with this year behind her, hardly realised the forces against which she was arrayed. Beware of the Gods after silence....

IV

And, after all, it was Clare herself who flung down the glove.

On a winter's evening she was engaged to some woman's party. Peter had planned an evening, snug and industrious, alone with a book. "The Stone House" awaited his attention—he had not worked at it for months. Also he knew that he owed Henry Galleon a visit. Why he had not been to see the old man lately he scarcely knew.

Clare, standing in the little hall, waiting for a cab, suggested an alternative.

"Peter dear, why don't you go round to Brockett's if you've nothing to do?"

"Brockett's!"

"Yes. You've never been since we married, and I had a letter from Norah this morning—not at all cheerful—I'm afraid she's been ill for months. They'd love to see you."

"Brockett's!" He stood astounded. Well, why not? A strange emotion—uncomfortable, alien, stirred him. He kissed her and saw her go with a half-distracted gaze. What a world away Brockett's seemed! Old Mrs. Lazarus, Norah (poor Norah!) Mrs. Brockett, young Robin Tressiter. They would be glad to see him—it was a natural thing enough that he should go—what was it that held him back? For the first time since his marriage, as he slowly and thoughtfully put on his greatcoat, he was distressed. He reproached himself—Norah, Stephen, Mr. Zanti!... he had not given them a thought.

He felt, as he went out, as though he were going, with key and candle, to unlock some old rusty door that led into secret rooms. It was a wet, windy night. The branches of the little orchard rattled and groaned, and doors and windows were creaking.

As he passed into the shadows and silence of Bloomsbury the impression weighed with increasing heaviness upon him that the old Peter had come back and that his married life with Clare had been a dream. He was still at Brockett's, still silent, shy, awkward, still poring over pages of "Reuben Hallard" and wondering whether any one would ever publish it—still spending so many hours in the old musty bookshop with Herr Gottfried's wild mop of hair coming so madly above the little counter.

The wind tugged at his umbrella, the rain lashed his face and at last, breathless, with the sharp corner of his upturned collar digging into his chin, he pulled the bell of the old grey remorseless door that he knew so well. There was no one in Bennett Square, only the two lamps dimly marked its desolation.

The door was opened by Mrs. Brockett herself and she stood there, stern and black peering into his face.

"What is it? What do you want?" she asked grimly.

He brushed past her laughing and stood back under the gas in the hall looking at her.

She gave a little cry. "No! It can't be! Why, Mr. Westcott!"

He had never, in all the seven years that he had been with her, seen her so strongly moved.

"But Mr. Westcott! To think of it! And the times we've talked of you! And you never coming near us all this while. You might have been dead for all we knew, and indeed if it hadn't been for Miss Monogue the other day we'd have heard no news since the day that wild man with the beard came walking in," she broke off suddenly—"and there you are, holding your umbrella with the point down and making a great pool on the carpet as though—" She took the umbrella from him but her hand rested for an instant on his arm and she said gruffly—

"But all the same, Mr. Peter, I'm more glad to see you than I can say—" She took him into her little room and looked at him. "But you've not changed in the least," she said, "not in the very least. And where, pray, Mr. Peter, have you been all this time and come nowhere near us?"

He tried to explain; he was confused, he said something about marriage and stopped. The room was filled with that subtle odour that brought his other life back to him in a torrent. He was bathed in it, overwhelmed by it—roast-beef, mutton, blacking, oil-cloth, decayed flowers, geraniums, damp stone, bread being toasted—all these things were in it.

He filled his nostrils with the delicious pathos and intimacy of it.

She regarded him sternly. "Now, Mr. Peter, it's of no use. Oh, yes, we've heard about your wedding. You wrote to Miss Monogue. But there were days before that, many of them, and never so much as a postcard. With some of, my boarders it would be natural enough, because what could you expect? We didn't want them, they didn't want us—only habit as you might say. But you, Mr. Peter—why just think of the way we were fond of you—Mrs. Lazarus and little Robin and Miss Monogue—as well as myself."

She stopped and pulled out her handkerchief and blew her nose.

"I dare say you're a famous man," she went on, "with your books and your marriage and the rest of it, but that doesn't alter your old friends being your old friends and it never will. There, I'm getting cross when all I mean to say is that I'm more delighted to see you than words."

He was humble before her. He felt, indeed, that he had been the most unutterable brute. How could he have stayed away all this time with these dear people waiting for him? He simply hadn't realised—

"And Miss Monogue?" he asked at last, "I'm afraid she's not been very well?"

"She's been very ill indeed—for months. At one time we were afraid that she would go. It's her heart. Poor dear, and she's been worrying so about her work—but she's better now and she'll be truly glad to see you, Mr. Peter—but you mustn't stay more than a few minutes. She's up on the sofa but it's the excitement that's bad for her."

But first Peter went to pay a visit to the Tressiter establishment. He knew, from old custom, that this would be the hour when the family would be getting itself, by slow and noisy degrees, to bed. So tremendous, indeed, was the tumult that he was able to open the door and stand, within the room, watching and un-noticed. Mrs. Tressiter was attempting to bathe a fat and very strident baby. Two small boys were standing on a bed and hitting one another with pillows; a little girl lay on her face on the floor and howled for no apparent reason; Robin, but little older than Peter's last impression of him had painted, was standing, naked save for his shirt and looking down, gravely, at his screaming sister.

Every now and again, Mrs. Tressiter, without ceasing from her work on the baby who slipped about in her hands like a stout eel, cried in a shrill voice: "Children, if you don't be quiet," or "Nicholas, in a moment I'll give you such a beating,"—or "Agatha, for goodness' sake!"...

Then suddenly Robin, looking up, caught sight of Peter, he gave a shout and was across the room in an instant. There was never a moment's doubt in his eyes. He flung himself upon Peter's body, he wound his arms round Peter's leg, he beat upon his chest with his bullet head, he cried: "Oh! Mr. Peter has come! Mr. Peter has come!"

Mrs. Tressiter let the baby fall into the bath with a splash and there it lay howling. The other members of the family gathered round.

But Peter thought that he had known no joy so acute for years as the welcome that the small boy gave him. He hoisted Robin on to his shoulder, and there Robin sat with his naked little legs dangling over, his hands in the big man's neck.

"Oh! Mr. Westcott, I'm sure..." said Mrs. Tressiter, smiling from ear to ear and wiping her wet hands on her apron—Robin bent his head and bit Peter's ear.

"Get on, horse," he cried and for a quarter of an hour there was wild riot in the Tressiter family. Then they were all put to bed, as good as gold,—"you might have heard a pin drop," said Mrs. Tressiter, "when Agatha said her prayers"—and at last the lights were put out.

Peter bent down over Robin's bed and the boy flung his arms round his neck.

"I dreamed of you—I knew you'd come," he whispered.

"What shall I send you as a present to-morrow?" asked Peter.

"Soldiers—soldiers on horses. Those with cannons and shiny things on their backs...." Robin was very explicit—"You'll be here to-morrow?" he asked.

"No—not to-morrow," Peter answered.

"Soon?"

"Yes, soon."

"I love you, more than Agatha, more than Dick, more than any one 'cept Daddy and Mummy."

"You'll be a good boy until I come back?"

"Promise ... but come back soon."

Peter gave him a long kiss and left him. Supposing, one day, he had a boy like that? A little boy in a shirt like that? Wouldn't it be simply too wonderful? A boy to give soldiers to....

He went across to Miss Monogue's door. A faint voice answered his knock and, entering the room, the scent of medicine and flowers that he always connected with his mother, met him. Norah Monogue, very white, with dark shadows beneath her eyes, was lying on the sofa by the fire.

Mrs. Brockett had prepared her for Peter's coming and she smiled up at him with her old smile and gave him her hand. How thin and white it was with its long slender fingers! He sat down by her sofa and he knew by the way that she looked at him that she was reproaching him—

"Naughty Peter," she said, "all these months and you have been nowhere near us."

"I, too, have a bone—you never sent me a word about my wedding."

She turned her head away. "I was frightfully ill just then. They didn't think I'd pull through. I did write afterwards to Clare, I told her how ill I'd been—"

"She never told me."

Peter bent over the sofa. "But I am ashamed, Norah, more ashamed than I can say. After I got well and went to live with the Galleons a new life seemed to begin for me and I was so eager and excited about it all. And then—" he hesitated for a moment—"there was Clare."

"Yes, I know there was Clare and I am so delighted about it—I know that you will both be so happy.... But, when one is lying here week after week and is worried and tired things take such a different outline. I thought that you and Clare—that you ... had given me up altogether and—"

Suddenly hiding her face in her hands she began to cry. It was inexpressibly desolate there in the dim bare little room, and the sharp sense of his neglect and the remembrance of the good friend that she had been to him for so many years overwhelmed Peter.

He knelt down and put his arms round her. "Norah—don't, please, I can't bear it. It's all right. I've been a beast, a selfish cad. But it shan't happen again. I'll come often—I'm ashamed."

She cried for a little and then she smiled at him. "I'm a fool to cry like that but you see I'm weak and ill— and seeing you again after all this time and your being so successful and happy upset me I suppose. Forgive it, Peter, and come again one day when I'm better and stronger—and bring Clare too."

She held tightly to his hand and her grasp was hot and feverish. He reassured her, told her that he would come soon again, that he would bring Clare and so left her.

He took a cab and drove back to Chelsea in a storm of agitation. Suddenly, out of nothing as it were, all these people, this old life had been thrust up in front of him—had demanded, made claims. About him once again was the old atmosphere: figures were filling his brain, the world was a wild tossing place ... one of those Roundabouts with the hissing lights, the screaming music, the horses going up and down. Plain enough now that the old life was not done with. Every moment of his past life seemed to spring before him claiming recognition. He was drunk with the desire for work. He flung the cabman something, dashed into the little house, was in his room. The lamp was lighted, the door was shut, there was silence, and in his brain figures, scenes, sentences were racing—"The Stone House," neglected for so long, had begun once more, to climb.

The hours passed, the white sheets were covered and flung aside. Dimly through a haze, he saw Clare standing in the doorway.

"Bad old boy!"

He scarcely glanced up. "I'm not coming yet—caught by work."

"Don't be at it too late."

He made no reply.

She closed the door softly behind her.

CHAPTER V

THE IN-BETWEENS

I

Then, out of the wind and rain, came Mr. Zanti.

II

Three days after Peter's visit to Brockett's he was finishing a letter before dressing for dinner. He and Clare were going on to a party later in the evening but were dining quietly alone together first. The storms that had fallen upon London three days before were still pommelling and buffeting the city, the trees outside the window groaned and creaked with a mysterious importance as though they were trying to tell one another secrets, and little branches tapped at the dripping panes. He was writing in the little drawing-room—warm and comfortable—and the Maria Theresa, so small a person in so much glory, looked down on him from her silver frame and gave him company.

Then Sarah—a minute servant, who always entered a room as though swept into it by a cyclone—breathlessly announced that there was a gentleman to see Mr. Westcott.

"'E's drippin' in the 'all," she gasped and handed Peter a very dirty bit of paper.

Peter read:—"Dear Boy, Being about to leave this country on an expedition of the utmost importance I feel that I must shake you by the hand before I go. Emilio Zanti."

Mr. Zanti, enormous, smiling from ear to ear, engulfed in a great coat from which his huge head, buffeted by wind and rain—his red cheeks, his rosy nose, his sparkling eyes—stood out like some strange and cheerful flower—filled the doorway.

He enfolded Peter in his arms, pressed him against very wet garments, kissed him on both cheeks and burst into a torrent of explanation. He was only in London for a very few days—he must see his dearest Peter—so often before he had wanted to see his Peter but he had thought that it would be better to leave him—and then he had heard that his Peter was married—well, he must see his lady—it was entirely necessary that he should kiss her hand and wish her well and congratulate her on having secured his "own, own Peter," for a life partner. Yes, he had found his address from that Pension where

Peter used to live; they had told him and he had come at once because at once, this very night, he was away to Spain where there was a secret expedition—ah, very secret—and soon—in a month, two months—he would return, a rich, rich man. This was the adventure of Mr. Zanti's life and when he was in England again he, Mr. Zanti, would see much of Peter and of his beautiful wife—of course she was beautiful—and of the dear children that were to come—

Here Peter interrupted him. He had listened to the torrent of words in an odd confusion. The last time that he had seen Mr. Zanti he had left him, sitting with his head in his hands sobbing in the little bookshop. Since then everything had happened. He, Peter, had had success, love, position, comfort—the Gods had poured everything into his hands—and now, to his amazement as he sat there, in the little room opposite his huge fantastic friend he was almost regretting all those glorious things that had come to him and was wishing himself back in the dark little bookshop—dark, but lighted with the fire of Mr. Zanti's amazing adventures.

But there was more than this in his thoughts. As he looked at Mr. Zanti, at his wild black locks, his flaming cheeks, his rolling eyes, his large red hands, he was aware suddenly that Clare would not appreciate him. It was the first time since his marriage that there had been any question of Clare's criticism, but now he knew, with absolute certainty, that Mr. Zanti was entirely outside Clare's range of possible persons. For the first time, almost with a secret start of apprehension, he knew that there were things that she did not understand.

"I'm afraid," he said, "that my wife is dressing. But when you come back you shall meet of course—that will be delightful." And then he went on—"But I simply can't tell you how splendid it is to look at you again. Lots of things have happened to me since I saw you, of course, but I'm just the same—"

Whilst he was speaking his voice had become eager, his eyes bright—he began to pace the room excitedly—

"Oh, Zanti! ... the days we used to have. I suppose the times I've been having lately had put it all out of my head, but now, with you here, it's all as though it happened yesterday. The day we left Cornwall, you and I—the fog when we got to London ... everything." He drew a great breath and stood in the middle of the room listening to the rain racing down the pipes beyond the dark windows.

Mr. Zanti, getting up ponderously, placed his hands on Peter's shoulders.

"Still the same Peter," he said. "Now I know zat I go 'appy. Zat is all I came for—I said I must zee my Peter because Stephen—"

"Stephen—" broke in Peter sharply.

"Yes, our Stephen. He goes with me now to Spain. He is now, until to-night, in London but he will not come to you because 'e's afraid—"

"Afraid?"

"Yes 'e says you are married now and 'ave a lovely 'ouse and 'e says you 'ave not written for a ver' long time, and 'e just asked me to give you 'is love and say that when 'e comes back from Spain, per'aps—"

"Stephen!" Peter's voice was sharp with distress. "Zanti, where is he now? I must go and see him at once."

"No, 'e 'as gone already to the boat. I follow 'im." Then Mr. Zanti added in a softer voice—"So when he tell me that you 'ave not written I say 'Ah! Mr. Peter forgets his old friends,' and I was zorry but I say that I will go and make sure. And now I am glad, ver' glad, and Stephen will be glad too. All is well—"

"Oh! I am ashamed. I don't know what has come over me all this time. But wait—I will write a note that you shall take to him and then—when he comes back from Spain—"

He went to his table and began to write eagerly. Mr. Zanti, meanwhile, went round the room on tip-toe, examining everything, sometimes shaking his huge head in disapproval, sometimes nodding his appreciation.

Peter wrote:

Dear, Dear Stephen,—I am furious, I hate myself. What can I have been doing all this time? I have thought of you often, but my marriage and all the new life have made me selfish, and always I put off writing to you because I thought the quiet hour would come to me—and it has never come. But I have no excuse—except that in the real part of myself I love you, just the same as ever—and it will be always the same. I have been bewildered, I think, by all the things that have happened to me during this last year—but I will never be bewildered again. Write to me from Spain and then as soon as you come back I will make amends for my wickedness. I am now and always, Your loving Peter.

Mr. Zanti took the letter.

"How is he?" asked Peter.

"I found 'im—down in Treliss. He wasn't 'appy. 'E was thinking of that woman. And then 'e was all alone. 'E got some work at a farm out at Pendragon and 'e was just goin' there when I came along and made 'im come to Spain. 'E was thinkin' of you a lot, Peter."

Mr. Zanti cast one more look round the room. "Pretty," he said. "Pretty. But not my sort of place. Too many walls—all too close in."

In the hall he said once more—a little plaintively:—

"I should like to see your lady, Peter," and then he went on hurriedly, "But don't you go and disturb her—not for anything—I understand...."

And, with his finger on his lip, wrapt in the deepest mystery, he departed into the rain.

As the door closed behind him, Peter felt a wave of chill, unhappy loneliness. He turned back into the cheerful little hall and heard Clare singing upstairs. He knew that they were going to have a delightful little dinner, that, afterwards, they would be at a party where every one would be pleased to see them—he knew that the evening in front of him should be wholly charming ... and yet he was uneasy. He felt now as though he ought to resign his evening, climb to his little room and work at "The Stone House." And yet what connection could that possibly have with Mr. Zanti?

His uneasiness had begun, he thought, after his visit to Brockett's. It seemed to him as he went upstairs to dress that the world was too full of too many things and that his outlook on it all was confused.

Throughout dinner this uneasiness remained with him. Had he been less occupied with his own thoughts he would have noticed that Clare was not herself; at first she talked excitedly without waiting for his answers—there were her usual enthusiasms and excitements. Everything in the day's history had been "enchanting" or "horrible," as a rule she waited for him to act up to her ecstasies and abhorrencies; to-night she talked as though she had no audience but were determined to fill up time. Then suddenly she was silent; her eyes looked tired and into them there crept a strange secret little shudder as though she were afraid of some thought or mysterious knowledge. She looked now like a little girl who knew, that to-morrow—the inevitable to-morrow—she must go to the dentist's to be tortured.

The last part of the meal was passed in silence. Afterwards she came into his study and sat curled upon the floor at his feet watching him smoke.

She thought as she looked up at him, that something had happened to make him younger. She had never seen him as young as he was to-night—and then because his thoughts were far away and because her own troubled her she made a diversion. She said:—

"Who was that extraordinary man you were talking to this evening?"

He came back, with a jerk, from Stephen.

"What man?"

"Why the man with all the black hair and a funny squash hat. I saw Sarah let him in."

"Ah, that," said Peter, looking down at her tenderly, "that was a great friend of mine."

She moved her head away.

"Don't touch my hair, Peter—it's all been arranged for the party. A friend of yours? What! That horrible looking man? Oh! I suppose he was one of those dreadful people you knew in the slums or in Cornwall."

Peter saw Mr. Zanti's dear friendly face, like a moon, staring at him, and heard his warm husky voice: "Peter, my boy...."

He moved a little impatiently.

"Look here, old girl, you mustn't call him that. He's one of the very best friends I've ever had—and I've been rather pulled up lately—ever since that night you sent me to Brockett's. I've felt ashamed of myself. All my happiness and—you—and everything have made me forget my old friends and that won't do."

She laughed. "And now I suppose you're going to neglect me for them—for horrid people like that man who came to-night."

Her voice was shaking a little—he saw that her hands were clenched on her lap. He looked down at her in astonishment.

"My dear Clare, what do you mean? How could you say a thing like that even in jest? You know—"

She broke in upon him almost fiercely—"It wasn't jest. I meant what I said. I hate all these earlier people you used to know—and now, after our being so happy all this time, you're going to take them up again and make the place impossible—"

"Look here, Clare, you mustn't speak of them like that—they're my friends and they've got to be treated as such." His voice was suddenly stern. "And by the way as we are talking about it I don't think it was very kind of you to tell me nothing at all about poor Norah's being so ill. She asked you to tell me and you never said a word. That wasn't very kind of you."

"I did speak to you about it but you forgot—"

"I don't think you did—I am quite sure that I should not have forgotten—"

"Oh, of course you contradict me. Anyhow there's no reason to drag Norah Monogue into this. The matter is perfectly clear. I will not have dirty old men like that coming into the house."

"Clare, you shall not speak of my friends—"

"Oh, shan't I? When I married you I didn't marry all your old horrid friends—"

"Drop it, Clare—or I shall be angry—"

She sprang to her feet, faced him. He had never in his life seen such fury. She stood with her little body drawn to its full height, her hands clenched, her breast heaving under her white evening dress, her eyes glaring—

"You shan't! You shan't! I won't have any of them here. I hate Cornwall and all its nasty people and I hate Brockett's and all those people you knew there. When you married me you gave them all up—all of them. And if you have them here I won't stay in the house—I'll leave you. All that part of your life is nothing to do with me. Nothing—and I simply won't have it. You can do what you like but you choose between them and me—you can go back to your old life if you like but you go without me!"

She burst from the room, banging the door behind her. She had behaved exactly like a small child in the nursery. As he looked at the door he was bewildered—whence suddenly had this figure sprung? It was some one whom he did not know. He could not reconcile it with the dignified Clare, proud as a queen, crossing a ball-room or the dear beloved Clare nestling into a corner of his arm-chair, her face against his, or the gentle friendly Clare listening to some story of distress.

The fury, the tempest of it! It was as though everything in the room had been broken. And he, with his glorious, tragical youth felt that the end of the world had come. This was the conclusion of life—no more cause for living, no more friendship or comfort or help anywhere. Clare had said those things to him. He stood, for ten minutes there, in the middle of the room, without moving—his face white, his eyes full of pain.

Sarah came to tell him that the hansom was there. He moved into the hall with the intention of sending it away; no party for him to-night—when, to his amazement he saw Clare coming slowly down the stairs, her cloak on, buttoning her gloves.

She passed him without a word and got into the hansom. He took his hat and coat, gave the driver the address, and climbed in beside her.

Once as they drove he put out his hand, touched her dress and said—"Clare dear—"

She made no reply, but sat looking, with her eyes large and black in her little white face, steadfastly in front of her.

III

Lady Luncon was a rich, good-natured woman who had recently published a novel and was anxious to hear it praised, therefore she gave a party. Originally a manufacturer's daughter, she had conquered a penniless baronet—spent twenty years in the besieging of certain drawing-rooms and now, tired of more mundane worlds, fixed her attention upon the Arts. She was a completely stupid woman, her novel had been exceedingly vulgar, but her good heart and a habit of speaking vaguely in capital letters secured her attention.

When Clare and Peter arrived people were filling her drawing-rooms, overflowing on to the stairs and pouring into the supper room. Some one, very far away, was singing "Mon coeur s'ouvre a ta voix," a babel of voices rose about Clare and Peter on every side, every one was flung against every one; heat and scent, the crackle and rustle of clothes, the soft voices of the men and sharp strident voices of the women gave one the sensation of imminent suffocation; people with hot red faces, unable to move at all, flung agonised glances at the door as though the entrance of one more person must mean death and disaster.

There were, Peter soon discovered, three topics of conversation: one was their hostess' novel and this was only discussed when Lady Luncon was herself somewhere at hand—the second topic concerned the books of somebody who had, most unjustly it appeared, been banned by the libraries for impropriety, and here opinions were divided as to whether the author would gain by the advertisement or lose by loss of library circulation. Thirdly, there was a new young man who had written a novel about the love affairs of a crocus and a violet—it was amazingly improper, full of poetry—"right back," as somebody said "to Nature." Moreover there was much talk about Form. "Here is the new thing in fiction that we are looking for ..." also "Quite a young man—oh yes, only about eighteen and so modest. You would never think...."

His name was Rondel and Peter saw him, for a moment, as the crowds parted, standing, with a tall, grim, elderly woman, apparently his mother, beside him. He was looking frightened and embarrassed and stood up straight against the wall as though afraid lest some one should come and snatch him away.

But Peter saw the world in a dream. He walked about, with Clare beside him, and talked to many people; then she was stopped by some one whom she knew and he went on alone. Now there had come back to him the old terror. If he went back, after this was over, and Clare was still angry with him, he did not know what he would do. He was afraid....

He smiled, talked, laughed and, in his chest, there was a sharp acute pain like a knife. He had still with him that feeling that nothing in life now was worth while and there followed on that a wild impulse to let go, to fling off the restraints that he had retained now for so long and with such bitter determination.

He wanted to cast aside this absurd party, to hurry home alone with Clare, to sit alone with her in the little house and to reach the divine moment when reconciliation came and they were closer to one another than ever before—and then there was the horrible suggestion that there would be no reconciliation, that Clare would make of this absurd quarrel an eternal breach, that things would never be right again.

He looked back and saw Clare smiling gaily, happily, at some friend. He saw her as she had faced him, furiously, an hour earlier ... oh God! If she should never care for him again!

He recognised many friends. There were the two young Galleons, Millicent and Percival, looking as important and mysterious as possible, taxing their brains for something clever to say....

"Ah, that's Life!" Peter heard Percival say to some one. Young fools, he thought to himself, let them have my trouble and then they may talk. But they were nice to him when he came up to them. The author of "Reuben Hallard," even though he did look like a sailor on leave, was worth respecting—moreover, father liked him and believed in him—nevertheless he was just a tiny bit "last year's sensation." "Have you read," said Percival eagerly, "'The Violet's Redemption'? It really is the most tremendous thing—all about a violet. There's the fellow who wrote it over there—young chap standing with his back to the wall...."

There was also with them young Tony Gale who was a friend of Alice Galleon. He was nice-looking, eager and enthusiastic. Rather too enthusiastic, Peter, who did not like him, considered. Full of the joy of life; everything was "topping" and "ripping." "I can't understand," he would say, "why people find life dull. I never find it dull. It's the most wonderful glorious thing—"

"Ah, but then you're so young," he always expected his companions to say; and the thing that pleased him most of all was to hear some one declare—"Tony Gale's such a puzzle—sometimes he seems only eighteen and then suddenly he's fifty."

It was rumoured that he had once been in love with Alice Galleon when she had been Alice du Cane—and that they had nearly made a match of it; but he was certainly now married to a charming girl whom he had seen in Cornwall and the two young things were considered delightful by the whole of Chelsea.

Tony Gale had with him a man called James Maradick whom Peter had met before and liked. Maradick was forty-two or three, large, rather heavy in build and expression and very taciturn. He was in business in the city, but had been drawn, Peter knew not how, into the literary world of London. He was often to be found at dinner parties and evening "squashes" silent, observant and generally alone. Many people thought him dull, but Peter liked him partly because of his reserve and partly because of his enthusiasm for Cornwall. Cornwall seemed to be the only subject that could stir Maradick into excitement, and when Cornwall was under discussion the whole man woke into sudden stir and emotion.

To-night, with his almost cynical observance of the emotions and excitement that surged about him, he seemed to Peter the one man possible in the whole gathering.

"Look here, Maradick, let's get somewhere out of this crush and have a cigarette."

People were all pouring into supper now and Peter saw his wife in the distance, on Bobby Galleon's arm. They found a little conservatory deserted now and strangely quiet after the din of the other rooms: here they sat down.

Maradick was capable of sitting, quite happily for hours, without saying anything at all. For some time they were both silent.

At last Peter said: "By jove, Maradick, yours is a fortunate sort of life—just going into the city every day, coming back to your wife in the evening—no stupid troubles that come from imagining things that aren't there—"

"How do you know I don't?" answered Maradick quietly. "Imagination hasn't anything to do with one's profession. I expect there's as much imagination amongst the Stock Exchange men as there is with you literary people—only it's expressed differently."

"What do you do," said Peter, "if it ever gets too much for you?"

"Do? How do you mean?"

"Well suppose you're feeling all the time that one little thing more, one little word or some one coming in or a window breaking—anything will upset the equilibrium of everything? Supposing you're out with all your might to keep things sane and to prevent your life from swinging back into all the storm and uncertainty that it was in once before, and supposing you feel that there are a whole lot of things trying to get you to swing back, what's the best thing to do?"

"Why, hold on, hold on—"

"How do you mean?"

"Fortitude—Courage. Clinging on with your nails, setting your teeth."

Peter was surprised at the man's earnestness. The two of them sitting there in that lonely deserted little conservatory were instantly aware of some common experience.

Maradick put his hand on Peter's knee.

"Westcott, you're young, but I know the kind of thing you mean. Believe me that it's no silly nonsense to talk of the Devil—the Devil is as real and personal as you and I, and he's got his agents in every sort and kind of place. If he once gets his net out for you then you'll want all your courage. I know," he went on sinking his voice, "there was a time I had once in Cornwall when I was brought pretty close to things of that sort—it doesn't leave you the same afterwards. There's a place down in Cornwall called Treliss...."

"Treliss!" Peter almost shouted. "Why that's where I come from. I was born there—that's my town—"

Before Maradick could reply Bobby Galleon burst into the conservatory. "Oh, there you are—I've been looking for you everywhere. How are you, Maradick? Look here, Peter, you've got to come down to supper with us. We've got a table—Alice, Clare, Millicent, Percival, Tony Gale and his wife and you and I—and—one other—an old friend of yours, Peter."

"An old friend?" said Peter, getting up from his chair and trying to look as though he were not furious with Bobby for the interruption.

"Yes—you'll never guess, if I give you a hundred guesses—it's most exciting—come along—"

Peter was led away. As he moved through the dazzling, noisy rooms he was conscious that there, in the quiet, dark little conservatory, Maradick was sitting, motionless, seeing Treliss.

IV

On his way down to the supper room he was filled with annoyance at the thought of his interrupted conversation. He might never have his opportunity again. Maradick was so reserved a fellow and took so few into his confidence—also he would, in all probability, be ashamed to-morrow of having spoken at all.

But to Peter at that moment the world about him was fantastic and unreal. It seemed to him that at certain periods in his life he was suddenly confronted with a fellow creature who perceived life as he perceived it. There were certain persons who could not leave life alone—they must always be seeing it as a key to something wider, bigger altogether. This was nothing to do with Christianity or any creed whatever, because Creeds implied Certainty and Definition of Knowledge, whereas Peter and the others like him did not know for what they were searching. Again, they were not Mystics because Mysticism needed a definite removal from this world before any other world were possible. No, they were simply Explorers and one traced a member of the order on the instant. There had been already in Peter's life, Frosted Moses, Stephen, Mr. Zanti, Noah Monogue, and now suddenly there was Maradick. These were people who would not laugh at his terror of Scaw House, at his odd belief that his father was always trying to draw him back to Treliss....

As he entered the supper-room and saw Clare sitting at a distant table, he knew that his wife would never be an Explorer. For her Fires and Walls, for her no questions, no untidiness moral or physical—the Explorer travelled ever with his life in his hands—Clare believed in the Stay-at-homes.

The great dining-room was filled with Stay-at-homes. One saw it in their eyes, in the flutter of useless and tired words that rose and fell; all the souls in that room were cushioned and were happy that it was so. The Rider on the Lion was beyond the Electric Lights—on the dark hill, over the darker river, under the stars. Somebody pulled a cracker and put on a paper cap. He was a stout man with a bald head and the back of his neck rippled with fat. He had tiny eyes.

"Look at Mr. Horset," cried the woman next to him—"Isn't he absurd?"

Peter found at the table in the corner Alice, Clare, Millicent and Percival Galleon, Tony Gale and his wife, waiting. There was also a man standing by Alice's chair and he watched Peter with amused eyes.

He held out his hand and smiled. "How do you do, Westcott?" he said. Then, with the sound of his voice, the soft almost caressing tilt of it, Peter knew who it was. His mind flew back to a day, years ago, when he had flung himself on the ground and cried his soul out because some one had gone away....

"Cards!" he cried. "Of all wonderful things!"

Cards of Dawson's—Cards, the magnetic, the brilliant, Cards with his World and his Society and now slim and dark and romantic as ever, making every one else in the room shabby beside him, so that Bobby's white waistcoat was instantly seen to be hanging loosely above his shirt and Peter's trousers were short, and even the elegant Percival had scarcely covered with perfect equality the ends of his white tie.

Instantly as though the intervening years had never been, Bobby took his second place beside Cards' glory—even Percival's intention of securing the wonderful Mr. Rondel, author of "The Violet's Redemption," for their table, failed of its effect.

They were enough. They didn't want anybody else—Room for Mr. Cardillac!

And he seized it. Just as he would have seized it years ago at school so he seized it now. Their table was caught into the most dazzling series of adventures. Cards had been everywhere, seen everybody and everything—seen it all, moreover, with the right kind of gaiety, with an appreciation that was intelligent and also humorous. There was humour one moment and pathos the next—deep feeling and the wittiest cynicism.

They were all swung about Europe and with Cards at their head pranced through the cities of the world. Meanwhile Peter fancied that once or twice Clare flung him a little glance of appeal to ask for forgiveness—and once they looked up and smiled at one another. A tiny smile but it meant everything.

"Oh! won't we have a reconciliation afterwards? How could I have said those things? Don't we just love one another?"

When they went upstairs again Peter and Cards exchanged a word:

"You'll come and see us?"

"My dear old man, I should just think so. This is the first time I've been properly in London for years and now I'm going to stay. Fancy you married and successful and here am I still the rolling-stone!"

"You! Why you can do anything!"

"Can't write 'Reuben Hallard,' old boy...." and so, with a laugh, they parted.

In the cab, afterwards, Clare's head was buried in Peter's coat, and she sobbed her heart out. "How I could have been such a beast, Peter, Peter!"

"Darling, it was nothing."

"Oh, but it was! It shall never, never happen again...but I was frightened—"

"Frightened!"

"Yes, I always think some one's going to take you away. I don't understand all those other people. They frighten me—I want you to myself, just you and I—always."

"But nobody can take me away—nobody—"

The cab jolted along—her hand was on his knee—and every now and again a lamp lighted her face for him and then dropped it back into darkness.

By the sharp pressure of her hand he knew that she was moved by an intensity of feeling, swayed now by one of those moods that came to her so strangely that it seemed that they belonged to another personality.

"Look... Peter. I'm seeing clearly as I think I never have before. I'm afraid—not because of you—but because of myself. If you knew—" here his hand came down and found hers—"if you knew how I despise myself, my real self. I've been spoilt always, always, always. I've always known it. My real self is ashamed of it. But there's another side of me that comes down suddenly and hides all that—and then—when that happens—I just want to get what I want and not to be hurt and ..." she pressed closer against him and went on in a whisper.

"Peter, I shall always care for you more than any one—always whatever happens. But think, a time will come—I know it—when you'll have to watch me, to keep me by you, and even let your work go—everything, just for a time until I'm safe. I suppose that moment comes to most women in their married lives. But to me, when it happens, it will be worse than for most women because I've always had my way. You mustn't let me have my way then—simply clutch me, be cruel, brutal, anything only don't let me go. Then, if you keep me through that, you'll always keep me."

To Peter it was almost as though she were talking in her sleep, something, there in the old, lumbering cab that was given to her by some one else to say something to which she herself would not give credit.

"That's all right, you darling, you darling, you darling." He covered her face, her eyes with kisses. "I'll never let you go—never." He felt her quiver a little under his arms.

"Don't mind, Peter, my horrible, beastly character. Just keep me for a little, train me—and then later I'll be such a wife to you, such a wife!"

Then she drew his head down. His lips touched her body just above her dress, where her cloak parted.

She whispered:

"There's something else."

She raised her face from his coat and looked up at him. Her cheeks were stained with crying and her eyes, large and dark, held him furiously as though he were the one place of safety.

He caught her very close.

"What is it?..."

That night, long after he, triumphant with the glory of her secret, had fallen asleep, she lay, staring into the dark, with frightened eyes.

CHAPTER VI

BIRTH OF THE HEIR

I

Peter's child was born on a night of frost when the stars were hard and fierce and a full moon, dull gold, flung high shadows upon the town.

During the afternoon the fear that had been in Clare's eyes for many weeks suddenly flamed into terror—the doctor was sent for and Peter was banished from the room.

Peter looked ludicrously, pitifully young as he sat, through the evening, in his room at the top of the house, staring in front of him, his face grey with anxiety, his broad shoulders set back as though ready for a blow; his strong fingers clutched the things on his writing-table, held them, dropped them, just like the hands of a blind man about the shining surface, tapping the wood.

He saw her always as he had seen her last night when she had caught his arm crying—"If I die, Peter.... Oh, Peter, if I die!"... and he had comforted and stroked her hair, warming her cold fingers.

How young she was, how tiny for this suffering—and it was he, he who had brought it upon her! Now, she was lying in her bed, as he had once seen his mother lie, with her hair spread about the pillow, her hands gripping the sheets, her eyes wide and black—the vast, hard bed-room closing her in, shutting her down—

She who loved comfort, who feared any pain, who would have Life safe and easy, that she should be forced—

The house was very still about him—no sound came up to him; it seemed to him that the hush was deliberate. The top branches of the trees in the little orchard touched his window and tapped ever and again; a fire burnt brightly, he had drawn his curtains and beyond the windows the great sheet of stars, the black houses, the white light of the moon.

And there, before him—what mockery! the neat pages of "The Stone House" now almost completed.

He stared into the wall and saw her face, her red-gold hair upon the pillow, her dark staring eyes—

Once the nurse came to him—Yes, she was suffering, but all went well ... it would be about midnight, perhaps. There was no cause for alarm....

He thought that the nurse looked at him with compassion. He turned fiercely upon Life that it should have brought this to them when they were both so young.

At last, about ten o'clock, able no longer to endure the silence of the house—so ominous—and the gentle tap-tap of the branches upon the pane and the whispering crackle of the fire, he went out....

A cold hard unreal world received him. Down Sloane Street the lines of yellow lamps, bending at last until they met in sharp blue distance, were soft and misty against the outline of the street, the houses were unreal in the moonlight, a few people passed quickly, their footsteps sharp in the frosty air—all the little painted doors of Sloane Street were blind and secret.

He passed through Knightsbridge, into the Park. As the black trees closed him in the fear of London came, tumbling upon him. He remembered that day when he had sat, shivering, on a seat on the Embankment, and had heard that note, sinister, threatening, through the noise and clattering traffic. He heard it again now. It came from the heart of the black trees that lined the moonlit road, a whisper, a thread of sound that accompanied him, pervaded him, threatened him. The scaly beast knew that another victim was about to be born—another woman was to undergo torture, so that when the day came and the scaly beast rose from its sleep then there would be one more to be devoured.

He, Peter, was to have a child. He had longed for a child ever since he could remember. He had always loved children—other people's children—but to have one of his own!... To have something that was his and Clare's and theirs alone, to have its love, to feel that it depended Upon them both, to watch it, to tend it—Life could have no gift like that.

But now the child was hidden from him. He thought of nothing but Clare, of her suffering and terror, of her waiting there so helplessly for the dreadful moment of supreme pain. The love that he had now for Clare was something more tender, more devoted, than he had ever felt for any human being. His mind flew back fiercely to that night of his first quarrel when she had told him. Now he was to be punished for his heartlessness and cruelty ... by her loss.

His agony and terror grew as he paced beneath the dark and bending trees. He sat down on a seat, at the other end of which was a little man with a bowler hat, spectacles and his coat collar turned up. He was a shabby little man and his thin bony hands beat restlessly upon his knees.

The little man said, "Good evening, sir."

"Good evening," said Peter, staring desperately in front of him.

"It's all this blasted government—"

"I beg your pardon—"

"This blasted government—This income tax and all—"

"It's more than that," said Peter, wishing that the man would cease beating his knees with his hands—

"It's them blasted stars—it's Gawd. That's what it is. Curse Gawd—that's what I say—Curse Gawd!"

"What's He done?" said Peter.

"I've just broken in my wife's 'ead with a poker. Killed 'er I expect—I dunno—going back to see in a minute—"

"Why did you do it?"

"'Ad to—always nagging—that's what she was—always nagging. Wanted things—all sorts o' things—and there were always children coming—So we 'ad a blasted argyment this evening and I broke 'er 'ead open—Gawd did it—that's what I say—"

Peter said nothing.

"You can call a bloomin' copper if you want to," the little man said.

"It's no business of mine," said Peter and he got up and left him. All shadows—only the sinister noise that London makes is real, that and Clare's suffering.

He left the Park turned into Knightsbridge and came upon a toyshop. The shutters had not been put up and the lights of a lamp shone full upon its windows. Against the iron railings opposite and the high white road these toys stood with sharp, distinct outline behind the slanting light of the glass. There were dolls—a fine wedding doll, orange blossom, lace and white silk, and from behind it all, the sharp pinched features and black beady eyes stared out.... There was a Swiss doll with bright red cheeks, red and green clothing and shoes with shining buckles. Then there were the more ordinary dolls—and gradually down the length of the window, their clothing was taken from them until at last some wooden creatures with flaring cheeks and brazen eyes kicked their limbs and defied the proprieties.

He would be a Boy ... he would not care about dolls....

There were soldiers—rows and rows of gleaming soldiers. They came from a misty distance at the top of the shop window, came marching from the gates of some dark, mediæval castle. Their swords caught the lamplight, shining in a line of silver and the precision with which they marched, the certainty with which they trod the little bridge ... ah, these were the fellows! He would be a Boy ... soldiers would enchant him! He should have boxes, boxes, boxes!

There were many other things in the window; teddy bears and animals with soft woolly stomachs and fat comfortable legs—and there were ugly, modern Horrors with fat bulging faces and black hair erect like wire; there were little devils with red tails, there were rabbits that rode bicycles and monkeys that climbed trees. There were drums—big drums and little drums—trumpets with crimson tassels, and in one corner a pyramid of balls, balls of every colour, and at the top of the pyramid a tiny ball of peacock blue, hanging, balancing, daintily, supremely right in pose and gesture.

It had gesture. It caught Peter's eye—Peter stood with his nose against the pane, his heart hammering— "Oh! she is suffering—My God, how she is suffering!"—and there the little blue ball caught him, held him, encouraged him.

"I will belong to your boy one day" it seemed to say.

"It shall be the first thing I will buy for him—" thought Peter.

He turned now amongst the light and crowds of Piccadilly. He walked on without seeing and hearing—always with that thought in his heart—"She is in terrible pain. How can God be so cruel? And she was so happy—before I came she was so happy—now—what have I done to her?"

Never, before to-night, had he felt so sharply, so irretrievably his sense of responsibility. Here now, before him, at this birth of his child, everything that he had done, thought, said—everything that he had been—confronted him. He was only twenty-seven but his shoulders were heavy with the confusion of his past. Looking back upon it, he saw a helpless medley of indecisions, of sudden impulses, sudden refusals; into the skeins of it, too, there seemed to be dragged the people that had made up his life—they faced him, surrounded him, bewildered him!

What right had he, thus encompassed, to hand these things on to another? His father, his grandfather ... he saw always that dark strain of hatred, of madness, of evil working in their blood. Suppose that as his boy grew he should see this in the young eyes? Suppose, most horrible of all, that he should feel this hatred for his son that his grandfather had felt for his father, that his father had felt for him.

What had he done?... He stopped, staring confusedly about him. The people jostled him on every side. The old devils were at him—"Eat and drink for to-morrow we die.... Give it up ... We're too strong for you and we'll be too strong for your son. Who are you to defy us? Come down—give it up—"

His white face caught attention. "Move along, guv'nor," some one shouted. A man took him by the arm and led up a dark side street. He turned his eyes and saw that the man was Maradick.

II

The elder man felt that the boy was trembling from head to foot.

"What's the matter, Westcott? Anything I can do for you?"

Peter seemed to take him in slowly, and then, with a great effort, to pull himself together.

"What, you—Maradick? Where was I? I'm afraid I've been making a fool of myself...." A church clock struck somewhere in the distance. "Hullo, I say, what's that? That's eleven. I must get back, I ought to be at home—"

"I'll come with you—"

Maradick hailed a hansom and helped Peter into it.

For a moment there was silence—then Maradick said—

"I hope everything's all right, Westcott? Your wife?"

Peter spoke as though he were in a dream. "I've been waiting there all the afternoon—she's been suffering—My God!... It got on my nerves.... She's so young—they oughtn't to hurt her like that." He covered his face with his hands.

"I know. I felt like that when my first child came. It's terrible, awful. And then it's over—all the pain—and it's magnificent, glorious—and then—later—it's so commonplace that you cannot believe that it was ever either awful or magnificent. Fix your mind on the glorious part of it, Westcott. Think of this time tomorrow when your wife will be so proud, so happy—you'll both be so proud, so happy, that you'll never know anything in life like it."

"Yes, yes, I know—of course it's sure to be all right—but I suppose this waiting's got on my nerves. There was a fellow in the Park just broken his wife's head in—and then everything was so quiet. I could almost hear her crying, right away in her room."

He stopped a moment and then went on. "It's what I've always wanted—always to have a boy. And, by Jove, he'll be wonderful! I tell you he shall be—We'll be such pals!" He broke off suddenly—"You haven't a boy?"

"No, mine are both girls. Getting on now—they'll soon be coming out. I should like to have had a boy—" Maradick sighed.

"Are they an awful lot to you?"

"No—I don't suppose they are. I should have understood a boy better,—but they're good girls. I'm proud of them in a way—but I'm out so much, you see."

Peter faced the contrast. Here this middle-aged man, with his two girls—and here too he, Peter, with his agonising, flaming trial—to slip, so soon, into dull commonplace?

"But didn't you—if you can look so far—didn't you, when the first child came, funk it? Your responsibility I mean. All the things one's—one's ancestors—it's frightening enough for oneself but to hand it on—"

"It's nothing to do with oneself—one's used, that's all. The child will be on its own legs, thrusting you away before you know where you are. It will want to claim its responsibilities—ancestors and all—"

Peter said nothing—Maradick went on:

"You know we were talking one night and were interrupted—you're in danger of letting the things you imagine beat the things you know. Stick to the thing you can grasp, touch—I know the dangers of the others—I told you that once in Cornwall, I—the most unlikely person in the world—was caught up by it. I've never laughed at morbidity, or nerves, or insanity since. There's such a jolly thin wall between the sanest, most level-headed beef-eating Squire in the country and the maddest poet in Bedlam. I know—I've been both in the same day. It's better to be both, I believe, if you can keep one under the other, but you must keep it under—"

Maradick talked on. He saw that the boy's nerves were jumping, that he was holding himself in with the greatest difficulty.

Peter said: "You don't know, Maradick. I've had to fight all my life—my father, grandfather, all of them have given in at last—and now this child ... perhaps I shall see it growing, see him gradually learning to hate me, see myself hating him ... at last, my God, see him go under—drink, deviltry—I've fought it—I'm always fighting it—but to-night—"

"Good heavens, man—you're not going to tell me that your father, your grandfather—the rest of them—are stronger than you. What about your soul, your own blessed soul that can't be touched by any living thing or dead thing either if you stick to it? Why, every man's got power enough in himself to ride heaven and earth and all eternity if he only believed he'd got it! Ride your scruples, man—ride 'em, drive 'em—send 'em scuttling. Believe in yourself and stick to it—Courage!..."

Maradick pulled himself in. They were driving now, down the King's Road. The people were pouring in a thick, buzzing crowd, out of the Chelsea Palace. Middle-aged stockbrokers in hansom cabs—talking like the third act of a problem play!—but Maradick had done his work. As they drove round the corner, past the mad lady's painted house, he saw that Peter was calmer. He had regained his self-control. The little house where Peter lived was very still—the trees in the orchard were stiff and dark beneath the stars.

Peter spoke in a whisper—"Good-night, Maradick, you've done me a lot of good—I shan't forget it."

"Good luck to you," Maradick whispered back. Peter stole into the house.

The little drawing-room looked very cosy; the fire was burning, the lamp lighted, the thick curtains drawn. Maria Theresa smiled, with all her finery, from the wall.

Peter sat down in front of the fire. Maradick was right. One must have one's hand on the bridle—the Rider on the Lion again. It's better that the beast under you should be a Lion rather than a Donkey, but let it once fling you off its back and you're done for. And Maradick had said these things! Maradick whom once Peter had considered the dullest of his acquaintances. Well, one never knew about people—most of the Stay-at-homes were Explorers and vice versa, if one only understood them.

How still the house was! What was happening upstairs? He could not go and see—he could not move. He was held by the stillness. The doctor would come and tell him....

He thought of the toyshop—that blue ball—it would be the first thing that he would buy for the boy—and then soldiers—soldiers that wouldn't hurt him, that he couldn't lick the paint from—

Now the little silver clock ticked! He was so terribly tired—he had never been tired like this before....

The stillness pressed upon the house. Every sound—the distant rattling of some cab, the faint murmur of trams—was stifled, extinguished. The orchard seemed to press in upon the house, darker and darker grew the forest about it—The stars were shut out, the moon... the world was dead.

Then into this sealed and hidden silence, a voice crying from an upper room, suddenly fell—a woman in the abandonment of utter pain, pain beyond all control, was screaming. Somewhere, above that dark forest that pressed in upon the house, a bird of prey hovered. It hung for a moment; it descended—its talons were fixed upon her flesh... then again it ascended. Shriek after shriek, bursting the silence, chasing the shadows, flooding the secrecy with horrible light, beat like blows upon the walls of the house—rose, fell, rose again. Peter was standing, his back against the wall, his hands spread out, his face grey.

"My God, my God... Oh! my God!"

The sweat poured from his forehead. Once more there was silence but now it was ominous, awful....

The little silver clock ticked—Peter's body stood stretched against the wall—he faced the door.

Hours, hours passed. He did not move. The screaming had, many years ago, ceased. The doctor—a cheerful man with blue eyes and a little bristling moustache—came in.

"A fine boy, Mr. Westcott—I congratulate you. You might see your wife for a moment if you cared—stood it remarkably well—"

Slowly the forest, dark and terrible, moved away from the house. Very faintly again could be heard the distant rattling of some cab, the murmur of trams.

CHAPTER VII

DECLARATION OF HAPPINESS

I

Extracts from letters that Bobby Galleon wrote to Alice Galleon about this time:

"... But, of course, I am sorrier than I can say that it's so dull. That's due to charity, my dear, and if you will go and fling yourself into the depths of Yorkshire because a girl like Ola Hunting chooses to think she's unhappy and lonely you've only yourself to thank. Moreover there's your husband to be considered. I don't suppose, for a single instant, that he really prefers to be left alone, with his infant son, mind you, howling at the present moment because his nurse won't let him swallow the glass marbles, and you can picture to yourself—if you want to make yourself thoroughly unhappy—your Robert sitting, melancholy throughout the long evening, alone, desolate, creeping to bed somewhere about ten o'clock.

"So there we are—you're bored to death and I've no one to growl at when I come back from the City—all Ola Hunting's fault—wring the girl's neck. Meanwhile here I sit and every evening I'll write whatever comes into my head and never look back on it again but stick it into an envelope and send it to you. You know me too well by now to be disappointed at anything.

"I'm quite sure that, if you were here with me now, sitting in that chair opposite me and sewing for all you were worth, that the thing that we'd be talking about would be Peter. If, therefore, these scrawls are full of Peter you won't mind, I know. He's immensely occupying my attention just now and you love him as truly and deeply as I do, so that if I go on at length about him you'll excuse it on that score. You who know me better than any one else in the world know that, in my most secret heart, I flatter myself on my ability as a psychologist. I remember when I told you first how you laughed but I think since then you've come round not a little, and although we both keep it to ourselves, it's a little secret that you're a tiny bit proud of. I can see how brother Percival, or young Tony Gale, or even dear Peter himself would mock, if I told them of this ambition of mine. 'Good, dear, stupid, old Bobby' is the way they think of me, and I know it's mother's perpetual wonder (and also, I think, a little her comfort) that I should be so lacking in brilliance when Percival and Millie are so full of it.

"You know Peter's attitude to me in these things—you've seen it often enough. He's patronising—he can't help it. That isn't, he considers, my line in the least, and, let me once begin to talk to him of stocks and shares and he'll open all his ears. Well, I can't blame him—but I do think these writers and people are inclined to draw their line a little too sharply with their Philistines—great big gulf, please—and Artists. At any rate, here goes for my psychology and good luck to it. Peter, in fact, is so interesting a subject if one sees anything of him at all that I believe he'd draw speculation out of any one. There was old Maradick talking about him the other night—fascinated by him and understanding him most amazingly well—another instance of your Philistine and Artist mixed.

"But I knew him—and knew him jolly well too—when he was about twelve, so that I really get a pull over the rest of you there, for it adds of course immensely to the interest and if ever child was Father of the Man, Peter was. You know how we both funked that marriage of his for him—you because you knew Clare so well, I because I knew Peter. And then for a time it really seemed that we were both entirely wrong. Clare's is a far simpler personality than Peter's, and if you work along one or two recognised lines—let her have her way, don't frighten her, above all keep her conventional—it's all right. Clare was, and is, awfully in love with him, and he madly with her of course—and that helped everything along. You know how relieved we both were and indeed it seemed, for a time, that it was going to be the making of both of them—going to make Clare braver and Peter less morbid.

"Well, it's since you've been away that everything's happened. Although the baby was born some weeks before you went, it's only lately that Clare has been up and about. She's perfectly well and the baby's splendid—promises to be a tremendous fellow and as healthy as possible. You can imagine, a little, the effect of it all on Clare. I don't suppose there's any girl in London been so wrapped in cotton wool all her life, and that old ass of a father and still more irritating ass of a mother would go on wrapping her still if they had their way. The fuss they've both made about this whole business is simply incredible— especially when the man's a doctor and brings Lord knows how many children into the world every week of his life. But it's all been awfully bad for Clare. Of course, she was frightened—frightened out of her wits. It's the very first time life ever had its wrappings off for her, and that in itself of course is a tremendously good thing. But you can't, unfortunately, wrap any one up for all those years and then take the wrappings off and not deliver a shock to the system. Of course there's a shock, and it's just this shock that I'm so afraid of. I'm afraid of it for one thing because Peter's so entirely oblivious of it. He was in an agony of terror on the day that the baby was born, but once it was there—well and healthy and promising—fear vanished. He could only see room for glory—and glory he does. I cannot tell you what that boy is like about the baby; at present he thinks, day and night, of nothing else. It is the most terrific thing to watch his feeling about it—and meanwhile he takes it for granted that Clare feels the same.... Well, she doesn't. I have been in a good deal during these last few days and she's stranger than words can say—doesn't see the child if she can help it—loves it, worships it, when it is there, and—is terrified of it. I saw a look in her eyes when she was nursing it yesterday that was sheer undiluted terror. She's been frightened out of her life, and if I know her the least little bit she's absolutely made up her mind never to be frightened like that again. She is going to hurl herself into a perfect whirlpool of excitement and entertainment and drag Peter with her if she can. Meanwhile, behind that hard little head of hers, she's making plans just as fast as she can make them. I believe she looks on life now as though it had broken the compact that she made with it—a compact that things should always be easy, comfortable, above all, never threatening. The present must be calm but the Future's absolutely got to be—and I believe, although she loves him devotedly in the depths of her strange little soul, that she half blames

Peter for all of this disturbance, and that there are a great many things about him—his earlier life, his earlier friends, even his work—that she would strip from him if she could.

"Well, enough for the present. I don't know what nonsense there isn't here. Into the envelope it all goes. I've been talking to you for an hour and a half and that's something...."

II

"... I've just come in from dinner with Peter and Clare and feel inclined to talk to you for hours ahead. However, that I can't do, so I shall write to you instead and you're to regard it all as a continuation of the things that I said in last night's letter. I am as interested as ever and indeed, after this evening's dinner more interested. The odd thing about it all is that Peter is so completely oblivious to any change that may be going on in Clare. His whole mind is centred now on the baby, he cannot have enough of it and it was he, and not Clare, who took me up after dinner to see it sleeping.

"You remember that they had some kind of a dispute about the name of the boy at the time of the christening. Peter insisted that it should be Stephen, after, I suppose, that odd Cornish friend of his, and Clare, weak and ill though she was, objected with all her might. I don't know why she took this so much to heart but it was all, I suppose, part of that odd hatred that she has of Peter's earlier life and earlier friends. She has never met the man Brant, but I think that she fancies that he is going to swoop down one of these days and carry Peter off on a broomstick or something. She gave in about the name— indeed I have never seen Peter more determined—but I think, nevertheless, that she broods over it and remembers it. My dear, I am as sorry for her as I can be. There she stands, loving Peter with all her heart and soul, terrified out of her wits at the possibilities that life is presenting to her, hating Peter's friends at one moment, his work the next, the baby the next—exactly like some one, walking on a window-ledge in his sleep and suddenly waking and discovering—

"Peter's a more difficult question. He's too riotously happy just at the moment to listen to a word from any one. His relation to the child is really the most touching thing you ever saw, and really the child, considering that it has scarcely begun to exist, has a feeling for him in the most wonderful way. It is as good as gold when he is there and follows him with its eyes—it doesn't pay much attention to Clare. I think it knows that she's frightened of it. Yes, Peter is quite riotously happy. You know that 'The Stone House' is coming out next week. There is to be a supper party at the Galleons'—myself, Mrs. Launce, Maradick, the Gales, some woman he knew at that boarding-house, Cardillac and Dr. and Mrs. Rossiter.

"By the way, Cardillac is there a great deal and I am both glad and sorry. He is very good for Clare and not at all good for Peter. He seems to understand Clare in the most wonderful way—far better than Peter does. He brings her out, helps her to be broader and really I think explains Peter to her and helps things along. His influence on Peter is all the other way. Peter, of course, worships him, just as he used to do in the old days at school, and Cards always liked being worshipped. He has an elegance, a savoir-faire that dear, square-shouldered rough-and-tumble Peter finds entrancing, but, of course, Peter's worth the dozen of him any day of the week. He drags out all Peter's worst side. I wonder whether you'll understand what I mean when I say that Peter isn't meant to be happy—at any rate not yet. He's got something too big, too tremendous in him to be carved easily into any one of our humdrum, conventional shapes. He takes things so hard that he isn't intended to take more than one thing at a time, and here he is with Clare and Cards both, as it seems to me, in a conspiracy to pull him into a thousand little bits and to fling each little bit to a different tea-party.

"He ought to be getting at his work and he isn't getting at it at all. 'The Stone House' is coming out next week and it may be all right, but I don't mind betting that the next one suffers. If he weren't in a kind of dream he'd see it all himself, and indeed I think that he'll wake one day soon and see that a thousand ridiculous things are getting in between him and his proper life.

"He was leading his proper life in those days at Dawson's when they were beating him at home and hating him at school, and it was that old bookshop and the queer people he met in it that produced 'Reuben Hallard.'

"He's so amazingly young in the ways of the world, so eager to make friends with everybody, so delighted with an entirely superficial butterfly like Cards, so devotedly attached to his wife, that I must confess that the outlook seems to me bad. There's going to be a tremendous tug-of-war in a minute and it's not going to be easy for the boy—nor, indeed for Clare.

"I hope that you don't feel so far removed from this in your Yorkshire desert that it has no interest for you, but I know how devoted you are to Peter and one doesn't want to see the boy turned into the society novelist creature—the kind of creature, God forgive me, that brother Percival is certain to become. You'll probably say when you read this that I am trying to drag out all the morbid side of Peter and make him the melancholy, introspective creature that he used to be, in fits and starts, when you first knew him. Of course that's the last thing I want to do, but work to a man of Peter's temperament is the one rock that can save him. He has, I do believe, a touch of genius in him somewhere, and I believe that if he's allowed to follow, devoutly and with pain and anguish, maybe, his Art, he'll be a great creature—a great man and a great writer. But he's in the making—too eager to please, too eager to care for every one, too desperately down if he thinks things are going badly with him. I notice that he hasn't been to see my father lately—I think too that all this reviewing is bad for him—other people's novels pouring upon him in an avalanche must take something from the freshness of his own.

"Anyhow I, Robert Galleon, your clever and penetrating husband, scent much danger and trouble ahead. Clare, simply out of love for him and anxiety for herself, will I know, do all she can to drag him from the thing that he should follow—and Cards will help her—out of sheer mischief, I verily believe.

"On their own heads be it. As to the carpets you asked me to go and look at...."

III

"... And now for the supper party. Although there's a whole day behind me I'm still quivering under the excitement of it. As I tell you about it it will in all probability, declare itself as a perfectly ordinary affair, and, indeed, I think that you should have been there yourself to have realised the emotion of it. But I'll try and give it you word for word. I was kept in the city and arrived late and they were all there. Mrs. Launce, twinkling all over with kindness, Maradick in his best Stock Exchange manner, the Gales (Janet Gale perfectly lovely), the old Rossiters, Cards, shining with a mixture of enterprise and knowledge of the world and last of all a very pale, rather nervous, untidy Irish woman, a Miss Monogue. Clare was so radiantly happy that I knew that she wasn't happy at all, had obviously taken a great deal of trouble about her hair and had it all piled up on the top of her head and looked wonderful. I can't describe these things, but you know that when she's bent on giving an impression she seems to stand on her toes all the time—well, she was standing on every kind of toe, moral, physical, emotional last night. Finally there was Peter, looking as though his evening dress had been made for something quite different from social dinner parties. It fitted all right, but it was too comfortable to be smart—he looked, beside Cards, like a good serviceable cob up against the smartest of hunters. Peter's rough, bullet head, the way that he stands with his legs wide apart and his thick body holding itself deliberately still with an effort as though he were on board ship—and then that smile that won all our hearts ages ago right out of the centre of his brown eyes first and then curving his mouth, at last seizing all his body—but always, in spite of it, a little appealing, a little sad somewhere—can't you see him? And Cards, slim, straight, dark, beautifully clothed, beautifully witty and I am convinced, beautifully insincere. Can't you see Cards say 'good evening' to me—with that same charm, that same ease, that same contempt that he had when we were at school together? Bobby Galleon—an honest good fellow—but dull—mon Dieu—dull (he rather likes French phrases)—can't you hear him saying it? Well from the very first, there was something in the air. We were all excited, even old Mrs. Rossiter and the pale Irish creature whom I remembered afterwards I had met that day when I went to that boarding—house after Peter. Clare was quite extraordinary—I have never seen her anything like it—she talked the whole time, laughed, almost shouted. The only person she treated stiffly was Cards—I don't think she likes him.

"He was at his most brilliant—really wonderful—and I liked him better than I've ever liked him before. He seemed to have a genuine pleasure in Peter's happiness, and I believe he's as fond of the boy as he's able to be of any one. A copy of 'The Stone House' was given to each of us (I haven't had time to look at mine yet) and I suppose the combination of the baby and the book moved us all. Besides, Clare and Peter both looked so absurdly young. Such children to have had so many adventures already. You can imagine how riotous we got when I tell you that dessert found Mrs. Rossiter with a paper cap on her head and Janet Gale was singing some Cornish song or other to the delight of the company. Miss Monogue and I were the quietest. I should think that she's one of the best, and I saw her look at Peter once or twice in a way that showed how strongly she felt about him.

"Well, old girl, I'm bothered if I can explain the kind of anxiety that came over me after a time. You'll think me a regular professional croaker but really I suppose, at bottom, it was some sort of feeling that the whole thing, this shouting and cheering and thumping the table—was premature. And then I suppose it was partly my knowledge of Peter. It wasn't like him to behave in this sort of way. He wasn't himself—excited, agitated by something altogether foreign to him. I could have thought that he was drunk, if I hadn't known that he hadn't touched any liquor whatever. But a man of Peter's temperament pays for this sort of thing—it isn't the sort of way he's meant to take life.

"Whatever the reason may have been I know that I felt suddenly outside the whole business and most awfully depressed. I think Miss Monogue felt exactly the same. By the time the wine was on the table all I wanted was to get right away. It was almost as though I had been looking on at something that I was ashamed to see. There was a kind of deliberate determination about their happiness and Clare's little body with her hair on the verge, as it seemed, of a positive downfall, had something quite pitiful in its deliberate rejoicing; such a child, my dear—I never realised how young until last night. Such a child and needing some one so much older and wiser than Peter to manage it all.

"Well, there I was hating it when the final moment came. Cards got up and in one of the wittiest little speeches you ever heard in your life, proposed Peter's health, alluded to 'Reuben Hallard,' then Clare, then the Son and Heir, a kind of back fling at old Dawson's, and then last of all, an apostrophe to 'The Stone House' all glory and honour, &c.:—well, it was most neatly done and we all sat back, silent, for Peter's reply.

"The dear boy stood there, all flushed and excited, with his hair pushed back off his forehead and began the most extraordinary speech I've ever heard. I can't possibly give you the effect of it at secondhand, in the mere repetition of it there was little more than that he was wildly, madly happy, that there was no one in the world as happy as he, that now at last the gods had given him all that he had ever wanted, let them now do their worst—and so crying, flung his glass over his shoulder, and smashed it on to the wall behind him.

"I cannot possibly tell you how sinister, how ominous the whole thing suddenly was. It swooped down upon all of us like a black cloud. Credit me, if you will, with a highly—strung bundle of nerves (not so solid matter-of-fact as I seem, you know well enough) but it seemed to me, at that moment, that Peter was defying, consciously, with his heart in his mouth, a world of devils and that he was cognisant of all of them. The thing was conscious—that was the awful thing about it, I could swear that he was seeing far beyond all of us, that he was hurling his happiness at something that he had there before him as clearly as I have you before me now. It was defiance and I believe the minute after uttering it he would have liked to have rushed upstairs to see that his baby was safe....

"Be that as it may, we all felt it—every one of us. The party was clouded. Cards and Clare did their best to brighten things up again, and Peter and Tony and Janet Gale played silly games and made a great deal of noise—but the spirit was gone.

"I left very early. Miss Monogue came away at the same time. She spoke to me before she said good-night: 'I know that you are an old friend of Peter's. I am so fond of him—we all are at Brockett's, it isn't often that we see him—I know that you will be his true friend in every sense of the word—and help him—as he ought to be helped. It is so little that I can do....'

"Her voice was sad. I am afraid she suffers a great deal. She is evidently greatly attached to Peter—I liked her.

"Well, you in your sober way will say that this is all a great deal of nonsense. Why shouldn't Peter, if he wishes, say that he is happy? All I can say is that if you yourself had been there...."

CHAPTER VIII

BLINDS DOWN

I

It was not until Stephen Westcott had rejoiced in the glories (so novel and so thrilling) of his first birthday and "The Stone House" had been six months before the public eye that the effect of this second book could be properly estimated. Second books are the most surely foredoomed creatures in all creation and there are many excellent reasons for this. They will assuredly disappoint the expectations of those who enjoyed the first work, and the author will, in all probability, have been tempted by his earlier success to try his wings further than they are, as yet, able to carry him.

Peter's failure was only partial. There was no question that "The Stone House" was a remarkable book. Had it been Peter's first novel it must have made an immense stir; it showed that he was, in no kind of way, a man of one book, and it gave, in its London scenes, proof that its author was not limited to one kind of life and one kind of background. There were chapters that were fuller, wiser, in every way more mature than anything in "Reuben Hallard."

But it was amazingly unequal. There were places in it that had no kind of life at all; at times Peter appeared to have beheld his scenes and characters through a mist, to have been dragged right away from any kind of vision of the book, to have written wildly, blindly.

The opinion of Mrs. Launce was perhaps the soundest that it was possible to have because that good lady, in spite of her affection for Peter, had a critical judgment that was partly literary, partly commercial, and partly human. She always judged a book first with her brain, then with her heart and lastly with her knowledge of her fellow creatures. "It may pay better than 'Reuben Hallard,'" she said, "there's more love interest and it ends happily. Some of it is beautifully written, some of it quite unspeakably. But really, Peter, it's the most uneven thing I've ever read. Again and again one is caught, held, stirred—then, suddenly, you slip away altogether—you aren't there at all, nothing's there, I could put my ringer on the places. Especially the first chapters and the last chapters—the middle's splendid—what happened to you?... But it will sell, I expect. Tell your banker to read it, go into lots of banks and tell them. Bank clerks have subscriptions at circulating libraries always given them ... but the wild bits are best, the wild bits are splendid—that bit about the rocks at night ... you don't know much about women yet—your girls are awfully bad. By the way, do you know that Mary Hollins is only getting £100 advance next time? All she can get, that last thing was so shocking. I hear that that book about an immoral violet, by that new young man—Rondel, isn't it?—is still having a most enormous success—I know that Barratt's got in a whole batch of new copies last night—I hear...."

Mrs. Launce was disappointed—Peter could tell well enough. He received some laudatory reviews, some letters from strangers, some adulation from people who knew nothing whatever. He did not know what it was exactly that he had expected—but whatever it was that he wanted, he did not get it—he was dissatisfied.

He began to blame his publishers—they had not advertised him enough; he even, secretly, cherished that most hopeless of all convictions—that his book was above the heads of the public. He noticed, also, that wherever he might be, this name of Rondel appeared before him, Mr. Rondel with his foolish face and thin mother in black, was obviously the young man of the moment—in the literary advertisements of any of the weekly papers you might see The Violet novel in its tenth edition and "The Stone House" by Peter Westcott, second edition selling rapidly.

He was again bewildered, as he had been after the publication of "Reuben Hallard" by the extraordinary variance of opinions amongst reviewers and amongst his own personal friends. One man told him that he had no style, that he must learn the meaning and feeling of words, another told him that his characters were weak but that his style was "splendid—a real knowledge of the value and meaning of words." Some one told him that he knew nothing at all about women and some one else that his women were by far the best part of his work. The variety was endless—amongst those who had appeared to him giants there was the same uncertainty. He seemed too to detect with the older men a desire to praise those parts of his work that resembled their own productions and to blame anything that gave promise of originality.

For himself it seemed to him that Mrs. Launce's opinion was nearest the truth. There were parts of it that were good, chapters that were better than anything in "Reuben Hallard" and then again there were many chapters where he saw it all in a fog, groped dimly for his characters, pushed, as it seemed to him, away from their lives and interests, by the actual lives and interests of the real people about him. This led him to think of Clare and here he was suddenly arrested by a perception, now only dimly grasped, of a change in her attitude to his writings. He dated it, thinking of it now for the first time, from the birth of young Stephen—or was it not earlier than that, on that evening when they had met Cards at that supper party, on that evening of their first quarrel?

In the early days how well he remembered Clare's enthusiasm—a little extravagant, it seemed now. Then during the first year of their married life she had wanted to know everything about the making of "The Stone House." It was almost as though it had been a cake or a pie, and he knew that he had found her questions difficult to answer and that he had had it driven in upon him that it was not really because she was interested in the subtleties of his art that she enquired but because of her own personal affection for him; if he had been making boots or a suit of clothes it would have been just the same. Then when "The Stone House" appeared her eagerness for its success had been tremendous—there was nothing she would not do to help it along—but that, he somewhat ironically discovered, was because she liked success and the things that success brought.

Then when the book had not succeeded—or only so very little—her interest had, of a sudden, subsided. "Oh! I suppose you've got to go and do your silly old writing ... I think you might come out with me just this afternoon. It isn't often that I ask anything of you...." He did not believe that she had ever really finished "The Stone House." She pretended that she had—"the end was simply perfect," but she was vague, nebulous. He found the marker in her copy, some fifty pages before the end.

She was so easily impressed by every one whom she met that perhaps the laughing attitude of Cards to Peter's books had something to do with it all. Cards affected to despise anything to do with work, here to-day, gone to-morrow—let us eat and drink ... dear old Peter, grubbing away upstairs—"I say, Mrs. Westcott, let's go and rag him...." And then they had come and invaded his room at the top of the house, and sometimes he had been glad and had flung his work down as though it were of no account ... and then afterwards, in the middle of some tea-party he had been suddenly ashamed, deeply, bitterly ashamed, as though he had actually wounded those white pages lying up there in his quiet room.

He was at this time, like a man jostled and pushed and turned about at some riotous fair; looking, now this way, now that, absorbed by a thousand sights, a thousand sounds—and always through it all feeling, bitterly in his heart, that something dear to him, somewhere in some place of silence, was dying—

Well, hang it all, at any rate there was the Child!

II

At any rate there was the Child!

And what a child! Did any one ever have a baby like it, so fat and round and white, with its head already covered with faint golden silk, its eyes grey and wondering—with its sudden gravities, its amazing joys and terrific humour, the beauty of its stepping away, as it did, suddenly without any warning, behind a myriad mists and curtains, into some other land that it knew of. How amazing to watch it as it slowly forgot all the things that it had come into the world remembering, as it slowly realised all the laws that this new order of things demanded of its obedience. Could any one who had been present ever forget its crow of ecstasy at the first shaft of sunlight that it ever beheld, at its first realisation of the blue, shining ball that Peter bought, at its first vision, through the window, of falling snow!

Peter was drunk with this amazing wonder. All the facts of life—even Clare and his work—faded before this new presence for whose existence he had been responsible. It had been one of the astonishing things about Clare that she had taken the child so quietly. He had seen her thrilled by musical comedy, by a dance at the Palace Music Hall, by the trumpery pathos of a tenth-rate novel—before this marvel she stood, it seemed to him, without any emotion.

Sometimes he thought that if it had not been for his reminder she would not have gone to kiss the child goodnight. There were many occasions when he knew—with wonder and almost dismay—that she was afraid of it; and once, when they had been in the nursery together and young Stephen had cried and kicked his heels in a tempest of rage, she had seemed almost to cling to Peter for protection.

There were occasions when Peter fancied that the baby seemed the elder of the two, it was at any rate certain that Stephen Westcott was not so afraid of his mother as his mother was of him. And yet, Peter fancied, that could Clare only get past this strange nervous fear she would love the baby passionately—would love him with that same fierceness of passion that she flung, curiously, now and again upon Peter himself. "Let me be promised," she seemed to say, "that I will never have any trouble or sorrow with my son and I will love him devotedly." Meanwhile she went into every excitement that life could provide for her....

It was on a March afternoon of early Spring after a lonely tea (Clare was out at one of her parties) that Peter went up to the nursery. He had just finished reading the second novel by that Mr. Rondel whose Violet sensation had occurred some two years before. This second book was good—there was no doubt about it—and Peter was ashamed of a kind of dim reluctance in his acknowledgment of its quality. The fellow had had such reviews; the book, although less sensational than its predecessor had hit the public straight in the middle of its susceptible heart. Had young Rondel done it all with bad work-well, that was common enough—but the book was good, uncommonly good.

He sent the nurse downstairs and began to build an elaborate fortress on the nursery floor. The baby lay on his back on a rug by the fire and contemplated his woollen shoe which he slowly dragged off and disdainfully flung away. Then, crowing to himself, he watched his father and the world in general.

He was amazingly like Peter—the grey eyes, the mouth a little stern, a little sulky, the snub nose, the arms a little short and thick, and that confident, happy smile.

He watched his father.

To him, lying on the rug, many, many miles away there was a coloured glory that ran round the upper part of the wall—as yet, he only knew that they gave him, those colours, something of the same pleasure that his milk gave him, that the warm, glowing, noisy shapes beyond the carpet gave him, that the happy, comfortable smell of the Thing playing near him on the floor gave him. About the Thing he was eternally perplexed. It was Something that made sounds that he liked, that pressed his body in a way that he loved, that took his fingers and his toes and made them warm and comfortable.

It was Something moreover from which delicious things hung—things that he could clutch and hold and pull. He was perplexed but he knew that when this Thing was near him he was warm and happy and contented and generally went to sleep. His eyes slowly travelled round the room and rested finally upon a round blue ball that hung turning a little from side to side, on a nail above, his bed. This was, to him, the final triumph of existence—to have it in his hand, to roll it round and round, to bang it down upon the floor and watch it jump, this was the reason why one was here, this the solution of all perplexities. He would have liked to have it in his hands now, so crowing, he smiled pleasantly at the Thing on the floor beside him and then looked at the ball.

Peter got up from his knees, fetched the ball down and rolled it along the floor. As it came dancing, curving, laughing along young Stephen shrieked with delight. Would he have it in his hands or would it escape him and disappear altogether? Would it come to him?... It came and was clutched and held and triumphed over.

Peter sat down by his son and began to tell him about Cornwall. He often did this, partly because the mere mentioning of names and places satisfied some longing in his heart, partly because he wanted Cornwall to be the first thing that young Stephen would realise as soon as he realised anything. "And you never can tell, you know, how soon a child can begin...."

Stephen, turning the blue ball round and round in his fingers, gravely listened. He was perfectly contented. He liked the sounds that circled about him—his father's voice, the rustle of the fire, the murmur of something beyond the walls that he could not understand.

"And then, you see, Stephen, if you go up the hill and round to the right you come to the market-place, all covered with shiny cobbles and once a week filled with stalls where people sell things. At the other end of it, facing you, there's an old Tower that's been there for ages and ages. It's got a fruit stall underneath it now, but once, years ago there was fighting there and men were killed. Then, if you go past it, and out to the right, you get into the road that leads out of the town. It goes right above the sea and on a fine-day—"

"Peter!"

The voice broke like a stone shattering a sheet of glass. The ball dropped from young Stephen's hands. He felt suddenly cold and hungry and wanted his woollen shoe. He was not sure whether he would not cry. He would wait a moment and see how matters developed.

Peter jumped to his feet and faced Clare: Clare in a fur cap from beneath which her golden hair seemed to burn in anger, from beneath which her eyes, furiously attacked his. Of course she had heard him talking to the baby about Cornwall. They had quarrelled about it before ... he had thought that she was at her silly tea-party. His face that had been, a few moments before, gentle, humorous, happy, now suddenly wore the sullen defiance of a sulky boy.

Her breast was heaving, her little hands beat against her frock.

"He shan't," she broke out at last, "hear about it."

"Of all the nonsense," Peter answered her slowly. "Really, Clare, sometimes I think you're about two years old—"

"He shan't hear about it," she repeated again. "You don't care—you don't care what I think or what I say—I'm his mother—I have the right—"

The baby looked at them both with wondering eyes and to any outside observer would surely have seemed the eldest of the three. Clare's breath came in little pants of rage—"You know—that I hate—all mention of that place—those people. It doesn't matter to you—you never think of me—"

"At any rate," he retorted, "if you were up here in the nursery more often you would be able to take care that Stephen's innocent ears weren't insulted with my vulgar conversation—"

It was then that he saw, behind Clare, in the doorway, the dark smiling face of Cards.

Cards came forward. "Really, you two," he said, laughing. "Peter, old man, don't be absurd—you too, Clare" (he called her Clare now).

The anger died out of Clare's eyes: "Well, he knows I hate him talking about that nasty old town to the baby—" Then, in a moment, she was smiling again—"I'm sorry, Peter. Cards is quite right, and anyhow the baby doesn't understand—"

She stood smiling in front of him but the frown did not leave his face.

"Oh! it's all right," he said sullenly, and he brushed past them up the stairs, to his own room.

III

From the silence of his room he thought that he could hear them laughing about it downstairs. "Silly old Peter—always getting into tempers—" Well, was he? And after all hadn't it been, this time, her affair? Stephen and he had been happy enough before the others had come in. What was this senseless dislike of Clare's to Cornwall? What could it matter to her? It was always cropping up now. He could think of a thousand occasions, lately, when she had been roused by it.

But, as he paced, with frowning face, back and forwards across the room, there was something more puzzling still that had to be thought about. Why did they quarrel about such tiny things? In novels, in good, reliable novels, it was always the big things about which people fought. Whoever heard of two people quarrelling because one of them wanted to talk about Cornwall? and yet it was precisely concerning things just as trivial that they were always now disputing. Why need they quarrel at all? In the first year there had always been peace. Why shouldn't there be peace now? Where exactly lay Clare's altered attitude to himself, to his opinions, to the world in general. If he yielded to her demands—and he had yielded on many more occasions than was good either for her or himself—she had, he fancied, laughed at him for being so easily defeated. If he had not yielded then she had been, immediately, impossible....

And yet, after their quarrels, there had been the most wonderful, precious reconciliations, reconciliations that, even now at his thought of them, made his heart beat faster. Now, soon, when he went downstairs to dress for dinner, she would come to him, he knew, and beg most beautifully, his pardon. But to-night it seemed suddenly that this kind of thing had happened too often lately. He felt, poor Peter, bewildered. There seemed to be, on every side of him, so many things that he was called upon to manage and he was so unable to manage any of them. He stopped in his treading to and fro and stared at the long deal writing-table at which he always worked.

There, waiting for him, were the first chapters of his new novel, "Mortimer Stant." In the same way, two years ago, he had stared at the early chapters of "The Stone House," on that morning before he had gone to propose to Clare. Now there flashed through his mind the wonderful things that he intended "Mortimer Stant" to be. It was to concern a man of forty (in his confident selection of that age he displayed, most stridently, his own youth) and Mortimer was to be a stolid, reserved Philistine, who was, against his will, by outside forces, dragged into an emotional crisis.

At the back of his mind he had, perhaps, Maradick for his figure, but that was almost unconscious. "Mortimer Stant" was to represent a wonderful duel between the two camps—the Artists and the Philistines—with ultimate victory, of course, for the Artists. It was to be.... Well what was it to be? At present the stolid Mortimer was hidden behind a phalanx of people—Clare, young Stephen, Cards, Bobby, Mrs. Rossiter (tiresome woman), Alice Galleon—That was it. It was hidden, hidden just as parts of "The Stone House" had been hidden, but hidden more deeply—a regular jungle of interests and occupations was creeping, stealthily, stealthily upon him.

And then his eye fell upon an open letter that lay on his table, and, at the sight of it, he was seized with a burning sense of shame. How could he have forgotten?

The letter ran—

My dear Mr. Westcott,

You have not been to see me for many months. Further opportunities may, by the hand of God, be denied you.

Come if you can spare the time.

Henry Galleon.

The words were written, feebly almost illegibly, in pencil. Peter knew that Bobby had been, for many weeks, very anxious concerning his father's health, and during the last few days he had abandoned the City and spent all his time at home. That letter had come this very morning and Peter had intended to go at once and inquire. The fact that he had left all these months without going to see the old man rose before him now like an accusing hand. He deserved, indeed, whatever the Gods might choose to send him, if he could so wilfully neglect his duty. But he knew that there had been, in the back of his mind, shame. His work had not, so he might have put it to himself, been good enough to justify his presence. There would have been questions asked, questions that he might have found it difficult, indeed, to answer.

But now the sight of that letter immediately encouraged him. Henry Galleon, even though he was too ill to talk, would put him right with all his perplexities, would give him courage to cut through all these complications that had been gathering, lately, so thickly about him. "This," the room seemed to whisper to him, "is your chance. After all, you are given this opportunity. See him once before he dies and your fate will be shown you, clearly, honestly."

He stepped out of the house unperceived and was immediately conscious of the Spring night. Spring—with a precipitancy and extravagance that seems to be—to own peculiar quality in London—had leapt upon the streets.

The Embankment was bathed in the evening glow. Clouds, like bales of golden wool, sailed down a sky so faintly blue that the white light of a departed sun seemed to glow behind it. The lamps were crocus-coloured against black barges that might have been loaded with yellow primroses so did they hint, through their darkness, at the yellow haze around them.

The silence was melodious; the long line of dark houses watched like prisoners from behind their iron bars. They might expect, it seemed, the Spring to burst through the flagstones at their feet.

Peter's heart was lightened of all its burden. He shared the glory, the intoxication of the promise that was on every side of him. On such a night great ambitions, great ideals, great lovers were created.

He saw Henry Galleon, from behind his window, watching the pageant. He saw him gaining new life, getting up from his bed of sickness, writing anew his great masterpieces. And he saw himself, Peter Westcott, learning at last from the Master the rule and discipline of life. All the muddle, the confusion of this lazy year should be healed. He and Clare should see with the same eyes. She should understand his need for work, he should understand her need for help. All should be happiness and victory in this glorious world and he, by the Master's side, should...

He stopped suddenly. The house that had been Henry Galleon's was blank and dead.

At every window the blinds were down....

CHAPTER IX

WILD MEN

I

To Peter's immediate world it was a matter of surprise that he should take Henry Galleon's death so hardly. It is a penalty of greatness that you should, to the majority of your fellow men, be an Idea rather than a human being. To his own family Henry Galleon had, of course, been real enough but to the outside world he was the author of "Henry Lessingham" and "The Roads," whose face one saw in the papers as one saw the face of Royalty. Peter Westcott, moreover, had not appeared, at any time, to take more than a general interest in the great man, and it was even understood that old Mrs. Galleon and Millicent and Percival considered themselves somewhat affronted because the Master had "been exceedingly kind to the young man. Taken trouble about him, tried to know him, but young Westcott had allowed the thing to drop—had not been near him during the last year."

Even Bobby and Alice Galleon were astonished at Peter's grief. To Bobby his father's death came as a fine ending to a fine career. He had died, full of honour and of years. Even Bobby, who thought that he knew his Peter pretty well by now, was puzzled.

"He takes it," Bobby explained to Alice, "as though it were a kind of omen, sees ever so much more in it than any of us do. It seems that he was coming round the very evening that father died to talk to him, and that he suddenly saw the blinds down; it was a shock to him, of course. I think it's all been a kind of remorse working out, remorse not only for having neglected my father but for having left other things—his work, I suppose, rather to look after themselves. But he won't tell me," Bobby almost desperately concluded, "he won't tell me anything—he really is the most extraordinary chap."

And Peter found it difficult enough to tell himself, did not indeed try. He only knew that he felt an acute, passionate remorse and that it seemed to him that the denial of that last visit was an omen of the anger of all the Gods, and even—although to this last he gave no kind of expression—the malicious contrivance of an old man who waited for him down there in that house by the sea. It was as though gates had been clanged in his face, and that as he heard them close he heard also the jeering laughter behind them.... He had missed his chance.

He saw, instantly, that Clare understood none of this, and that, indeed, she took it all as rather an affectation on his part, something in him that belonged to that side of him that she tried to forget. She hated, quite frankly, that he should go about the house with a glum face because an old man, whom he had never taken the trouble to go and see when he was alive, was now dead. She showed him that she hated it.

He turned desperately to his work. There had been a hint, only the other day, from the newspaper for which he wrote, that his reviews had not, lately, been up to his usual standard. He knew that they seemed to him twice as difficult to do as they had seemed a year ago and that therefore he did them twice as badly.

He flung himself upon his book and swore that he would dissipate the shadows that hid it from him. One of the shadows he saw quite clearly was Cards' attitude to his work. It was strange, he thought almost pathetically, how closely his feeling for Cards now resembled the feeling that he had had, those years ago, at Dawson's. He still worshipped him—worship was the only possible word—worshipped him for all the things that he, Peter, was not. One could not be with him, Peter thought, one could not watch his movements, hear his voice without paying it all the most absolute reverence. The glamour about Cards was, to Peter, something almost from another world. Peter felt so clumsy, so rough and ugly and noisy and out-of-place when Cards was present that the fact that Cards was almost always present now made life a very difficult thing. How could Peter prevent himself from reverencing every word that Cards uttered when one reflected upon the number of things that Cards had done, the things that he had seen, the places to which he had been. And Cards' attitude to Peter's work was, if not actually contemptuous, at least something very like it. He did not, he professed, read novels. The novelists' trade at the best, he seemed to imply, was only a poor one, and that Peter's work was not altogether of the best he almost openly asserted. "What can old Peter know about life?" one could hear him saying— "Where's he been? Who's he known? Whatever in the world has he done?"

Against this, in spite of the glitter that shone about Cards' head, Peter might, perhaps, have stood. He reminded himself, a hundred times a day, that one must not care about the things that other people said, one must have one's eyes fixed upon the goal—one must be sure of oneself—what had Galleon said?...

But there was also the effect of it all upon Clare to be considered. Clare listened to Cards. She was, Peter gloomily considered, very largely of Cards' opinion. The two people for whom he cared most in the world after young Stephen who, as a critic, had not yet begun to count, thought that he was wasting his time.

Sometimes, as he sat at his deal table, fighting with a growing sense of disillusionment that was like nothing so much as a child's first discovery that its beautiful doll is stuffed with straw, he would wish passionately, vehemently for the return of those days when he had sat in his little bedroom writing "Reuben Hallard" with Norah Monogue, and dear Mr. Zanti and even taciturn little Gottfried, there to encourage him.

That had been Adventure—but this ...? And then he would remember young Stephen and Clare—moments even lately that she had shared with him—and he would be ashamed.

II

It was on an afternoon of furious wind and rain in early April that the inevitable occurred. All the afternoon the trees in the little orchard had been knocking their branches together as though they were in a furious temper with Somebody and were indignant at not being allowed to get at Him; they gave you the impression that it would be quite as much as your life would be worth to venture into their midst.

Peter had, during a number of hours, endeavoured to pierce the soul of Mortimer Stant—meanwhile as the wind howled, the rain lashed the windows of his room, and the personality of Mr. Stant faded farther and farther away into ultimate distance, Peter was increasingly conscious that he was listening for something.

He had felt himself surrounded by this strange sense of anticipation before. Sometimes it had stayed with him for a short period only, sometimes it had extended over days—always it brought with it an emotion of excitement and even, if he had analysed it sufficiently, fear.

He was suddenly conscious, in the naked spaces of his barely-furnished room, of the personality of his father. So conscious was he that he got up from his table and stood at the rain-swept window, looking out into the orchard, as though he expected to see a sinister figure creeping, stealthily, from behind the trees. In his thoughts of his father there was no compunction, no accusing scruples of neglect, only a perfectly concrete, active sense, in some vague way, of force pitted against force.

It might be summed up in the conviction that "the old man was not done with him yet"—and as Peter turned back from the window, almost relieved that he had, indeed, seen no creeping figure amongst the dark trees, he was aware that never since the days of his starvation in Bucket Lane, had he been so conscious of those threatening memories of Scaw House and its inhabitants.

At that, almost as he reached his table, there was a knock on his door.

"Come in," he cried and, scorning himself for his fears, faced the maid with staring eyes.

"Two gentlemen to see you, sir," she said. "I have shown them into the study."

"Is Mrs. Westcott in?"

"No, sir. She told me that she would not be back until six o'clock, sir."

"I will come down."

In the hall, hanging amongst the other things as a Pirate might hang beside a company of Evangelist ministers, was Stephen Brant's hat....

As Peter's hand turned on the handle of the study door he knew that his heart was beating with so furious a clamour that he could not hear the lock turn.

III

He entered the room and found Stephen Brant and Mr. Zanti facing him. The little window between the dim rows of books showed him the pale light that was soon to succeed the storm. The two men seemed to fill the little room; their bodies were shadowy and mysterious against the pale colour, and Peter had the impression that the things in the room—the chairs, the books, the table—huddled against the wall, so crowded did the place seem.

For himself, at his first sight of them, he was compelled, instantly, to check a feeling of joy so overwhelming that he was himself astonished at the force of it. To them, as they stood there, smiling, feeling that same emotion to which he, also, was now succumbing! He checked himself. It was as though he were forced suddenly, by a supreme effort of will, to drive from the room a tumultuous crowd of pictures, enthusiasms and memories, that, for the sake of the present and of the future, must be forbidden to stay with him. It was absurd—he was a husband, a father, a responsible householder, almost a personage... and yet, as he looked at Stephen's eyes and Mr. Zanti's smile, he was the little boy back again in Tan's shop with the old suit of armour, the beads and silver and Eastern cloths, and out beyond the window, the sea was breaking upon the wooden jetty....

He put the picture away from him and rushed to greet the two of them. "Zanti!... Stephen!... Oh! how splendid! How perfectly, perfectly splendid!"

Mr. Zanti's enormous body was enclosed in a suit of bright blue, his broad nose stood out like a bridge, his wide mouth gaped. He wore white spats, three massive rings of twisted gold and in his blue tie a glittering emerald. He was a magnificent, a costly figure and in nothing was the geniality of his nature more plainly seen than in his obvious readiness to abandon, at any moment, these splendid riches for the sake of a valued attachment. "I love wearing these things," you might hear him say, "but I love still better to do anything in the world that I can for you, my friend."

Stephen presented a more moderate appearance, but he was brown with health and shining with strength. He was like the old Stephen of years and years ago, so different from the—man who had shared with Peter that room in Bucket Lane.

He carried himself with that air of strong, cautious reserve that Cornishmen have when they are in some other country than their own; his eyes, mild, gentle, but on the alert, ready at an instant to be hostile. Then, when Peter came in, the reserve instantly fled. They had, all three of them, perhaps, expected embarrassment, but at that cry of Peter's they were suddenly together, Mr. Zanti, waving his hands, almost shouting, Stephen, his eyes resting with delight on Peter, Peter himself another creature from the man who had pursued Mortimer Stant in the room upstairs, half an hour before.

"We thought that ze time 'ad come, dear boy... we know zat you are busy." Mr. Zanti looked about him a little anxiously, as though he expected to find Mrs. Peter hiding under a chair or a sofa.

"Oh! Stephen, after all this long long while! Why didn't you come before when Mr. Zanti came?"

"Too many of us coming, Mr. Peter, and you so busy."

"Nonsense. I'm not in the least busy. I'm sorry to say my wife's out but the baby's in, upstairs, and there's the most terrific woman up there too, the nurse—I'm frightened out of my life of her—but we'll get rid of her and have the place to ourselves... you know the kid's called after you, Stephen?"

"No, is he really?" Stephen's face shone with pleasure. "I'm keen to see him."

"Oh, he's a trump! There never really was such a baby."

"And your books, Mr. Peter?"

"Oh! the books!" Peter's voice dropped, "never mind them now. But what have you been doing, you two? Made heaps of money? Discovered treasure?..." He pulled himself up shortly. He remembered the bookshop, the girl leaning against the door looking into the street, then the boys crying the news....

If Mr. Zanti had been mixing himself up with that sort of thing again! And then the bright blue suit, the white spats, were reassuring. As if one could ever take such a child seriously about anything!

Mr. Zanti shook his head, ruefully. "No, not ezackly a fortune! There was a place I 'eard of, right up in the Basque country—'twas an old deserted garden, where zey 'ad buried treasure, centuries ago—I 'ad it quite certainly from a friend. We came up there for a time but we found nothing." He sighed and then was instantly cheered again. "But it's all right. I've got a plan now—a wonderful plan." He became very mysterious. "It's a certain thing—we're off to Cornwall, Mr. Brant and myself—"

"Cornwall?"

"Come too, Peter."

"Ah! don't I wish that I could!" He suddenly saw his life, his books—everything in London holding him, tying him—"But I can't go now, my father being there makes it impossible. But in any case, I'm a family man now—you know."

As he said the words he was conscious that, in Stephen's eyes at any rate, the family man was about the last thing that he looked. He was wondering, with intense curiosity, what were the things that Stephen was finding in him, for the things that Stephen found were most assuredly the things that he was. No one knew him as Stephen knew him. Against his will the thought of Clare came driving upon him. How little she knew him! or was it only that she knew another side of him?

But he pulled himself away from that. "Now for the nursery—Stephen Secundus. But you'll have to support me whilst I get rid of Mrs. Kant—perhaps three of us together—"

As he led the way upstairs he knew that Stephen was not entirely reassured about him.

Mrs. Kant was a large, busy woman, like a horse—a horse who dislikes other horses and sniffs an enemy in every wind. She very decidedly sniffed an enemy now, and Mr. Zanti's blue suit paled before her fierce eyes. He stepped back into the doorway again, treading upon Stephen. Peter, who was always conscious that Mrs. Kant looked upon himself and Clare as two entirely ridiculous and slightly impertinent children, stammered a little.

"You might go down and have your tea now, Mrs. Kant. I'll keep an eye upon Stephen."

"I've had my tea, thank you, sir."

"Well, I'll relieve you of the baby for a little." She was sewing. She snapped off a piece of thread with a sharp click of her teeth, sat silently for a moment staring in front of her, then quietly got up. "Thank you, sir," she said and left the room.

All three men breathed again as the door closed—then they were all conscious of young Stephen.

The thing was, of course, absurd, but to all three of them there came the conviction that the baby had been laughing at them for their terror of Mrs. Kant. He was curled up on a chair by the fire, looking at them with his wide eyes over his shoulder, and he seemed to say, "I don't care a snap for the woman— why should you?" The blue ball was on the floor at the foot of the chair, and the firelight leapt upon the frieze that Peter had so carefully chosen—giants and castles, dwarfs and princesses running round the room in red, and blue and gold.

Young Stephen looked at them, puzzled for an instant, then with a shout he would have acclaimed his father, but his gaze was suddenly arrested by the intense blueness of Mr. Zanti's clothes. He stared at it, fascinated. Into his life there had suddenly broken the revelation that you might have something far larger than the blue ball that moved and shone in so fascinating a manner. His eyes immediately glittered with the thought that he would presently have the joy of rolling something so big and shining along the floor. He could not bear to wait. His fat fingers curved in the air with the eager anticipation of it—words, actual words had not as yet come to him, but, crowing and gurgling, he informed the world that he wanted, he demanded, instantly, that he should roll Mr. Zanti.

"Well, old man, how are you?" said Peter. But he would not look at his father. His arms stretched toward Mr. Zanti.

"You've made a conquest right away, Zanti," Peter said laughing.

It was indeed instantly to be perceived that Mr. Zanti was in his right element. Any pretence of any kind of age fell away from him, his arms curved towards young Stephen as young Stephen's curved towards him. He was making noises in his throat that exactly resembled the noises that the baby made.

He looked down gravely upon the chair—"'Ow do you do?" he said and he took young Stephen's fat fingers in his hand.

"'E says," he remarked, looking at Peter and Stephen, "that 'e would like to roll me upon the floor—like that ball there—"

"Well, let him," said Peter laughing.

The baby then dug his fingers into Mr. Zanti's hair and pulled down his head towards the chair, intense satisfaction flooding his face as he did so.

The baby seemed, for a moment, to whisper into Mr. Zanti's ear, then, chuckling it climbed down from the chair, and, on all fours, crawled, its eyes and mouth suddenly serious as though it were conscious that it was engaged upon a very desperate adventure. The three men watched it. Across the absolute silence of the room there came the sound of the rain driving upon the pane, of the tumbling chatter of the fire, of the baby's hands falling upon the carpet.

Mr. Zanti was suddenly upon his knees. "Here," he cried, seizing the blue ball. He rolled it to young Stephen. It was caught, dropped and then the fat fingers had flung themselves upon Mr. Zanti's coat. He let himself go and was pulled back sprawling upon the floor, his huge body stretching from end to end of the rug.

Then, almost before they had realised it, the other two men were down upon their knees. The ball was picked up and tossed from hand to hand, the baby, sitting upon Mr. Zanti's stomach, watched with delight these extraordinary events.

Then they played Hunt the Slipper, sitting round in a ring upon the carpet, young Stephen trying to catch his own slipper, falling over upon his back, kicking his legs in the air, dashing now at Stephen the Elder's beard, now at his father's coat, now at Mr. Zanti's legs.

The noise of the laughter drowned the rain and the fire. Mr. Zanti had the slipper—he was sitting upon it. Peter made a dash for it, Mr. Zanti rolled over, they were all in a heap upon the floor.

"I've got it." Mr. Zanti was off on all fours round the room, the baby on his back clutching on to his hair. A chair was over, then a box of bricks, the table rocked and then was suddenly down with a crash!

What had come to them all? Stephen, so grave, so solemn, had caught the baby into the air, had flung him up and caught him again. Peter and Mr. Zanti looking up from the floor saw him standing, his legs wide, his beard flowing, his arms stretched with young Stephen shouting between them.

Behind him, around him was a wrecked nursery....

The baby, surveying the world from this sudden height, wondered at this amazing glory. He had never before beheld from such a position the things that bounded his life. How strange the window seemed! Through it now he could see the tops of the trees, the grey sky, the driving lines of rain! Only a little way above him now were pictures that had always glowed before from so great a distance. Around him, above him, below him space—a thing to be frightened of were one not held so tightly, so safely.

He approved, most assuredly, of the banishment of Mrs. Kant, and the invasion of these splendid Things! He would have life always like this, with that great blue ball to roll upon the floor, with that brown beard, near now to his hand, to clutch, with none of that hideous soap-in-the-eyes-early-to-bed Philosophy that he was becoming now conscious enough to rebel against.

He dug his hands into the beard that was close to him and, like the sons of the morning, shouted with joy.

Peter, looking up at the two Stephens, felt his burdens roll off his back. If only things could be like this always! And already he saw himself, through these two, making everything right once more with Clare. They should prove to her that, after all, his past life had not been so terrible, that Cornwall could produce heroes if it liked. Through these two he would get fresh inspiration for his work. He felt already, through them, a wind blowing that cleared all the dust from his brain.

And how splendid for the boy! To have two such men for his friends! Already he was planning to persuade them to stay in London. He had thought of the very place for them in Chelsea, near the Roundabout, the very house....

"Of course you'll stay for dinner, you two—"

"But—" said Mr. Zanti, mopping his brow from which perspiration was dripping.

"No, nonsense. Of course you'll stop. We've got such heaps to talk about—"

Stephen had got the baby now on his shoulder. "Off to Cornwall," he shouted and charged down the room.

It was at that instant that Peter was conscious that Clare had been standing, for some moments, in the room. She stood, quite silently, without moving, by the door, her eyes blazing at him....

His first thought was of that other time when she had found him in the nursery, of the quarrel that they had had. Then he noticed the state of the room, the overturned chairs and table. Then he saw Mr. Zanti still wiping his forehead, but confusedly, and staring at Clare in a shocked hushed way, as though he were a small boy who had been detected with his fingers in a jam-pot.

Stephen saw her at last. He put the baby down and came slowly across the floor. Peter spoke: "Why, Clare! You're back early. We've been having such a splendid time with Stephen—let me introduce my friends to you—Mr. Zanti and Mr. Brant... you've heard me speak of them—"

They came towards her. She shook hands with them, regarding them gravely.

"How do you do?"

There was silence. Then Mr. Zanti said—"We must be goin'—longer than we ought to stop—we 'ave business—"

Peter felt rising in him a cold and surging anger at her treatment of them. These two, the best friends that he had in the world—that she should dare!

"Oh! you'll stay to dinner, you two! You must—"

"I'm afraid, ver' afraid," Mr. Zanti said bowing very low and still looking at Clare with apologetic, troubled eyes, "we 'ave no time. Immediate business."

Still Clare said nothing.

There was another moment's silence, and then Peter said:

"I'll come down and see you off." Still without moving from her place she shook hands with them.

"Good-bye."

They all three went out.

Peter could say nothing. The words seemed to be choked in his throat by this tide of anger that was like nothing he had ever felt before.

He held their hands for a moment as they stood outside in the dusk.

"Where are you staying? I must see you again—"

"We go down to Cornwall to-morrow."

Stephen caught Peter's shoulder:

"Come down to us, Peter, if you get a chance." They all stared at one another; they were all, absolutely, entirely without words. Afterwards they would regret that they had said nothing, but now—!

They vanished into the dusk and Peter, stepping into the house again, closed very softly the hall door behind him.

CHAPTER X

ROCKING THE ROUNDABOUT

I

As he climbed, once more, the stairs to the nursery, he was conscious of the necessity for a great restraint. Did he but relax for an instant his control he was aware that forces—often dimly perceived and shuddered at—would now, as never in his life before, burst into freedom.

It was as though a whole life of joy and happiness had been suddenly snatched from him and it was Clare who had robbed him—Clare who had never cared what the things might be that she demanded from him—Clare who gave him nothing.

But his rage now, he also felt, was beyond all reason, something that belonged to that other part of him, the part that Scaw House and its dark room understood and so terribly fostered.

He was afraid of what he might do.

II

On opening the nursery door he saw the straight, thin, shining back of Mrs. Kant as she bent to put things straight. Young Stephen was quietly asleep. He closed the door, and, turning in the narrow passage, found Clare coming out of her room. In the dim light they faced one another, hostility flaming between them. She looked at him for a moment, her breast heaving, her mouth so tight and sharp, her eyes so fierce that her little stature seemed to be raised by her anger to a great height.

At that moment Peter felt that he hated her as he had never hated any one in his life before.

She went back, without a word, into her room.

She did not come down again that night and he had his evening meal, miserably, alone.

He slept in his dressing-room. Long before morning his rage had gone. He looked at her locked door and wished, miserably, that he might die for her....

III

Later, as he sat, hopelessly, over the dim and sterile pages of "Mortimer Slant," Mrs. Rossiter came, heavily, in to talk with him. Mrs. Rossiter always entered the room with an expression of stupid benignity that hid a good deal of rather sharp perception. The fact that she was not nearly so stupid as she looked enabled her to look all the stupider and she covered a multitude of brains with a quantity of hard black silk that she spread out around her with the air of one who is filling as much of the room as she can conveniently seize upon. Her plump arms, her broad and placid bosom, her flat smooth face, her hair, entirely negative in colour and arrangement, offered no clue whatever to her unsuspected sharpnesses. Smooth, broad, flat and motionless she carried, like the Wooden Horse of Troy, a thousand dangers in the depths of her placidity.

She had come now to assist her daughter, the only person for whom she may be said to have had the slightest genuine affection, for Dr. Rossiter she had long-despised and Mrs. Galleon was an ally and companion but never a friend. She had allowed Clare to marry Peter, chiefly because Clare would have married him in any case, but also, a little, because she thought that Peter had a great career in front of him. Now that Peter's career seemed already to be, for the most part, behind him, she disliked him and because he appeared to have made Clare unhappy suddenly hated him... but placidity was the shield that covered her attack and, for a symbol, one might take the large flat golden brooch that she wore on her bosom—flat, expressionless and shining, with the sharpest pin behind it that ever brooch possessed.

Peter, whose miseries had accumulated as the minutes passed, was ready to seize upon anything that promised a reconciliation. He did not like Mrs. Rossiter—he had never been able to get to close quarters with her, and he was conscious that his roughness and occasional outbursts displeased her. He felt, too, that the qualities that he had resented in Clare owed their origin to her mother. That brooch of hers was responsible for a great deal.

Fixing his eyes upon it he said, "You've come about Clare?"

"Yes, Peter." Mrs. Rossiter settled herself more comfortably, spread her skirts, folded her hands. "She's very unhappy."

The mild eyes baffled him.

"I'm terribly sorry. I will do anything I can, but I think—that I had a right"—he faltered a little; it was so like talking to an empty Dairy—"had a right to mind. Two old friends of mine—two of the best friends that I have in the world were here yesterday and Clare—"

"I don't think," the soft voice broke in upon him whilst the eyes searched his body up and down, "that, even now, Peter, you quite understand Clare—"

"No," he said eagerly, "I know. I'm blundering, stupid. Lots of times I've irritated her, and now again." He paused, but then added, with a touch of his old stubbornness—"But they were friends of mine—she should have treated them so."

Mrs. Rossiter felt that she did indeed hate the young man.

"Clare is very unhappy," she repeated. "She tells me that she has been crying all night. You must remember, Peter, that her life has been very different to yours—"

He wished that she would not repeat herself; he wished that she would not always use the same level voice; he wanted insanely to tell her that she ought to say "different from"—he could not take his eyes from the brooch. But the thought of Clare came to him and he bowed himself once more humbly.

"I will see that things are better," he said earnestly. "I don't know what has been the matter lately—my work and everything has been wrong, and I expect my temper has been horrible. You know," he said with a little crooked smile, "that I've got to work to keep it all going, and when I'm writing badly then my temper goes to pieces."

Mrs. Rossiter, with no appearance of having heard anything that he had said, continued—

"You know, Peter, that your temperament is very different to Clare's. You are, and I know you will forgive my putting it so plainly, a little wild still—doubtless owing to your earlier years. Clare is gentle, bright, happy. She has never given my husband or myself a moment's trouble, but that is because we understood her nature. We knew that she loved people about her to be happy—she flourished in the sun, she drooped under the clouds... under the clouds" Mrs. Rossiter repeated again softly, as she searched, with care, for her next words.

Irritation was rising within Peter. Why should it be concluded so inevitably that the fault was all on Peter's side and not at all on Clare's—after all, there were reasons... but he pulled himself up. He had behaved like a beast.

"I've tried very hard—" he began.

"Clouds—" said Mrs. Rossiter. "And you, Peter, are at times—I have seen it myself and I know that it is apparent to others—inclined to be morose—gloomy, a little gloomy—" Her fingers tapped the silk of her dress. "Dear Clare, considering what her own life has been, shrinks, I must confess it seems to me quite naturally, from any reminder of what your own earlier circumstances have been. Look at it, Peter, for an instant from the outside and you will see, at once, I am sure, what it must have been to her, yesterday, to come into her nursery, to find tables, chairs overturned, strange men shouting and flinging poor little Stephen towards the ceiling—some talk about Cornwall—really, Peter, I think you can understand..."

He abandoned all his defences. "I know—I ought to have realised... it was quite natural..."

In the back of his head he heard her words "You're morose—you're wild. Other people find you so—you're making a mess of everything and every one knows it—"

He was humbled to the dust. If only he might make it all right with Clare, then he would see to it—Oh! yes he would see to it—that nothing of this kind ever happened again. From Mrs. Rossiter's standpoint he looked back upon his life and found it all one ignoble, selfish muddle. Dear Clare!—so eager to be happy and he had made her miserable.

"Will she forgive me?"

"Dear Clare," said Mrs. Rossiter, rising brightly and with a general air of benevolence towards all the sinners in existence, "is the most forgiving creature in the world."

He went down to her bedroom and found her lying on a sofa and reading a novel.

He fell on his knees at her side—"Clare—darling—I'm a beast, a brute—"

She suddenly turned her face into the cushions and burst into passionate crying. "Oh! it's horrible—horrible—horrible—"

He kissed her hand and then getting on to his feet again, stood looking at her awkwardly, struggling for words with which to comfort her.

IV

And then at luncheon, there was a little, pencilled feeble note for Peter from Norah Monogue. "Please, if you can spare half an hour come to me. In a day or two I am off to the country."

Things had just been restored to peace and happiness—Clare had just proposed that they should go, that afternoon, to a Private View together—they might go and have tea with—

For an instant he was tempted to abandon Norah. Then his courage came:—

"Here's a note from Miss Monogue," he said. "She's awfully ill I think, I ought—"

Clare's face hardened again. She got up from the table—

"Just as you please—" she said.

He climbed on to the omnibus that was to stumble with him down Piccadilly with a. hideous, numbing sense of being under the hand of Fate. Why, at this moment, in all time, should this letter of Norah Monogue's have made its unhappy appearance? With what difficulty and sorrow had he and Clare reached once more a reconciliation only, so wantonly, to be plucked away from it again! From the top of his omnibus he looked down upon a sinister London. It was a heavy, lowering day; thick clouds like damp cloths came down upon the towers and chimneys. The trees in the Green Park were black and chill and in and out of the Clubs figures slipped cautiously and it seemed furtively. Just beyond the Green Park they were building a vast hotel, climbing figures and twisting lines of scaffolding pierced the air, and behind the rolling and rattling of the traffic the sound of many hammers beat rhythmically, monotonously....

To Peter upon his omnibus, suddenly that sound that he had heard before—that sound of London stirring—came back to him, and now more clearly than he had ever known it. Tap-tap-tap-tap... Clamp-clamp-tap-tap-tap-tap—whir! whir!... Clamp-clamp....

It seemed to him that all the cabs and the buses and the little black figures were being hurried by some power straight, fast, along Piccadilly to be pitched, at the end of it, pell-mell, helter-skelter into some dark abysmal pit, there to perish miserably.

Yes, the beast was stirring! Ever so little the pavements, the houses were heaving. Perhaps if one could see already the soil was cracking beneath one's feet. "Look out! London will have you in a minute." Tap-tap-tap-tap—clamp-clamp—tap-tap-tap-tap—whir-whir—clamp-clamp....

Anyhow it was a heavy, clammy day. The houses were ghosts and the people were ghosts, and grey shadows, soon perhaps to be a yellow fog, floated about the windows and the doors and muffled all human sounds.

He passed the great pile of scaffolding, saw iron girders shining, saw huge cranes swinging in mid-air, saw tiny, tiny black atoms perched above the noise and swallowed by the smoke... tap-tap-clamp-clamp....

Yes, the beast was moving... and, out and in, lost and then found again, crept that twisting chain of beggars to whose pallid army Peter himself had once so nearly belonged.

"I suppose I've got a headache after all that row with Clare," Peter thought as he climbed off the omnibus.

V

He realised, as he came into the Bloomsbury square, and saw Mrs. Brockett gloomily waiting for him, that the adventures of his life were most strangely bound together. Not for an instant did he seem to be able to escape from any one of them. Now it would be Cornwall, now the Bookshop, now Stephen, now Mr. Zanti, now Bucket Lane, now Treliss—all of them interweaving, arresting his action at every moment. Because he had done that once now this must not be permitted him; he felt, as he rang the old heavy bell of Brockett's that his head would never think clearly again. As the door opened and he stepped into the hall he heard, faintly, across the flat spaces of the Square "Tap-tap-tap-tap-clamp-clamp...."

Even Mrs. Brockett, who might be considered if any one in the world, immune from morbid imaginations, felt the heaviness of the day, suggested a prevalence of thunder, and shook her head when Peter asked about Miss Monogue.

"She's bad, Mr. Peter, very bad, poor dear. There's no doubt about that. It's hard to see what can be done for her—but plucky! That's a small word for it!"

"I'm sure she is," said Peter, feeling ashamed of having made so much of his own little troubles.

"She must get out of London if she's to improve at all. In a week or two I hope she'll be able to move."

"How's every one else?"

"Oh, well enough." Mrs. Brockett straightened her dress with her beautiful hands in the old familiar way—"But you're not looking very hearty yourself, Mr. Peter."

"Oh! I'm all right," he answered smiling; but she shook her head after him as she watched him go up the stairs.

And then he was surprised. He came into Norah Monogue's room and found her sitting up by her window, looking better than he had ever seen her. Her face was full of colour and her eyes bright and smiling. Only on her hands the blue veins stood out, and their touch, when she shook hands with him, was hot and burning.

But he was reassured; Mrs. Brockett had exaggerated and made the worst of it all.

"You're looking splendid—I'm so glad. I was afraid from your letter-"

"Oh! I really am getting on," she broke in gaily, "and it's the nicest boy in the world that you are to come in and see me so quickly. Only on a day like this London does just lie heavily upon one doesn't it? and one just longs for the country—"

A little breath of a sigh escaped from her and she looked through her window at the dim chimneys, the clouds hanging like consolidated smoke, the fine, thin dust that filtered the air.

"You're looking tired yourself, Peter. Working too hard?"

"No," he shook his head. "The work hasn't been coming easily at all. I suppose I've been too conscious, lately, of the criticisms every one made about 'The Stone House.' I don't believe one ought really to listen to anybody and yet it's so hard not to, and so difficult to know whose opinion one ought to take if one's going to take anybody's. I wish," he suddenly brought out, "Henry Galleon were still alive. I could have followed him."

"But why follow anybody?"

"Ah! that's just it. I'm beginning to doubt myself and that's why it's getting so difficult."

Her eyes searched his face and she saw, at once, that he was in very real trouble. He looked younger, just then, she thought, than she had ever seen him, and she felt herself so immensely old that she could have taken him into her arms and mothered him as though he'd been her own son.

"There are a lot of things the matter," she said. "Tell me what they all are."

"Well," he said slowly, "I suppose it's all been mostly my own fault—but the real difficulty is that I don't seem to be able to run the business of being married and the business of writing together. I don't think Clare in the least cares now about my writing—she almost resents it; she cared at first when she thought that I was going to make a huge success of it, but now—"

"But, of course," said Miss Monogue, "that success comes slowly—it must if it's going to be any use at all—"

"Well, she doesn't see that. And she wants me to go out to parties and play about all the time—and then she doesn't want me to be any of the things that I was before I met her. All my earlier life frightens her—I suppose," he suddenly ended, "I want her to be different and she wants me to be different and we can't make a compromise."

Then Miss Monogue said: "Have any outside people interfered at all?"

Peter coloured. "Well, of course, Mrs. Rossiter stands up for Clare. She came and talked to me this morning and I think the things that she said were quite true. I suppose I am morose and morbid sometimes—more than I realise—and then," he added slowly, "there's Cards—"

"Cards?"

"Cardillac—a man I was at school with. I'm very fond of him. He's the best friend I've got, and he's been all over the place and done everything and, of course, knows ever so much more about the world than I do. The fact is he thinks really that my novels are dreadful nonsense, only he's much too kind to say so—and, of course, Clare looks up to him a lot. Although he's only my own age he seems so much older than both Clare and myself. I don't believe she'd have lost interest in my work so quickly if he hadn't influenced her—and he's influenced me too—" Peter added sighing.

"Well—and is there anything else?"

"Yes. There's Stephen. I can't begin to tell you how I love that kid. There haven't been many people in my life that I've cared about and I've never realised anything so intensely before. Besides," he went on laughing proudly, "he's such a splendid kid! I wish you could see him, Norah. He'll do something one day—"

"Well, what's the trouble about Stephen?"

"Clare's so odd about him. There are times when I don't believe she cares for him the least little bit. Then there are other times when she resents fiercely my interfering about him. Sometimes she seems to love him more than anything in the world, but it's always in an odd defiant way—just as though she were afraid that something would hurt her if she showed that she cared too much."

There was silence between them for a minute and then Peter summed it all up with:—"The fact is, Norah, that every sort of thing's getting in between me and my work and worries me. It's as though I were tossing more balls in the air than I could possibly manage. At one moment I think it's Clare that I've got especially to hang on to—another time it's the book—and then it's Stephen. The moment I've settled down something turns up to remind me of Cornwall or the Bookshop. Fact is I'm getting battered at by something or other and I never can get my breath. I oughtn't ever to have married—I'm not up to it."

Norah Monogue took his hand.

"You are up to it, Peter, but I expect you've got a lot to go through before you're clear of things. Now I'm going to be brutal. The fact is that you're too self-centred. People never do anything in the world so long as they are wondering whether the world's going to hurt them or no. Those early years of yours made you morbid. You've got a temper and one or two other things that want a lot of holding down and that takes up your attention—And then Clare isn't the woman to help you—"

Peter was about to break in but she went on:—"'Oh! I know my Clare through and through. She's just as anxious as you are not to be hurt by anything and so she's being hurt all the time. She's out for happiness at any cost and you're out for freedom—freedom from every kind of thing—and because both of you are denied it you are restive. But you and Clare are both people whose only salvation is in being hurt and knocked about and bruised to such an extent that they simply don't know where they are. Oh! I know—I'm exactly the same sort of person myself. We can thank the Gods if we are knocked about—"

Suddenly she paused and, falling back in her chair, put her hand to her breast, coughing. Something seized her, held her in its grip, tossed her from side to side, at last left her white, speechless, utterly exhausted. It had come so suddenly that it had taken Peter entirely by surprise. She lay back now, her eyes closed, her face a grey white.

He ran to the door and called Mrs. Brockett. She came and with an exclamation hurried away for remedies.

Peter suddenly felt his hand seized—a hoarse whisper was in his ear—"Peter—dear—go—at—once—I can't bear—you—to see me—like this. Come back—another day."

He knelt, moved by an affection and tenderness that seemed stronger than any emotion he had ever known, and kissed her. She whispered:

"Dear boy—"

On his way back to Chelsea, the orange lamps, the white streets powdered with the evening glow, the rustling plane trees whispered to him, "You've got to be knocked about—you've got to be knocked about—you've got to be knocked about—" but the murmur was no longer sinister.

Still thinking of Norah, he went up to the nursery to see the boy in bed. He remembered that Clare was going out alone to a party and that he would have the evening to himself.

On entering the room, dark except for a nightlight by the boy's bed, some unknown fear assailed him. He was instantly, at the threshold, conscious of it. He stood for a moment in silence. Then realised what it was. The boy was moaning in his sleep.

He went quickly over to the cot and bent down. Stephen's cheeks were flaming, his hands very hot.

Peter rang the bell. Mrs. Kant appeared.

"Is there anything the matter with Stephen?"

Mrs. Kant looked at him, surprised, a little offended. "He's had a little cold all day, sir. I've kept him indoors."

"Have you taken his temperature?"

"Yes, sir, nothing at all unusual. He often goes up and down."

"Have you spoken to your mistress?"

"Yes, sir. She agrees with me that there is nothing unusual—"

He brushed past the woman and went to his wife's bedroom.

She was dressed and was putting on a string of pearls, a wedding present from her father. She smiled up at him—

"Clare, do you know Stephen's ill?"

"No, it's only a cold. I've been up to see him—"

He took her hand—she smiled up at him—"Did you enjoy your visit?" She fastened the necklace.

"Clare, stay in to-night. It may be nothing but if the boy got worse—"

"Do you want me to stay?"

"Yes."

"I wanted you to go with me this afternoon—"

"That was different. The boy may be really ill—"

"You didn't do what I wanted this afternoon. Why should I do what you want now?"

"Clare, stay. Please, please—"

She took her hand gently out of his, and, as she went out of the door switched off the electric light.

He heard the opening of the hall door and, standing where she had left him in the dark bedroom, saw, shining, laughing at him, her eyes.

CHAPTER XI

I

There are occasions in our life when the great Wave so abruptly overwhelms us that before we have recovered our dazed senses it has passed and the water on every side of us is calm again.

There are other occasions when we stand, it may seem through a lifetime of anticipation bracing our backs for the inevitable moment. Every hour before it comes is darkened, every light is dimmed by its implacable shadow. Then when at last it is upon us we meet it with an indifference, almost with a relief, because it has come at last.

So was it now with Peter. During many weeks he had been miserable, apprehensive, seeing an enemy in every wind. Now, behold, his adversary in the open.

"This," he might cry to that old man, down in Scaw House, "this is what you have been preparing for me, is it? At last you've shown me—well, I'll fight you."

Young Stephen was very ill. Peter was strangely assured that it was to be a bad business. Well, it rested with him, Peter, to pull the boy through. If he chose to put his back into it and give the kid some of his own vigour and strength then it was bound to be all right.

Standing there in the dark, he stripped his mind naked; he flung from it every other thought, every other interest—his work, Clare, everything must go. Only Stephen mattered and Stephen should be pulled through.

For an instant, a little cold trembling fear struck his heart. Supposing...? Then fiercely, flinging the thought from him he trampled it down.

He went to the telephone and called up a doctor who lived in Cheyne Walk. The man could be with him in a quarter of an hour.

Then he went back into the nursery. Mrs. Kant was there.

"I've sent for Dr. Mitchell."

"Very well, sir."

"He'll be here in quarter of an hour."

"Very well, sir."

He hated the woman. He would like to take her thin, bony neck and wring it.

He went over to the cot and looked down. The little body outlined under the clothes was so helpless, the little hands, clenched now, were so tiny; he was breathing very fast and little sounds came from between his teeth, little struggling cries.

Peter saw that moment when Stephen the Elder had held Stephen the younger aloft in his arms. The Gods appear to us only when we claim to challenge their exultation. They had been challenged at that moment.... Young Stephen against the Gods! Surely an unequal contest!

II

Dr. Mitchell came and instantly the struggle was at its height. Appendicitis. As they stood over the cot the boy awoke and began to cry a little, turned his head from side to side as though to avoid the light, beating with his hands on the counterpane.

"I must send for a nurse at once," Dr. Mitchell said.

"Everything is in your hands," Peter answered.

"You'd better go down and have something to eat."

The little cry came trembling and pitiful, driving straight into Peter's heart.

"Temperature 105—pretty bad." Mitchell, who was a stout, short man with red cheeks, grey eyes and the air of an amiable Robin, was transformed now into something sharp, alert, official.

Peter caught his arm—

"It's all right?... you don't think—?"

The man turned and looked at him with eyes so kind that Peter trembled.

"Look here, we've got to fight it, Westcott. I ought to have been called hours ago. But keep your head and we'll pull the child through.... Better go down and have something to eat. You'll need it."

Outside the door Peter faced a trembling Mrs. Kant.

"Look here, you lied just now. You never took the boy's temperature."

"Well, sir—"

"Did you or not?"

"Well, sir, Mrs. Westcott said there was no need. I'm sure I thought—"

"You leave the house now—at once. Go up and pack your things and clear out. If I see you here in an hour's time the police shall turn you out."

The woman began to cry. Peter went downstairs. To his own surprise he found that he could eat and drink. Of so fundamental an importance was young Stephen in his life that the idea that he could ever lose him was of an absurd and monstrous incredibility. No, of that there was no question—but he was conscious nevertheless of the supreme urgency of the occasion. That young Stephen had ever been delicate or in any way a weakling was a monstrous suggestion. Always when one thought of him it was a baby laughing, tumbling—or thoughtfully, with his hand rolled tightly inside his father's, taking in the world.

Just think of all the tottering creatures who go on and on and snap their fingers at death. The grotesque old men and women! Or think of the feeble miserables who never know what a day's health means—crowding into Davos or shuddering on the Riviera!

And young Stephen, the strongest, most vital thing in the world! Nevertheless, suddenly, Peter found that he could eat and drink no more. He put the food aside and went upstairs again.

In the darkened nursery he sat in a chair by the fire and waited for the hours to pass. The new nurse had arrived and moved quietly about the room. There was no sound at all save the monotonous whispering beseeching little cries that came from the bed. One had heard that concentration of will might do so much in the directing of such a battle, and surely great love must help. Peter, as he sat in the half-darkness thought that he had never before realised his love for the boy—how immense it was—how all-pervading, so that if it were taken from him life would be instantly broken, without colour, without any rhythm or force.

As he sat there he thought confusedly of a great number of things of his own childhood—of his mother—of a boy at Dawson's who had asked him once as they gazed up at a great mass of apple blossoms in bloom, "Do you think there is anything in all that stuff about God anyway, Westcott?"—of a night when he had gone with some loose woman of the town and of the wet miry street that they had left behind them as she had closed the door—of that night at the party when he had seen Cardillac again—of the things that Maradick had said to him that night when young Stephen was born—and so from that to his own life, his own birth, his father, Scaw House, the struggle that it had all been.

He remembered a sentence out of a strange novel of Dostoieffsky's that he had once read, "The Brothers Karamazoff": "It's a feature of the Karamazoffs ... that thirst for life regardless of everything—" and the Karamazoffs were of a sensual, debased stock—rotten at the base of them with an old drunken buffoon of a father—yes, that was like the Westcotts. All his life, struggle ... and young Stephen—all his life, struggle... and yet, even in the depths of degradation, if the fight were to go that way there would still be that lust for life.

So many times he had been almost under. First Stephen Brant had saved him, then at Brockett's Norah Monogue, then in Bucket Lane his illness, then in Chelsea his marriage, lately young Stephen... always, always something had been there to keep him on his feet. But if everything were taken from him, if he were absolutely, nakedly alone—what then? Ah, what then!

He buried his head in his hands. "God, you don't know what young Stephen is to me—or, yes, of course you do know, God—and because you do know, you will not take him from me."

The little tearing pain at his heart held him—every now and again it turned like some grinding key.

Mitchell entered with another doctor. Peter went over to the window, and whilst they made their examination, stared through the glass at the fretwork of trees, the golden haze of London beyond, two stars that now, when the storm had spent itself, showed in a dark dim sky. Very faintly the clanging note of trams, the clatter of a hansom cab, the imperative call of some bell came to him.

The world could thus go on! Mitchell crossed to him and put his hand on his shoulder—

"He's pretty bad, Westcott. An operation's out of the question I'm afraid. But if you'd like another opinion—"

"No thanks. I trust you and Hunt." The doctor could feel the boy's body trembling beneath his touch.

"It's all right, Westcott. Don't be frightened. We'll do all mortals can. We'll know in the early morning how things are going to be. The child's got a splendid constitution."

He was interrupted by the opening of the nursery door and, turning, the men saw Clare with the light of the passage at her back, standing in the doorway. Her cloak was trailing on the floor—around her her pink filmy dress hung like shadows from the light behind her. Her face was white, her eyes wide.

"What—?" she whispered in the voice of a frightened child.

Peter crossed the room, and took her with him into the passage, closing the door behind him.

She clung to him, looking up into his face.

"Stephen's very bad, dear. No, it's something internal—"

"And I went out to a party?" her voice was trembling, she was very near to tears. "But I was miserable, wretched all the time. I wanted to come back, I knew I oughtn't to have gone.... Oh Peter, will he die? Oh! poor little thing! Poor little thing!"

Even at that moment, Peter noticed, she spoke as though it were somebody else's baby.

"No, no, dear. It'll be all right. Of course it will. Mitchell's here, he'll pull him through. But you'd better go and lie down, dear. I promise to come and tell you if anything's the matter. You can't do any good—there's an excellent nurse!"

"Where's Mrs. Kant?"

"I dismissed her this evening for lying to me. Go to bed. Clare—really it's the best thing."

She began to cry with her hands up to her face, but she went, slowly, with her cloak still trailing after her, to her room.

She had not, he noticed, entered the nursery.

III

He went back and sat down again in the arm-chair by the fire. Poor Clare! he felt only a great protecting pity for her—a strange feeling, compounded of emotions that were unexpectedly confused. A feeling that was akin to what he would have felt had she been his sister and been insulted by some drunken blackguard in the street. Poor Clare! She was so young—simply not up to these big grown-up troubles.

Those little cries had ceased—only every now and again an echo of a moan—so slight was the sound that broke the silence. The hours advanced and there settled about the house that chilly ominous sense of anticipation that the early morning brings in its grey melancholy hands. It was a little house but it was full, now, of expectancy. Up the stairs, through the passages, pressing against the windows there were many presences waiting for the moment when the issue of this struggle would be decided. The air was filled with their chill breath. The struggle round the bed was at its height. On one side doctors, nurses, the father, the mother—on the other that still, ironic Figure, in His very aloofness so strong, in His indifference so terrible.

With Peter, as the grey dawn grew nearer, confidence fled. He was suddenly conscious of the strength and invisibility of the thing that he was fighting. He must do something. If he were compelled to sit, silently, quietly, with his hands folded, much longer, he would go mad. But it was absurd—Stephen, about whom he had made so many plans, Stephen, concerning whom there had been that struggle to bring about his very existence ... surely all that was not now to go for nothing at all.

If he could do something—if he could do something!

There were drops of sweat on his forehead—inside his clothes his body was hot and dry and had shrunk, it seemed, into some tiny shape, like a nut, so that his things hung loosely all about him.

He could not bear that dark cavernous nursery, with the faint lights and the stairs and passages beyond it so crowded with urgent silence!

He caught Mitchell on the shoulder.

"How is it?"

"Oh! we're fighting it. It's the most rapid thing I've ever known. If we only could have operated! Look here, go and lie down for a bit—I'll let you know if there's any change!"

He went to his dressing-room, all ghostly now with the first struggling light of dawn. He closed the door behind him and then fell down on his knees by the bed, pressing his face into his hands.

He prayed: "Oh! God, God, God. I have never wanted anything like this before but Stephen is more to me, much, much more to me than anything that I have ever had—more, far more than my own life. I haven't much to offer but if you will let me keep Stephen you can have all the rest. You can send me back to Bucket Lane, take my work, anything ... I want Stephen ... I want Stephen. God, he is such a good boy. He has always been good and he will make such a fine man. There won't be many men so fine as he. He's good as gold. God I will die myself if he may live, I'm no use. I've made a mess of things—but let him live and take me. Oh! God I want him, I want him!"

He broke into sobs and was bowed down there on the floor, his body quivering, his face pressed against the bed.

He was conscious that Clare had joined him. She must have heard him from her room. He tried as he felt her body pressed against his, to pull himself together, but the crying now had mastered him and he could only feel her pushing with her hand to find his—and at last he let her take his hand and hold it.

He heard her whisper in his ear.

"Peter dear, don't—don't cry like that. I can't bear to hear you like that. I'm so miserable, Peter. I've been so wicked—so cross and selfish. I've hurt you so often—I'm going to be better, Peter. I am really."

At that moment they might have come together with a reality, an honesty that no after-events could have shaken. But to Peter Clare was very far away. He was not so conscious of her as he was of those presences that thronged the house. What could she do for him now? Afterwards perhaps. But now it was Stephen—Stephen—Stephen—

But he let her hold his hand and he felt her hair against his cheek, and at last he put his arm around her and held her close to him, and she, with her face against his, went fast asleep. He looked down at her. She looked so young and helpless that the sight of her leaning, tired and beaten, against him, touched him and he picked her up, carried her into her room and laid her on her bed.

How light and tiny she was!

He was conscious of his own immense fatigue. Mitchell had told him that he would wake him; good fellow, Mitchell! He lay down on the bed in his dressing-room and was instantly asleep.

He was outside Scaw House. He was mother-naked and the howling wind and rain buffeted his body and the stones cut his feet. The windows of the house were dark and barred. He could just reach the lower windows with his hands if he stood on tiptoe.

He tapped again and again.

He was tired, exhausted. He had come a long, long way and the rain hurt his bare flesh. At last a candle shone dimly behind the dark window. Some one was there, and instantly at the moment of his realising that aid had come he was conscious also that he must, on all accounts, refuse it. He knew that if he entered the house Stephen would die. It depended on him to save Stephen. He turned to flee but his father had unbarred the door and was drawing him in. He struggled, he cried out, he fought, but his father was stronger than he. He was on the threshold—he could see through the dark ill-smelling hall to the door beyond. His father's hand fastened on his arm like a vice. His body was bathed in sweat, he screamed ... and woke to find the room dim in the morning light and Mitchell shaking him by the arm.

IV

He was still dreaming. Now he was in the nursery. Clare was kneeling by Stephen's bed. One doctor was bending down—the nurse was crying very softly.

He looked down on his son. As he looked the little face was, for an instant, puckered with pain. The mouth, the eyes, the throat struggled.

The tiny hands lifted for a moment, hung, and then like fluttering leaves, fell down on to the counterpane. Then the body was suddenly quiet, the face was peaceful and the head had fallen gently, sideways against the pillow.

At that moment of time, throughout the house, the Presences departed. The passages, the rooms were freed, the air was no longer cold.

At that moment also Peter awoke. Mitchell said: "The boy's gone, Westcott."

Peter, turning his back upon them all, drove from him, so softly that they could scarcely hear, but in a voice of agony that Mitchell never afterwards forgot:—

"I wanted him so—I wanted him so."

CHAPTER XII

A WOMAN CALLED ROSE BENNETT

I

The days that followed were dead—dead in more than any ordinary sense of the word. But perhaps it was Peter who was dead. He moved, ate, drank, even wrote his reviews, slept—he thanked gravely all those who offered him condolences—wrote letters in answer to kind friends.... "Dear S—— It was just like you to write so kindly and sympathetically...." And all this time he was without any kind of emotion. He was aware that there was something in the back of his brain that, were it once called upon to awake, might stir him into life again. What it would tell him he did not know, something about love, something intensely sorrowful, something that had occurred very probably to himself. He did not want to live—to think, to feel. Thinking meant pain, meant a sudden penetrating into that room shrouded now by heavy, black curtains but containing, were those curtains drawn, some great, phantasmal horror.

He was dimly aware that the people about him were frightened. Clare, Bobby Galleon, Cardillac. He knew that they would be glad for him to draw those curtains aside and penetrate into that farther room. That was unkind of them. He had no other emotion but that it was unkind of them. Beyond that unkindness, they did not exist.

He was thinner. His shoulders seemed to pierce sharply his clothes; his cheeks were white and hollow, there were dark lines beneath his eyes, dark, grey patches. His legs were not so straight, nor so strong. Moreover his eyes were as though they were covered with a film. Seeing everything they yet saw nothing at all. They passed through the world and were confronted by the heavy, veiling curtains....

This condition lasted for many days. Of all about him none understood him so well as Bobby Galleon. Bobby had always understood him, and now he felt for him with a tenderness that had both the past and the future to heighten its poignancy. It seemed to Bobby that nothing more tragic than the death of this child could possibly have occurred. It filled him with anxiety for the future, it intensified to a depth that only so simple and affectionate a character as his could feel, the love that he had always had for Peter.

He was with him during these days continually, waiting for the relief to come.

"It's got to come soon," he said, "or the boy'll go mad."

At last it came.

One day about tea-time they were sitting in Peter's upstairs study. It had been a day of showers and now the curtains were not drawn and a green-grey dusk glimmered beyond the windows.

Peter was writing letters, and as Bobby watched him he seemed to him like some automaton, something wound into life by some clever inventor. The hand moved across the paper—the dead eyes encountered nothing in their gaze, the shoulders were the loosely drooping shoulders of an old man.

"Can you see, Peter?"

"Yes, thanks. Switch on the light if you like."

Bobby got up and moved to the door. The dusk behind Peter's face flung it into sharp white outline.

Another shower! The rain at first in single drops, then more swiftly, fell with gentle, pattering fingers up and down the window. It was the only sound, except the scraping of Peter's pen. The pen stopped. Peter raised his head, listening.

Bobby switched on the light and as he did so Peter in a strangled breathless mutter whispered—

"The rain! The rain! It was like that that night. Stephen! Stephen!"

His head fell on to his hands and he burst into a storm of tears.

II

And now Peter was out to be hurt, hurt more horribly than he could have ever believed possible. It was like walking—as they did in the days of the Ordeal—on red-hot iron, every step an agony. Always there was something to remind him! He could go nowhere, see nobody, summon no kind of recollection out of the past without this coming to him. There were a thousand things that Stephen had done, that he, Peter, had never noticed at the time. He was haunted now with regrets, he had not made enough of him whilst he was there! Ah! had he only known that the time was to be so short! How he would have spent those precious, precious moments! It was as though he had flung away, wilfully, possessions of the utmost price—cast them off as though it had been his very intention to feel, afterwards, this burning regret. The things in the nursery were packed away, but there remained the room, the frieze with the dragons and princesses, the fire-place, the high broad window. Again and again he saw babies in the streets, in the parks and fancied that Stephen had come back again.

The thing had happened to him so swiftly that, behind reason, there lurked the thought that perhaps, with equal suddenness, Stephen would be restored. To come back one afternoon and to find him there! To find him lying there on his back in his cot looking up at the ceiling, to find him labouring unsteadily on his feet, clinging to the sides of his bed and shouting—to find him laughing at the jumping waves in the fire—to find him!... No, never to be found again—gone, hopelessly, cruelly, for no reason, for no one's good or benefit—simply for some one's sport.

But, strangely, more than the actual Stephen did he miss the imaginary future Stephen at school, hero of a thousand games, winner of a thousand prizes, the Stephen grown up, famous already at so young an age, loved by men and women, handsome, good.... Oh! the folly of it! No human being could carry all the glories that Peter had designed for his son—no human being, then how much less a Westcott. It might be best after all, young Stephen had been spared. Until every stone of Scaw House was level with the ground no Westcott could be termed safe—perhaps not then.

Now he realised how huge a place in his heart the boy had filled dimly, because as yet he refused to bring it to the open light he was conscious that, during these past two years he had been save for Stephen, a very lonely man. It was odd that Stephen the elder and Stephen the younger should have been the only two persons in his life to find the real inside of him—they, too, and perhaps Norah Monogue. But, otherwise, not Bobby, nor Cards, nor Alice Galleon, nor Mr. Zanti—nor Clare.

Not Clare. He faced the fact with a sudden shudder. Now that Stephen was gone he and Clare were face to face—face to face as they had never been since that first happy year of their marriage. That first year of their marriage—and now!

With an instant clenching of his teeth he pulled down the blinds upon that desolating view.

III

With teeth still clenched he set himself to build up his house again. Clare was very quiet and submissive during those first weeks. Her little figure looked helpless and appealing in its deep black; she was prettier than she had ever been in her life before. People said, "Poor Mrs. Westcott, she feels the loss of her baby so dreadfully"—and they didn't think about Peter. Indeed some people thought him callous. "Mr. Westcott seemed to be so fond of the child. Now I really believe he's forgotten all about him." Bobby was the only person in the world who knew how Peter suffered.

Clare was, indeed, after a time, reassured. Peter, after all, seemed not to mind. Did he mind anything? He was so often glum and silent that really you couldn't tell. Clare herself had been frightened on that night when the baby had died. She had probably never in all her life felt a more genuine emotion than she had known when she knelt by Peter's side and went to sleep in his arms. She was quite ready to feel that emotion again would Peter but allow her. But no. He showed no emotion himself and expected no one else to show any, for he was ready to share it but in her heart of hearts she longed to fling away from her this emotional atmosphere. She had loved the baby—of course she had loved it. But she had always known that something would happen to it—always. If Peter would insist on having those horrid Cornishmen.... At heart she connected that dreadful day when those horrible men had played about in the nursery with baby's death. Of course it was enough to kill any baby.

So, ultimately, it all came back to Peter's fault. Clare found real satisfaction in the thought. Meanwhile she emphatically stated her desire to be happy again.

She stated it always in Peter's absence, feeling that he would, in no way, understand her. "It can't help poor dear little Stephen that we should go on being melancholy and doing nothing. That's only morbid, isn't it, mother?"

Mrs. Rossiter entirely agreed, as indeed she always agreed with anything that Clare suggested.

"The dear thing does look lovely in black, though," she confided to Mrs. Galleon. "Mr. Cardillac couldn't take his eyes off her yesterday at luncheon."

Mrs. Rossiter and Jerry Cardillac had, during the last year, become the very best of friends. Peter was glad to see that it was so. Peter couldn't pretend to care very deeply about his mother-in-law, but he felt that it would do her all the good in the world to see something of old Cards. It would broaden her understanding, give her perhaps some of that charity towards the whole world that was one of Cards' most charming features. Cards, in fact, had been so much in the house lately that he might be considered one of the family. No one could have been more tender, more sympathetic, more exactly right about young Stephen's death. He had become, during those weeks almost a necessity. He seemed to have no particular interest of his own in life. He dressed very perfectly, he went to a number of parties, he had delightful little gatherings in his own flat, but, with it all, he was something more—a great deal more—than the mere society idler. There was a hint at possible wildness, an almost sinister suggestion of possible lawlessness that made him infinitely attractive. He was such good company and yet one felt that one didn't know nearly the whole of him.

To Peter he was the most wonderful thing in the world, to Clare he was rapidly becoming so—no wonder then that the Roundabout saw him so often.

IV

It would need a very acute perception indeed to pursue precisely the train of cause and effect in Mrs. Rossiter's mind after young Stephen's death. Her black garments added, in the most astonishing fashion, to her placid flatness. If she had gloried before in an armour that was so negative that it became instantly exceedingly dangerous, her appearance now was terrifying beyond all words. Her black silk had apparently no creases, no folds—it almost eliminated terms and boundaries. Mrs. Rossiter could not now be said to come into a room—she was simply there. One was sitting, gazing it might be at the fire, a looking-glass, a picture or two, when suddenly there came a black shadow, something that changed the colour of things a little, something that obscured certain objects, but scarcely anything more definite. The yellow brooch was definite, cold, stony eyes hung a little above it, over those a high white forehead—otherwise merely a black shadow putting out the fire.

She was in the Roundabout now all the time. How poor Dr. Rossiter fared it was difficult to imagine, but he cared for Clare as deeply as his wife did and was quite ready for everything to be sacrificed to her at this crisis of her history.

Mrs. Rossiter, meanwhile, was entirely convinced that Peter was responsible for his son's death. Had you suddenly challenged her and demanded her reasoned argument with regard to this matter she would probably have failed you—she did not like reasoned arguments—but she would also have been most sincerely indignant had you called her a liar and would have sworn to her convictions before a court of law.

"Those Cornishmen" had frightened the poor little thing into fits and it was only to be expected. Moreover it followed from this that a man who murdered his only child would most assuredly take to beating his wife before very long. After that, anything might happen. Peter was on a swift road to being a "Perfect Devil."

Indeed, allow Mrs. Rossiter two consecutive hours of peace and quiet, she, sitting like the personification of the English climate, alone before her fire, and she could make any one into anything—once made so they remained.

It mattered nothing to her that poor Peter was, during these weeks, the most subdued and gently courteous of husbands—that was as it might be (a favourite phrase of hers). She knew him ... and, so knowing, waited for the inevitable end.

But the more certain she was of his villainous possibilities the more placid she became. She spread her placidity over everything. It lay, like an invisible glue, upon everything in the Roundabout—you could feel it on the door-handles, as you feel the jammy reminiscences of incautious servant-maids. Peter felt it but did not know what it was that he had to deal with.

He had determined, when the sharpest shock of Stephen's death had passed, and he was able to think of other things, that the supremely important thing for him now to do was to get back to his old relations with Clare. There was, he grimly reflected, "Mortimer Stant" to be finished within a month or two and he knew, perfectly well, with the assurance of past experience that whilst Clare held the stage, Mortimer had the poorest of chances—nevertheless Clare was, at this moment, the thing to struggle for.

He must get her back—he must get her back.

Behind his brain, all this time, was the horror of being left alone in the world and of what he might do—then.

To get Clare back he must have the assistance of two people—Mrs. Rossiter and Cards.

It was at this point that he perceived Mrs. Rossiter's placidity.

He could not get at her at all—he could not get near her. He tried in every way, during these weeks, to please her. She apparently noticed nothing. He could force no direct opinion about anything from her and yet he was conscious of opposition. He was conscious of opposition, increasingly, every day.

"I believe she wants Clare to hate me," he suddenly revealed to himself, and, with that, all hope of her as an ally vanished.

Then he hated her—he hated her more bitterly every day.

He wanted to tell her not to call him "Peter dear"—she loved to put him in positions that showed him in the worst light to Clare.

At luncheon for instance: "Peter dear, it would be a nice thing for you and Clare to go to that Private View at the Carfax this afternoon. You've nothing to do, Clare, have you?"

Peter knew that Mrs. Rossiter had already ascertained that he was engaged. He knew also that Clare had had no thought of Peter's company before but that now she would very speedily feel herself injured.

"I'm afraid—" Peter would begin.

"Peter's too engaged to take you, Clare dear."

"I dare say Jerry will come—" this from Clare.

"Ah! yes, Mr. Cardillac is always ready to take any trouble, Peter."

"If you'd let me know earlier, Clare, that you wanted me."

Mrs. Rossiter. "Oh! don't put yourself out, Peter. It would never do to break an engagement. Only it seems such a long time since you and Clare—"

Peter. "We'll go to-morrow afternoon, Clare."

Clare. "You're so gloomy when you do come, Peter. It's like going out with a ghost."

Mrs. Rossiter. "Ah! Peter has his work, dear—so much hangs on the next book, doesn't it, Peter? Naturally the last one didn't quite—"

Peter. "Look here, Clare, I'll chuck this engagement."

Clare. "No, thank you, Peter—Jerry and I will be all right. You can join us if you like—"

The fact was that Peter wasn't tactful. He showed Mrs. Rossiter much too plainly that he disliked her intensely. He had no idea that he showed it her. He thought, indeed, that he was very skilful in his disguise of his feelings but Mrs. Rossiter knew and soon Clare knew also.

Peter had no conception of subtlety in the matter. It was clear to him that he had once been devoted to Clare and she to him, it was clear also that that relationship had recently been dimmed. Now that Stephen was gone that early intimacy must be restored and the fact that he was willing on his side to do anything to bring it back seemed to him reason enough for its restoration. That the whole matter was composed of the most delicate and intricate threads never occurred to him for an instant. Clare had loved him once. Clare would love him again—and the sooner it happened the better for him.

Meanwhile Mrs. Rossiter being enemy rather than ally there remained Cards.

But Cards was strange. Peter could never claim to have been intimate with him—their relationship had been founded on an inequality, on a recognition from Peter of Cards' superiority. Cards had always laughed at Peter, always patronised him. But now, although Cards had been in the place so much of late, the distance seemed farther than ever before.

Cards was as kind as he could be—always in good spirits, always ready to do anything, but Peter noticed that it was only when Clare was present that Cards changed from jest to earnest. "He thinks Clare worth talking to seriously.... I suppose it's because he was at Dawson's ... but after all I'm not an imbecile."

This attitude of Cards was in fact as vague and nebulous as all the other things that seemed now to stand between Peter and Clare.

Peter tried to talk to Cards—he was always prevented—held off with a laughing hand.

"What's the matter with me?" thought Peter. "What have I done? It's like being out in a fog."

At last one evening, after dinner, when Clare and Mrs. Rossiter had gone upstairs he demanded an answer.

"Look here, Cards, what have I done? You profess to be a friend of mine. Tell me what crime I've committed?"

Cards' eyes had been laughing. Suddenly he was serious. His dark, clean-cut face was stern, almost accusing.

"Profess, Peter? I hope you don't doubt it?"

"No, of course not. You know you're the best friend I've got. Tell me—what have I done?"

"Done?"

"Yes—you and Clare and her mother—all of you keep me at arms' length—why?"

"Do you really want a straight talking?"

"Of course."

"Well, I can only speak for myself—but—to tell the truth, old boy—I think you've been rather hard on poor little Clare."

For the first time since his marriage Peter resented Cards' words. "Poor little Clare"—wasn't that a little too intimate?

"What do you mean?" he asked, his voice a little harder.

"Well—I don't think you understand her, Peter."

"Explain."

"She's a happy, merry person if ever there was one in this world. She wants all the happiness you can give her—"

"Well?"

"Well, you don't seem to see that. Of course young Stephen's death—"

"Let's leave that—" Peter's voice was harder again.

"Oh, all right—just as you please. But most men would have seen what a shock it must be to a girl, so young, who knew so little about the cruelty of life. You didn't—you don't mind, Peter, do you?—you didn't seem to think of that. Never tried to cheer her up, take her about, take her out of herself. You just wrapped yourself up—"

"You don't understand," muttered Peter, his eyes lowered. "If I'd thought that she'd really minded Stephen's death—"

"Oh! come Peter—that's grossly unfair. Why, she felt it all most horribly. That shows how little you've understood her, how little you've appreciated her. You've always been a gloomy, morbid devil and—"

"All right, Cards—that'll do."

Cards stood back from the table, his mouth smiling, his eyes hard and cold.

"Oh! no, it won't. You asked for it and now you're going to get it. You've not only been gloomy and morbid all your life, you've been selfish as well—always thinking of yourself and the books you were going to write, and then when they did come they weren't such great shakes. You oughtn't to have married at all—you've never considered Clare at all—your treatment of her—"

Peter stood up, his face white, so that his eyes and the lines of his mouth showed black in the shadow.

"Clear out—I've heard enough."

"Oh! that's just like you—ask me for my opinion and then lose your temper over it. Really, Peter, you're like a boy of ten—you don't deserve to be treated as a grown-up person."

Peter's voice shook. "Clear out—clear out or I'll do for you—get out of my house—"

"Certainly."

Cards opened the door and was gone. Peter heard him hesitate for a moment in the hall, get his hat and coat and then close the hall-door after him.

The house was suddenly silent. Peter stood, his hands clenched. Then he went out into the hall.

He heard Mrs. Rossiter's voice from above—"Aren't you two men ever coming up?"

"Jerry's gone."

"Gone?"

"Yes—we've had a row."

Mrs. Rossiter made no reply. He heard the drawing-room door close. Then he, too, took his coat and hat and went out.

V

The night was cool and sweet with a great silver haze of stars above the sharply outlined roofs and chimneys. The golden mist from the streets met the night air and mingled with it.

Peter walked furiously, without thinking of direction. Some clock struck half-past nine. His temper faded swiftly, leaving him cold, miserable, regretful. There went his damnable temper again, surging up suddenly so hot and fierce that it had control of him almost before he knew that it was there. How like him, too! Now when things were bad enough, when he must bend all his energies to bringing peace back into the house again, he must needs go and quarrel with the best friend he had in the world. He had never quarrelled with Cards before, never had there been the slightest word between them, and now he had insulted him so that, probably, he would never come into their house again.

And behind his immediate repentance at the quarrel there also bit into his heart the knowledge that there was truth in the accusation that Cardillac had flung at him. He had been morbid, he had been selfish. Absorbed by his own grief at Stephen's loss he had given no thought to any one else. He had expected Clare to be like himself, had made no allowance for differences of temperament, had.... Poor Peter had never before known an hour of such miserable self-condemnation. Had he known where to find him he would have gone that very instant to beg Cards' pardon.

Now, in comparison with his own black deeds, Mrs. Rossiter seemed an angel. He should show her in the future that he could mend his ways. Clare should make no further complaint of him. He found himself in Leicester Square and still wrapt in his own miserable thoughts went into the Empire. He walked up and down the Promenade wondering that so many people could take the world so lightly. Very far away a gentleman in evening dress was singing a song—his mouth could be seen to open and shut, sometimes his arms moved—no sound could be heard.

The Promenade was packed. Up and down ladies in enormous hats walked languidly. They all wore clothes that were gorgeous and a little soiled. They walked for the most part in couples and appeared to be absorbed in conversation, but every now and again they smiled mechanically, recognised a friend or saw somebody who was likely very shortly to become one.

There was a great deal of noise. There were numbers of men—old gentlemen who were there because they had always been there, young gentlemen who were there because they had never been there before and a few gentlemen who had come to see the Ballet.

The lights blazed, the heat and noise steadily accumulated, corks were popped in the bar behind, promises were broken in the Promenade in front, and soon after eleven, when everything had become so uncomfortable that the very lights in the building protested, the doors were opened and the whole Bubble and Squeak was flung out into the cool and starlit improprieties of Leicester Square.

Peter could not have told you if he had been asked, that he had been there, felt a devouring thirst and entered a building close at hand where there were rows of little round tables and numbers of little round waiters.

Peter sat down at the first table that occurred to him and it was not until he looked round about him that he discovered that a lady in a huge black hat was sitting smiling opposite him. Her cheeks were rouged, her gloves were soiled and her hair looked as though it might fall into a thousand pieces at the slightest provocation, but her eyes were pathetic and tired. They didn't belong to her face.

"Hullo, dear, let's have a drink. Haven't had a drink to-night."

He asked her what she would like and she told him. She studied him carefully for quite a long time.

"Down on your luck, old chum?" she said at last.

"Yes, I am," Peter said, "a bit depressed."

"I know. I'm often that way myself. We all catch it. Come home and have a bit of supper. That'll cheer you up."

"No, thanks," said Peter politely. "I must get back to my own place in a minute."

"Well," said the lady. "Please yourself, and I'll have another drink if you don't very much mind."

It was whilst he was ordering another drink that he came out of his own thoughts and considered her.

"That's right," she said smiling, "have a good look. My name's Rose Bennett. Here's my card. Perhaps you'd like to come and have tea with me one day."

She gave him a very dirty card on which was written "Miss Rose Bennett, 4 Annton Street, Portland Place."

"You're Cornish," he suddenly said, looking at her.

She moved her soiled gloves up and down the little table—"Well, what if I am?" she said defiantly, not looking at him.

"I knew it," said Peter triumphantly, "the way you rolled your r's—"

"Well, chuck it, dear," said Miss Bennett, "and let's talk sense. What's Cornwall got to do with us anyhow?"

"I'm Cornish too," said Peter, "it's got a good deal to do with us. You needn't tell me of course—but what part do you come from?"

Still sullenly she said: "Almost forgotten the name of it, so long ago. You wouldn't know it anyway, it's such a little place. They called it Portergwarra—"

"I know," cried Peter, "near the Land's End. Of course I know it. There are holes in the rocks that they lift the boats through. There's a post-box on the wall. I've walked there many a time—"

"Well, stow it, old man," Miss Bennett answered decisively. "I'm not thinking of that place any more and I don't suppose they've thought of me since. Why, it's years—"

She broke off and began hurriedly to drink. Peter's eyes sought her eyes—his eyes were miserable and so were hers—but her mouth was hard and laughing.

"It's funny talking of Cornwall," she said at last. "No one's spoken of the place since I came up here. But it's all right, I tell you—quite all right. You take it from me, chucky. I enjoy my life—have a jolly time. There's disadvantages in every profession, and when you've got a bit of a cold as I have now why—"

She stopped. Her eyes sought Peter's. He saw that she was nearly crying.

"Talking of Cornwall and all that," she muttered, "silly rot! I'm tired—I'm going home."

He paid for the drinks and got a hansom.

At that moment as he stood looking over the horse into the dimly-lit obscurities of the Square he thought with a sudden beating of the heart that he recognised Cardillac looking at him from the doorway of a neighbouring restaurant. Then the figure was gone. He had got Cardillac on the brain! Nevertheless the suggestion made him suddenly conscious of poor Miss Bennett's enormous hat, her rouge, her soiled finery that allowed no question as to her position in the world.

Rather hurriedly he asked her to get into the cab.

"Come that far—" she said.

He got in with her and she took off one glove and he held her hand and they didn't speak all the way.

When the hansom stopped at last he got down, helped her out and for a moment longer held her hand.

"We're both pretty unhappy," he said. "Things have been going wrong with me too. But think of Cornwall sometimes and remember there's some one else thinking of it."

"You're a funny kid," she said, looking at him, "sentimental, I don't think!"

But it was her eyes—tired and regretful that said goodbye.

She let herself in and the door closed behind her.

He turned and walked the streets; it was three o'clock before he reached his home.

CHAPTER XIII

"MORTIMER STANT"

I

Next morning Peter went round to Cardillac's flat and made his apologies. Cardillac accepted them at once with the frankest expressions of friendship.

"My dear old Peter, of course," he said, taking both Peter's hands in his, "I was horribly blunt and unpleasant about the whole thing. I didn't mean half what I said, but the fact is that you got angry and then I suppose I got angry—and then we both said more than we meant."

"No," said Peter slowly, "for you were quite right. I have been selfish and morbid. I see it all quite clearly. I'm going to be very different now, Cards, old man."

Cards' flat was splendid—everything in it from its grey Ascot trouserings kind of wall paper to its beautiful old chairs and its beautiful old china was of the very best—and Cards himself, in a dark blue suit with a black tie and a while pearl and white spats on his shining gleaming shoes, just ready to go out and startle Piccadilly was of the very best. He had never, Peter thought, looked so handsome.

At the door Cards put a hand on Peter's shoulder.

"Get in late this morning, Peter?"

"Why?" said Peter, turning round.

"Oh, nothing," Cards regarded him, smiling. "I'll see you to-night at the Lesters. Until then, old man—"

Neither Mrs. Rossiter nor Clare made any allusion to the quarrel but it had nevertheless, Peter felt, made reconciliation all the more difficult. Mrs. Rossiter now seemed to imply in her additional kindnesses to Cardillac that she felt for him deeply and was sorry that he, too, should have been made to suffer under Peter's bear-like nature.

There was even an implied atmosphere of alliance in the attitude of the three to Peter, an alliance fostered and cemented by Mrs. Rossiter and spread by her, up and down, in and out about the house.

It was obvious indeed now that Mrs. Rossiter was, never again, under any terms, to be won over. She had decided in her own slow mind that Peter was an objectionable person, that he neglected his wife, quarrelled with his best friends and refused to fulfil the career that he had promised to fulfil. She saw herself now in the role of protectress of her daughter, and that role she would play to the very end. Clare must, at all costs, be happy and, in spite of her odious husband, happy she should be.

Peter discerned Mrs. Rossiter's state of mind on the whole clearly enough, but with regard to Clare he was entirely in the dark. He devoted his days now to her service. He studied her every want, was ready to abandon his work at any moment to be with her, and was careful also to avoid too great a pestering of her with attentions.

"I know women hate that," he said to himself, "if you go down on your knees to them and hang around them they simply can't stand it. I won't show her that I care."

And he cared, poor fellow, as he had never cared for her before during their married life. The love that he had had for Stephen he would now give to Stephen's mother would she but let him.

But it was a difficult business. When Mrs. Rossiter was present he could do nothing right. If he were silent she would talk to Clare about people being morose; and what a pity it was that some people didn't think of other people a little instead of being miserable about things for which they had nobody to thank but themselves, and if he tried to be light-hearted and amusing Mrs. Rossiter bore with his humour in so patient and self-denying a spirit that his efforts failed lamentably and only made the situation worse than it had been before.

Clare seemed to be now entirely in her mother's hands; she put her mother's large flat body between herself and Peter and, through that, they were compelled to talk.

Peter also knew now that Clare was exceedingly uncomfortable in his presence—it was almost as though she had something to conceal. On several occasions he had noticed that his sudden entrance into a room had confused her; once he had caught her hurriedly pushing a letter out of sight. She was now strangely timid when he was there; sometimes with a sudden furious beating of the heart he fancied that she was coming back to him again because she would make little half movements towards him and then draw back. Once he found her crying.

The impulse to beg her to confide in him was almost stronger than he could resist, and yet he was terrified lest by some sudden move he should frighten her and drive her back and so lose the little ground that he had gained. The strangest thing of all was that Mrs. Rossiter herself did not know what Clare's trouble was. She, of course, put it all down to Peter, but she could accuse him of nothing specific. Clare had not confided in her.

Did Cards know? Peter suddenly asked himself with a strange pang of jealousy. That he should be jealous of Cards, the most splendid, most honourable fellow in the world! That, of course, was absurd. And yet they were together so often, and it was with Jerry Cardillac alone that Clare seemed now at ease.

But Peter put all such thoughts at once away from him. Had it been any other man but Cards he might have wondered... but he would trust Cards alone with his wife in the wilderness and know that no ill could come of it. With—other women Cards might have few scruples—Peter had heard such stories— but with Peter's wife, no.

Peter wondered whether perhaps Clare did not miss young Stephen more than they knew! Oh, if that were the reason how he could take her into his arms and comfort her and love her! Poor little Clare... the time would come when she would show him that she wanted him.

Meanwhile the months passed, the proofs of "Mortimer Stant" had been corrected and the book was about to appear. To Peter now everything seemed to hang upon this event. It became with him, during the weeks before its appearance, a monomania. If this book were a success why then dare and Mrs. Rossiter and all of them would come round to him. It was the third book which was always so decisive, and there was ground to recover after the comparative failure of the second novel. As he corrected the proofs he persuaded himself that "Mortimer Stant" wasn't, after all, so bad. It had been ambitious of him, of course, to write about the emotions and experiences of a man of forty and there was perhaps rather an overloaded and crude attempt at atmosphere, but there was life in the book. It had, he thought, more swing in the telling of it than the other two.

It is possible, when one is correcting proofs to persuade oneself of anything. The book appeared and was, from the first moment, loaded with mishap. On the day of publication there was that terrible fire at the Casino theatre—people talked of nothing else for a fortnight. Moreover by an unlucky chance young Rondel's novel, "The Precipice," was published on the very same day, and as the precipice was a novel one and there were no less than three young ladies prepared to fall over it at the same moment, it of course commanded instant attention. It was incidentally written with an admirable sense of style and a keen sense of character.

But Peter was now in a fever that saw an enemy round every corner. The English News Supplement only gave him a line:—"'Mortimer Stant.' A new novel by the author of 'Reuben Hallard,' depicting agreeably enough the amorous adventures of a stockbroker of middle-age." To this had all his fine dreams, his moments of exultation, his fevered inspiration come! He searched the London booksellers but could find no traces of "Mortimer Stant" at any of them. His publishers told him that it was only the libraries that bought any fiction, with the exception of volumes by certain popular authors—and yet he saw at these booksellers novels by numbers of people who could not lay claim to the success that "Reuben Hallard" had secured for its writer.

The reviews came in slowly, and, excepting for the smaller provincial papers, treated him with an indifference that was worse than neglect. "This interesting novel by Mr. Westcott"—"A pleasant tale of country life by the author of 'Reuben Hallard.' Will please those who like a quiet agreeable book without too much incident."

One London weekly review—a paper of considerable importance—took him severely to task, pointed out a number of incoherences of fact, commented on carelessness of style and finally advised Mr. Westcott, "if he is ever to write a book of real importance to work with greater care and to be less easily contented with a superficial facility."

But worse than these were the opinions of his friends. Henry Galleon was indeed gone, but there were a few—Mrs. Launce, Alfred Lester, William Trent, Alfred Hext—who had taken a real and encouraging interest in him from the beginning. They took him seriously enough to tell him the truth, and tell him the truth they did. Dear Mrs. Launce, who couldn't bear to hurt anybody and saw perhaps that he was taking the book a great deal more hardly than he had taken the others, veiled it as well as she could:—"I do think it's got splendid things in it, Peter dear—splendid things. That bit about the swimming and the character of Mrs. Mumps. But it doesn't hang together. There's a great deal of repetition. It's as though you'd written it with your mind on something else all the time."

And so he had—oh! so he had! What cruel irony that because his mind was set to winning Clare back to him the chief means for gaining her should be ruined by his very care for her.

What to do when all the things of life—the bustle and hurry, the marriages and births and deaths—came in between him and his work so that he could scarcely see it, so many things obscured the way. Poor Mortimer! Lost indeed behind a shifting, whirring cloud of real life—never to emerge, poor man, into anything better than a middle-aged clothes' prop.

For six weeks the book lingered in the advertisements. A second edition, composed for the most part of an edition for America, was announced, there were a belated review or two ... and then the end. The end of two years' hopes, ambitions, struggles, sweat and tears—and the end, too, of how much else?

From the beginning, so far back as he could remember, he had believed that he would one day write great books; had believed it from no conceit in him but simply because he clung so tenaciously to ambition that it had become, again and again, almost realised in the intensity of his dreams of it. He had known that this achievement of his would take a long time, that he must meet with many rebuffs, that he must starve and despair and be born again, but, never at any moment, until now, had he, in his heart of hearts, doubted that that great book was in front of him.

He had seen his work, in his dreams, derided, flouted, misunderstood. That was the way with most good work, but what he had never seen was its acceptance amongst the ranks of the "Pretty Good," its place given it beside that rising and falling tide of fiction that covered every year the greedy rocks of the circulating libraries and ebbed out again leaving no trace behind it.

Now, after the failure of "Mortimer Stant" for the first time, this awful question—"What if, after all, you should be an Ordinary Creature? What if you are no better than that army who fights happily, contentedly, with mediocrity for its daily bread and butter? That army, upon whose serried ranks you have perhaps, unconsciously, but nevertheless with pity, looked down?... What if you are never to write a word that will be remembered, never even to cause a decent attention, amongst your own generation?"

What if after all this stir and fluster, this pain and agony and striving, there should be nothing exceptional about Peter? What rock to stand on then?

He had never, perhaps, analysed his feelings about it all. He had certainly never thought himself an exceptional person ... but always in his heart there had been that belief that, one day, he would write an exceptional book.

He was very young, not yet thirty, but he had had his chance. It seemed to him, in these weeks following the death of "Mortimer Stant," that his career was already over. There was also the question of ways and means. Just enough to live on with the reviewing and a column for an American paper and Clare's income, but if the books were all of them to fail as this one had failed—why then it was a dreary future for them both.

In fact there were now, at his feet, pits of so dismal and impenetrable a blackness that he refused to look down, but clung rather to his determination to make all things right with Clare again, and then things would come round.

If that failed him—why then, old black-faced father in Scaw House with your drunken cook and your company of ghosts, you shall have your merry way!

II

Henry Galleon was dead. Mrs. Launce was, unfortunately, during the whole of this period of Peter's career, away in the country, being burdened with work, children and ill-health. He turned then once again to Bobby.

He had seen very little of Bobby and Alice Galleon lately; he was as fond of Bobby as he had ever been, but Bobby had always been a background, some one who was there, one liked to think, if one wanted him—but if there was any one more exciting, then Bobby vanished. Lately—for quite a long time now—there had been Cardillac—and somehow Cards and Bobby did not get on together and it was impossible to have them both at the same time. But now Peter turned to Bobby with the eagerness of a return to some comfortable old arm-chair after the brilliant new furniture of a friend's palace. Bobby was there waiting for him. It is not to be denied that the occasional nature of Peter's appearances had hurt them both—wounded Bobby and made Alice angry.

"He's given us up, Bobby, now that he's found so many new friends. I shouldn't have expected him to do that. I'm disappointed."

But Bobby nodded his head. "The boy's all right," he said, "he's just trying to forget young Stephen and he forgets things better in Cardillac's company than he does in mine—I'm not lively enough for that kind of thing. He'll come back—"

But, at the same time, Bobby was anxious. Things were wrong up there at The Roundabout, very wrong. He knew Clare and Cards and Peter and Mrs. Rossiter, in all probability better than any one alive knew them—and he was no fool.

Then Peter came back to him and was received as though he had never left him; and Alice, who had intended to tell Mr. Peter what she thought of his disloyalty, had no word to say when she saw his white drawn face and his tired eyes.

"There's something awfully wrong up there," said Alice to Bobby that night. "Bobby, look after him."

But Bobby who had heard by that time what Peter had to say shut his mouth tight. Then at last:

"Our friend Cardillac has a good deal to answer for," and left Alice to make what she could out of it.

Meanwhile up in Bobby's dusty old room, called by courtesy "The Study" but having little evidence of literature about it save an edition of Whyte-Melville and a miscellaneous collection of Yellow-backs, Peter had poured out his soul:

"Bobby, I feel as though I'd just been set up with my back against the wall for every one to make shies at. Everything's going wrong—everything. The ground's crumbling from under my feet. First it's young Stephen, then it's Clare, then my book fails (don't let's humbug—you know it's an utter failure) then I quarrel with Cards, then that damned woman—" he stopped at the thought of Mrs. Rossiter and drove his hands together. Then he went on more quietly. "It's like fighting in a fog, Bobby. There's the thing I want somewhere, just beside me—I want Clare, Clare as she used to be when we were first married— but I can't get at her and yet, through it all, I don't know what it is that stops me.

"I know I hadn't thought of her enough—with the book and Stephen and everything. Cards told me that pretty straight—but now I've seen all that and I'm ready to do anything—anything if she'll only love me again."

"Go directly to her and tell her," said Bobby; "have it all out in the open with her."

"That's just it," Peter answered, "I never seem to get her alone. There's always either her mother or Cards there. Cards sees her alone much more than I do, but, of course, she likes his company better than mine just now. I'm such a gloomy beggar—"

"Nonsense," said Bobby roughly. "You believe anything that any one tells you. They tell you that you're gloomy and depressing and so you think you are. They didn't find you gloomy at Brockett's did they?

And Alice and I have never found you depressing. Don't listen to that woman. Clare's always been under her influence and it's for you to take her out of it—not to lie down quietly and say she's too much for you—but there's another thing," he added slowly and awkwardly, after a moment's pause.

"What's that?" asked Peter.

"Well—Cards," said Bobby at last. "Oh! I know you'll say I hate him. But I don't. I don't hate him. I've always known him for what he was—in those days at Dawson's when if you flattered him he was kind, and if you didn't he was contemptuous. At Cambridge it was the same. There was only one fellow there I ever saw him knock under to—a man called Dune—and he was out and away exceptional anyhow, at games and work and everything. Now he made Cards into a decent fellow for the time being, and if he'd had the running of him he might have turned all that brilliance into something worth having.

"But he vanished and Cards has never owned his master since. Everything was there, ready in him, to be turned one way or the other, and after he left Cambridge there was his silly mother and a sillier London waiting to finish him—now he's nothing but Vanity and Fascination—and soon there'll be nothing but Vanity."

"You're unjust to him, Bobby, you always have been."

"Well, perhaps I am. He's always treated me with such undisguised contempt that it's only human that I should be a little prejudiced. But that's neither here nor there—what is the point, Peter, is that he's too much up at your place. Too much for his own good, too much for yours, and—too much for—Clare's."

"Bobby!"

"Oh yes—I know I'm saying a serious thing—but you asked me for my advice and I give it. I don't say that Cards means any harm but people will talk and it wouldn't do you any damage in Clare's eyes either, Peter, if you were to stand up to him a little."

Peter smiled. "Dear old Bobby! If any one else in the world had said such a thing of course I should have been most awfully angry, but I've always known how unfair you were about Cards. You never liked him, even in the Dawson days. You just don't suit one another. But I tell you, Bobby, that I'd trust Cards more than I'd trust any one in the world. Of course Clare likes to be with him and of course he likes to be with her. They suit one another exactly. Why, he's splendid! The other day when I'd been a perfect beast— losing my temper like a boy of ten—you should have heard the way he took it. One day, Bobby, you'll see how splendid he is."

Bobby said no more.

Peter went on again: "No, it's my mother-in-law's done the damage. You're right, the thing to do is to get Clare alone and have it right out with her. We'll clear the mists away."

Bobby said: "You know Peter, both Alice and I would do anything in the world to make you happy— anything."

Peter gripped his hand.

"I know you would. If I could forget young Stephen," he caught his breath—"Bobby, I see him everywhere, all the time. I lie awake hours at night thinking about him. I see him in my sleep, see him sometimes grown-up—splendid, famous.... Sometimes I think he comes back. I can see him, lying on his back and looking up at the ceiling, and I say to myself, 'Now if you don't move he'll stay there' ... and then I move and he's gone. And I haven't any one to talk about him to. I never know whether Clare thinks of him or not. He was so splendid, Bobby, so strong. And he loved me in the most extraordinary way. We'd have been tremendous pals if he'd lived.

"I could have stood anything if I'd been able to see him growing up, had him to care about.... I'm so lonely, Bobby—and if I don't make Clare come back to me, now that the book's failed, I—I—I'll go back to Scaw House and just drink myself to the devil there with my old father; he'll be glad enough."

"You once told me," Bobby said, "about an old man in your place when you were a kid, who said once, 'It isn't life that matters but the courage you bring to it—' Well, that's what you're proving now, Peter."

"Yes, but why me? I've had a bad time all my life—always been knocked about and cursed and kicked. Why should it go on all the time—all the time?"

"Because They think you're worth it, I suppose," said Bobby.

III

And the result of that conversation was that, on that very night Peter made his appeal. They had had a silent evening (Mrs. Rossiter was staying in the house at this time), and at last they all had gone up to bed. Peter stayed for a moment in his dressing-room, seeing his white face in the looking-glass, hearing the beating of his heart and then with a hand that strangely trembled, knocked on Clare's door.

Her voice sounded frightened, he thought, as she called to him to come in. Indeed, as he entered she folded a letter that she had been reading, and put it in a drawer in the dressing-table at which she was sitting.

It was only seldom now that he disturbed her in that room. She had turned on the electric light over her dressing-table; the rest of the room was in darkness. She seemed to Peter very fragile and tiny as she sat there in her black evening frock, her breast rising and falling as though something had suddenly frightened her, her eyes wide and startled. He felt a gross, coarse brute as he stumbled, coming across the dark floor to her.

"My God," he cried in his heart, "put everything right now—let this make everything right."

His big square body flung huge fantastic shadows upon the wall, but he looked, as he faced her, like a boy who had come to his master to confess some crime.

Apparently she was reassured now, for she took off her necklace and moved about the things on her table as though to show him that she was on the point of undressing.

"Well, Peter, what is it?" she said.

"I've come—Clare—just a moment—I want a talk."

"But it's late, I'm tired—won't some other time do?"

"No, I want it now."

"What is it?"

She was looking into the glass as she spoke to him.

He pulled a little chair over to her and sat forward so that his knees nearly touched her thin black dress. He put out his big hand and caught one of her little ones; he thought for a moment that she was going to resist—then it lay there cold as ice.

"Clare—darling—look here, everything's been wrong with both of us—for ages. And I've come—I've come—because I know it's been very largely my fault. And I've come to say that everything will be different now and I want you to let things—be—as they were before—"

For a moment he fancied that he saw a light leap into her eyes; he felt her hand tremble for a moment in his. Then the expression was gone.

"How do you mean?" she said, still looking into the glass. "What do you mean, Peter? I haven't noticed anything different."

"Oh yes, you have. You know that—ever since Stephen died and before that really—you've avoided me. You'd rather be without me than with me. You've all thought me selfish and glum and so I suppose I was. But I missed—the kid—a lot." Again Peter felt her hand tremble. He pressed it. Then he went on, leaning more toward her now and putting an arm out to touch her dress.

"Clare—it's been like a fog all these weeks—we've never had it out, we've never talked about it, but you've been disappointed in me. You thought I was going to write great books and I haven't—and then your mother—and I—don't get on. And then I suppose I'm stupid in society—I can't talk a lot to any one who comes along as all you people can. I've been brought up differently and—and—I know you don't like to think about that either, and so I'll never bring my old friends into the house and I'll see that I'm not such a gawk at your parties—"

He paused for a moment; she was looking down now and he couldn't see her eyes. He bent forward more closely—his arm caught her waist—his hand crushed hers—

She tried desperately to pull herself together to say something—

"No—there's nothing. Well, if there is—Of course I suppose it happens to all married people—"

"What happens?"

"Why, they find one another out a little. Things aren't quite as they thought they'd be. That must happen always."

"But tell me—tell me the things in me that have disappointed you and then I can alter—"

"Well—it's a little as you say. You have been rather rude to Mother. And then—your quarrel—"

"What! You mean with Cards!"

"With—Jerry—yes. And then," her voice was high and sharp now—her eyes avoided his—"I've always—been happy, until I married. Things frighten me. You don't understand me, Peter, how easily I'm frightened—you never seemed to see that. Other people—know."

"I've been selfish—I—"

"Yes," she went on still in that high voice, "and you never consider me in little things. And you laugh at me as though I were stupid. I don't suppose it's all your fault. You were brought up—roughly. But you are rough. You hurt me often. I can't bear," her lip was trembling and she was nearly crying—"I can't bear being unhappy—"

"My God!" cried Peter, "what a beast I am! What a brute I've been!"

"Yes—and you never seemed to think that I minded poor little Stephen's death—the dear little thing—of course it hurt me dreadfully—and you never thought of me—"

"It's all going to be different now. Love me, Clare—love me and it will all come back. And then if you'll only love me I'll be able to write the most wonderful books. I'll be famous all the world over—if you'll only love me, Clare darling—"

He dropt on to his knees before her and looking up at her whispered—"Clare—darling, darling—you're all that I've got now—everything in the world. And in return I'll try to be everything to you. I'll spend my life in making you happy. I'll care for only one thing and that is to be your servant. Clare—Clare—"

She gave a little protesting cry—"Peter, Peter—don't—I—I—can't—" and then in a shuddering whisper—"Peter—I'm not good enough—I don't love you now—I—can't—"

But he had caught her, was holding her to him now, with both his arms round her, pressing her against his shirt, hurting her—at last covering her mouth, her eyes, her cheeks with kisses.

He had not heard those words now, in the triumph of having her back again, his as she had been on the first day of their marriage, did not feel her body unresponsive, her hands cold, nor did he see the appeal, wild and desperate, in her eyes....

At last he left her, closing, softly her door between them.

CHAPTER XIV

PETER BUYS A PRESENT

I

Peter did not hesitate now. He should win Clare back with his strong right hand and he would rule The Roundabout with a rod of iron. Ruling The Roundabout meant ruling Mrs. Rossiter and he was surprised at the ease with which he won his victory over that lady. Had he considered it more deeply that easy victory might have seemed to him ominous.

At luncheon on the day after his talk with Clare they three sat together—Mrs. Rossiter silent, Clare silent, Peter silent.

Suddenly Peter said: "Oh by the way, Clare, I telephoned for seats this morning for the new thing at the Criterion. I got two stalls."

They had not been to the theatre together since Stephen's death.

Clare lifted a white face—"I don't think I—"

"Oh yes," said Peter, smiling across at her—"you'll enjoy it."

Mrs. Rossiter stroking her large bosom with a flat white hand said, "I don't think Clare—"

"Oh yes," said Peter again, "it will do her good."

Mrs. Rossiter smiled. "Get another stall, Peter, and I will come too."

"I'm afraid," said Peter very politely, "that it's too late. The piece is a thumping success. I was very lucky to get any seats at all."

And then Mrs. Rossiter subsided, absolutely subsided ... very strange.

That was not a very happy evening. Clare scarcely spoke, she answered him with "Yes" and "No," she sat in the stalls looking like a little unhappy ghost. She did not in any way repulse him—she let him take her hand coming home in the cab. She shivered and he asked whether she were cold and she said, Yes, she thought that she was. That night he came in, took her for a moment in his hands, kissed her very gently on the lips, and said—

"Clare, you're not angry with me for last night?"

"No" she answered him. Then she added slowly, as though she were repeating a part that she'd learnt, "Thank you for taking me to the play, Peter. I was rather tired. But thank you for taking me."

He went to bed thanking God for this change in her. "I'll make her love me just as she used to, those days on our honeymoon. God bless her."

Yes, Mrs. Rossiter was strangely altered. It all shows what one can do with a woman when one tries. Her hostile placidity had given place to something almost pathetic. One would have thought, had one not known that lady's invariable assurance of movement, that she was perplexed, almost distressed.

Peter was conscious that Clare was now as silent with her mother as she was with him. He perceived that Mrs. Rossiter was disturbed at Clare's reticence. He fancied that he sometimes interrupted little conversations between the mother and the daughter the intention of which was, on Mrs. Rossiter's part at any rate, that "Clare should tell her something." There was no doubt at all, that Mrs. Rossiter was anxious. Even—although this seemed impossible—she appeared to be ready to accept Peter as a friend and ally now—now after these many weeks of hostility. Surely women are strange creatures. In any case, one may observe the yellow brooch agitated now and ill at ease.

Very soon, too, Cards came to make his farewells—he was going to Paris for the whole of May.

"What! Won't you be back for the beginning of the Season?" cried Peter astonished.

"No," Cards answered, laughing. "For once the Season can commence without me."

He was especially affectionate but seemed anxious to be gone. His dark eyes avoided Peter's gaze. He didn't look well—a little anxious: and Cards was generally the soul of light-hearted carelessness.

What a splendid fellow he was! Peter looked him up and down taking that same delight that he had always taken in his distinction, his good looks, his ease. "He ought to have been born king of somewhere," Peter used to think, "he ought really—no wonder people spoil him."

"There's another thing," Peter said, "you're forgetting Clare's birthday next week. She'll be dreadfully disappointed at your not being here for it."

"I'll have to remember it from Paris," Cards said.

"Well—it's an awful pity that you're going for a whole month. I don't know what we shall do without you. And you cheer Clare up—she's rather depressed just now. Thinks of the kid a bit, I expect."

"Well, I'll write," said Cards, and was gone.

II

Peter received at this time a letter that showed him that he had, at any rate, one friend, in the world who believed in him. It was from James Maradick and it was strangely encouraging—now at this period of yawning pits from whose blackness he so resolutely turned away.

It asked him to go with Maradick as his guest to some Club dinner. Then it went on.... "You know, Westcott, we don't meet as often as we should. Like ships in the night, we signal every now and again and then pass. But I am quite sure that we have plenty to say to one another. Once or twice—you remember that party when I gassed about Cornwall?—we have nearly said it, but something has always prevented. I remember that you divided the world once in a fit of youthful confidence, into Explorers and Stay-at-homes. Well, those words will do as well as any others to describe the great dividing line. At any rate, you're an Explorer and you're trying to get on terms with the Stay-at-homes, and I'm a Stay-at-home and I'm trying to get on terms with the Explorers and that's why we're both so uncomfortable. The only happy people, take my word for it, are those who know the kind of thing they are—Explorers or Stay-at-homes, and just stick at that and shut their eyes tight to the other kind of people—il n'existe pas, that other world. Those are the happy people, and, after all most people are like that. But we, you and I, are uncomfortably conscious of the other Party—want to know them, in fact, want them to receive us.

"Well, I'm getting on and it's late days for me, but you've got all your life before you and will do great things, take my word for it. Only don't be discouraged because the Stay-at-homes don't come to you all at once. Give 'em time—they'll come...."

This seemed to Peter, at this moment of a whole welter of doubt and confusion and misunderstanding of people's motives and positions, to explain a great deal. Was that the reason why he'd been so happy in old Zachary Tan's shop years ago? Why he'd been happy through all that existence at the bookshop, those absurd unreal conspirators—happy, yes, even when starving with Stephen in Bucket Lane.

He was then in his right company—explorers one and all. Whereas here?—Now? Had he ever been happy at The Roundabout except during the first year, and afterwards when Stephen came? And was not that, too, the explanation of young Stephen's happiness upon the arrival of Mr. Zanti and Brant? Did he not recognise them for what they were, explorers? He being a young explorer himself.

On the other side Mrs. Rossiter, Clare, Cards, old Bobby who in spite of his affection never understood half the things that Peter did or said, the Galleons, old Mrs. Galleon and Percival and his sister?... Had Henry Galleon known that dividing-line and suffered under it all his life, and borne it and perhaps conquered it?

And Peter suddenly, standing at his window watching London caught by the evening light, saw for an instant his work in front of him again. London with her towers, her roofs and chimneys—smoke and mist and haze weaving a web—and then beneath it, humming, buzzing, turning, all the lives, all the comedies, all the tragedies—Kings and princes, guttersnipes and duchesses, politicians and newsboys, criminals and saints—

Waiting, that golden top, for some hand to set it humming.

In that moment Peter Westcott, aged twenty-nine, with a book just behind him that had been counted on every side the most dismal of failures, saw himself the English Balzac, saw London open like a book at his feet, saw heaven and all its glories... himself the one and only begetter of a thousand masterpieces!

But the sun set—the towers and roofs and chimneys were coldly grey, a ragged wind rose through the branches of the orchard, dark clouds hid the risen moon, newsboys were crying a murder in Whitechapel.

"I hate this house," Peter said, turning away from the window, into a room crowded now with dusk.

III

It was the first of May, and the day before Clare's birthday. It was one of the most beautiful days of the year, with a hint of summer in its light and shadow, a shimmer of golden sun shaking through the trees in the orchard, flung from there on to the windows of The Roundabout, to dance in twisting lines along the floors and across the walls.

All doors and windows seemed to be open; the scent of flowers—a prophecy of pinks and roses where as yet there were none—flooded the little Chelsea streets.

The Velasquez on the walls of The Roundabout danced in her stiff skirts, looking down upon a room bathed in green and gold shadow.

It was three o'clock in the afternoon and Peter was going out to buy Clare a present. He had seen a ruby pendant many months ago in a window in Bond Street. He had thought of it for Clare but he had known that, with young Stephen's education and the rest of the kid's expenses, he could not dare to afford it. Now... things were different.

It should sign and seal this new order....

He came downstairs. He looked into the little sitting-room. Clare was standing there by the window looking at the gay trees in the orchard. On the opposite wall the Velasquez danced....

She had not heard him come in and she was standing by the window with her hands clasped tightly behind her, her body strung up, so it seemed, by some height of determination. She wore a black dress with a little white round her neck and at the sleeves. Her hair was rolled into a pile on the top of her head and the sunlight from the orchard was shining upon it.

When Peter called her name she turned round with a startled cry and put her hand to her throat. Then she moved back against the window as though she were afraid that he was going to touch her.

He noticed her movement and the words that he had intended to say were checked on his lips. He stammered, instead, something about going out. She nodded her head; she had pulled herself together and walked towards him from the window.

"Won't you come, too? It is such a lovely day," he asked her.

"I've got a headache."

"It'll do your headache good."

But she shook her head—"No, I'm going upstairs to lie down."

She moved past him to the door. Then with her hand on it she turned back to him:—

"Peter, I—" she said.

She seemed to appeal to him with her eyes beseeching, trying to say something, but the rest of her face was dumb.

The appeal, the things that she would have said suddenly died, leaving her face utterly without expression.

"Bobby and mother are coming to dinner to-night, aren't they?"

"Yes—"

She passed through the door across the sunlit hall, up the dark stairs. She walked with that hesitating halting step that he knew so well: her small, white hand lay, for a moment on the banisters—then she had disappeared.

IV

Coming through the hall Peter noticed that there was a letter in the box. He took it out and found, with delight, that it was from Stephen Brant. He had had no word from him since the day when he and Mr. Zanti had paid their fateful visit.

The letter said:—

Dear Mr. Peter,

This is a hurried line to tell you that He is dead at last, died in drink cursing and swearing and now her mother and she, poor dear, are going to America and I'm going to look after her hoping that we'll be marrying in a few months' time and so realise my heart's wish.

Dear Peter I sail on Thursday from Southampton and would be coming to see you but would not like to inconvenience you as you now are, but my heart is ever the same to you, Dear Boy, and the day will come when we can talk over old times once again.

Your affectionate friend, sir,

Now about to be made the happiest man in all the world,

Stephen.

N.B. I hope the little kid is strong and happy.

N.B. Zanti goes with us to America having heard of gold in California and is to be my best man when the day comes.

So Stephen's long wait was ended at last. Peter's eyes were dimmed as he put the letter away in his pocket. What a selfish beast, to be sure, must this same Peter Westcott, be, for here he was wishing— yes, almost wishing—that Stephen's happiness had not come to him. Always at the back of everything there had been the thought of Stephen Brant. Let all the pits in the world gape and yawn, there was one person in the world to whom Peter was precious. Now—in America—with a wife... some of the sunlight had gone out of the air and Peter's heart was suddenly cold with that old dread.

Another friend taken from him! Another link gone! Then he pulled himself together, tried to rejoice with Stephen at his happiness, failed dismally, walked down Piccadilly defiantly, with swinging shoulders and a frowning face, like a sailor in a hostile country, and went into the Bond Street jeweller's.

He had been there on several former occasions and a large stout man who looked as though he must have been Lord Mayor several years running came forward and gave Peter an audience. Precious stones were of no account in such a place as this, and the ruby pendant looked quite small and humble when it was brought to Peter—nevertheless it was beautiful and would suit Clare exactly. It seemed to appeal personally to Peter, as though it knew that he wanted it for a very especial occasion. This wasn't one of those persons who would come in and buy you as though you were dirt. It meant something to Peter. It meant something indeed—it meant exactly sixty pounds—

"Isn't that rather a lot?" said Peter.

"It's as fine a ruby—" said the dignitary, looking over Peter's head out of the window, as though he were tired of the affair and wanted to see whether his car were there.

"I'll take it," said Peter desperately.

Sixty Pounds! Did one ever hear of such a thing? Sixty pounds ... Never mind, it marked an occasion. The ruby smiled at Peter as it was slipped into its case; it was glad that it was going to somebody who hadn't very many things.

He had several other matters to settle and it was nearly five o'clock when he turned out of Knightsbridge down Sloane Street. The sun was slipping behind the Hyde Park Hotel so that already the shadows were lying along the lower parts of the houses although the roofs were bright with sunshine.

It was the hour when all the dogs were taken for the last exercise of the day. Every kind, of dog was there, but especially the fat and pampered variety—Poms, King Charles, Pekinese, Dachshunds—a few bigger dogs, and even one mournful-eyed Dane who walked with melancholy superiority, as a king amongst his vassals.

The street stirred with the patterings of dogs. The light slid down the sky—voices rang in the clear air softly as though the dying day had besought them to be tender. The colours of the shops, of the green trees, of slim and beautifully-dressed houses were powdered with gold-dust; the church in Sloane Square began to ring its bells.

Peter, as he turned down the street, was cold—perhaps because Knightsbridge had been blazing with sunshine and the light here was hidden.... No, it was more than that....

"They say," he thought, "that Cornishmen always know when a disaster's coming. If that's true, something ought to be going to happen to me."

And then, in a flash, that sound that he had been half-subconsciously expecting, came—the sound of the sea. He could hear it quite distinctly, a distant, half-determined movement that seemed so vast in its roll and plunge, so sharp in the shock with which it met the shore, and yet so subdued that it might be many thousands of miles away. It was as though a vast tide were dragging back a million shells from an endless shore—the dragging hiss, the hesitating suspense in mid-air, and then the rattle of the returning wave.

As though hypnotised he closed his eyes. Yes, he was walking along the Sea Road. There was that range of rock that lay out at sea like a crouching dog. There was that white twisting circle of foam that lay about the Ragged Stone—out there by itself, the rock with the melancholy bell. Then through the plunging sea he could hear its note—the moan of some one in pain. And ever that rattle, that hiss, that suspense, that crash.

"I beg your pardon—" he had run into a lady's maid who was leading a pompous King Charles. The spaniel eyed him with hatred, the maid with distrust. He passed on—but the Sea had departed.

To chase away his gathering depression he thought that he would go in and have tea with Bobby and Alice. It was quite late when he got there, and stars were in a sky that was so delicate in colour that it seemed as though it were exhausted by the glorious day that it had had; a little sickle moon was poised above the Chelsea trees.

To his disgust he found that Percival and Millicent Galleon were having tea with their brother. Their reception of him very quickly showed him that "Mortimer Stant" had put a final end to any hopes that they might have had of his career as an artist.

"How's the book doing, Westcott?" said Percival, looking upon Peter's loose-fitting clothes, broad shoulders and square-toed shoes with evident contempt.

"Not very well thank you, Galleon."

"Ah, well, it didn't quite come off, did it, Westcott?—not quite. Can't hit the nail every time. Now young Rondel in this Precipice of his has done some splendid work. We had him to tea the other day and really he seemed quite a nice unassuming fellow—"

"Oh! shut up," Bobby growled. "You talk too much, Percival."

Peter was growing. Quite a short time ago he would have been furious, would have gone into his shell, refused to speak to anybody, been depressed and glowering.

Now, smiling, he said:

"Alice, won't you consider it and come up and dine with us after all to-night? It's only my mother-in-law beside ourselves—"

"No, thanks, Peter. I mustn't. The boy's not quite the thing."

"Well, all right—if you must."

Nevertheless, it hurt, although it was only that young ass of a Galleon. That, though, was one of the pits into which one must not look.

He felt the little square box that contained the ruby, lying there so snugly in his pocket. That cheered him.

"I must be getting back. Good-night, everybody. See you at dinner, Bobby."

He went.

After Percival and his sister had also gone Alice said:—

"Dear Peter's growing up."

"Yes," said Bobby. "My sweet young brother wants the most beautiful kicking and he'll get it very soon." Then he looked at the clock. "I must go up and dress."

"I'm rather glad," said Alice, "I'm not coming. Clare gets considerably on my nerves just at present."

"Yes," said Bobby, "but thank God Mr. Cardillac's in Paris—for the time being." Then he added, reflectively—

"Dear old Peter—bless him!"

CHAPTER XV

MR. WESTCOTT SENIOR CALLS CHECKMATE

I

Peter felt as he closed the hall door behind him that The Roundabout was both cold and dark. The little hall drew dusk into its corners very swiftly and now, as he switched on the electric light, he was conscious almost of protest on the part of the place, as though it wished that it might have been left to its empty dusk.

A maid passed him.

"Has your mistress gone upstairs?" he asked her.

"I don't think she has come in, sir."

"Not come in?"

"No, sir, she went out about three o'clock. I don't think she's come back, sir."

She's running it pretty close, he thought as he looked at his watch—then he went slowly up to dress.

He had been more irritated by the superiorities of young Percival Galleon than he had cared to confess. Peter had, at the bottom of his soul, a most real and even touching humility. He had no kind of opinion of his abilities, of his work in comparison with the other workers that counted. Moreover he would not, were his ultimate critical sense aroused, fail to admit to himself some certain standard of achievement. Nothing that young Galleon could say mattered from the critical standpoint—nevertheless he seemed to represent, in this case, a universal opinion; even in his rejection of Peter one could see, behind him, a world of readers withdrawing their approval.

"Peter Westcott's no good.... Peter Westcott's no good.... Peter Westcott's no good...."

In any case that was quite enough to account for the oppression that he was feeling—feeling with increasing force as the minutes passed. He undressed and dressed again slowly, wondering vaguely, loosely, in the back of his mind, why it was that Clare had not come in. Perhaps she had come in and the maid had not heard her. He took the ruby out of his pocket, opened the little case, looked at the jewel shining there under the electric light, thought of Clare with a sudden rush of passionate affection. "Dear thing, won't she look lovely in it? Her neck's so white and she's never worn much jewellery—she'll be pleased. She'll know why I'm giving it to her now—a kind of seal on what we agreed to the other night. A new life ... new altogether...."

He was conscious as he took his shirt off that his windows were open and a strange scent of burning leaves was with him in the room. It was quite strong, pungent—very pleasant, that sense of burning. Burning leaves in the orchard.... But it was rather cold. Then he came back to his looking-glass and, standing there, naked save for his dress trousers, he saw that he was looking in much better health than he had looked for weeks. The colour had returned to his face, his eyes were brighter and more alert— the lines had gone. He was strong and vigorous as he stood there, his body shining under the glow. He opened and shut his hands feeling the strength, force, in his fingers. Thick-set, sturdy, with his shoulders back again now, straight, not bent as they had been.

"Oh, I'm all right—I'm all right you know. I'll write some stuff one day..." and even behind that his thought was—"that young Galleon, by jove, I could jolly well break him if I wanted to—just snap him up."

And then the odour of the burnt leaves filled his nostrils again; when he had dressed he turned out the light, opened the windows more widely, and stood for a moment there smelling the smoke, feeling the air on his forehead, seeing the dark fluttering shadows of the trees, the silver moon, the dim red haze of the London sky....

II

He went down to his study. Clare must be in now. Bobby would be here in a few minutes. He took up the Times but his mind wandered. "Mr. Penning Bruce was at his best last night in the new musical Comedy produced at the Apollo Theatre—the humour of his performance as Lieutenant Pottle, a humour never exaggerated nor strained...."

But he couldn't attend. He looked up at the little clock and saw that it was nearly dinner-time. Bobby ought to be here.

He stood up and listened. The house was profoundly silent. It was often silent—but to-night it was as though everything in the house—the furniture, the pictures—were listening—as though The Roundabout itself listened.

He went into the hall—stood for a moment under the stairs—and then called "Clare—Clare." He waited and then again "Clare, Clare—I say, it's late. Come along—"

There was no answer.

Then, crossing the hall, he opened the door of the little drawing-room and looked in. It was black and empty—here, too, he could smell the burning leaves.

He switched on the light and instantly, perched against the Velasquez Infanta, saw the letter, white and still before the pink and grey of the picture. At the sight of the letter the room that had been empty and cold was suddenly burning hot and filled with a thousand voices. "Take it—take it—why don't you take it? It's been waiting there for you a long time and we've all been wondering when you were coming in for it. It's waiting there for you. Take it—take it—take it!"

At the sight of it too, the floor of the room seemed instantly to pitch, slanting downwards, like the deck of a sinking ship. He caught on to the back of a chair in order that he might not slip with it. His hands shook and there was a great pain at his heart, as though some one were pulling it tight, then squeezing it in their fingers and letting it go again.

Then, as suddenly, all his agitation fled. The room was cold and empty again, and his hands were steady. He took the letter and read it.

It was written in great agitation and almost illegible, and at the bottom of the paper there was a dirty smudge that might have been a tear stain or a finger mark. It ran:

I must go. I have been so unhappy for so long and we don't get on together, Peter, now. You don't understand me and I must be happy. I had always been happy until I married you—perhaps it's partly my fault but I only hinder your work and there is some one else who loves me. He has always said so.

I would not have gone perhaps if it had not been for what you did on April 12. I know because some one saw you getting into a cab at midnight with that horrible woman. That shows that you don't care about me, Peter. But perhaps I would have gone anyhow. Once, the night I told you about baby coming, I told you there'd be a time when you'd have to hold me. It came—and you didn't see it. You didn't care—you can't have loved me or you would have seen.... But anything is better than staying here like this. I am very unhappy now but you will not care. You are cruel and hard, Peter. You have never understood what a woman wants.

I am going to Jerry in Paris. You can divorce me. I don't care about anything now. I won't come back—I won't, I won't—Clare.

He read this all through, very carefully with a serious brow. He finished it and then knew that he had not read a word of it. He went, slowly, to the window and opened it because the room was of a stifling heat. Then he took the letter again and read it. As he finished it again he was conscious that the door-bell was ringing. He wondered why it was ringing.

He was standing in the middle of the room and speaking to himself: "The humour of his performance as Lieutenant Pottle, a humour never exaggerated nor strained ..."

"The humour of his Lieutenant Pottle as a performer—never strained... never exaggerated... never strained..."

Bobby came in and found him there. Peter's face was so white that his collar and shirt seemed to be a continuation of his body—a sudden gruesome nakedness. Both his hands were shaking and his eyes were puzzled as though he were asking himself some question that he could not solve.

Bobby started forward—

"God, Peter, what—"

"She's gone away, Bobby," Peter said, in a voice that shook a little but was otherwise grave and almost a whisper, so low was it. "She's gone away—to Cardillac." Then he added to himself—"Cardillac is my best friend."

Then he said "Listen," and he read the letter straight through. He repeated some of the phrases—"What you did on April 12." "That shows that you don't care.... You are cruel and hard, Peter.... I am going to Jerry in Paris...."

"Jerry—that's Cardillac, you know, Bobby. He's in Paris and she's going over to him because she can't stand me any more. She says I don't care about her. Isn't that funny, when I love her so much?"

Bobby went to him, put his arm round his neck—

"Peter—dear—Peter—wait," and then "Oh my God! we must stop her—"

He drew himself away from Bobby's arm and, very unsteadily, went across the room and then stood against the farther wall, his head bent, motionless.

"Stop her? Oh! no, Bobby. Stop her when she wants to go! I—" His voice wasn't Peter's voice, it was a thin monotonous voice like some one speaking at a great distance.

Then it seemed that intelligence was flashed upon him. He lurched forward and with a great voice—as though he had been struck by some sudden agonising, immortal pain—

"Bobby—Bobby—My wife—Clare—"

And at that instant Mrs. Rossiter was shown into the room.

III

The maid who opened the door had apparently some suspicion that "things were odd," because she waited for a moment before she closed the door again, staring with wide eyes into the room, catching, perhaps, some hint from her master's white face that something terrible had occurred.

It was obvious enough that Mrs. Rossiter had herself, during the last week, been in no easy mind. From the first glances at Peter and Bobby she seemed to understand everything, for, instantly, at that glimpse of their faces she became, for the first time in her life, perhaps, a personality, a figure, something defined and outlined.

Her face was suddenly grey. She hesitated back against the door and, with her face on Peter, said in a whisper, to Bobby:

"What—what has happened?"

Bobby was not inclined to spare her. As an onlooker during these last months he felt that she, perhaps, was more guiltily responsible for the catastrophe than any other human being.

"Clare," he said, trying to fix her eyes. "She's gone off to Cardillac—to Paris."

Then he was himself held by the tragedy of those two faces. They faced each other across the room. Peter, with eyes and a mouth that were not his, eyes not sane, the eyes of no human being, mouth smiling, drawn tight like a razor's edge, with his hands spread out against the wall, watched Mrs. Rossiter.

Mrs. Rossiter, at Bobby's words, had huddled up, suddenly broken, only her eyes, in her great foolish expressionless face, stung to an agony to which the rest of her body could not move.

Her little soul—a tiny scrap of a thing in that vague prison of dull flesh—was suddenly wounded, desperately hurt by the only weapon that could ever have found it.

"Clare!" that soul whispered, "not gone! It's not possible—it can't be—it can't be!"

Peter, without moving, spoke to her.

"It's you that have sent her away. It's all your doing—all your doing—"

She scarcely seemed to realise him, although her eyes never left his face—she came up to Bobby, her hands out:

"Bobby—please, please—tell me. This is absurd—there's a mistake. Clare, Clare would never do a thing like that—never leave me like that—why—" and her voice rose—"I've loved her—I've loved her as no mother ever loved her girl—she's been everything to me. She knows it—why she often says that I'm the only one who loves her. She'd never go—"

Then Peter came forward from the wall, muttering, waving his hands at her—"It's you! You! You! You've driven her to this—you and your cursed interference. You took her from me—you told her to deceive me in everything. You taught her to lie and trick. She loved me before you came into it. Now be proud, if you like—now be proud. God damn you, for making your daughter into a whore—That's what you've done, you with your flat face, your filthy flat face—you've made your daughter a whore, I tell you—and it's nothing but you—you—you—!"

He lifted his hand as though he would strike her across the face. She said nothing but started back with her hands up as though to protect herself. He did not strike her. His hand fell. But she, as though she had felt a blow had her hand held to her face.

He stood over her for a moment laughing, his head flung back. Then still laughing he went away from them out into the hall.

Then, through the open door they heard him. He passed through the upper rooms crying out as he went—"Clare! Clare! Where are you? Come down! They're here for dinner! You're wanted! It's time, Clare!—where are you? Clare! Clare!"

They heard him, knocking furniture over as he went. Then there was silence. Mrs. Rossiter seemed, at that, to come to herself. She stood up, feeling her cheek.

"It's sent him off his head, Bobby. Go after him. He'll hurt himself." Then as though to herself, she went on—"I must find Clare—she'll be in Paris, I suppose. I must go and find her, Bobby. She'll want me badly."

She went quietly from the room, still with her hand to her cheek. She listened for a moment in the hall.

She turned round to Bobby:

"It doesn't say—the letter—where Clare's gone?"

"No—only Paris."

He helped her on with her cloak and opened the front door for her. She slipped away down the street.

Bobby turned back and saw that Peter was coming down the stairs. But now the fury had all died from his face, only that look, as of some animal wounded to death, a look that was so deep and terrible as almost to give his white face no expression at all, was with him.

It had been with him at Stephen's death, it was with him far more intensely now. He looked at Bobby.

"She's gone," in a tired, dull voice as of some one nearly asleep, "gone to Cardillac. I loved Cards—and all the time he loved Clare. I loved Clare and all the time she loved Cards. It's damned funny isn't it, Bobby, old man?"

He stood facing him in the hall, no part of him moving except his mouth. "She says I treated her like a brute. I don't think I did. She says there was something I did one night—I don't know. I've never done anything—I've never been with another woman—something about a cab—Perhaps it was poor Rose Bennett. Poor Rose Bennett—damned unhappy—so am I—so am I. I'm a lonely fellow—I always have been!"

He went past Bobby, back into the little drawing-room. Bobby followed him.

He turned round.

"You can go now, Bobby. I shan't want you any more."

"No, I'm going to stay."

"I don't want you—I don't want any one."

"I'm going to stay."

"I'd rather you went, please."

"I'm going to stay."

Peter paid no more attention. He went and sat down on a chair by the window. Bobby sat down on a chair near him.

Once Peter said: "They took my baby. They took my work. They've taken my wife. They're too much for me. I'm beaten."

Then there was absolute silence in the house. The servants, who had heard the tumbling of the furniture, crept, frightened to bed.

Thus The Roundabout, dark, utterly without sound, stayed through the night. Once, from the chair by the window in the little drawing-room a voice said, "I'm going back to Scaw House—to my father. I'm going back—to all of them."

During many hours the little silver clock ticked cheerfully, seeing perhaps with its little bright eyes, the two dark figures and wondering what they did there.

BOOK IV — SCAW HOUSE

CHAPTER I

THE SEA

I

Peter Westcott was dead.

They put his body into the 11.50 from Paddington.

II

It was a day of high, swinging winds, of dappled skies, of shining gleaming water. Bunches now and again of heavy black clouds clustered on the horizon, the cows and horses in the fields were sharply defined, standing out rigidly against a distant background. The sun came and was gone, laughed and was instantly hidden, turned the world from light to shadow and from shadow back to light again.

Peter's body was alone in the compartment. It was propped up against red velvet that yielded with a hard, clenched resistance, something uncomfortable, had the body minded. The eyes of the body were the high blank windows of a deserted house. Behind them were rooms and passages, but lately so gaily crowded, so eager, with their lights and fires, for hustling life—now suddenly empty—swept of all its recent company, waiting for new, for very different inhabitants.

The white hands motionless upon the knees, the eyes facing the light but blind, the body still against the velvet, throughout the long, long day....

III

There were occasions when some one came and asked for his ticket. Some one came once and asked him whether "He would take lunch." Once a woman, flushed and excited, laden with parcels, tumbled into his carriage and then, after a glance at the white face, tumbled out again.

Then, from very, very far away, came the first whispered breath of returning consciousness. The afternoon sun now had banished the black clouds—the wind had fallen—the sky was a quiet blue and birds rose and fell, rivers shone and had passed, roads were white like ribbons, broad and brown like crinkled paper, then ribbons again as the train flung Devonshire, scornfully, behind its back. Peter was conscious that his body was once more to be tenanted. But by whom?

Here was some one coming to him now, some one who, as the evening light fell about the land, dark with his cloak to his face, came softly upon the house and knocked at the door. Peter could hear his knock—it echoed through the empty passages, the deserted rooms, it was a knock that demanded, imperatively, admittance. The door swung back, the black passages gaped upon the evening light and were closed again. The house was once more silent—but no longer untenanted.

IV

Peter was now conscious of the world. That was Exeter that they had left behind them and soon there would be Plymouth and then the crossing of the bridge and then—Cornwall!

Cornwall! His lips were dry—he touched them with his tongue, and knew, suddenly, that he was thirsty, more thirsty than he had ever been. He would never be hungry again, but he would always be thirsty. An attendant passed. What should he drink? The attendant suggested a whisky and soda. Yes ... a large whisky....

It was very long indeed since he had been in Cornwall—he had not been there since his boyhood. What had he been doing all the time in between? He did not know—he had no idea. This new tenant of the house was not aware of those intervening years, was only conscious that he was returning after long exile, to his home—Scaw House, yes, that was the name ... the house with the trees and the grey stone walls—yes, he would be glad to be at home again with his father. His father would welcome him after so long an absence.

The whisky and soda was brought to him and as he drank it they crossed the border and were in Cornwall.

V

They were at Trewth, that little station where you must change for Treliss. It stood open to all the winds of heaven, two lines of paling, a little strip of platform, standing desolately, at wistful attention in the heart of gently breathing fields, mild skies, dark trees bending together as though whispering secrets ...

all mysterious, and from the earth there rose that breath—sea-wind, gorse, soil, saffron, grey stone—
that breath that is only Cornwall.

Peter—somewhere in some strange dim recesses of his soul—felt it about his body. The wind, bringing
all these scents, touched his cheek and his hair and he was conscious that that dark traveller who now
tenanted his house closed the doors and windows upon that breath. It might waken consciousness, and
consciousness memory, and memory pain ... ah! pain!—down with the shutters, bolt the doors—no
vision of the outer world must enter here.

The little station received gratefully the evening light that had descended upon it. A few men and
women, dim bundles of figures against the pale blue, waited for the train, a crescent moon was stealing
above the hedges, from the chimneys of two little cottages grey smoke trembled in the air.

Suddenly there came to Peter, waiting there, the determination to drive. He could not stand there,
surrounded by this happy silence any longer. All those shadows that were creeping about the dark
spaces beyond his house were only waiting for their moment when they might leap. This silence, this
peace, would give them that moment. He must drive—he must drive.

In the road outside the station a decrepit cab with a thin rake of a man for driver was waiting for a
possible customer. The cab was faded, the wheels encrusted with ancient mud, the horse old and
wheezy, but the cabman, standing now thinner than ever against the sky, was, in spite of a tattered top
hat, filled with that cheerful optimism that belongs to the Cornishman who sees an opportunity of
"doing" a foreigner.

"I want to drive to Treliss," said Peter.

They bargained. The battered optimist obtained the price that he demanded and cocked his eye,
derisively, at the rising moon.

Peter surveyed the cab.

"I'll sit with you on the box," he said.

The thin driver made way for him. It was a high jolting cab of the old-fashioned kind, a cab you might
have sworn was Cornish had you seen it anywhere, a cab that smelt of beer and ancient leather and salt
water, a cab that had once driven the fashion of Treliss to elegant dances and now must rattle the roads
with very little to see, for all your trouble, at the end of it.

The sleeping fields, like grey cloths, stretched on every side of them and the white road cut into the
heart of the distance. It was a quarter to eight and a blue dusk. The driver tilted the top hat over one ear
and they were off.

"I know this road as yer might say back'ards. Ask any one down along Treliss way. Zachy Jackson they'll
say—which is my name, sir, if yer requirin' a good 'orse any time o' day. Zachy Jackson! which there ain't
no man,—tarkin' of 'orses, fit to touch 'im, they'll tell yer and not far wrong either."

But now with every stumbling step of that bony horse Peter was being shaken into a more active
consciousness, consciousness not of the past, very slightly of the present, but rather of an eager, excited

anticipation of events shortly to befall him, of the acute sense—the first that had, as yet, come to him—that, very shortly, he was to plunge himself into an absolute abandonment of all the restraints and discipline that had hitherto held him. He did not know, he could not analyse to himself—for what purpose those restraints had been formerly enforced upon his life. Only now—at this moment, his body was being flooded with a warm, riotous satisfaction at the thought of the indulgences that were to be his.

Still this fortress of his house was bare and desolated, but now in some of the rooms there were lights, fire, whispers, half-hidden faces, eyes behind curtains.

The wind struck him in the face. "Enough of this—you're done for—you're beaten—you're broken... you're going back to your hovel. You're creeping home—don't make a fine thing of it—" the wind said.

The top of the hill rolled up to them and suddenly with the gust that came from every quarter there was borne some sound. It was very delicate, very mysterious—the sound, one might fancy, that the earth would make if all spring flowers were to pierce the soil at one common instant—so fugitive a whisper.

"That's the sea," said Mr. Jackson, waving his whip in the air, "down to Dunotter Cove. There's a wind to-night. It'll blow rough presently."

Now from their hilltop in the light of a baby moon puddles of water shone like silk, hedges were bending lines of listeners, far on the horizon a black wood, there in one of those precipitous valleys cottages cowering, overhead the blue night sky suddenly chequered with solemn pompous slowly moving clouds. But here on the hilltop at any rate, a bustle of wind—such a noise amongst the hedges and the pools instantly ruffled and then quiet again; and so precipitous a darkness when a cloud swallowed the moon. In the daylight that landscape, to any who loved not Cornwall, would seem ugly indeed, with a grey cottage stuck here and there naked upon the moor, with a bare deserted engine house upon the horizon, with trees, deep in the little valley, but scant and staggering upon the hill—ugly by day but now packed with a mystery that contains everything that human language has no name for, there is nothing to do, on beholding it, but to kneel down and worship God. Mr. Jackson had seen it often before and he went twice to chapel every Sunday, so he just whipped up his horse and they stumbled down the road.

"Dirty weather coming," he said.

Peter was disturbed. That whispering noise that had crept across the country frightened him. If it went on much longer it would make him remember—he must not remember.

They turned down into a deep, mysterious lane and the whisper was hidden. Now there was about them only the urgent crowding of the hedges, the wild-flowers flinging their scent on to the night air, and above and below and on every side of the old cab there streamed into the air the sweet smell of crushed grass, as though many fields had been pressed between giant's fingers and so had been left.

Peter sat there and about him, like flames licking woodwork, evil thoughts devoured his body. He was going now at last to do all those things that, these many years, he had prevented himself from doing. That at any rate he knew.... He would drink and drink and drink, until he would never remember anything again ... never again.... Meanwhile as the cab slowly began to climb the hill again Mr. Jackson was telling a story.

He rolled his r's as though life were indeed a valuable and happy thing, and now and again, waving his thin whip in the air, he would seem to appeal to the moon.

"'Twas down to Dunotter Cove and I, a lad, my father bein' a fisherman, and one night, I mind it as though it were yesterday, there was a mighty wreck. Storm and wind and rain there was that night and there we were, out in it, suddenly, all the village of us. I but a slip of a boy, you must know, which it was thirty year back now and the rain sizzling on the cobbles and the wind blawin' the chimneys crooked. Well—she were a mighty wreck blawn right up against the Dunotter rocks, you understand, and sendin' up rockets and we seein' her clear enough, black out to sea which she seemed enormous in the night time and all. My father and the rest of 'em went out in the boat—we waited and we waited and they didn't come back.... They never come back—none of them only a crazed luny, Bill Tregothny—'e was washed up against the rocks down to Bosillian and 'e were just livin' ... And when it come daylight,"—Mr. Jackson cleared his throat and paused—"when it come daylight there wasn't no wreck—nothing—nor no bodies neither—nothing—only Bill Tregothny the fool...."

Peter had heard no single word of this. His ears were straining for the return of that whisper. They were nearly once again at the hilltop. Then in front of them there would be the sea—at the top of the hill there would be the sea.... He was seized with a great terror—frightened like a child in the dark.... "Bill Tregothny, you must understand sir, 'ad always been a idiot—always, born so. When 'e was all well again 'e told strange tales about the lot of them havin' boarded the vessel and there bein' gold all over the decks—bars of it with the rain fallin' all about it—piled in 'eaps and 'e said the sailors weren't like common sailors yer knew, but all in silks with cocked hats and the gold lyin' all about—

"O course Bill was the idiot you must understand, but it's true enough that there were no vessel in the marnin'—no vessel at all—and my father and the rest were never seen again—nor no bodies neither.... And they do say—"

Here Mr. Jackson dropped his voice—

They were just at the top of the hill now. Peter was sitting with his hands clenched, his body trembling.

"... They do say that up in the potato field over Dunotter they've seen a man all in a cocked hat and red silk and gold lace—a ghost you must understand, sir—which Bill Tregothny says ..."

The sea broke upon them with an instant, menacing roar. Between them and this violence there was now only moorland, rough with gorse bushes, uneven with little pits of sand, scented with sea pinks, with stony tracks here and there where the moonlight touched it.

But across it, like a mob's menace, fell the thunder, flung up to them from below, swelling from a menace to a sudden crash, then from crash to echo, dying to murmur again. It had in it anger and power, also pity and tenderness, also scorn and defiance. It cared for no one—it loved every one. It was more intimate than any confidence ever made, and then it shouted that intimacy to the whole world. It flung itself into Peter's face, beat his body, lashed his soul—"Oh! you young fool—you've come slinking back, have you? After all these years you've come slinking back. Where are all your fine hopes now, where all those early defiances, those vast ambitions?—Worthless, broken, defeated—worthless, broken, defeated."

And then it seemed to change:

"Peter—Peter—Hold out a little longer—the battle isn't over yet—struggle on for a little, Peter—I'll help you—I'll bring your courage back to you—Trust me, Peter—trust me...."

Through the rattle of the surf there came the sick melancholy lowing of the Bell Rock; swinging over a space of waters it fell across fields, unutterably, abominably sad.

And in the boy there instantly leapt to life his soul. Maimed and bruised and stunned it had been—now alive, tearing him, bringing on to his bending shoulders an awful tide of knowledge: "Everything is gone—your wife, your boy, your friend, your work.... We have won, Peter, we have won. The House is waiting for you...."

And above those dreadful voices the thundering echo, indifferent to his agonies, despising his frailties, flinging him, sea-wreck of the most miserable, to any insignificant end....

Peter suddenly stood up, rocking on his box. He seized the whip from the driver's hands. He lashed the miserable horse.

"Get on, you devil, get on—leave this noise behind you—get out of it, get out of it—"

The cab rocked and tossed, Mr. Jackson caught the boy about the shoulders, held him down. The horse, tired and weary, paid no heed to anything that might be happening but stumbled on.

"Good Lord, sir," Mr. Jackson cried, "you might have had us over—What's it all about, sir?"

But Peter now was huddled down with his coat about his ears and did not move again.

"Catchin' the whip like that—might 'ave 'ad us right into the 'edge," muttered Mr. Jackson, wishing his journey well over.

As they turned the corner the lights of Treliss burst into view.

CHAPTER II

SCAW HOUSE

I

Mr. Jackson inquired as to the hotel that Peter preferred and was told to drive anywhere, so he chose The Man at Arms.

The Man at Arms had been turned, by young Mr. Bannister, from a small insignificant hostelry into the most important hotel in the West of England. It stood above the town, looking over the bay, the roofs of the new town, the cottages of the old one, the curving island to the right, the lighthouse to the left—all Cornwall in those grey stones, that blue sea, the grave fishing boats, the flocks of gulls, far, far below.

Mr. Bannister had spared no trouble over The Man at Arms, and now it was luxuriously modern Elizabethan, with an old Minstrels' Gallery kept studiously dusty, and the most splendid old oak and deep fire-places with electric light cunningly arranged, and baths in every passage. Of course you paid for this skilful and comfortable romance, but Mr. Bannister always managed his bills so delicately that you expected to find a poem by Suckling or Lovelace on the back of them. When Peter had been last in Treliss The Man at Arms had scarcely existed, but he was now utterly unconscious of it, and stood in the dim square hall talking to Mr. Bannister like a man in a dream.

He was aware now that he was exhausted with a fatigue that was beyond anything that he had ever experienced. It was a weariness that was not, under any conditions, to be resisted. He must lie down— here, anywhere—now, at once and sleep ... sleep ... sleep.

Mr. Bannister caught him by the arm as he swayed.

"You looked played out, sir."

"Done up... done up!"

His eyes were closed. Then suddenly he had touched Mr. Bannister's shoulder. He was looking at a wire letter rack, hanging by the superintendent's little office. There were some telegrams and many letters stretched behind the wire netting. One envelope was addressed—

Miss Norah Monogue, The Man at Arms Hotel. Treliss, Cornwall.

"Miss Monogue ... Miss Monogue ... have you any one here called Miss Monogue?"

"Yes, sir—been here some weeks. Poor lady, she's very ill I'm afraid. Something to do with her heart— strained it in some way. Seemed much better ... but the last few days...."

Peter stumbled upstairs to his room.

II

Some clock was striking five when he awoke and looking vaguely about his room saw, by the light, that it must be late afternoon. He must have slept for a day and a night. As he lay back on his bed his first moments of consciousness were filled with a pleasant sense of rest and ease. He remembered nothing ... he only knew that in the air there was the breath of flowers and that through the open window there floated up to him a song, a murmur of the sea, a rattle of little carts.

He looked about his room. On a distant wall there was a photograph—"Dunotter Rocks, from the East." Then he remembered.

He flung the bed-clothes off him and hurried to dress. He must go up to Scaw House at once, at once, at once. Not another moment must be wasted. His hands trembled as he put on his clothes and when he came downstairs he was dishevelled and untidy. He had eaten nothing for many hours but food now would have choked him. He hurried out of the hotel.

The town must have had many recollections to offer him had he observed it but he passed through it, looking neither to the right nor the left, brushing people aside, striding with great steps up the steep cobbled street that leads out of the town, on to the Sea Road.

Here on the Sea Road he paused. The wind, tearing, as it had always done, round the corner met him and for a moment he had to pull himself together and face it. He remembered, too, at that instant, Norah Monogue. Where had he seen her? What had brought her to his mind quite lately? What did she mean by interfering?—interfering? Then he remembered. It was her name in the letter rack. She was at The Man at Arms ill. Impatiently, he would have driven her from him, but all the way down the Sea Road she kept pace with him.

"I'm done with her.... I'm done with everybody. Damn it all, one keeps thinking...."

In the evening light the sea below the road was a pale blue and near the shore a calm green. It was all very peaceful. The water lapped the shore, the Bell Rock sighed its melancholy note across space; out a little way, when some jagged stones sprang like shoulders from the blue, gentle waves ringed them in foam like lace and broke with a whisper against their sides.

Except for the sea there was absolute silence. Peter alone seemed to walk the world. As he strode along his excitement increased and his knees trembled and his eyes were burning. He did not think of the earlier days when he had walked that same road. That was another existence that had nothing to do with him as he was now. The anticipation that possessed him was parallel with the eager demand of the opium-smoker. "Soon I shall be drugged. I'm going to forget, to forget, to forget. Just to let myself go— to sink, to drown."

He had still with him the consciousness of keeping at bay an army of thoughts that would leap upon him if he gave them an opportunity. But soon that would be all over—no more battle, no more struggle. He turned the corner and saw Scaw House standing amongst its dark trees, with its black palings in front of its garden and the deserted barren patch of field in front of that again. The sun was getting low and the sky above the house was flaming but the trees were sombre and the house was cold.

It did not seem to him to have changed in any way since he had left it. The windows had always been of a grim hideous glass, the stone shape of the place always squat and ugly, and the short flight of steps that led up to the heavy beetling door had always hinted, with their old hard surface, at a surly welcome and a reluctant courtesy. It was all as it had been.

The sky, now a burning red, looked down upon an utterly deserted garden, and the silence that was over all the place seemed to rise, like streaming mist, from the heart of the nettles that grew thick along the crumbling wall.

The paint had faded from the door and the knocker was rusty; as Peter hammered his arrival on to the flat silence a bird flew from the black bunch of trees, whirred into the air and was gone....

For a long time after the echo of his knock had faded away there was silence, and it seemed to him that this could be only another of those dreams—those dreams when he had stood on the stone steps in the heart of the deserted garden and woken the echoes through the empty house. At last there were steps; some one came along the passage and halted on the other side of the door and listened. They both waited on either side, and Peter could hear heavy thick breathing. He caught the knocker again and let it go with a clang that seemed to startle the house to its foundations. Then he heard bolts, very slowly drawn back, again a pause and then, stealthily the door swung open.

A scent of rotten apples met him as the door opened, a scent so strong that it was confused at once with his vision of the woman who stood there, she, with her gnarled and puckered face, her brown skin and crooked nose standing, as it were, for an actual and visible personification of all the rotten apples that had ever been in the world.

He recognised also a sound, the drunken hesitating hiccough of the old clock that had been there when he had come in that evening long ago ready to receive his beating, that had kept pace with his grandfather's snorings and mutterings and had seemed indeed, the only understanding companion that the old man had ever had. The woman was, he saw, the arms-akimbo ferocious cook of the old days, but now how wrinkled and infirm!—separated by so many more years than the lapse of time allowed her from the woman of his past appearance there. There was more in her than the mere crumbling of her body, there was also the crumbling of her spirit, and he saw in her old bleared eyes the sign of some fierce battle fought by her, and fought to her own utter defeat.

In her eyes he saw the thing that his father had become....

What did he want, she asked him, coming disturbing them at that hour, but in her face there was, he fancied, something more than the surly question justified, some curiosity, some eagerness that seemed to show that she did not have many visitors here and that their company might be an eager relief.

"I'm Peter Westcott and I've come to see my father."

She did not answer this, but only, with her hand to her breast stood back a little and watched him with frightened eyes. She was wearing an old, faded, green blouse, open at her scraggy neck and her skirt was a kind of bed-quilt, odd bits of stuffs of many colours stuck together. Her scanty hair was pulled into a bunch on the top of her head, her face where it was not brown was purple, and her hands were always shaking so that her fingers rattled together like twigs. But her alarmed and startled eyes had some appeal that made one pity her poor battered old body.

"You don't remember me," he said, looking into her frightened eyes. But she shook her head slowly.

"You'd much better have kept away," she said.

"Where is he?" he asked her.

She shuffled in front of him down the dark hall. Except for this strange smell of rotting apples it was all very much as it had been. The lamp hanging at the foot of the stairs made the same spluttering noise and there was the door of the room that had once been his grandfather's, and Peter fancied that he could still see the old man swaying there in the doorway, laughing at his son and his grandson as they struggled there on the floor.

The woman pushed open the dining-room door and Peter went in.

Peter's first thought was that his father was not there. He saw standing in front of the well-remembered fireplace a genial-looking gentleman clothed in a crimson dressing-gown—a bald gentleman, rather fat, with a piece of toast in one hand and a glass of something in the other. Peter had expected he knew not what—something stern and terrible, something that would have answered in one way or another to those early recollections of terror and punishment that still dwelt with him. He had remembered his father as short, spare, black-haired, grim, pale—this gentleman, who was now watching him, bulged in the cheeks and the stomach, was highly coloured with purple veins down the sides of his nose and his rather podgy hands trembled. Nevertheless, it was his father. When the red dressing-gown spoke it was in a kind of travesty of that old sharp voice, those cutting icy words—a thickened and degenerate relation:

"My boy! At last!" the gentleman said.

The room presented disorder. On the table were scattered playing cards, a chair was overturned, under the cactus plant lay what looked like a fiddle, and the only two pictures on the wall were very indecent old drawings taken apparently from some Hogarthian prints.

Peter stared at all this in amazement. It was, after the grim approach and the deserted garden, like finding an Easter egg in a strong box. Peter saw that his father was wearing under the dressing-gown a white waistcoat and blue trousers, both of them stained with dark stains and smelling very strongly of whisky. He noticed also that his father seemed to find it difficult to balance himself on both his legs at the same time, and that he was continually shifting his feet in an indeterminate kind of way, as though he would like to dance but felt that it might not be quite the thing.

Mr. Westcott closed up both his eyes, opened his mouth and shut it again and shook Peter excitedly by the hand. At the same time Peter felt that his father was shaking his hand as much because he wanted to hold on to something as for reasons of courtesy.

"Well, I am glad. I wondered when you would come to see your poor old father again—after all these years. I've often thought of you and said to myself, 'Well, he'll come back one day. You only be patient,' I've said to myself, 'and your son will come back to you—your only son, and it isn't likely that he's going to desert you altogether.'"

"Yes, father, I've come back," said Peter, releasing his hand. "I've come back to stay."

He thought of the many times in London when he'd pictured his father, stern and dark, pulling the wires, dragging his wicked son back to him—he thought of that ... and now this. And yet....

"Well now, isn't that pleasant—you've come to stay! Could I have wanted anything better? Come and sit down—yes, that chair—and have something to drink. What, you won't? Well, perhaps later. So you've come to keep your old father company, have you? I'm sure that's delightful. Just what a son ought to do. We shall get along very well, I'm sure."

All the while that his father talked, still holding the toast and the glass of something, Peter was intensely conscious of the silent listening house. After all that grimness, that desertion, the old woman's warning had gone for something. And yet, in spite of a kind of dread that hung about him, in spite of a kind of perception that there was a great deal more in his father than he at present perceived, he could not resist a kind of warm pleasure that here at any rate was some sort of a haven, that no one else in the world might want him, but here was some one who was glad to see him.

"Well, my boy, tell me all you've been doing these years."

"I've been in London, writing—"

"Dear, dear—have you really now? And how's it all turned out?"

"Badly."

"Dear me, I'm sorry for that. But there are better things in the world than writing, believe me. I dare say, my boy, you thought me unkind in those old days but it was all for your best—oh dear me, yes, entirely for your best."

Here, for an instant, his father's voice sounded so like his old grandfather's that Peter jumped.

"Married?" said his father.

"My wife has left me—"

"Dear me, I am sorry to hear that." Mr. Westcott finished the toast and wiped his fingers on a very old and dirty red handkerchief. "Women—bless them—angels for a time, but never to be depended on. Poor boy, I'm sorry. Children?"

"I had a son. He died."

"Well now, I am indeed sorry, I'd have liked a grandson too. Don't want the old Westcott stock to die out. Dear me, that is a pity."

It was at this point that Peter was aware, although he could not have given any reasonable explanation of his certainty, that his father had been perfectly assured beforehand of all the answers to these questions. Peter looked at the man, but the eyes were almost closed, and the smile that played about the weak lips—once so stern and strong—told one nothing.

It was dark now. Mr. Westcott got, somewhat unsteadily, to his feet.

"Come," he said, "I'll show you the house, my boy. Not changed much since you were here, I'm sure. Wanted a woman's care since your dear mother died of course—and your poor old grandfather—"

He whispered over again to himself as he shuffled across the room—"your poor old grandfather—"

It had seemed to grow very suddenly dark. Outside in the hall, under the spluttering lamp, Mr. Westcott found a candle. The house was intensely silent.

As they climbed the stairs, lighted only by the flickering candle-light, Peter's feelings were a curious mixture of uneasiness and a strange unthinking somnolence. Some part of him, somewhere, was urging him to an active unrest—"Norah ... what does she want interfering? I'll just go and see her and come back.... No, I won't, I'll just stay here ... never to bother again ... never to bother again...."

He was also, in some undefined way, expecting that at any moment his father would change. The crimson dressing-gown swayed under the flickering candle-light. Let it turn round and what would one see inside it? His father never stopped talking for an instant—his thick wandering voice was the only sound in the deserted house.

The rooms were all empty. They smelt as though the windows had not been opened for years. It was in the little room that had once been his bedroom that the apples were stored—piles upon piles of them and most of them rotten. The smell was all over the house.

Mr. Westcott, standing with the apples on every side of him, flung monstrous shadows upon the wall— "This used to be your room. I remember I used to whip you here when you were disobedient. The only way to bring up your child. The Westcotts have always believed in it. Dear me, how long ago it all seems ... you can have this room again if you like. Any room in the house you please. We'll be very good company for one another...."

All about Peter there was an atmosphere of extraordinary languor—just to sit here and let the days slip by, the years pass. Just to stay here with no one to hurt one, no need for courage....

They were out in the long passage. Mr. Westcott came and placed his hand upon Peter's arm. The whole house was a great cool place where one slept. Mr. Westcott smiled into Peter's face ... the house was silent and dark and oh! so restful. The candle swelled to an enormous size—the red dressing-gown seemed to enfold Peter.

In another moment he would have fallen asleep there where he stood. With the last struggle of a drowning man he pulled back his fading senses.

"I must go back to the hotel and fetch my things." He could see his father's eyes that had been wide open disappear.

"We can send for them."

"No, I must go for them myself—"

For a moment they faced one another. He wondered what his father intended to do. Then—with a genial laugh, Mr. Westcott said: "Well, my boy, just as you please—just as you please. I know you'll come back to your old father—I know you'll come back—"

He blew the candle out and put his arm through his son's and they went downstairs together.

CHAPTER III

NORAH MONOGUE

I

Peter found, next morning, Miss Monogue sitting by her window. She gave him at once the impression of something kept alive by a will-power so determined that Death himself could only stand aside and wait until it might waver.

She was so thin that sitting there in the clear white colours of the sky beyond her window she seemed like fine silk, something that, at an instant's breath, would be swept like a shadow, into the air. She wore something loose and white and over her shoulders there was a grey shawl. Her grey hair was as untidy as of old, escaping from the order that it had been intended to keep and falling over her beautiful eyes, so that continually she moved her hand—so thin and white with its deep purple veins—to push it back. In this still white figure the eyes burnt with an amazing fire. What eyes they were!

One seemed, in the old days, to have denied them their proper splendour, but now in this swiftly fading body they had gathered more life and vigour, showing the soul that triumphed over so slender a mortality.

She seemed to Peter, as he came into the room, to stand for so much more than he had ever hitherto allowed her. Here, in her last furious struggle to keep a life that had given to her nothing worth having, he saw suddenly emblazoned about him, the part that she had played in his life, always from the first moment that he had known her—a part that had been, by him, so frequently neglected, so frequently denied.

As she turned and saw him he was ashamed at the joy that his coming so obviously brought her. He felt her purity, her unselfishness, her single-heartedness, her courage, her nobility in that triumphant welcome that she gave him. That she should care so much for any one so worthless, so fruitless as he had proved himself to be!

He had come to her with some dim sense that it was kind of him to visit her; he advanced to her now across the room with a consciousness that she was honouring him by receiving him at all.

That joy, with which she had at first greeted him, had in it also something of surprise. He had forgotten how greatly these last terrible days must have altered his appearance—he told much more than he knew, and the little sad attempt that he made, as he came to her, to present as careless and happy an appearance as he had presented in the old Brockett days was more pathetic and betraying than anything he could have done.

But she just closed both her burning hands about his cold one, made him sit down in a chair by her side and, trembling with the excited joy of having him with her, forced him to determine that, whatever came of it, he would keep his troubles from her, would let her know nothing of his old chuckling father and the shadowy welcome that Scaw House had flung over him, would be still the Peter that he had been when he had seen her last in London.

"Peter! How splendid to have you here! When Mr. Bannister told me last night I could have cried for happiness, and he, dear little man, was surely as pleased to see me happy as though I'd been his own sister."

"I'd just come down—" Peter began, trying to smile and conscious with an alarm that surprised him, of her fragility and the way that her hand went now and again to her breast, as though to relieve some pain there. "Are you sure—" he broke off, "that I'm not doing you harm coming like this—not agitating you too much, not exciting you?"

"Harm! Why, Peter," she was smiling but he noticed too that her eyes were searching his face, as though to find some clue to the change that they saw there—"Why it's all the good in the world. It's what I've been wanting all this time. Some change, a little excitement, for I've been here, you know, quite a number of weeks alone—and that it should be you—you! of all people in this lovely exciting surprising world."

"How did it happen?" he asked, "your coming down?"

"After I saw you last—I was very bad. My stupid old heart.... And the doctor said that I must get away, to the sea or somewhere. Then—what do you think?—the dears, all of them in Brockett's put their heads together and got me quite a lot of money.... Oh! the darlings, and they just as poor as church mice themselves. Of course I couldn't insult them by not taking it. They'd have been hurt for ever—so I just pocketed my pride and came down here."

"Why Treliss?" asked Peter.

"Well, hadn't you so often talked about it? Always, I'd connected you with it in my mind and thought that one day I'd come down and see it. I suggested it to the doctor—he said it was the very place. I used to hope that one day you'd be with me here to explain it, but I never expected it... not so soon... not like this."

Her voice faltered a little and her hand held his more tightly.

They were silent. The sounds of the world came, muffled, up to their window, but they were only conscious of one another.

Peter knew that, in another instant, he would tell her everything. He had always told her everything— that is what she had been there for, some one, like an elder sister, to whom he might go and confess.

At last it came. Very softly she asked him:

"Peter, what's the matter? Why are you here? What's happened?"

Staring before him out of the window, seeing nothing but the high white light of the upper sky, his heart, as it seemed to him, lying in his hands like a stone to be tossed lightly out there into space, he told her:

"Everything's happened. Clare has run off with my best friend.... It has just happened like that. I don't blame her, she liked him better—but I—didn't know—it was going... to happen."

He didn't look at her, but he heard her catch her breath sharply and he felt her hand tighten on his. They were silent for a long time and he was dimly aware in some unanalysed way that this was what she had expected ever since he had come into the room.

"Oh!" she said at last, holding his hand very tightly, "I'm sorry, I'm sorry—"

He had seen, of course, from the beginning that this business must be told her, but his one desire was to hurry through it, to get it done and banished, once and for all, from their conversation.

"It happened," he went on gruffly, "quite suddenly. I wasn't in any way prepared for it. She just went off to Paris, after leaving a letter. With the death of the boy and the failure of my book—it just seemed the last blow—the end."

"The end—at thirty?" she said softly, almost to herself, "surely, no—with the pluck that you've got—and the health. What are you going to do—about it all?"

"To do?" he smiled bitterly. "Do you suppose that I will ask her to come back to me? Do you suppose that I want her back? No, that's all done with. All that life's finished." Then he added slowly, not looking at her as he spoke—"I'm going to live with my father."

He remembered, clearly enough, that he had told her many things about his early life at Scaw House. He knew that she must now, as he flung that piece of information at her, have recalled to herself all those things that he had told her. He felt rather than perceived, the agitation that seized her at those last words of his. Her hand slowly withdrew from his, it fell back on to her lap and he felt her whole body draw, as it were, into itself, as though it had come into contact with some terror, some unexplained alarm.

But she only said:

"And what will you do at home, Peter?"

He answered her with a kind of bravado—"Oh, write, I suppose. I went up to see the old man yesterday. Changed enormously since the old days. I found him quite genial, seemed very anxious that I should come. I expect he's a bit lonely."

She did not answer this and there was a long awkward pause. He knew, as they sat there, in troubled silence that his conscience was awake. It had seemed to be so quiescent through his visit yesterday; it had been drugged and dimmed all these last restless days. But now it was up again. He was conscious that it was not, after all, going to be so easy a thing to abandon all his energies, his militancies, the dominant vigorous panoply of his soul. He knew as he sat there, that this sick shadow of a woman would not let him go like that.

He said good-bye to her for the moment, but, as he left the room he knew that Scaw House would not see him again until he had done everything for her that there was to be done.

II

That evening he saw the doctor who attended on her. He was a nice young fellow, intelligent, eager, with a very real individual liking for his patient. "Ah! she's splendid—brave and plucky beyond anything I've ever seen; so full of fun that you'd think that she'd an idea that another three weeks would see her as well as ever again—whereas she knows as well as I do that another three weeks may easily see her out of the world altogether!"

"There's no hope then?" asked Peter.

"None whatever. There's every kind of complication. She must have always had something the matter with her, and if she'd been cared for and nursed when she was younger she might have pulled out of it. Instead of that she's always worn herself to a thread—you can see that. She isn't one of those who take life easily. She ought to have gone before this, but she holds on with her pluck and her love of it all.... Lord! when one thinks of the millions of people who just 'slug' through life—not valuing it, doing nothing with it—one grudges the waste of their hours when a woman like Miss Monogue could have done so much with them."

"Am I doing her any harm, going in to see her?"

"No—doing her good. Don't excite her too much—otherwise the company's the best thing in the world for her."

The days then, were to be dedicated to her service. He knew, of course, that at the end of it—and the end could not be far distant—he would go to Scaw House and remain there; meanwhile the thing was postponed. He would not think about it.

But on his second meeting with Norah Monogue he saw that he was not to be allowed to dismiss it. He found her sitting still by her window; she was flushed now with a little colour, her eyes burning with a more determined fire than ever, her whole body expressing a dauntless energy.

The sight of her showed him that there was to be battle and, strangely enough, he found that there was something in himself that almost welcomed it. Before he knew where he was he found that he was "out" to defend his whole life.

The first thing that she did was to draw from him a minute, particular account of all that had happened during these last months. It developed into a defence of his whole married life, as though he had been pleading before a jury of Clare's friends and must fight to prove himself no blackguard.

"Ah! don't I know that I've made a mess of it all? Do you think that I'm proud of myself?" he pleaded with her. "Honestly I cannot see where, as far as Clare is concerned, I'm to blame. She didn't understand—how could she ever have understood?—the way that my work mattered to me. I wanted to keep it and I wanted to keep her too, and every time I tried to keep her it got in the way and every time I tried to keep it she got in the way. I wasn't clever enough to run both together."

Norah nodded her head.

"But there was more than that. Life has always been rough for me. Rough from the beginning when my father used to whip me, rough at school, rough when I starved in London, roughest of all when young Stephen died. I'd wanted to make something out of it and I suppose the easiest way seemed to me to make it romantic. This place, you know, was always in my bones. That Tower down in the Market Place, old Tan's curiosity shop, the sea—these were the things that kept me going. Afterwards in London it was the same. Things were hard so I made them into a story—I coloured them up. Nothing hurt when everything was romance. I made Clare romance too—that was the way, you see, that all my life was bound up so closely together. She was an adventure just as everything else had been. And she didn't like it. She couldn't understand the Adventure point of view. It was, to her, immoral, indecent. I went easily along and then, one day, all the romance went out of it—clean—like a pricked bubble. When young

Stephen died I suddenly saw that life was real—naked—ugly, not romantic a bit. Then it all fell to pieces like a house of cards. It's easy enough to be brave when you're attacking a cardboard castle—it's when you're up against iron that your courage is wanted. It failed me. I've funked it. I'm going to run away."

He could see that Norah Monogue's whole life was in the vigour with which she opposed him—

"No, no, no. To give it up now. Why, you're only thirty—everything's in front of you. Listen. I know you took Clare crookedly, I saw it in the beginning. In the first place you loved her, but you loved her wrong. You've been a boy, Peter, all the time, and you've always loved like a boy. Don't you know that there's nothing drives a woman who loves a man more to desperation than that that man should give her a boy's love? She'd rather he hated her. Clare could have been dealt with. To begin with she loved you— all the time. Oh! yes, I'm as certain of it as I can be of anything. I know her so well. But the unhappiness, the discomfort—all the things, the ugly things, that her mother was emphasising to her all the time— frightened her. Knowing nothing about life she just felt that things as they were were as bad as things could be. It seems extraordinary that any one so timid as she should dare to take so dangerous a plunge as running off to another man.

"But it was just because she knew so little about Life that she could do it. This other man persuaded her that he could give her the peace and comfort that you couldn't. She doesn't know—poor thing, poor thing—what it will mean, that plunge. So, out of very terror, she took it. And now—Oh! Peter, I'm as certain as though I could see her, she's already longing for you—would give anything to get back to you. This has taught her more than all the rest of her life put together. She was difficult—selfish, frightened at any trouble, supersensitive—but a man would have understood her. You wanted affection, Peter— from her, from me, from a lot of people—but it was always because of the things that it was going to bring to you, never because of the things that you were going to give out. You'd never grown up—never. And now, when suddenly the real world has come to you, you're going to give it up."

"I don't give it up," he said to her—"I shall write—I shall do things—"

She shook her head. "You've told me. I know what that means." Then almost below her breath—"It's horrible—It's horrible. You mustn't do it—you must go back to London—you must go back—"

But at that he rose and faced her.

"No," he said, "I will not. I've given the other things a chance—all these years I've given them a chance. I've stood everything and at the end everything's taken away from me. What shall I go back to? Who wants me? Who cares? God!" he cried, standing there, white-faced, dry-eyed, almost defying her— "Why should I go? Just to fail again—to suffer all that again—to have them take everything I love from me again—to be broken again! No, let them break the others—I'm done with it...."

"And the others?" she answered him. "Is it to be always yourself? You've fought for your own hand and they've beaten you to your knees—fight now for something finer—"

She seemed as she appealed to him to be shining with some great conquering purpose. Here, with her poor body broken and torn, her spirit, the purer for her physical pain, confronted him, shamed him, stretched like a flaming sword before the mean paths that his own soul would follow.

But he beat her down. "I will not go back—you don't know—you don't understand—I will not go."

The little dusty Minstrels' Gallery saw a good deal of him during these days. It was a lonely place at the top of the hotel, once intended to be picturesque and romantic for London visitors, but ultimately left to its own company with its magnificent view appreciated by no one.

Here Peter came. Every part of him now seemed to be at war with every other part. Had he gone straight to Scaw House with bag and baggage and never left it again, then the Westcott tradition might have caught him when he was in that numbed condition—caught him and held him.

Now he had stayed away just long enough for all the old Peter to have become alive and active again.

He looked back upon London with a great shuddering. The torment that he had suffered there he must never undergo again. Norah was now the one friend left to him in the world. He would cut himself into pieces to make these last days of hers happy, and yet the one thing that could give her happiness was that he should promise to go back.

She did not understand—no one could understand—the way that this place, this life that he contemplated, pulled him. The slackness of it, the lack of discipline in it, the absence of struggle in it. All the strength, the fighting that had been in him during these past years, was driven out of him now. He just wanted to let things drift—to wander about the fields and roads, to find his clothes growing shabby upon him, to grow old without knowing even that he was alive—all this had come to him.

She, on the other side, would drive him back into the battle of it all once more. To go back a failure—to be pointed out as the man whose wife left him because she found him so dull—to hear men like young Percival Galleon laughing at his book—to sell his soul for journalism in order to make a living—to see, perhaps, Clare come back into the London world—to break out, ultimately, when he was sick and tired of it all, into every kind of debauch ... how much better to slip into nothing down here where nobody knew nor cared!

And yet, on the other hand, he had never known until now the importance that Norah Monogue had held in his life.

Always, in everything he had done, in his ambitions and despairs, his triumphs and defeats, she had been behind him. He'd just do anything in the world for her!—anything except this one thing. Up and down, up and down he paced the little Minstrels' room, with its dusty green chair and its shining floor—"I just can't stand it all over again!"

But every time that he went in to see her—and he was with her continually—made his resistance harder. She didn't speak about it again but he knew that she was always thinking about it.

"She's worrying over something, Westcott—do you happen to know what it is?" the doctor asked him. "It's bad for her. If you can help her about it in any way—"

The strain between them was becoming unbearable. Every day, when he went in to sit with her, they would talk about other things—about everything—but he knew that before her eyes there was that picture of himself up at Scaw House, and of the years passing—and his soul and everything that was fine in him, dying.

He saw her growing daily weaker. Sometimes he felt that he must run away altogether, go up to Scaw House and leave her to die alone; then he knew that that cruelty at any rate was not in him. One day he thought her brutal and interfering, another day it seemed that it was he who was the tyrant. He reminded himself of all the things that she had done for him—all the things, and he could not grant her this one request.

Then he would ask himself what the devil her right was that she should order his life in this way?... everyday the struggle grew harder.

The tension could not hold any longer—at last it broke.

IV

One evening they were sitting in silence beside her window. The room was in dusk and he could just see her white shadow against the dim blue light beyond the window.

Suddenly she broke down. He could hear her crying, behind her hands. The sound in that grey, silent room was more than he could bear. He went over to her and put his arms round her.

"Norah, Norah, please, please. It's so awfully bad for you. I oughtn't to come if I—"

She pulled herself together. Her voice was quite calm and controlled.

"Sit over there, Peter. I've got to talk to you."

He went back to his chair.

"I've only got a few more weeks to live. I know it. Perhaps only a few more days. I must make the very utmost of my time. I've got to save you...."

He said nothing.

"Oh! I know that it must all have seemed to you abominable—as though I were making use of this illness of mine to extort a promise from you, as though just because I'm weak and feeble I can hold an advantage over you. Oh! I know it's all abominable!—but I'll use everything—yes, simply everything—if I can get you to leave this place and go back!"

He could feel that she was pulling herself together for some tremendous effort.

"Peter, I want you now just to think of me, to put yourself out of everything, absolutely, just for this half-hour. After all as I've only a few half-hours left I've got that right."

Her laugh as she said it was one of the saddest things he'd ever heard.

"Now I'm going to tell you something—something that I'd never thought I'd tell a soul.

"I've not had a very cheerful life. It hasn't had very much to make it bright and interesting. I'm not complaining but it's just been that way—" She broke off for a moment. "I don't want you to interrupt or say anything. It'll make it easier for me if I can just talk out into the night air, as it were—just as though no one were here."

She went on: "The one thing that's made it possible, made it bearable, made it alive, has been my love for you. Always from the first moment I saw you I have loved you. Oh! I haven't been foolish about it. I knew that you'd never care for me in that kind of way. I knew from the very first that we should be pals but that you'd never dream of anything more romantic. I've never had any one in love with me—I'm not the kind of woman who draws the romance out of men.

"No, I knew you'd never love me, but I just determined that I'd make you, your career, your success, the pivot, the centre of my life.

"I wasn't blind about you—not a bit. I knew that you were selfish, weak, incredibly young about the world. I knew that you were the last person in existence to marry Clare—all the more reason it seemed to me why I should be behind you. I was behind you so much more than you ever knew. I wonder if you've the least idea what most women's lives are like. They come into the world with the finest ideals, the most tremendous energies, with a desire for self-sacrifice that a man can't even begin to understand. Then they discover slowly that none of those things, those ideals, those energies, those sacrifices, are wanted. The world just doesn't need them—they might as well never have been born. Do you suppose I enjoyed slaving for my mother, day and night for years? Do you suppose that I gladly yielded up all my best blood, my vitality, to the pleasure of some one who never valued it, never even knew that such things were being given her? Before you came I was slowly falling into despair. Think of all the women who are haunted by the awful thought—'The time will come when death will be facing me and I shall be forced to own that for any place that I have ever filled in the world I might never have been born.' How many women are there who do not pray every day of their lives, 'God, give me something to do before I die—some place to fill, some work to carry out, something to save my self-respect.'

"I tell you that there is a time coming when women will force those things that are in them upon the world. God help all poor women who are not wanted!

"I wasn't wanted. There was nothing for me to do, no place for me to fill... then you came. At once I seized upon that-God seemed to have sent it to me. I believed that if I turned all those energies, those desires, those ambitions upon you that it would help you to do the things that you were meant to do. I was with you always—I slaved for you—you became the end in life to which I had been called.

"All the time you were only a boy—that was partly I think why I loved you. You were so gauche, so ignorant, so violent, so confident one moment, so plunged into despair the next. For a while everything seemed to go well. I had thought that Clare was going to be good for you, was going to make you unselfish. I thought that you'd got the better of all that part of you that was your inheritance. Even when I came down here I thought that all was well. I knew that I had come down to die and I had thanked God because He had, after all, allowed me to make something of my life, that I'd been able to see you lifted into success, that I'd seen you start a splendid career.... Then you came and I knew that your life was broken into pieces. I knew that what had happened to you might be the most splendid thing in the world for you and might be the most terrible. If you stay down here now with your father then you are done for—you are done for and my life has, after all, gone for nothing."

Her voice broke, then she leaned forward, catching his hands:

"Peter, I'm dying—I'm going. If you will only have it you can take me, and when I am gone I shall still live on in you. Let me give you everything that is best in me—let me feel that I have sent you back to London, sent you with my dying breath—and that you go back, not because of yourself but because of everything that you can do for every one else.

"Believe me, Peter dear, it all matters so little, this trouble and unhappiness that you've had, if you take it bravely. The courage that you've wanted before is nothing to the courage that you want now if you're going back. Let me die knowing that we're both going back.

"Think of what your life, if it's fine enough, can mean to other people. Go back to be battered—never mind what happens to your body—any one can stand that. There's London waiting for you, there's life and adventure and hardship. There are people to be helped. You'll go, with all that I can give you, behind you ... you'll go, Peter?"

He sat with his teeth set, staring out into the world. He had known from the first sentence of her appeal to him that she had named the one thing that could give him courage to fight his cowardice. Some one had once said: "If any one soul of us is all the world, this world and the next, to any other soul, then whoever it may be that thus loves us, the inadequacy of our return, the hopeless debt of us, must strike us to our knees with an utter humility."

So did he feel now. Out of the wreck there had survived this one thing. He remembered what Henry Galleon had once said about Fortitude, that the hardest trial of all to bear was the consciousness of having missed the Finest Thing. All these years she had been there by the side of him and he had scarcely thought of her—now, even as he watched her, she was slipping away from him, and soon he would be left alone with the consciousness of missing the greatest chance of his life.

The one thing that he could do in return was to give her what she asked. But it was hard—he was under no illusion as to the desperate determination that it would demand. The supreme moment of his life had come. For the first time he was going to fling away the old Peter Westcott altogether. He could feel it clinging to him. About him, in the air, spirits were fighting. He had never before needed Courage as he was needing it now. It seemed to him that he had to stand up to all the devils in the world—they were thick on every side of him.

Then, with a great uplifting of strength, with a courage that he had never known before, he picked up Peter Westcott in his hands, held him, that miserable figure, high in air, raised him, then flung him with all his strength out, away, far into space, never to return, never to encumber the earth again.

"I'll go back," Peter said—and as he said it, there was no elation in him, only a clear-sighted vision of a life of struggle, toil, torment, defeat, in front of him, something so hard and arduous that the new Peter Westcott that had now been born seemed small indeed to face it.

But nevertheless he knew that at the moment that he said those words he had broken into pieces the spell that had been over him for so many years. That Beast in him that had troubled him for so long, all the dark shadows of Scaw House ... these were at an end.

He felt tired, discouraged, no fine creature, as he turned to her, but he knew that, from that moment, a new life had begun for him.

He put his arms round Norah Monogue and kissed her.

V

He got up very early next morning and went down to the Harbour. The fishing-boats were coming in; great flocks of gulls, waiting for the spoil that was soon to be theirs, were wheeling in clouds about the brown sails.

The boats stole, one after another, around the pier. The air was filled with shrill cries—the only other sound was the lapping of the water as it curled up the little beach.

As Peter stood there there crept upon him a sensation of awe. He took off his hat. The gulls seemed to cease their cries.

As another brown sail stole round the white point, gleaming' now in the sun, he knew, with absolute certainty, that Norah Monogue was dead.

CHAPTER IV

THE GREY HILL

I

The day of Norah Monogue's funeral was fine and clear. Peter and little Mr. Bannister were the only mourners and it was Peter's wish that she should be buried in the little windy graveyard of the church where his mother had been buried.

There was always a wind on that little hill, but to-day it was gentler than he had ever known it before. His mind went back to that other funeral, now, as it seemed, such a lifetime ago. Out of all the world these two women only now seemed to abide with him. As he stood beside the grave he was conscious that there was about him a sense of peace and rest such as he had never known before. Could it be true that some of Norah Monogue's fine spirit had come to him? Were they, in sober fact to go on together during the remainder of his days?

He lingered for a little looking down upon the grave. He was glad to think that he had made her last hours happy.

Indeed she had not lived in vain.

Heavy black clouds were banking upon the horizon as he went down the hill and struck the Sea Road in the direction of Scaw House. Except in that far distance the sky was a relentless, changeless blue. Every detail in the scene was marked with a hard outline, every sound, the sea, the Bell Rock, the cries of sheep, the nestling trees, was doubly insistent.

He banged the knocker upon the Scaw House door and when the old woman came to open to him he saw that something had occurred. Her hair fell about her neck, her face was puckered with distress and her whole appearance was dismayed.

"Is my father in?" he asked.

"He is, but he's ill," she answered him, eyeing him doubtfully. "He won't know yer—I doubt he'll know any one. He's had a great set-back—"

Peter pushed past her into the hall—"Is he ill?"

"Indeed he is. He was suddenly took—the other evenin' I being in my kitchen heard a great cry. I came runnin' and there in the dining-room I found him, standing there in the midst, his hands up. His eyes, you must understand, sir, were wide and staring—'They've beaten me,' he cried, 'They've beaten me'— just like that, sir, and then down he tumbled in a living fit, foaming at the mouth and striking his poor head against the fender. Yer may come up, sir, but he won't know yer which he doesn't me either."

Peter followed her up to the dreary room that his father inhabited. Even here the paper was peeling off the walls, some of the window-glass was broken and the carpet was torn. His father lay on his back in an old high four-poster. His eyes stared before him, cheeks were ashen white—his hands too were white like ivory.

His lips moved but he made no sound. He did not see Peter, nor did his eyes turn from the blank stare that held them.

"Has he a doctor?" Peter asked the old woman.

"Ay—there's a young man been coming—" the old woman answered him. She was, he noticed, more subservient than she had been on the former occasion. She obviously turned to him now with her greedy old eyes as the one who was likely soon to be in authority.

Peter turned back to the door. "This room must be made warmer and more comfortable. I will send a doctor from the hotel this evening—I will come in again to-night."

As he looked about the poor room, as he saw the dust that the sunlight made so visible, he wondered that the house of cards could so recently have held him within its shadow. He felt as though he had passed through some terrible nightmare that the light of day rendered not only fantastic but incredible. That old Peter Westcott had indeed been flung out of the high window of Norah Monogue's room.

Leaving Scaw House on his right he struck through the dark belt of trees and came out at the foot of the Grey Hill. The dark belt of cloud was spreading now fast across the blue—soon it would catch the sun—the Tower itself was already swallowed by a cold grey shadow.

Peter began to climb the hill, and remembered that he had not been there since that Easter morning when he had kissed an unknown lady and so flung fine omens about his future.

Soon he had reached the little green mound that lay below the Giant's Finger. Although the Grey Hill would have been small and insignificant in hilly country here, by its isolation, it assumed importance. On every side of it ran the sand-dunes—in front of it, almost as it seemed up to its very feet, ran the sea. Treliss was completely hidden, not a house could be seen. The black clouds now had caught the sea and only far away to the right the waves still glittered, for the rest it was an inky grey with a touch of white here and there where submerged rocks found breakers. For one moment the sun had still evaded the cloud, then it was caught and the world was instantly cold.

Peter, as he sat there, felt that if he were only still enough the silence would soon be vocal. The Hill, the Sea, the Sky—these things seemed to have summoned him there that they might speak to him.

He was utterly detached from life. He looked down from a height in air and saw his little body sitting there as he had done on the day when he had proposed to Clare. He might think now of the long journey that it had come, he might watch the course of its little history, see the full circle that it had travelled, wonder for what new business it was now to prepare.

For full circle he had come. He, Peter Westcott, sat there, as naked, as alone, as barren of all rewards, of all success, of all achievements as he had been when, so many years ago he had watched that fight in the inn on Christmas Eve. The scene passed before him again—he saw himself, a tiny boy, swinging his legs from the high chair. He saw the room thick with smoke, the fishermen, Dicky the Fool, the mistletoe swinging, the snow blocking in from outside, the fight—it was all as though it passed once more before his eyes.

His whole life came to him—the scenes at Scaw House, Dawson's, the bookshop, Brockett's, Bucket Lane, Chelsea, that last awful scene there ... all the people that he had known passed before him—Stephen Brant, his grandfather, his father, his mother, Bobby Galleon, Mr. Zanti, Clare, Cards, Mrs. Brockett, Norah, Henry Galleon, Mrs. Rossiter, dear Mrs. Launce ... these and many more. He could see them all dispassionately now; how that other Peter Westcott had felt their contact; how he had longed for their friendship, dreaded their anger, missed them, wanted them, minded their desertion....

Now, behold, they were all gone. Alone on this Hill with the great sea at his feet, with the storm rolling up to him, Peter Westcott thought of his wife and his son, his friends and his career—thought of everything that had been life to him, yes, even his sins, his temptations, his desires for the beast in man, his surly temper, his furious anger, his selfishness, his lack of understanding—all these things had been taken away from him, every trail had been given to him—and now, naked, on a hill, he knew the first peace of his life.

And as he knew, sitting there, that thus Peace had come to him, how odd it seemed that only a few weeks ago he had been coming down to Cornwall with his soul, as he had then thought, killed for ever.

The world had seemed, utterly, absolutely, for ever at an end; and now here he was, sitting here, eager to go back into it all again, wanting—it almost seemed—to be bruised and battered all over again.

And perceiving this showed him what was indeed the truth that all his life had been only Boy's History. He had gone up—he had gone down—he had loved and hated, exulted and despaired, but it was all with a boy's intense realisation of the moment, with a boy's swift, easy transition from one crisis to another.

It had been his education—and now his education was over. As he had said those words to Norah Monogue, "I will go back," he had become a man. Never again would Life be so utterly over as it had been two months ago—never again would he be so single-hearted in his reserved adoption of it as he had been those days ago, at Norah Monogue's side.

He saw that always, through everything that boy, Peter Westcott had been in the way. It was not until he had taken, on that day in Norah Monogue's room, Peter Westcott in his hands and flung him to the four winds that he had seen how terribly in the way he had been. "Go back," Norah had said to him; "you have done all these things for yourself and you have been beaten to your knees—go back now and do something for others. You have been brave for yourself—be brave now for others."

And he was going back.

He was going back, as he had seen on that day, to no easy life. He was going to take up all those links that had been so difficult for him before—he was going to learn all over again that art that he had fancied that he had conquered at the very first attempt—he was going now with no expectations, no hopes, no ambitions. Life was still an adventure, but now an adventure of a hard, cruel sort, something that needed an answer grim and dark.

The storm was coming up apace. The wind had risen and was now rushing over the short stiff grass, bellowing out to meet the sea, blowing back to meet the clouds that raced behind the hill.

The sky was black with clouds. Peter could see the sand rising from the dunes in a thin mist.

Peter flung himself upon his back. The first drops of rain fell, cold, upon his face. Then he heard:

"Peter Westcott! Peter Westcott!"

"I'm here!"

"What have you brought to us here?"

"I have brought nothing."

"What have you to offer us?"

"I can offer nothing."

He got up from the ground and faced the wind. He put his back to the Giant's Finger because of the force of the gale. The rain was coming down now in torrents.

He felt a great exultation surge through his body.

Then the Voice—not in the rain, nor the wind, nor the sea, but yet all of these, and coming as it seemed from the very heart of the Hill, came swinging through the storm—

"Have you cast This away, Peter Westcott?"

"And this?"

"That also—"

"And this?"

"This also?"

"And this?"

"I have flung this, too, away."

"Have you anything now about you that you treasure?"

"I have nothing."

"Friends, ties, ambitions?"

"They are all gone."

Then out of the heart of the storm there came Voices:—

"Blessed be Pain and Torment and every torture of the Body ... Blessed be Plague and Pestilence and the Illness of Nations....

"Blessed be all Loss and the Failure of Friends and the Sacrifice of Love....

"Blessed be the Destruction of all Possessions, the Ruin of all Property, Fine Cities, and Great Palaces....

"Blessed be the Disappointment of all Ambitions....

"Blessed be all Failure and the ruin of every Earthly Hope....

"Blessed be all Sorrows, Torments, Hardships, Endurances that demand Courage....

"Blessed be these things—for of these things cometh the making of a Man...."

Peter, clinging to the Giant's Finger, staggered in the wind. The world was hidden now in a mist of rain. He was alone—and he was happy, happy, as he had never known happiness, in any time, before.

The rain lashed his face and his body. His clothes clung heavily about him.

He answered the storm:

"Make of me a man—to be afraid of nothing ... to be ready for everything—love, friendship, success ... to take if it comes ... to care nothing if these things are not for me—

"Make me brave! Make me brave!"

He fancied that once more against the wall of sea-mist he saw tremendous, victorious, the Rider on the Lion. But now, for the first time, the Rider's face was turned towards him—

Hugh Walpole – A Short Biography

Sir Hugh Seymour Walpole, CBE was born in Auckland, New Zealand, on March 13th, 1884.

His parents had moved to New Zealand in 1877, but his mother, Mildred, unable to settle there, eventually persuaded, in 1889, her husband, Somerset, an Anglican clergyman, to accept another post, this time in New York.

Walpole's early years involved being educated by a Governess until, in 1893, his parents decided he needed an English education and the young Walpole was sent to England.

He first attended a preparatory school in Truro. He naturally missed his family but was reasonably happy. A move to Sir William Borlase's Grammar School in Marlow in 1895, found him bullied, frightened and miserable. He later said, "The food was inadequate, the morality was 'twisted', and Terror—sheer, stark unblinking Terror—stared down every one of its passages ... The excessive desire to be loved that has always played so enormous a part in my life was bred largely, I think, from the neglect I suffered there".

In 1896 Somerset Walpole, hearing of his son's unhappiness, moved him to the King's School, Canterbury. For two years he settled but was undistinguished as a pupil. The following year, 1897, Walpole senior was appointed principal of Bede College, Durham, and his son was moved again; to be a day boy for four years at Durham School. Day boys were regarded as the underclass by boarders, and Bede College was the subject of snobbery within the university. His sense of isolation increased. He continually took refuge in the local library, where he read all the novels of Austen, Fielding, Scott and Dickens and many others. He was voracious in reading.

Walpole wrote in 1924: "I grew up ... discontented, ugly, abnormally sensitive, and excessively conceited. No one liked me—not masters, boys, friends of the family, nor relations who came to stay; and I do not in the least wonder at it. I was untidy, uncleanly, excessively gauche. I believed that I was profoundly misunderstood, that people took my pale and pimpled countenance for the mirror of my soul, that I had marvellous things of interest in me that would one day be discovered".

From 1903 to 1906 Walpole studied history at Emmanuel College, Cambridge and there, in 1905, had his first work published, the critical essay "Two Meredithian Heroes". Here he met and fell under the spell of A C Benson. Walpole's religious beliefs, previously sacrosanct, were fading, and Benson helped him through that personal crisis. Walpole was also attempting to cope with his homosexual feelings, which, for a while, focused on Benson.

Benson gently declined Walpole's advances. They remained friends, but Walpole, feeling rebuffed, gradually downgraded the relationship. Two years later Benson's diary entry on Walpole's subsequent social career reveals his thoughts on his protégé's progress: "He seems to have conquered Gosse completely. He spends his Sundays in long walks with H G Wells. He dines every week with Max Beerbohm and R Ross ... and this has befallen a not very clever young man of 23. Am I a little jealous?– no, I don't think so. But I am a little bewildered ... I do not see any sign of intellectual power or perception or grasp or subtlety in his work or himself. ... I should call him curiously unperceptive. He does not, for instance, see what may vex or hurt or annoy people. I think he is rather tactless–though he is himself very sensitive. The strong points about him are his curiosity, his vitality, his eagerness, and the emotional fervour of his affections. But he seems to me in no way likely to be great as an artist.

Somerset Walpole, himself the son of an Anglican priest, hoped that his eldest son would follow him into the ministry. Walpole was concerned for his father's feelings. So much so that on graduation from Cambridge in 1906 he took a post as a lay missioner at the Mersey Mission to Seamen in Liverpool. He described that as one of the "greatest failures of my life". Walpole resigned after six months.

From April to July 1907 Walpole was in Germany, privately tutoring children before returning, in 1908, to teach French at Epsom College.

Walpole now found the desire to fully immerse himself in the literary world. He moved to London to become a book reviewer for The Standard and to write fiction in his spare time. He had by this time come to terms with his homosexuality. His encounters were discreet, as they were illegal in Britain. He was constantly searching for "the perfect friend".

In 1909, Walpole published his first novel, The Wooden Horse, the story of a staid, snobbish English family shaken by the return of one of their own from a more out-going New Zealand. The book received good reviews but sold little.

Better was to come in 1911 when he published Mr Perrin and Mr Traill. The Guardian observed that "the setting of Mr Perrin and Mr Traill was clearly drawn from life". The boys of Epsom College were delighted with the thinly disguised version of their school, but the authorities were not, and Walpole was persona non grata there for many years. It was an early illustration of his capacity, noted by Benson, for unthinkingly giving offence, though being hypersensitive to criticism himself.

In early 1914 Henry James wrote an article for The Times Literary Supplement surveying the younger generation of British novelists and comparing them with their eminent elders. In the latter category James put Bennett, Conrad, Galsworthy, Hewlett and H G Wells. The four new authors were Walpole, Gilbert Cannan, Compton Mackenzie and D H Lawrence. From Walpole's point of view one of the greatest living authors had publicly ranked him among the finest young British novelists.

As war approached, Walpole realised that his poor eyesight would disqualify him from serving in the armed forces. He volunteered for the police, but was turned down. He then accepted an appointment, based in Moscow, reporting for The Saturday Review and The Daily Mail. Although he was allowed to visit the front in Poland, these dispatches were not enough to stop hostile comments at home that he was not doing his bit for the war effort.

Walpole was ready with a counter; an appointment as a Russian officer, in the Sanitar. He explained they were "part of the Red Cross that does the rough work at the front, carrying men out of the trenches, helping at the base hospitals in every sort of way, doing every kind of rough job. They are an absolutely official body and I shall be one of the few Englishmen in the world wearing Russian uniform".

While training Walpole spent many hours gaining fluency in Russian, and writing a literary biography of Joseph Conrad.

In the summer of 1915 he worked on the Austrian-Russian front, assisting at operations in field hospitals and retrieving the dead and wounded from the battlefield. Writing home to Arnold Bennett he said "A battle is an amazing mixture of hell and a family picnic—not as frightening as the dentist, but absorbing, sometimes thrilling like football, sometimes dull like church, and sometimes simply physically sickening like bad fish. Burying the dead afterwards is worst of all."

During a skirmish in June 1915 Walpole rescued a wounded soldier; his Russian comrades refused to help and this meant Walpole had to carry one end of a stretcher, dragging the man to safety. He was awarded the Cross of Saint George.

In October 1915 he returned to England to visit family and friends and to stay at a cottage he had purchased in Cornwall. In January 1916 he was asked by the Foreign Office to return to Petrograd.

Before going his novel, The Dark Forest, was published. It drew on his experiences in Russia, and was more sombre than much of his earlier fiction. Reviews were highly favourable; The Daily Telegraph commented on "a high level of imaginative vision ... reveals capacity and powers in the author which we had hardly suspected before."

Back in Petrograd his diary entry for March 13th records "Thirty two today! Should have been a happy day but was completely clouded for me by reading in the papers of Henry James' death. This was a terrible shock to me."

By late 1917 it was clear to Walpole and the authorities that his work was at an end. On November 7th he left, missing the Bolshevik Revolution, which began that very day.

In London Walpole was appointed to a post at the Foreign Office and remained there until resigning in February 1919. For his wartime work he was awarded the CBE in 1918.

Walpole continued to write and publish and now also began a career on the highly lucrative lecture tour in the United States.

He made his first lecture tour in 1919, receiving an enthusiastic welcome wherever he went. It was noted that Walpole's "genial and attractive appearance, his complete lack of aloofness, his exciting fluency as a speaker and his obvious and genuine liking for his hosts" combined to win him a large American following. The success of his talks led to an increase in lecturing fees, greater sales of his books, and large sums from American publishers keen to print his latest fiction.

A keen music lover, Walpole, in 1920, heard a new tenor at the Proms, impressed he sought him out. Lauritz Melchior became one of the most important friendships of his life, and Walpole did much to foster the singer's budding career. Wagner's son Siegfried engaged Melchior for the Bayreuth Festival in 1924 and succeeding years. Walpole attended, and met Adolf Hitler, then recently released from prison after an attempted putsch.

In 1924 Walpole moved to a house, Brackenburn, near Keswick in the Lake District. His large income enabled him to maintain his London flat in Piccadilly, but Brackenburn was his main home for the rest of his life.

At the end of 1924 Walpole met Harold Cheevers, who soon became his friend and companion and remained so for the rest of his life. Cheevers, a policeman, with a wife and two children, left the police force and entered Walpole's service as his chauffeur. Walpole trusted him completely, and gave him extensive control over his affairs. Whether Walpole was at Brackenburn or Piccadilly, Cheevers was almost always with him, and often accompanied him on overseas trips. Walpole provided a house in Hampstead for Cheevers and his family.

During the mid-twenties Walpole produced two of his best-known novels in the macabre vein that he drew on from time to time, exploring the fascination of fear and cruelty. The Old Ladies (1924) is a study of a timid elderly spinster exploited and eventually frightened to death by a predatory widow. Portrait of a Man with Red Hair (1925) depicts the malign influence of a manipulative, insane father on his family and others.

Walpole continued a series of stories for children, begun in 1919 with Jeremy, taking the young hero's story forward with Jeremy and Hamlet (the boy's dog) in 1923, and Jeremy at Crale in 1927.

In 1930 Walpole wrote possibly his best-known work, Rogue Herries, a historical novel set in the Lake District. The Daily Mail considered it "not only a profound study of human character, but a subtle and intimate biography of a place." He followed it with four sequels and an almost finished fifth.

Hollywood, in the shape of MGM, invited him in 1934 to write the script for a film of David Copperfield. Walpole enjoyed life in Hollywood, but as one who rarely revised any of his work he found it a bore to produce sixth and seventh drafts at the behest of the studio. He also had a small acting role in the film; he played the Vicar of Blunderstone delivering a boring sermon that sends David to sleep.

Walpole's performance was a success. The sermon was improvised and the producer, David O Selznick, had mischievously called for retake after retake to try to make him dry up, but Walpole fluently delivered a different extempore address each time.

The critical and commercial success of the film led to a return in 1936. Arriving, he found the studio had no idea which films they wanted him to work on, and he had eight weeks of highly paid leisure, during which he wrote a short story and worked on a novel. He was eventually asked to write the script for Little Lord Fauntleroy. He spent most of his fees on paintings; he was an avid collector and left many to the Tate in London on his death. His last lecture tour, also in 1936, was primarily to raise funds to pay US taxes which he had neglected to pay earlier.

In 1937 Walpole was offered a knighthood. He accepted although Kipling, Hardy, Galsworthy had all refused. "I'm not of their class... Besides I shall like being a knight," he said.

Walpole's taste for adventure did not diminish in his last years. In 1939 he was commissioned to report for William Randolph Hearst's newspapers on the funeral in Rome of Pope Pius XI, the conclave to elect his successor, and the subsequent coronation. In the weeks between the funeral and Pius XII's election Walpole, with his customary fluency, wrote much of Roman Fountain, a mixture of fact and fiction about the city. It was his last overseas visit.

After the outbreak of the Second World War Walpole remained in England, dividing his time between London and Keswick, where he continued to write with his usual speed. He completed a fifth novel in the Herries series and began work on a sixth.

Unfortunately his health was undermined by diabetes. He overexerted himself at the opening of Keswick's fund-raising "War Weapons Week" in May 1941, making a speech after taking part in a lengthy march.

Sir Hugh Seymour Walpole, CBE died of a heart attack at Brackenburn, aged 57 on June 1st, 1941. He was buried in St John's churchyard in Keswick.

Hugh Walpole – A Concise Bibliography

Books
The Wooden Horse (1909)
Maradick at Forty: A Transition (1910)
Mr Perrin and Mr Traill (1911) (Revised for the US version as The Gods and Mr Perrin)
The Prelude to Adventure (1912)
Fortitude (1913)
The Duchess of Wrexe, Her Decline and Death (1914)
The Golden Scarecrow (Short Stories) (1915)
Prologue
Hugh Seymour
Henry Fitzgeorge Strether
Ernest Henry
Angelina
Bim Rochester
Nancy Ross
'Enery
Barbara Flint
Sarah Trefusis
Young John Scarlet
Epilogue
The Dark Forest (1916)
Joseph Conrad (1916)
The Green Mirror (1918)
The Secret City (1919)
Jeremy (1919)
The Art of James Branch Cabell (1920)
The Captives (1920)

The Thirteen Travellers (Short Stories) (1920)
Absalom Jay
Fanny Close
The Hon Clive Torby
Miss Morganhurst
Peter Westcott
Lucy Moon
Mrs Porter and Miss Allen
Lois Drake
Mr Nix
Lizzie Rand
Nobody
Bombastes Furioso
The Young Enchanted (1921)
The Cathedral (1922)
Jeremy and Hamlet (1923)
The Crystal Box (1924) Privately published by Walpole – limited edition of 150 copies
The Old Ladies (1924)
The English Novel: Some Notes on its Evolution (1924)
Portrait of a Man with Red Hair (1925)
Harmer John (1926)
Reading: An Essay (1926)
Jeremy at Crale (1927)
Anthony Trollope (1928)
My Religious Experience (1928)
The Silver Thorn (Short Stories) (1928)
The Little Donkeys with the Crimson Saddles
The Tiger
No Unkindness Intended
Ecstasy
A Picture
Old Elizabeth (A Portrait)
The Etching
Chinese Horses
The Tarn
Major Wilbraham
A Silly Old Fool
The Enemy
The Enemy in Ambush
The Dove
Bachelors
Wintersmoon (1928)
Farthing Hall (1929) With J B Priestley
Hans Frost (1929)
Rogue Herries (1930)
Above the Dark Circus (1931) Published in the US as Above the Dark Tumult
Judith Paris (1931)
The Apple Trees: Four Reminiscences (1932) Limited edition of 500 copies

The Fortress (1932)
A Letter to a Modern Novelist (1932)
All Souls' Night (Short Stories) 1933
The Whistle
The Silver Mask
The Staircase
A Carnation for an Old Man
Tarnhelm – or The Death of my Uncle Robert
Mr Oddy
Seashore Macabre – A Moment's Experience
Lilac
The Oldest Talland
The Little Ghost
Mrs Lunt
Sentimental but True
Portrait in Shadow
The Snow
The Ruby Glass
Spanish Dusk
Vanessa (1933)
Extracts from a Diary (1934) Privately published by Walpole
Captain Nicholas (1934)
Cathedral Carol Service (1934) An episode from "The Inquisitor"
The Inquisitor (1935)
Claude Houghton: Appreciations (1935) With Clemence Dane
A Prayer for My Son (1936)
John Cornelius: His Life and Adventures (1937)
Head in Green Bronze and Other Stories (1938)
Head in Green Bronze
The German
The Exile
The Train
The Haircut
Let The Bores Tremble
The Honey-Box
The Fear of Death
The Field with Five Trees
Having No Hearts
The Conjurer
The Joyful Delaneys (1938)
The Sea Tower (1939)
Roman Fountain (1940)
The Bright Pavilions (1940)
The Blind Man's House (1941)
Open Letter of an Optimist (1941)
The Killer and the Slain (1942)
Katherine Christian (1943)
Mr Huffam and Other Stories (1948)

The White Cat
The Train to the Sea
The Perfect Close
Service for the Blind
The Faithful Servant
Miss Thom
Women are Motherly
The Beard
The Last Trump
Green Tie
The Church in the Snow
Mr Huffam – A Christmas Story

Short Stories

The following stories appeared in the Windsor Magazine

The Dog and the Dragon In Reminiscence (October 1923)
Red Amber (December 1923)
The Garrulous Diplomatist (December 1924)
The Adventure of Mrs Farbman (January 1925)
The Adventure of the Imaginative Child (February 1925)
The Happy Optimist (March 1925)
The Dyspeptic Critic (April 1925)
The Man Who Lost His Identity (May 1925)
The Adventure of the Beautiful Things (June 1925)
The War Babies are Growing Up! (November 1934)

Plays

The Young Huntress (1933)
The Cathedral (adaptation of his 1922 novel) (1936)
The Haxtons (1939)

Editor

In 1932 Walpole edited The Waverley Pageant: Best Passages from the Novels of Sir Walter Scott. In 1937 he edited a compilation of short stories, A Second Century of Creepy Stories (Hutchinson, 1937), by a range of writers including Guy de Maupassant, M. R. James, Henry James, Walter de la Mare, Oliver Onions, Walpole himself ("Tarnhelm") and twenty-one others.